A SENSE
OF
SILENCE

The first of the Sam Wright adventures

Peter Reisz

There are those who believe that we are all born with a telepathic gift, but almost always fail to discover it.

Even if we do find it, other people's fear, cynicism and hostility to the unknown will prevent us from living at ease with an ability that is not regarded as 'normal'.

If you have the gift, keep it secret.

Thank you to my wife who persuaded me to take the big leap and publish this.

Peter Reisz

ISBN: 9781549853128

CONTENTS

CHAPTER 1 - THE START OF A JOURNEY

I t's the scream that changes Sam Wright's life for ever. And eventually, the future of the world.

Cycling home, Sam's breaths form clouds in the cold winter air. He notes idly that the windows of the bus on the other side of the road are misted with condensation.

Of greater interest is the mother who signalled for the bus to stop. She bends to unstrap her baby from his pushchair and Sam senses her feeling of relief - the bus is on time and she can get her son out of the cold.

Sam no longer asks why he can sense peoples' feelings like that. It's something he has lived with for years. Perhaps he's good at reading body language. No matter.

The woman is looking down, so she never sees what hits her.

"Idiot!"

Sam skids his bike to a halt as a bright orange Ford Focus hurtles past the bus, travelling absurdly and dangerously fast towards him. The driver's-side front wheel jars against the kerb and its tyre explodes.

Sparks stream from underneath as metal scrapes on road. Out of control, the car careers in front of the bus. Sam catches the briefest glimpse of a wide-eyed driver uselessly wrestling with the wheel. Laughing? Is he laughing?

"Look out!" Sam shouts to warn the mother, but it's futile. The Ford smashes into the bus stop. With a thud like a bass drum, felt as much as heard, it demolishes the post in an instant.

The woman is thrown into the road.

The pushchair is crushed.

The remains of the Focus rebound from a garden wall and spin towards Sam. Desperately he throws his bike down.

No time!

His bike is twisted into a madman's sculpture of buckled wheels and mangled tubing. The spinning wreckage of the Ford scoops Sam up and throws him into the path of the bus.

It can't stop in time. He'll be crushed.

As he catapults through the air, taking in every last detail of the world he is about to leave, Sam screams in terror.

It is that scream that changes his life for ever.

* * *

"Oh my ..." The metal tray and the drinks on it fall to the floor with a crash.

"Mum, are you alright? You're shaking."

"Sorry?"

"Are you alright?"

"I ... I think so. No, I don't know. I had the strangest feeling."

"They could have heard that clatter in Lagos."

"I'm sorry."

"Look - go and sit down. I'll clear this up."

"No, I'll be ..."

"Mum, you're shaking. Go and sit down!"

"You're right. I will. Just for a minute. Thank you."

* * *

"Oh my God!" Helen Wright's hands freeze, mid-sentence, above her computer keyboard. A sense of terror overwhelms her, and then stops. Kicking back her chair she runs downstairs and throws open the front door. "George", she shouts.

On the drive her husband is vacuuming the car, the high-pitched whine drowning out any other sound.

"GEORGE" she screams, and bangs him on the shoulder.

"Shit!" Her husband straightens too quickly and hits his head on the car roof. "What did you do that for?"

With insolent slowness, the noise of the cleaner dies. Puzzled and annoyed, her husband rubs the back of his head. "What's up?"

"Did you hear anything?"

5

"What? With this thing going?" he snaps. Then, seeing that his wife is agitated he softens his tone "No, of course not."

"Something bad has happened."

"What?"

"I don't know. Something terrible. Come quickly."

George runs into the house after his wife. She is pulling on her shoes.

"Will you tell me what the hell is going on?"

"I don't know. Something's happened ... to Sam, I think. Something bad. I think it must be there." She points.

A hundred metres down the road is the rear of a stationary bus. Clearly something has happened there. Something serious. People are running from their homes, gathering round, staring at the road. There's a pall of smoke rising slowly into the air.

"Sam's there."

"How do you know?"

"I just do. Come on!"

Helen and George Wright sprint, leaving the doors of their house and the car gaping open.

For the passengers already standing to get off the bus, it's a trauma. Cursing, they are thrown to the floor as it judders to a halt, acrid smoke rising from its overheated tyres.

"Sorry" shouts the driver as he leaps from his seat. "Emergency." They'll sort themselves out - at least they're still alive. What's happened to the boy?

Shaking with fear, he stumbles down onto the road. Steeling himself for his worst nightmare - the sight of a young body mangled and broken under the wheels of the bus - HIS bus - he is already rehearsing what he will have to say.

"Couldn't stop: didn't stand a chance. He fell in front of me. Nothing I could do. The young lad - is he ... dead?"

As Sam instinctively calculated, the bus couldn't stop in time. But by luck or his own presence of mind, he twists as he tumbles through the air and falls between, not under, the front wheels. Missing them by a whisker, he hits his head against the hard cold metal of the suspension and then the road. The world spins. Dazed, unable to move, he lies still. Then slowly, and trembling with shock, he crawls backwards from under the bus, shivering and bleeding, but alive.

Miraculously, impossibly alive.

Desperate to be seen helping, the driver helps Sam to the opposite side of the road. Sam sits on the kerb, shaking uncontrollably.

"You all right, lad?"

Sam nods weakly. He is shivering too violently to talk. He feels the relief of the driver wash over him, the release of the fear.

"Thank God. I was sure ..." The sentence remains unfinished as the man rushes to the nearest drain to throw up. Sam puts his head between his knees, hoping not to do the same.

Alarmed by the noises, people race from their homes. Some stand, their hands to their mouths, frozen in horror. Others have cooler heads and reach down to help the injured woman lying in the road. But most pull away quickly. She will never stand again on those shattered and twisted legs, which are folded under her at impossible angles. Worse – a pool of blood is forming round her and it is slowly, thickly and ominously getting larger.

Too much blood.

"Harry! My baby, where is he?" she whispers hoarsely.

A bystander disentangles the wrecked pushchair from the car and lifts from it a tiny, motionless bundle. He groans sadly and shakes his head at the people watching. With exaggerated gentleness he closes the baby's eyes and hands the body to his mother. She moans sadly and holds him close, murmuring softly, stroking his still warm face.

The Focus has come to rest against a lamp post that is now leaning at a dangerous angle. A wisp of steam curls from the engine and a green liquid is dripping onto the road. Scrawled on the dirty surface above the number plate are the words 'CAN'T CATCH ME!'

The young driver kicks open the door and staggers out. Someone shouts "stop him!"

A large man in a rugby shirt tackles the fleeing driver to the ground. "Oh no you don't. You are going nowhere."

The young man writhes and twists and kicks, desperate to free himself. Sam senses his panic. He swears and screams and bites and punches the man who is holding him. Sam senses his panic.

"Cut that out. Stay still or I'll punch your lights out. I'm warning you, you little shit!"

The driver ignores the warning, frantic to escape.

The man is as good as his word and the noise stops abruptly.

"Look out!"

A voice warns Sam to move. A second car, impatient to leave the scene of the accident has mounted the pavement. Sam scrambles to his feet and steps backwards. The car narrowly misses him.

He looks around to thank whoever warned him. No idea. It could have been any one of the watching crowd. But that's twice in a few minutes he's narrowly escaped being killed.

Panting and ashen-faced, Sam's parents come running. "Oh my God – Sam" screams his mother.

George takes a handkerchief from his pocket and holds it to his son's head. Sam pulls it away. He doesn't want to be treated like a child in front of all these people. With surprise he notices a large bloodstain. He turns the handkerchief over and holds it back in place.

"You alright, son?"

"Think so. But the baby - the woman - can you do anything?"

Helen takes a few steps towards the mother and child lying in the road. She turns back, grimly shaking her head.

The woman is silent now, unconscious. The dark pool has flowed all the way to the gutter. The symbolism is potent - the life-blood of a dying person, flowing into the drain. A man is using his belt as a tourniquet, trying to stop the bleeding from her mangled leg. It's futile. A shocked hush descends on the watching crowd. In silence they watch the tragedy unfold to its inevitable conclusion.

Police arrive, then an ambulance. Then two more of each. They shepherd the watching crowd back as medics attend to the injured woman. But they don't work for long. They stand back and gently lay a blanket over the mother and her baby. A groan rises from the watching crowd.

"Did anyone witness what happened here?" a police officer asks.

Sam raises his hand. "I did."

The officer takes his name and address and a brief description of what he saw. They are grateful - they will take a full statement later. "But you need to get to hospital right away, Sir. You're hurt."

"No. I'll be OK."

No discussion is allowed. Against his will, trained hands lay Sam on a stretcher and, with skill born of practice, lift him into an ambulance. His father rides with him. Carefully, softly, the paramedics check his temperature, heartrate and blood pressure and bathe his cuts.

As the ambulance jerks towards the hospital and he realises that the flashing blue light is for him – for him – the full reality dawns of how close to death he had been. A few centimetres – that's all. He'd actually brushed against the moving wheel of the bus before it stopped.

He feels numb.

Ugly lumps and cuts on his head show where he hit the road and the bus. Blood from his legs is soaking through his jeans and congealing. He is still shivering violently. The motion of the ambulance is the last straw: he throws up.

At the hospital he is wheeled quickly down long corridors, the bright lights stinging his eyes. Fresh sets of skilled hands take his pulse, his blood pressure, blood samples. Then an injection in his thigh. He doesn't fight now. He doesn't even ask.

Distant voices discuss him as if he isn't there ... lucky to be alive ... should have been wearing a helmet ... another teenager too proud to wear one ... nasty bruises on his head ... X-Rays ... check for a skull fracture ... possible concussion ... could have been avoided ... friction burns ... shock.

"You've had a lucky escape." A doctor smiles at Sam. "Don't worry, you're going to be fine. But just to be sure we'll finish cleaning you up, run some more tests and make you comfortable."

No, he can't go home just yet. Not till they're sure. They'll keep him in overnight and think about things tomorrow.

Great!

Sam's parents sit with him. A thick bandage circles his head. He doesn't want to talk: the images of the lifeless baby and the broken body of the dying mother are imprinted on his mind. He remembers the loving caresses she gave her dead child as she slipped away herself.

Sam has seen two innocent people die.

Two innocent people! Dead.

His numbness morphs to anger. What an asshole! The driver was unhurt, of course. Why is it always the innocents that die and the guilty that survive?

The police come. Painstakingly, they take down every detail of what he saw. They write the statement for him and read it back. They ask Sam to sign each page.

"My writing's not normally this bad. I can't hold the pen very well – sorry." Sam's hand is swollen, numb and bandaged: it hurts to move.

"Please, don't worry. You've been really helpful."

"I feel guilty - I should have done something to help her and the baby."

"Nothing you could have done, Sir." The officer shakes his head. "Nothing anyone could have done. You mustn't feel bad about it."

"Did you arrest the driver?"

"Oh yes. He'll be put away this time."

"This time?"

The Officer realises he's said too much. "Let's just say he's known to us, Sir."

Sam boils with suppressed anger. He's never watched anyone die before – not a real person, anyway. And no-one should have to witness the death of an innocent baby under any circumstances.

Later, lying alone in the unfamiliar hospital bed, Sam hears and re-hears the dying mother calling for her baby. He's certain that he won't be able to sleep.

But he does.

Clearly he does.

Because that night, in the hospital, Sam's dream comes for the first time.

He'd forgotten that he screamed himself.

CHAPTER 2 - EXTRACT FROM NEW YEAR'S LECTURE

"If we are to escape the confines of this planet, the human race must evolve. We are not well equipped for travel through interstellar space and we are still constrained by the law that states that nothing can travel faster than the speed of light. Science has so far failed to supply a solution to this limitation. But evolution might.

"Consider the shape that such evolution might take. It will not be enough for the human animal simply to grow taller, faster and cleverer or to live longer or more healthily. That is not evolution in the sense that Darwin would have recognised it, but merely the by-product of better food, improved living conditions, effective medicines and accessible education - at least in the developed world.

"Evolution of a species isn't about doing the same things better. It's about developing new skills. When early life acquired the ability to live on land and thereby left the water - that was evolution. When our ancestors learnt to walk upright and to manufacture tools, that was evolution too.

"Future humans must acquire skills that none of us currently possess. Such abilities, till now confined to the imagination of creative authors and film-makers, may help the human race reach outwards, to populate other planets and to spread among the stars.

"Some people believe that technological advances will suffice. They are wrong. We cannot vest our future in inanimate machines. They are not the answer.

"Indeed, over-reliance on technology may send the human race backwards, lazing itself towards extinction. No: to leave this Earth we must develop skills of which we currently only dream.

"I predict that we will learn the ability to communicate without the use of speech or machines, through the power of thought alone. I believe there may be people living among us today who can already do this.

"It is expansion of the mind in which we must place our hopes for human survival. That, ladies and gentlemen, is the Destination of the Species.

"But here's the tragedy of the human way. If there are people out there today who can do these things, my advice to them is to keep very quiet about it. It is the nature of man to destroy anything that he perceives as abnormal or different. We are the first species in the history of our planet to have developed the power to halt our own evolution."

Extract from New Year Lecture
Delivered by Professor Stamford Harkness to the Royal Society.

CHAPTER 3 – FIRST CONTACT

B ack home and lone in his bedroom, Sam buries his face in hands. He's in trouble. He's not coping. For the first time in his life, he has a problem he can't control.

He needs to talk to someone – but who?

"George, I'm worried about Sam."

George puts down his book and looks at his wife. "He's not ill, is he?"

"Not physically. But he's burning up inside, ever since the accident. He's so angry. I feel it when he walks in the room. That idiot killed two people but walked away without a scratch."

"But that's natural: I feel angry too when I think about it. Don't worry - Sam's got his head screwed on. He'll sort things out."

"No. He's not coping." Helen shakes her head. "Just look at him. He's exhausted. He's not sleeping properly: I hear him calling out at night. He's got a real problem. Surely you've noticed?"

"Oh." George pauses. Perhaps he hasn't been paying enough attention. "What do you suggest? Counselling? Some professional advice?"

"If only! You know he won't do that. He says he's talked to his friends a bit, but they're bored now. You know how sensitive he is to people and their feelings."

George nods; their son has always been perceptive that way. "Witnessing an accident like that was awful. Anyone would be affected; they wouldn't be human otherwise."

George can see that this attempt at offering comfort hasn't worked. "Look, do you think I should talk to him?"

"Please. He might listen to you. You might be able to get through to him. He has to talk to someone. The thing is - this was for real, wasn't it? He's seen people die in films and in computer games but this time two real people died and he was almost killed himself. That's not fiction."

"I almost died." Sam can't get the thought out of his head. The demonstration of his mortality – it shocks him. The tragic event is changing him and he knows it. In one unwanted and unplanned leap he's being forced to cope with thoughts and emotions he's never had to face before.

But he can't. It was too early for him. Too sudden.

He wasn't ready.

What makes things worse is that he now knows more about the crash. How come someone racing a stolen car – a stolen car - can destroy the lives of two innocent people but get away himself without a scratch? Why the hell was he driving at all? Sam's Facebook contacts say he was disqualified and uninsured. Why aren't morons like that just locked away?

And he knows the answer to that question too. An idiot judge gave him 'one final chance' and let him walk free. Within days he'd stolen another car. Basically, the bastard didn't give a toss about other people. All he cared about was the thrill of stealing and racing fast cars.

Sam wants to rant and scream about the injustice and the stupid, stupid, stupid judge.

But to whom?

Maddy is great; warm and caring, as always.

His parents are there for him, of course, but you don't share your innermost thoughts with your parents. Not when you're almost fourteen. Parents tell you what to think. Sam needs to work things out for himself.

There are teachers at school, but he doesn't trust them. They might report him to the social services or shrinks. He's not going there.

For the first time in his life, though he is surrounded by people who care about him, Sam feels alone. Alone and angry and guilty ... and desperately sad.

Sitting at the computer in his room, Sam looks with distaste at the shoot-em-up games he enjoyed playing till recently. He curses, gathers them into a pile and throws them angrily into the bin.

Never again.

Death is not a game. He knows that now.

Against his parents' advice, Sam attends the funeral of the woman and her baby. "You've been through enough already, son: you don't need to put yourself through that as well" they say. "Besides, it's your birthday. You should go out; enjoy yourself – take your mind off things."

But Sam wants to say goodbye to two people he never knew in life and only met in death. He hopes it might help.

Standing back from the mourners, he watches as the single coffin containing two bodies is lowered into the ground. He sees the woman's husband discreetly brush a tear from his eye. He notes with deep shock the pale-faced little girl in the black coat gripping his hand as she steps forward and solemnly drops a small teddy into the grave. The baby boy had a sister.

She looks up at her father. Has she done it right? He nods and picks her up, holding close to him what is left of his family. She looks just four years old and will never see her mother or brother again. She'll grow up hardly even remembering them. That's so sad.

Standing beside Sam, Madeleine James whispers. "You OK?"

Sam nods.

It's a lie. He's not OK. He's angry and confused and miserable.

And exhausted.

He hasn't slept properly since the accident.

Not even one night.

* * *

Sam Wright is searching. In his sleep, he is looking for something. But what? He doesn't know.

Whatever it might be, he is failing to find it. With failure comes a sense of deep frustration. So he searches on ...

... and on

... and on ...

... for hour after hour after interminable hour.

Where is he? His dream is taking him to places he doesn't recognise: grey, deserted towns; shadowy buildings; office blocks he knows will be empty even before he walks in.

He roams long, empty, echoing corridors lined by anonymous doors. He tries to check them all. At first he walks, carefully opening each door to peer in. But as the night wears on, he runs frantically, kicking them open. Each slam, bang and crash reverberates down the hollow corridors and with each failure his disappointment and dejection mount.

Sam tries searching the rooms. He looks behind the curtains and feels under the beds. But ... nothing.

He tries standing quietly to listen.

Nothing. A thick, glutinous silence wraps itself round him.

He tries calling.

No answer. Just the reverberating echo of his voice reflecting back at him.

He tries to defy the dream.

"I won't do this" he shouts in his sleep. He backs away from the hostile, threatening buildings. But a deep chasm opens behind him. For a moment he teeters on the brink and then, with a dread inevitability, he falls. Sheer black walls speed past him and he tenses himself for the agonizing, bone-breaking crash when he reaches the bottom.

It never comes.

He never reaches the bottom.

Instead, he wakes, bathed in sweat and panting with terror. He is in his bedroom, exactly where he should be. Rain is pounding on the window and a glance at his clock tells him that the night has more interminable, exhausting hours with which to torture him.

Helen Wright lies in bed, awake but with her eyes shut. She had heard her son cry out in his sleep. He is quiet now. Should she go to see how he is? She will if he cries out again.

With a feeling of deep foreboding Sam sighs and lays his head back on the pillow. Fearfully he closes his eyes, praying that the dream won't return.

But it does. It comes back straight away.

Oh God. Sam wakes feeling ill. His head aches - a horrible nagging pain in one side. He swears again. If he feels like this first thing, what will the rest of the day be like?

He knows the answer: today will be a little bit worse than yesterday and tomorrow will be slightly worse than today.

Every night since the accident he's had the same, repetitive dream. It started that first evening in the hospital. It's intense. It's like it's being injected straight into his head, taking him over. It's like it's someone else's dream and he is being forced to endure it.

And to make it worse, he has no idea what it means.

As he laboriously brushes his teeth, Sam is shocked at his gaunt and haggard reflection. His skin is pale. There are dark rings under his deep blue eyes. His long, light brown hair lies lank round his ears. It's a stranger looking back at him: a pallid, drained and ill relative – but not him.

He forces himself to shower and dress for school. Should he take the day off, pleading sickness? Heaven knows, that's the truth. But today is important. He can't afford to miss the football match, if he wants to make the school team.

Besides, the alternative is to go back to bed. No: he shudders at the thought of experiencing the dream again.

He has no choice. He drags himself downstairs.

Helen Wright has dressed for the office today. In her early forties, she writes part-time for the local paper, a journalistic career that allows her to work from home most days. But, as Sam enters the kitchen, she doesn't need a reporter's powers of observation to see that this is the worst morning yet.

"Another bad night?" she asks tentatively, not knowing exactly what to say.

"Uh." Sam nods.

"You could take the day off. Have a rest."

"Don't want to miss" - Sam almost says 'football' but that would invite an argument – "important lessons." Please, stop talking!

"Look – one day won't hurt. I'll phone the doctor if you want – make you an appointment. I think you should talk to him again."

"That won't help."

"I think you should see him. Really."

Sam slams his spoon on the table. "Mum - no! He'll try again to fill me up with pills - anti-depressants or sleeping tablets or something. I'm not doing that. Those things mess with your head."

His mother has taken an involuntary step backwards. Sam realises he overreacted and adds, more softly: "Sorry. Look, I'll handle this. I'll be alright - I just need a decent night's sleep."

But even as he reassures her, Sam has no idea how he can get it.

On the bus Madeleine James is sitting in her regular place. She shifts along to make room for Sam. She smiles. "Alright?"

"Bit rough."

Maddy and Sam have known each other since playschool. Sam doesn't think of her as his girlfriend – but they're friends and she is most certainly a girl. Very attractive too: a couple of inches shorter than Sam, with long golden hair, a turned-up nose, large and piercing green eyes, a wicked smile, an infectious sense of humour ... and a foul temper.

The bus is crowded and hot and stuffy because of the rain. Maddy is talking quietly. Something about being worried ... something about her father...

"Uh!"

Sam starts. Two things just happened. Even on the bus, his dream began again. And Maddy dug her elbow into his ribs.

Hard.

"What the hell's got into you?" she hisses. "Bloody rude, isn't it, snoring when I'm talking to you?"

"I don't snore."

"You were asleep! That boring am I? For God's sake, Sam, I'm trying to tell you something important and you don't even have the decency to stay awake!"

"Look, I'm sorry. I had a bad night again. Feeling really rough. I'm not good company today. Better just leave me alone." Sam winces as soon as he says the words – they came out more sharply than he intended. He needs to say something else.

Too late.

"You're telling me! You haven't been worth talking to for weeks. I've tried to be here for you but OK, have it your way: I'll leave you alone."

Other passengers look round curiously to see who's arguing. Embarrassed, Maddy swears, snatches her bag and stamps forward to sit with two girls. They look round at Sam.

Sitting alone, plagued by a dream he doesn't understand and issues he can't talk about, Sam feels more miserable than he can ever remember.

I've shouted at Mum and now I've fallen out with Maddy. What's happening to me?

"What's happening to you, Wright?" The teacher is furious. "No, leave it. Stand back. Leave it, I say!" Sam watches miserably as the spilt acid is treated and cleaned away.

"Shit!" Sam stares at the dinner plate he's dropped. He tries to ignore the cheers echoing round the school hall. Miserably, he clears up the mess.

"For God's sake, Wright!" He's just missed an open goal and Masterson, the school team coach, is furious. The other players glower. He's letting them down.

Lewis Squires, in the other team's goal, looks at Sam contemptuously. Sam wants to hit him, to wipe the disdainful look from his face.

But he doesn't have the energy.

Usually Maddy and Sam walk home together. But this evening she hasn't stayed. Miserably, he trudges back alone, head bowed.

This has to stop.

Oh hell – bedtime. Sam looks at his bed with foreboding. Before the accident he would throw himself into it. Now he dreads it.

"My God! I'm frightened of going to bed. I am ... I'm going mad!" His once-comfortable room stares malevolently back at him, threatening more endless hours of bad dreams and lost sleep.

It can't go on.

It mustn't.

He has to put an end to the dream before it puts an end to him.

"No more. Please. No more!" he mutters and wipes his face on the pillow to remove the tears from his eyes. He takes a breath to compose himself.

"This stops tonight." he mutters as he nervously puts out the light.

Sam is in an unknown, deserted town. In his dream he searches, but he finds nothing. He always finds nothing.

No, Sam, fight this! He turns his back and walks away. The road before him curls upwards and swoops down, forcing him to turn and run back.

He stands at a junction of many long corridors, each lined with doors. Which should he take?

No! For goodness sake, stop!

In the small hours of the morning and in the half-awake state between sleep and reality, Sam Wright determines to take control of his life again.

The scene fades. Take control, Sam. Take control!

Sam imposes himself on the dream. Go somewhere I know. Somewhere I recognise.

This is different.

Yes; for the first time he recognises where he is. It's the seaside hotel he visited as a child.

Why here? Happy memories? If so, it's not happy now. The hotel he remembers as lively and colourful, warm and exciting is now deserted and grey, cold and depressing.

He's alone in a ghost hotel.

Here's the corridor where his father told him to be quiet in case other children were sleeping. It's empty and sad now - there are no children in the rooms.

Here's a door that Sam recognises. He turns the handle. Silently, it opens. This is the room where they stayed. He slept in here – over there on the sofa bed. But now it's different: sombre and unwelcoming. Everything is grey. No-one has brought happiness to this monochrome, forbidding place for years.

Here's the wardrobe where he kept his clothes. Is there something in there? In his dream Sam slides open the door and peers in.

Nothing. Total blackness. No light at all. The darkness envelops him.

And yet ...

Hesitantly Sam stretches his arm forward and reaches into the emptiness. His fingers tingle with anticipation.

Still nothing. Just the thump, thump, thump of his heart beating.

He steps into the wardrobe. The blackness surrounds him. His senses jangle.

"Is someone there?" Sam whispers into the darkness.

And booming back from the pitch black a voice answers him. *"Oh thank heavens. Is that really you? I've been trying to find you for weeks."*

CHAPTER 4 – A VOICE IN THE DARK

G asping in terror, Sam sits bolt upright.

His bedroom.

He's in his bedroom.

At home.

Alone.

That's right. That's how it should be.

Through a crack in the curtains, the moonlight gives his room an eerie, blue-tinged glow. It's enough, though, to see that everything looks normal.

But if he's alone, where did that voice come from?

His heart is pounding. He wipes his clammy forehead with his hand. He feels more scared than at any time since his accident.

"Who's there?" he whispers again, fearfully.

"*A friend.*"

Oh my God! The lack of sleep has got to me. I really am going mad! Sam gasps and clamps his hands over his ears. Voices in my head! This is crazy!

But the voice continues: "*No, no, no. Please stay calm. You're not going mad, it's not crazy, believe me. I'm a friend. My name is Ngozi. Ngozi Agalaba. I understand that you're afraid. Just stay calm and whatever you do, don't break contact. I'll explain everything.*"

A woman's voice!

Is this part of his awful dream?

It can't be – he's awake now.

Frantically, Sam looks round again. He gets out of bed and nervously looks under it.

Nothing. Everything is normal. This is madness!

"No, you haven't gone mad. I promise."

She's answering a question he never asked! Get away! He has to get away! Sam runs from his bedroom to the bathroom.

"Hello? Are you still there?"

The voice – it followed him! It's not in the bedroom - it's in his head! Sam splashes cold water on his face to make sure he's awake. "What's happening to me?" he whispers to himself.

"Something very special. Stay calm and whatever else you do, keep talking to me. It's taken me so long to find you. Don't let me lose you now. Take a deep breath. Believe me, there's nothing wrong. Just stay with me and I'll explain everything, I promise. Start by telling me your name."

"Samuel. Samuel Wright", he whispers.

What the hell am I doing? What's happening to me? He walks quietly back to his bedroom.

The voice continues. *"Well done, Samuel. Just try to relax. Then I'll tell you what's happening."*

There it goes again – answering a question I haven't asked.

"Are you starting to feel calmer?"

"No! I'm scared shitless. Shaking like a leaf. Just get on with it and tell me what the hell is going on." Sam pauses. "Please."

"OK. I know how you feel. This is telepathy."

"You're taking the piss."

"No I'm not, Samuel. You are telepathic. If you've been whispering, you can stop. There's no need. Just think the words. I'll hear them. Try it."

Yes, he'd been whispering. Sam forces himself not say his next words out loud. It seems strange.

"OK. I'm not whispering anymore."

"And I'm still hearing you. Think about that – you're making no sound, but I'm answering you. Are you starting to believe me?"

"Bloody hell ..."

"Good. Now listen carefully: you're not going mad, you're not dreaming and you're not imagining things. But it's very frightening the first time."

"Too right!"

"I sympathise. I felt the same when this happened to me."

That's a comfort.

"Samuel, I'm so relieved to have found you. I was ready to give up on you. You've been difficult to find."

Sam shakes his head, trying to clear it. *"Contact me? Why? Why me, I mean? How do you know about me?"* The questions tumble out.

"Right – let's take this one step at a time. I know about you because you screamed. A few weeks ago. Do you remember?"

"No?"

"Well you did. You scared me half to death. I was in the kitchen when I heard this awful shriek in my head like someone was about to die. I dropped a tray of glasses. And 'bus'. I think I heard the word 'bus'. It was terrifying. My daughter made me go and sit down.

"Ever since then I've been trying to contact you, to find out who you are and what happened. I was starting to think you'd been killed."

Sitting on his bed again, Sam leans his head back against the wall. *"I was knocked off my bike. You're right about the bus – I fell under it and, yes, I did think I was going to die. I don't remember screaming though."*

"Oh, believe me, you did. That's how I knew about you."

"OK, let's assume I believe you about that, 'cos I don't see how you could have made it up, can you please tell me how you are you doing this? How can I hear you?"

"I'm not doing this. We both are. It takes two people to make a conversation. We are talking to each other – right?"

"Suppose ..."

"As to how we do it – sorry, I can't help. No-one knows. People have theories but the plain truth is that no-one has worked it out yet. It just, well, happens."

"I thought telepathy was just a wild idea. Science fiction films, that sort of thing. But not for real."

"That's what most people think, mainly because they can't do it. But some people can - you're one, I'm another. And scientists – they're experimenting with machines to transmit thoughts straight into peoples' brains. There's a University in Sweden working on it right now. Urgh!"

"So we're not asleep? I'm not dreaming?"

The Ngozi voice sounds irritated. *"No, of course not. Do you feel like you're asleep? As for me - it's early morning here. I work night shifts. I'm certainly not asleep!"*

"But I keep getting this dream - searching."

"That will have been me, looking for you. I've been trying to contact you at all times of the day and night: these last few weeks I've been working nights. I had to try at every time I could - you could be anywhere in the world, for all I knew. You sensed me in your sleep - that's not unusual for someone new to our community."

"You live in a community?"

"No, nothing like that. There's not enough of us, even if we wanted to. Across the world, there are only twenty or so at most. Like I said, very rare. Most of us never even meet. But you've just joined us – so you're a very special person, Sam!"

"I don't feel special. Thanks to you I'm knac - exhausted."

"I'm sorry."

She's sorry? Is that it? After what he's been through? Nevertheless, Sam is relieved. Incredible though it might be, he may have an answer.

"I was really starting to worry that the accident had damaged me and I had – you know, psychological problems."

"Well, you don't. No, let me be more accurate: you have no more than you had before."

For the first time in days, Sam smiles. *"But how can I be sure? How do I know I'm not imagining this? How do I know I haven't just made you up and I really am going mad and you really are just a voice in my head?"*

"Good questions. I'll prove it to you. Are you on the internet?"

"Not right now."

"Can you log on now?"

"I could. Why?"

"Please, just do it."

Sam picks up his phone. He'll log in from there.

"Sorry, it's taking a long time ..."

"OK. Whilst it's loading, tell me your e-mail address."

Again Sam does as he is told.

"OK, I'm online."

"Me too. Right. Now ask me a question - an easy one."

"What for?"

"Just do it. Don't type it, or say it out loud. Just think it."

This is crazy! *"OK. What's the capital of America?"*

"Not crazy at all. That's a good one."

Sam's phone beeps. He has an e-mail. He opens it. "Washington DC."

"Bloody hell!"

"Ah, I thought that might make an impression. Do it again. Make it easy."

"OK. I see what you're doing. Simple one: what are nine times three?"

The phone beeps. The message says "27".

Sam is astounded. This is no party trick: the person at the other end is definitely answering his unspoken questions and using his e-mail address.

"Who was the first man on the moon?"

Beep. Neil Armstrong.

"Tallest mountain in the world?"

Beep. Everest.

"Oh my God!"

"Believe me now?"

Sam looks at the list of e-mails he has just read. Physical evidence! *"OK. No choice now, have I? It's incredible!"*

"I'm glad that worked. We used to have one hell of struggle making people believe before e-mails were invented. But those are real, Samuel. From someone you've never contacted or met. In the morning, I suggest you look at them again and remind yourself that this wasn't a dream. You're telepathic, Samuel. And I have to tell you ... your life is never going to be the same. After today it's going to be a thousand times more interesting."

Sam wants to ask more. But he's too tired. *"OK. We'll have to do this again. But not now. Look, I don't want to be rude, but I HAVE to get some sleep. I haven't been sleeping properly for weeks, thanks to you. I'm falling apart - can't think straight. Can I speak to you tomorrow? I mean, can we do this again?"*

"Yes, let's talk again tomorrow."

"Can we do this – telepathy - any time we want?"

"Pretty well."

"By the way, you said it was the morning where you are. Where is that?"

"Nigeria, just outside Lagos. And you?"

"Nigeria? That's in Africa: thousands of miles away! I'm in Winchester, England."

"But I can hear you like we're in the same room. That's quite extraordinary. Hold on. Winchester - isn't that a famous place?"

"It's the old capital of England. But stop now, please. Do me a big favour, will you? You've found me. Stop looking. I've weeks of sleep to catch up, and only a few hours to do it."

"OK. I'll wait to hear from you tomorrow. And Samuel – "

"Yes?"

"I'm so pleased to have found you."

Sam lies back. Even the excitement of his discovery can't compete with his physical exhaustion. The next thing he knows, his father is shaking him awake. "Sam! Come on, son, you'll miss the bus."

Sam feels likes cheering. The dream - it didn't return. Not only that – he's overslept! Luxury!

And for the first time in weeks, he has woken without a headache.

CHAPTER 5 – THE GHOST TRAIN

Matt Lawson is keeping his promise and he feels good about it. OK, it's not a big promise, but it's important. Tonight, he's taking his daughters to the fair. They've been looking forward to it for weeks.

How many times has he let them down? How often has he disappointed them? Matt forced himself long ago to stop counting. Tonight is a new start.

But he can't help feeling guilty. Were the reasons for letting them down really good enough? Covering for a short shift; he didn't have to volunteer. Leave being cancelled – OK, he couldn't do anything about that. But staying late to complete paperwork? He should have kept on top of that part of his job better. The list of excuses is embarrassingly long. It was never his intention to see so little of the girls.

Julie Lawson is pleasantly surprised when Matt meets them, exactly on time, in the far corner of the car park as agreed, away from other cars. "Hi, luv", she says awkwardly. Lauren and Tamsin throw their arms round their father's waist.

Matt gives his wife a peck on the cheek. He still hasn't come to terms with them living apart. It's a strain.

Julie allows herself to smile and her hand lingers on his. He's here as promised, the girls are delighted and she's pleased to see him too.

Of course she is. She misses him.

"You'll keep a close eye on them? Keep them with you all the time?"

"Of course I will. Don't worry."

"But I do worry. I can't help it. I hate fairs, otherwise I'd come with you. There are so many people there – you know – dodgy – you hear stories."

"We'll be perfectly OK. Hey – it's my job to spot dodgy people, remember? More to the point, they know me, so they'll stay out of my way. Back here at ten? That's the deal, yeah?"

Their parents talk too much - Lauren and Tamsin interrupt impatiently. "Come on, Dad. I'm going on every ride tonight."

"That you're not. You're not old enough." Matt says this firmly for Julie's benefit as much as anything else and looks to check that she agrees.

"Julie, you don't think ...?"

"No, Matt. You know we can't. Not till it's safe again. We can't risk the safety of the girls."

A million times they've had this conversation. Matt purses his lips and nods sadly. So much to say ... so much happiness sacrificed ...

Matt gives his wife a longer, lingering kiss. Strange, but familiar. Eight years, they've been married. Happy as well. Very happy. But now they've been forced apart. "Love you" he whispers.

"Love you, too."

For the benefit of the children, Matt turns away. "Right then, my little misses, let's get going."

It's a perfect night for being outdoors. The air is clear and crisp but not too cold, as long as they keep moving. As they walk, the sounds of the fair float invitingly on the slight breeze.

Then the bright lights, the sweet and sour smells of candy floss and overcooked onions in old oil, the noises of generators, badly-recorded music struggling through blown speakers, sirens and excited screams all combining to overwhelm the senses and create the tingle of excitement that only a fair at night can produce. The girls tug their father eagerly into the cacophony and set about working their way through the rides and the stalls. This will be an expensive evening for their Dad.

Matt smiles; he knows perfectly well what they're doing and he's in the mood to indulge his daughters tonight. And himself too. Evenings like this are few and precious. What's more, with so many people around, he can relax. Here he'll be secure. Among all these people, he'll be safe.

Half an hour later, each girl has an inflatable hammer and a cuddly toy: treasures to be guarded tonight; junk to be discarded tomorrow.

"The Ghost Train! I've never been on that, Dad!"

"And you won't tonight, either. Too scary. Mum would have a fit."

"But we're eight now. We won't be frightened."

"Of course you will. That's what it's there for, to frighten you. That's why it's called 'the Ghost Train'. And then you'll have nightmares and Mum will give me a hard time for months. Not yet. When you're older."

The twins now eye the forbidden ride with a new longing, the yearning of denial. This is now a point of principle.

A carriage clatters out of the dark, its two young occupants laughing and giggling. Lauren is always the one with the compelling argument. "Look, Dad. They're the same age as us – they go to our school." She has no idea whether that's true or not. "They've been on it and they're alright - look. And, if you got in the carriage behind us, Tamsin and I could go together and you could follow to check that we're OK. Mum wouldn't mind then. Please, Dad: it's not often that we get to come out with you."

Ouch! That hurt.

Just like it was meant to.

Against his better judgement, Matt hears himself saying. "OK then. But don't go landing me in it with Mum. This is strictly between you and me, and no-one else. Deal?"

Deal! The girls squeal with delight. Hurdle overcome. They'll handle any fall-out later.

Getting to the head of a short queue, Matt pays for three. He sees his daughters into their seats and settles himself into the carriage behind. Dammit, how did he end up here? He hates this sort of thing. Why do people pay to get themselves frightened? It's ridiculous.

Excitedly, the girls wave as they move off. He watches them disappear through the rubber swing doors into the black beyond. A brief delay and then his car jerks forward too. He braces himself. As the doors swing shut behind him, he grips the handrail tightly. Ahead of him, in the dark, he can hear Lauren and Tamsin squealing and laughing. He hopes he's made the right decision for them. Yes, they sound like they're enjoying themselves.

The car twists and turns its way through the pitch black. Just as he thinks his eyes are adjusting, a bright light flashes and the darkness becomes denser and more enveloping.

Unseen fronds touch his face in the dark. He grimaces.

He jumps. Has someone just got in beside him? That's a good effect. Better than he is expecting.

"Hello, Matt. It's been too long."

Lauren and Tamsin's car crashes through the heavy rubber doors and back into the night air. They jump out, laughing and shouting, and step down onto the grass.

"I almost died when that hand touched my shoulder."

"And that skeleton thing! Was it a real one?"

"Course not. Plastic."

"Do you think Dad will get us a hot dog?"

"Yes. He'll want one himself. It's his night out too."

Matt Lawson's car swings through the rubber doors and stops. The girls wait for him to get out.

"Come on Dad. We're hungry." Tamsin is impatient. He's taking an age.

The attendant stamps over. "Out you get then, squire. There's people waiting."

Matt Lawson's hand is still gripping the rail tightly. The man pokes him, none too gently, in the shoulder. "Right we are, guv – can't wait all night."

At the man's touch, Matt's head lolls back on the seat. The attendant jumps back. "What the ..."

The girls approach now, wide-eyed, cautious.

"Dad?" Something isn't right.

The man snarls. "Stay down there, you two."

Matt Lawson eyes are wide open, unmoving, unblinking, unseeing. And his face ...

Frozen at the moment of his death, Matt Lawson's face is contorted into a silent, frantic, never-ending rictus of pure terror.

Tamsin screams.

Lauren uses her phone. "Mum, come quickly. Something terrible's happened. It's Dad. Please, Mum, we're at the fair – the ghost train - come straight away."

That night, Julie Lawson sends an e-mail. Her face streaked with tears, she writes: "It's happened. Everything we feared. Matt died tonight. For God's sake, protect yourself." She sends it to coombrayj@parliament.uk.

A few moments later her phone rings.

"Mrs. Lawson?

"Yes."

"Forgive me for phoning so late. This is Jonathan Coombray. I picked up your e-mail on my phone. I'm so sorry. Are you certain it was ..."

"Yes."

"Oh God. Matt was good man. Brave."

"Thank you. Yes, he was. Please, don't let this happen to you too."

"I can't go into hiding like Matt did. I'm a public figure."

"You must do something. You're on the list."

"The Police know about tonight?"

"Yes. Matt's one of them. Was."

"Of course. Sorry. I'll talk to them again. See what they recommend. But please, let's not talk about me. What about you? Is there anything I can do to help?"

"No. Not really. What could you do? He's dead."

"Is someone with you tonight?"

"My brother and his wife have come. They'll stay tonight. They're upstairs now with the girls."

"I'm glad you're not alone. Look, I'll phone again tomorrow. When the dust has settled, I'm come and see you. Are you still in Woking?"

"That's right."

"My office will have your address. I can't tell you how sorry I am. Matt was a good man. He didn't deserve this. But you know you did everything you could."

"Thank you."

Julie Lawson switches off the phone. "Everything we could."

But everything wasn't enough. The widow buries her face in her hands.

The phone falls to the floor and breaks open. The batteries roll slowly across the carpet.

CHAPTER 6 – PRESS STATEMENT

The following statement has been released by Professor Stamford Harkness.

START

"As many people already know, an attempt was made on my life yesterday. A bomb destroyed my car. Luckily no-one was in it at the time. It would appear that a passing lorry set off a motion sensor in the device. I understand that the driver of the lorry is uninjured, but understandably shaken.

"I have no doubt that this criminal act was linked to the death-threats I received following my televised New Year interview. Some people cannot accept my suggestion that man, as he evolves, may develop new abilities.

"I count among these abilities the power to communicate without the use of speech or machines, but through thought alone. I even suggested, perhaps a little over-eagerly, that there may be people living among us today who can already do this. Let me make it clear: I was speculating. I know of no-one who can do this.

"To all of you who assumed that I must have been talking about myself, I must disappoint you. I can't do it. There is no secret society plotting to take over the world and no super-beings aiming to manipulate you through control of your minds. I am merely putting forward the idea that telepathic communication could and will happen.

"So, to everyone who has sent me hate mail: please save your energy. Yes, you may believe that man was made in the image of God and is destined to stay in his current form forever. I do not. I believe that man is a species that has evolved remarkably and is capable of evolving still further, just as every other species on Earth today has evolved over millions of years.

"I believe that, if we are ever to leave this crowded planet and spread across the galaxy, we will need abilities that we do not yet have. Open your minds to that possibility and don't be scared by it. Imagine instead the benefits it could bring in terms of expanding the knowledge of the human race and preserving our future as a species.

"Even so, in the light of my experience, I advise anyone who develops these abilities to keep very quiet about them. There are people out there who would kill you for being able to do such things.

"They tried to kill me simply for daring to think it."

END

CHAPTER 7 – A PROBLEM

Once again, Sam is finding it impossible to concentrate. Yesterday it was exhaustion. Today his head is whirling as he goes over and over again the events of last night.

Telepathy? For goodness sake!

But, yes: telepathy! He has given up trying to think of alternative explanations. His looks for the twentieth time at the e-mails on his phone. There they are - answers he received from the Ngozi woman. Real replies to questions he never asked, from a person he's never met.

He checks his sent items again. No, he sent nothing. He gave her his e-mail address telepathically and she used it.

But how? It's impossible! I'm just an ordinary fourteen-year-old. Things like this don't happen to people like me.

Maddy is still ignoring him. The football players are glaring at him with genuine contempt. OK then; Sam needs some time to himself anyway. Time to think. At lunchtime he retreats to the school library. Perhaps there's a book, or something on the internet that will help him make sense of what happened last night.

Good. The library is deserted apart from a bored-looking supervisor who watches him with mild surprise for being there, and then feigns a studied disinterest.

No, bad. It isn't deserted. Tariq Alufi is there. Of course he is. Tariq; a legend in his own lunchtime. Tariq with the pushy parents. Tariq whose father is obsessed with him winning a scholarship to

Oxford or Cambridge. Tariq, the sad case who lives and breathes his coursework and nothing else.

Tariq glances up momentarily, expecting to see a member of staff. Hell no - Sam Wright of all people. He's delighted. He smiles. Tariq would like nothing better than to be Sam Wright's friend and move in his social circle – to be good at socialising as well as coursework and, well, popular. But he harbours no such hopes. So he keeps himself to himself and concentrates on his studies.

Sam nods. He senses that Tariq is pleased to see him but also nervous. Deliberately choosing a seat at the back of the room, he logs on and searches 'telepathy'.

"Telepathy", the first article says, "involves the passing of messages from one person to another without using conventional communication methods based on sound, vision, smell or touch. Instead communication is direct: mind-to-mind. Despite considerable research and experimentation, science remains uncertain whether telepathy is a concept or a reality."

You don't say! Sam sighs and reads on.

"Most people experiment unsuccessfully at some time, but the accepted scientific view is that telepathy has never been sufficiently proven under controlled conditions to be acknowledged as a demonstrable fact of human life. That said, some experiments in controlled conditions have aroused interest, reporting positive results, higher than chance would allow or logic explain. These suggest that telepathy might be possible, perhaps even an evolving skill, but there has never been a demonstration under controlled conditions that achieves a level of consistency at which telepathic powers might be considered a practical or reliable method of communication.

"Recent scientific developments have shown that simple machines can be controlled using thought waves, and these are being enthusiastically received by organisations representing disabled groups. But whilst human-to-machine interaction is proving possible, nothing has yet shown that reliable human-to-human thought exchange is achievable.

"Telepathy has been given a bad name by stage acts presenting themselves as 'mind readers', when they are in fact speaking in code.

"There is limited evidence that twins are more likely to succeed in passing messages to each other in controlled exercises.

"The so-called 'sixth sense' is an important part of folklore, often linked to discussions of telepathy. It causes a mother to know instinctively when her baby is distressed, even though she has heard no sound. Some people claim to have 'dreamt' real events.

"But no-one knows for certain whether human minds have the ability, consciously or subconsciously, to exchange thoughts without resort to the traditional means of communication."

Sam leans back with another sigh. There's nothing here that he couldn't have predicted for himself. Perhaps there is someone he could talk to, instead?

One of the teachers? Who does he trust most? Mr. Masterson?

Not a chance! After the accident - just think what people will say. Sam can just picture what reaction he will get if he tells anyone about this: "... bad thump on the head, it was - he's not been sleeping - LOOKS just awful - did you see his last game? He was like a zombie. Now he says he's hearing voices in his head. Reckon that accident did for him, know what I mean? Going off the rails. Heading for the funny-farm. Keep away till the men in white coats come."

Sam shudders. He'll keep this to himself, at least for now.

A light touch on his arm makes Sam jump. Deep in thought, he hadn't seen Tariq approach.

"Hi." Tariq whispers. The supervisor looks in their direction. She has one opportunity to exercise power in her job and that's by imposing herself on the library users. The fact that Tariq and Sam are the only people there and can't be disturbing anybody else doesn't matter.

"Oh, hi Tariq."

"Don't normally see you here." He looks curiously at Sam's open page. Sam hurriedly minimises the screen.

"Researching something - for a project." Did he manage to make that sound nonchalant?

"A project!" exclaims Tariq gleefully. It seems he did.

The supervisor taps her pen, apparently meaningfully. Perhaps it's Morse code? Tariq lowers his voice again. "Need any help?" he offers in an intense whisper. Please say yes! Please say yes!

"Er, no thanks. I found what I needed."

"Oh." Tariq looks disappointed. "What's it about?"

"It's, well, kind of personal. Look, I don't want to be rude, but I have to dash now. See you." Sam logs off and hurries out.

Wistfully, Tariq watches Sam go, then settles wearily back to his work. He sighs. He'd been hoping for a break from the usual monotony.

Too bad.

Desperately wanting to make his peace with his friend, Sam seeks out Maddy after school. "Want to walk home?"

"Walk home - yes. With you - no." She stalks away.

Time to eat humble pie. Sam matches steps with her. "Look - I'm sorry."

Maddy doesn't break stride and looks straight ahead.

"Maddy, I apologise for being such a bore yesterday. I've been having a really hard time sleeping lately - since the accident."

Maddy stops and turns, her green eyes flashing with anger. "Hard time sleeping? Well good news, Sam – there's a cure. I start talking about something that matters to me, you start sleeping. Problem solved. Any time you can't nod off, just give me a ring and ask me to tell you something important. Sorted." She storms ahead again.

Ouch.

Sam winces and matches steps with her for a second time. "Look, I felt really ill yesterday. Should've stayed home, I really should. I only came in because of the football and I ballsed that up as well. But I'm better today. And you wanted to tell me something about your Dad. Why don't you tell me now? I'd like to help if I can."

Maddy doesn't respond. She marches on.

The tensions of the last few days finally boil over. Sam stops and shouts after her. "Suit yourself. But I'm not apologising again, OK?"

He takes a deep breath. Calm down. You don't want to say things that will lose her friendship forever. Leave it at that. He leans miserably against the wall and lets Maddy walk on.

Maddy slows down. Has she pushed it too far? Probably. He did apologise, after all. And nothing's changed; she still needs to talk with someone. She has a problem she desperately wants to share.

She turns. "Look, I'm glad you're feeling better." She beckons. "Come on."

Sam breathes a sigh of relief and catches up with her. "Look, I am really sorry ..."

"Yes, I know. Let's drop it."

Maddy and Sam live about twenty minutes' walk from the school. For a few moments they amble in awkward silence. Then Maddy says quietly: "Sam, what I wanted to tell you ... I think Dad's in trouble."

"What kind of trouble?"

"I don't know. He's acting weird. Has been for weeks. Months actually."

"Weird? How?"

"He gets secret phone calls. Always in the evening. He goes to another room so no-one can hear."

"People get private calls ..."

"No, I didn't say 'private', Sam. I said 'secret'. He doesn't want people to know who he's talking to. But that's not all of it. Every time he takes one, he goes out later that night. By himself. Without saying anything."

"Where?"

"I don't know! That's another part of how he's acting strange. He doesn't say anything – not to Mum, not to me. He just slips out quietly and comes back half an hour later, sits down and acts like nothing has happened. Normally when he goes out he says something: 'going to the shops', 'going to see George' – that sort of thing. But these nights – the phone call nights - nothing. It's quite obvious. He doesn't want us - or me at least - to know what he's doing."

"Ask your Mum. She's bound to know."

"I did. She mumbled something him having business at the office."

"There you go then."

"No. She was lying. I could tell. Anyhow, I checked. I can see his office from my room and no light came on. He wasn't there – I'd bet my life on it."

"Phew" says Sam. "You don't think he's having an affair, do you?"

"Dad? Cheat on Mum? No! He wouldn't. At least I don't think he would. Besides, she's covering for him. And anyway he's not gone long enough – you know – for..." Maddy's voice tails off, embarrassed.

Sam is relieved. He's known Edward and Jan James for as long as he can remember. Jan and his own mother have been friends for over ten years, since they first met at the play school that Maddy and Sam attended.

They walk in silence for a few more minutes. They pass the building where Edward James works. Instinctively Sam lowers his voice and whispers: "There could be thousands of explanations. What makes you think he's in trouble?"

"He went out two nights ago. That's when I checked whether the light was on at his office, and it wasn't. And I checked his phone to see who had called."

"And?"

"It said 'unknown'"

"Big deal! You can't read anything into that! Loads of people hide their numbers."

"I know that! But why would they phone Dad regularly, at home, in the evenings, causing him to talk so quietly that no-one can hear, and then go out?"

Sam doesn't even attempt to answer that one.

"It's the secrecy; it makes no sense. It's not like him."

"Have you tried asking him?"

"Oh come on! How can I ask him?" Maddy snaps. "If there really is something wrong - and I reckon there is - and I let on that I'm worried about it, he'll just clam up even more." She kicks angrily at a stone. It rattles into the road, and she stops to watch as it spins to a stop. Without looking up she blurts out: "Sam, will you do something for me?"

"Yes. What?"

Maddy leans close and speaks quickly and quietly. "I can't ask Dad where he's going and I can't very well follow him."

Sam nods.

Abruptly she grabs Sam's arm, gripping it with a ferocity that surprises him. "But you could."

Sam is shocked. "Me? Follow him?" Sam rubs his arm.

"If you don't want to do that, could you watch from your bedroom window? Next time he goes out - if I ring you, you could watch from your room. If he's going to the office, he'll come past your house and you'll see him."

"You want me to spy on your Dad?"

"Yes. No. Not spy, exactly. Oh, call it what you like but just do that, will you? Better leave your light off so he can't see you. Will you do it? And then tell me? Will you do that for me? Please?" The words tumble out.

"So you DO want me to spy on your Dad! How'd you like it if someone did that to you?"

"For God's sake Sam – you're being a real jerk, you know that?" Maddy pushes him away. "First you fall asleep and then when I tell you there's something wrong and my Dad's mixed up in it and I'm worried sick - oh, forget it. I should have known better. I'll find another way. Screw you, Sam Wright." She's red in the face.

"Hey! Calm down! I said I'd help if I could, didn't I?" Sam purses his lips. "OK, I'll do it, because you're my friend and because I said I would. That doesn't mean I have to like it."

"Right then. Thanks." Maddy is still angry. She walks to her front door. She turns: "look, Sam ... "

Sam puts up his hand. "Forget it. You're worried. But I'm telling you - there'll be a perfectly ordinary explanation and you'll find there's nothing going on - nothing serious anyway."

But, as Sam is to find out, he is wrong.

Very wrong.

Dangerously wrong.

CHAPTER 8 – A CRASH OF HEADS

To Sam's relief, Maddy doesn't phone that evening. Good. He has something more important to do. His heart is beating rapidly ... what happens in the next few minutes could be crucial for the rest of his life.

His parents are watching the news; something about a strange death – a man who died on a fairground ride. A ghost train. Apparent heart failure. Sam didn't know the rides were that scary.

Still, it suits Sam that his parents seem unusually interested and don't react when he says he's going to take an early night. His father mumbles "Good idea", but doesn't move his eyes from the news.

Sam has no intention of sleeping - not straight away. He intends to keep his date with the Ngozi woman – if he can.

Sitting on his bed he closes his eyes.

"Hello? Are you there?"

No answer.

He tries again. *"Hello. Ngozi?"*

Still nothing.

He must be doing something wrong.

Sam feels a sense of panic. What if he can't contact her again? Will he have to live the rest of his life with a hundred questions unanswered? Was it all a dream, after all?

No. Stay calm. Try again - do what you did last night.

Sam imagines himself in the hotel: the corridor: the room, the dark wardrobe. He steps into the blackness. He can sense someone. Reaching out, he thinks: *"Ngozi, are you there?"*

"Samuel? Yes, I'm here."

Sam jumps. The reply comes so quickly and so clearly that it startles him. It's like wearing headphones - her voice is being played straight into his head.

"Good grief! How? You answered quickly."

"I've been waiting for you. I'm so pleased that you've been able to do this again. How're you feeling after last night?"

"Better, thanks."

"Really?"

"I actually got some sleep after we spoke. First time in weeks. Even those few hours made a difference."

"Ah."

"I still can't believe what we're doing."

"I felt exactly the same when I started."

"Look, I have loads of questions..."

"Sure you have, and I'll try to answer them, but I'm sorry - they'll have to wait. First you must listen to me very carefully. I need to tell you something vitally important and I'm furious with myself for not saying it yesterday. It was all so sudden and unexpected and rushed last night. I just hope it's not too late. I want you to make me a promise."

"OK, what?"

"Whatever happens, no matter how tempted you are - don't tell anyone about this. No-one. Not a word. And I mean that - absolutely no-one! Not your parents, the rest of your family, your best friend, your doctor, your schoolteacher, not the person you trust most in the world. No-one. Don't hint about it, joke about it, or do anything that might make people even think about it. You understand what I'm saying?"

"Yes. Wow, you're fired up about this."

"With good reason, Samuel. If you do, one day you may wake up dead."

"Seriously?"

"Seriously. Believe me. People don't understand. Even if they half believe you, it means trouble."

Sam smiles thinly. *"People will think I have brain damage after my accident."*

"In your case, that's a possibility. If that's what they assume, you'd be very lucky. If you were unlucky ..."

"Are you seriously suggesting that people would try to kill me?"

"Yes, Samuel, I am. People like us get persecuted. It's been going on for centuries. Every time one of us talks about having telepathic abilities, hoping

that in their case the people in whom they're confiding will be sympathetic and understand – well, they're wrong."

"Every time?"

"Every single time without exception, poor fools. We're all given this advice but some just can't live with such a big secret. It burns them up inside. So they just have to tell someone. They convince themselves that their confidant will be different from the rest and understand where nobody else has. But they're wrong. People don't understand, Samuel. They never do. When people don't understand things, they get frightened. Frightened people do really bad things."

"But killing people? Really?"

"In the old days - you've heard of witch hunts? You've seen the stories?"

"Yes."

"That's what happened. People like you and me were burnt at the stake, or put in ducking stools, or tortured. Luckier ones were just run out of town – chased away because they were possessed by evil spirits. The killings - they still happen in some parts of the world."

"But not here. Not now, surely? We're past all that."

"You reckon? You think nothing bad could happen in sophisticated, liberal-minded England? You're so wrong. In so-called 'educated' countries they have different ways to persecute people like us. OK, they don't burn us at the stake any more – instead, they get us certified with mental health problems and lock us away. That's today's 'civilised' way of getting rid of people who frighten you: dose them so full of drugs they don't know what time of day it is. Are you insane, Samuel?"

"No! At least I don't think so."

"And neither am I. But perfectly sane people have wasted away under unnecessary treatment because they talked too much. Believe me, once the authorities get involved, it's danger all the way for people like us. They'll either lock you away or medicate you till you don't know your own name."

Sam winces. "But that's just ignorance."

"Ignorance – prejudice – stupidity. Call it what you like. Basically it boils down to one thing - fear. Fear of people who are different. Samuel, people are scared of us. Do you understand what I'm saying?"

"Absolutely."

"And you promise?"

"Of course I do. I'd pretty well worked it out for myself."

"Well done. That's such a relief. I'm sorry; I should have said this yesterday. You definitely haven't told anyone?"

"That's right. No-one."

"Thank goodness. I shouldn't have exposed you to the risk."

"Forget it. Now can I ask my questions?"

"OK. I'll do my best ..."

"Did you say there are other people you can talk to like this?"

Ngozi pauses for a moment. *"Two. Well, one reliably. A man in Mexico – my first contact. There's also a woman but she drifts in and out. She's in New Zealand. I haven't heard from her for six months. You're my clearest contact, by a long way."*

"How come I haven't known about this before?"

"Good question. We think it's an ability we're born with, but it usually develops when we reach adulthood. Did you say you're fourteen?"

"Yes. Just had my birthday."

"Well, it's a bit late, but about right. I was thirteen when it happened to me. Sometimes really young children have the ability. We have to be very careful then – we give their voice a name and encourage them to talk about 'their imaginary friend' until they're old enough to understand the importance of secrecy. Then they stop talking about it and people assume they've grown out of it."

"That's amazing." Sam pauses. *"So children with imaginary friends; they're not imaginary at all?"*

"Most are. One or two aren't, that's all."

Sam pauses. Did he have an imaginary friend? He doesn't think so.

"Can you tell me a bit about yourself?"

"Right. I am Ngozi Agalaba. I'm 45..."

"Oh, I assumed you were younger..."

"Sorry to disappoint you, then. Exciting things happen to grown-ups too, you know. I'm married. I have two children. My husband works for an oil company. We live outside Lagos, like I told you yesterday. We have been married for thirty years."

"Thirty? That means you were..."

"Yes. Things work differently in different countries, Sam. I've been married for thirty years and I'm a children's nurse at our local hospital."

"Ngozi – that's an interesting name."

"Thank you. It's an Ibo word and it means 'blessing'. Now, your turn."

"Sam Wright..."

"Samuel or Sam?"

"My friends call me Sam. Sam's better."

"OK, Sam it is..."

"I've just had my 14th birthday. Sorry, I've already told you that. I have a sister called Rachel – she's eleven. I go to Queen's School. I play football and

I'm hoping to get into the school team. My other hobby is riding my bike but I haven't been doing that since the accident."

"Lost your nerve?"

"Lost my bike! It was crushed by the car. Mum and Dad gave me money for my birthday to put towards a new one but I haven't done anything about it yet. Haven't been out much. No energy, thanks to you."

"Tell me about the accident."

Vivid, frightening memories flood back into Sam's mind. This will be the first time he has really opened up to anyone about that day - his feelings, his anger and his sense of guilt. But it's what he needs – someone to talk to.

"Did it help, going to the funeral?"

"Oh, I don't know. Might have. It was really upsetting, seeing the father and the little girl. Maddy came with me – I was grateful."

"She sounds like a good friend. Girlfriend?"

"No. Yes. Well, we've known each other pretty well all our lives."

The mention of Maddy reminds Sam of their conversation earlier in the day. *"Ngozi, can I ask you a question – I mean ask your advice? On a totally different subject? About Maddy?"*

"If you like."

So it is that Sam finds himself telling a woman he's never met about Maddy's father and his strange behaviour and how Maddy wants him, Sam, to spy on a family friend. In later months, he'll look back on this conversation as the first time he shared his inner secrets with her and they started the process of becoming the closest of friends.

Later than night, as he lies in bed, Sam feels an inner contentment. It's a new feeling. At last, an emptiness in his life is being filled. He has a friend, a confidant; someone detached from him and yet so close that he can talk to her at any time, about anything. He knows she will keep their conversations secret because, like him, she can't talk about them to anyone.

Now it will be easier to cope.

For the first time in weeks, Sam enjoys a full, relaxed and unbroken night's sleep. In the morning, he whistles softly to himself as he showers and dresses.

He feels at ease with himself.

That makes a change.

On Monday morning, Helen is relieved to see her son so much improved. "Feeling back to normal now?"

"Pretty much, thanks." Sam senses her relief and happiness.

"You know, if there was ever anything you needed to talk about - your father and I - you can always - I mean, you don't have to bottle things up ..."

Sam smiles, as much to put her out of her embarrassment as anything else. "Yes, I know. Thanks. But there's nothing. Not any more. I'm good. Promise."

He churns up inside as he says it. He'd love to share his secret with his parents but Ngozi has made it quite clear that he can't. As much for his own benefit as hers he adds, truthfully: "I'm getting back to normal now. In fact", he smiles, "I feel the best I have since the accident. I think it shook me up more than I realised."

His mother nods. It is an explanation that's easy to believe.

Sam finishes breakfast and leaves for school, humming softly. Helen smiles for a moment, curiously but happily. It's good to see her son back to his old self.

And yet, she senses something different – deeper – mysterious. Private. Dark, even. It's in his eyes, she thinks.

She shakes her head.

He's been through a horrible experience. And he's growing up.

Yes, that's what it must be.

On the bus, Maddy is also more like her usual self. Her father had taken no furtive phone calls.

They talk instead about the House football match scheduled for that afternoon. "I'm really worried that I'll be dropped. I was useless in the last game. That would be a disaster - the match against Fairbrother Hill is in a few weeks and today's my last chance to impress Hardcastle."

"Don't worry. You'll keep your place. You're White House's best striker. You've scored more goals this season than the rest of the team put together."

"Hope you're right."

"Course I'm right."

"No!" Sam swears under his breath. The House team has been posted on the notice board and he is listed as substitute. OK, it's not as bad as being dropped altogether, but it's still awful - he'll have to sit on the bench and watch, at least for a while.

It's a humiliation; everyone will see. They'll all know why.

Sam bangs his head angrily against the wall, much to the delight of Lewis Squires who happens to appear in the corridor at the exact moment. How long has he been there? Surely it's coincidence? Yes, it has to be – they don't like each other but surely he wouldn't hang around just for the chance to gloat?

Or would he?

Sam can't remember why he and Squires dislike each other so much. He vaguely remembers an argument at primary school. But he feels a deep contempt for this boy and, no question, the feeling is mutual. Everyone knows it.

Lewis Squires has short-cropped red hair, dark eyes and freckled skin. Their studies bring them into only intermittent contact but their shared passion for football should unite them. However, football is a competitive sport and somehow they use it to maintain the antagonism between them.

"Serves you right. If you ask me, Masterson's being generous to even let you sit on the bench."

"Good job nobody's asking you." Sam struggles to keep his anger and disappointment under control.

"If he had any sense he'd drop you completely. You were pathetic last week."

"He probably reckons that with you in goal we won't need our best striker."

"Best striker? You?" Squires curls his lip contemptuously. "Did you see yourself? You made a complete fool of yourself and if you weren't such a stuck-up little shit you'd admit it. Ask anyone." Squires turns and stalks away.

Sam swears again under his breath. Is that really what people think of him? Stuck up? Or is he letting Squires get to him? No: the contempt on Squires' face was real. This is a double humiliation. Worst of all, Sam knows Squires is right, and how badly he played last time.

His worried thoughts are interrupted by a soft voice beside him. "Reckon you're off his Christmas card list then."

Sam jumps. "Oh, hi Tariq." He's surprised that Tariq has approached him like this. "You could say that. Don't think I was ever on it – he hates me."

"Know the feeling. How's the project?"

"Project?"

"The one you were working on in the library. Remember?"

"Oh – that. Yes, it's good. Found the stuff I need. I'm on the right track, I think. Quite interesting really", he adds as an afterthought, which is true.

Tariq looks pleased. Perhaps they have something in common after all. "Great. Look, if I can help, anytime, just let me know. If you want ..." His voice tails off.

"I will."

As Tariq walks away, Sam calls after him. "And Tariq ... thanks." He means it too. What with his disappointment over the team and Squires' stinging comments, it's good to have someone being genuinely friendly.

The atmosphere in the changing room is frosty as Sam gets changed into the House strip with the rest of his team. Time to clear the air.

"Look, I'm sorry about last week. I know I played like shit ..."

Stephen Kettler snorts. "Shit? You cocky bastard - you really think you were that good?" The others murmur their agreement.

"You know, a one-legged blind man in a blindfold on a black night could have scored! Bloody hell, Wright, you only had to touch it!" The noises of agreement are louder this time.

"I know. Look, I was feeling rough that day. I'd had no sleep. I'm better now. If Masterson puts me on today, I'll be OK."

"Then you're a bloody selfish git. If you were sick, you should have said, and let someone else play. We're meant to be a team - you know T - E - A - M."

The rebuke is true. Sam had been selfish. Too focused on himself.

"You're right. I'm sorry. But I'm up for it today, if I get on."

"Bloody well hope so. We can't afford another shambles like that."

Sam hates being a spectator. The teams are evenly matched and Sam is sure he could make a difference. The first half ticks by and with every passing minute his frustration mounts. With Stephen Kettler's angry reproach still burning in his ears, being powerless to do anything is totally frustrating. He wants to prove to everyone that he's back to normal. That he deserves his place.

Half time. No score. Surely he'll be brought on now to break the deadlock? Sam looks pointedly at Mr. Masterson, hoping to catch his eye, but the coach isn't looking. Is that deliberate? Hell - is this just a wake-up call? Or has he really blown his chances? Either way, the game restarts without him and the ordeal continues. He's being made to sit and watch the match, in full view of everyone.

The coach is teaching him a lesson. OK, he recognises what's happening. He'll take his punishment. That last game - he should have stood down. He really should.

It's fifteen minutes into the second half before Sam is able to run onto the pitch, but the circumstances are neither what he expects nor wants. Richard Hartson floats a high cross from the right corner flag into the penalty area. Lewis Squires sprints from his line, straining to reach a ball that is curling away from him. He jumps high and punches it. But his momentum takes him hard into Mr. Masterson, who is refereeing.

There is a sickening thud as their heads crash together. Man and boy collapse, Squires hitting the turf head-first. Neither makes a sound as he falls – the first sign that something is wrong.

Applause turns to silence.

Silence turns to gasps of horror.

The game stops as players gather round. "Masterson's out cold" says one.

"There's something wrong with Squires!" shouts another. "He's choking. He's going blue ..."

Clearly something is dangerously wrong. "Ambulance. Anyone got a phone out here?" Heads shake. "Right, I'm going to the school office." Stephen Kettler sprints across the field.

"He can't breathe" shouts one of the players. "He won't last till the ambulance gets here. He'll be dead before they get here."

No! Not again! He can't stand by and watch another death - not without trying to help.

What would the ambulance men do?

Artificial respiration. He's seen it on television, but doesn't remember it well enough.

Ngozi! Didn't she say she was a nurse or something? He recalls their conversation the previous evening. He closes his eyes and concentrates on calling her.

"Ngozi?"

"Sam. What's going on? It's a really bad time."

"Sorry. Can you help me? There's an emergency here. Did you say you're a nurse?"

"A children's nurse, yes. Why?"

"*There's been a football accident here. One of the players is unconscious. He's not breathing right. He's choking and turning blue. He's going to die. Can you tell me what to do?*"

"*Oh! Right. I'll instruct you - do exactly as I say. Lay him on his back.*"

The other players watch in astonishment as Sam shouts "out of my way" and pushes them aside. He kneels beside Lewis Squires, who is now ominously still.

"*OK. He's on his back.*"

"*Tip his head back ... open his mouth. Has he swallowed his tongue?*"

"*Sorry?*"

Ngozi speaks quickly and urgently. "*His mouth. Look in his mouth. If his tongue is curled backwards and going down his neck, he's swallowed it. That's really dangerous. You'll need to hook it out, otherwise he can't breathe. Check it - quickly.*"

Sam does as Ngozi has told him. Some of the watching boys murmur.

"*Yes, he has. His tongue's all twisted back on itself.*"

"*Use your fingers to uncurl it - get his airway free.*"

Sam feels uncomfortable as he puts his fingers into Squire's mouth.

"*Hold on. Yes, I've freed it. Now what?*"

"*With a bit of luck he'll start breathing normally again.*"

Sam puts his ear close to Squires' mouth. "*No. He's not breathing at all. Oh my God, Ngozi! He's dead!*"

"*Stay calm. How long since the accident?*"

"*A minute. Two?*"

"*Then he's not dead. Not yet. But if he's not breathing, he's dying. Do as I say and you can save him. Tip his head back so his airway is free.*"

"*Done that.*"

"*Now squeeze his nose so that no air can get out. Take a deep breath, put your mouth on his and blow air into his lungs. You are going to do his breathing for him.*"

"*I am?*"

"*Yes. Some people don't support doing this nowadays, but I do.*"

Sam does as Ngozi has directed. It feels horrible putting his mouth onto Squires' but it has to be done."

"What's he doing?"

"Kiss of life, I think."

"*Sam, have you done that?*"

"*Yes, I've blown into his mouth.*"

"Did you see his chest move up?"

"When I breathed into him? Yes."

"Good. Count to three. Take a deep breath and do it again. As if you were breathing normally."

Ngozi pauses.

"Have you done that? Sam, speak to me."

"Yes. Yes, I've done that."

"And is he breathing now?"

"No."

"Oh dear. Is his heart still beating? Can you feel a pulse?"

"How do I do that? His wrist?"

"No. Check the artery on his neck – to the side of his Adam's apple. Quickly."

Sam feels for a pulse. *"Can't feel anything. Perhaps I'm doing it wrong?"*

"No, you'd feel it. This is very serious. You need to do chest compressions. Put the heel of your hand on his chest, three finger-widths up from his breastbone. Put your other hand on top, and keep your fingers in the air. Have you done that?"

"Yes."

"Push down hard on his chest and let it rise again. Do it fifteen times, quickly. It's to massage his heart and keep his blood circulating. Count it out to me as you're doing it."

Cautiously, Sam pushes down *"one... two... three... "*

"No, no, that's no good at all. Go faster, Sam."

"OK. Seven... eight... nine..."

"Faster. Come on, his life depends on you doing this right."

There are more mutterings around him from the other boys. Sam ignores them and concentrates on following Ngozi's instructions.

"Thirteen, fourteen, fifteen - I've done that."

"OK. Now breathe for him again, twice. And then fifteen more chest compressions. Keep doing them in turn. Then check for a pulse again."

Sam does as directed.

"Nothing."

"Then do it again. Two breaths: make them big ones. Then fifteen chest compressions."

"For how long?"

"For as long as it takes."

It seems like for ever that Sam repeats the routines that Ngozi has described to him. Artificial breathing – chest compressions – breathing

– compressions – check for a pulse – nothing - breathing - compressions - more breathing.

It's exhausting.

"Nothing's happening, Ngozi. I must be doing it wrong."

"Not if you're doing exactly as I've told you. Don't give up. Sometimes it takes a while. Keep at it." But she sounds worried.

Sam is starting to feel light-headed. He forces himself to keep going ... he has to, until the ambulance arrives. He longs to hear its siren, but so far there's nothing.

He becomes oblivious to the others standing around and watching. All that matters now is him and Squires. He has descended into his own closed world, isolated from everyone other than his patient and Ngozi.

Artificial breathing – chest compressions – breathing – compressions – check for a pulse.

Nothing. Sam stifles a sob.

"Stay calm Sam. Panicking won't help anyone. Just do it again. Keep at it. Work quickly."

Sam fights to keep his emotions under control. He feels sick with exhaustion and worry. He becomes vaguely aware of a commotion at the edge of the crowd. Dr. Rhodes, the Headmaster, has arrived. His imposing red face is positively scarlet from sprinting across the field. He looks dishevelled from the unaccustomed exercise and angrily tells the boys to stand back. He observes the scene before him with disbelief.

"Wright, what the hell do you think ...?" He stops. He can see for himself. He watches as his fourteen-year-old pupil works silently.

Sam doesn't stop. Artificial breathing – chest compressions – breathing – compressions – check for a pulse.

Nothing.

"I must be doing it wrong."

"I can't tell. Keep going. Be firm with those chest compressions. Even if you're doing it not quite right, it's better than doing nothing and just watching him die."

Too right! Sam bends to his work again. Breathing – chest compressions – breathing – compressions – check for a pulse.

Still nothing.

Again.

Nothing.

Again.

Nothing ... no, wait!

There!

Is that a pulse?

Could be! Faint though.

"*Ngozi! I think I feel a pulse! Very weak though.*"

"*Thank goodness! I was getting worried. Stop doing the chest compressions. Is he breathing for himself yet?*

"*No.*"

"*OK. Continue with the breathing routine until he does.*"

Sam's head is swimming, but he keeps going as Ngozi has instructed. Then, to his great relief, the Squires gives a weak sigh and a cough and takes a breath.

The crowd of boys gasps. One of them cheers.

"Shut up!" the Headmaster snaps. It's out of character for him to speak like that. The boys go silent.

Sam feels like fainting - both with fatigue and with relief. He tips forward and rests his head on the grass.

"*Ngozi! He's just coughed and he's breathing again.*"

"*Thank goodness. You've done really well. That was a long time. Just a couple more things to do now. When you're sure he's breathing steadily again, lay him on his side, slightly curled up, as if he was in bed. Have you got something to cover him with, to keep him warm?*"

"*No. Wait - yes. There are some towels on the touch line. I'll get someone to fetch them.*"

Sam looks up at the other players. He speaks for the first time in ten minutes. "Towels. To keep him warm." He points weakly to the side of the pitch. "Please", he adds.

A member of the other team, who has been watching wide-eyed, jumps to his feet and speeds off. No way is he arguing with Sam Wright - he clearly knows this stuff.

"*Good. Keep him warm. If he wakes before the medical people get there, it's important he stays still. Tell him to do that and to keep calm. Don't let him get up — he could have other injuries. I take it that someone has sent for help?*"

"*Yes. Before I called you.*"

"*Very well. When the medics get there, they'll take charge. Tell them his heart and breathing had stopped. Tell them you did mouth-to-mouth breathing and chest compressions. Until then, make sure he's lying down and keeping warm.*"

"*Yes. Thanks Ngozi. You've saved his life.*"

"*Well actually, Sam, you have. I'm glad you called me. Good thinking. I'm sorry, I have to go. I'm running really late now. Tell me later how your friend recovers. Bye.*"

Two other staff members join the crowd. One of the boys says: "Wright just saved Squire's life." The silence is broken again by a sudden burst of chatter.

Dr. Rhodes snaps at them, exasperation clear in his voice: "For goodness sake, be quiet." He turns. "Mr. Blakely, Mr. Gilbert - please be good enough to take everyone back to the changing rooms. Wright, Kettler - you will stay. Tell me exactly what happened and what you did before I arrived."

"In a minute, Sir." Sam sees Lewis Squires starting to move. Sam stays down, kneeling beside him. Squires' eyes widen when he sees who's next to him and he struggles to get up. Sam places his hand gently on his shoulder to stop him. "You've been in an accident. You need to lie still. Wait for the ambulance."

Squires murmurs something weakly that Sam can't make out, but he stops trying to get up.

Sam's instinct is to stand to talk to Dr. Rhodes but his head is swimming and he's not sure he can. Besides, Lewis Squires is his main concern – Sam feels a commitment to him now. So he stays kneeling on the grass and listens as Stephen Kettler describes the collision. He then adds what he did.

Now, only now, in the distance he hears sirens wailing – the ambulance is arriving. It would have been far too late.

The ambulance drives straight onto the field and stops where Squires is lying. The paramedics stoop to take his pulse and blood pressure. They cover him with a metalised sheet and transfer him to a stretcher.

"What happened?"

Sam explains and the paramedics nod. "Will he be alright?"

"Should be. We'll get him in the ambulance and do some more checks."

By the time he returns slowly to the changing room, the other players are dressed. They've been waiting for him. They surround him as soon as he walks through the door. Josh Hunter says "Bloody hell, Sam, you saved his life, you know."

Richard Hartson asks "where did you learn to do that?"

There's no way Sam can tell him. Instead he replies simply "I'm glad he's OK" and leaves it at that.

The other boys look at him curiously. There is something – different – about Wright today. Still, no-one can argue about what he's done. Let him be modest if that's what he wants – better than pushy, any day.

Sam has finished changing and is ready to leave when an ashen-faced Mr. Masterson and the Headmaster join them. The boys fall silent.

Dr. Rhodes speaks: "I am pleased to tell you that Squires was fully conscious, and able to speak when he was carried onto the ambulance. The medical staff complimented the school on the actions taken to care for him after the accident." He nods appreciatively in Sam's direction.

Mr. Masterson has an angry red lump on his forehead, made even more prominent because he is deathly pale. He says nothing but he manages a weak smile and thumps Sam on the back.

"Thank God that's over" mutters Sam under his breath.

But it isn't. Today's episode has started a chain of events more frightening than anything Sam has experienced before.

CHAPTER 9 – LYING

Maddy hasn't waited to walk home with Sam. Slowly he trudges back by himself, head bowed in thought. What will he say to his parents about today's events? What can he say? He saved Lewis Squires' life, but how can he possibly explain how he knew what to do?

Ngozi had told him that his life would be different now. She was dead right if today is anything to go by. What other unexpected surprises might his telepathy have in store for him?

At the scene of the accident, the wrecked bus stop has been removed but not yet replaced. A new street light is in position but it's a different colour to the others and looks out of place – a jarring reminder of the tragedy. The sad remnants of flowers placed by sympathetic neighbours now lie faded and forlorn on the pavement.

Tragedy has turned to history. How quickly life moves on!

A woman's voice is raised in anger. Sam looks up.

"The stupid bastards! Stan helped them. I don't know what this bloody country's coming to!" A large woman, red in the face, is sounding off to her neighbour, who nods silently, not that she has much choice in the matter. "That nutcase shouldn't have been allowed anywhere near a car ever again – he's the one who needs locking away, not my Stan."

She sees Sam and points. "You! You were there, weren't you?"

Sam stops. "Sorry?"

"You were there when that idiot killed the woman and her baby."

"Yes. He almost got me, too."

"That's right." She points again. "That's right! He knocked you down too - you went under the bus. Do you know what the police have done now? Come on – guess."

"No. Sorry." Sam shakes his head. Why is he apologising? How could he know? And thanks for asking how I am.

"They've only gone and arrested my Stan. The little bastard's complained that Stan assaulted him. He says Stan used 'unjustifiable force'. Unjustifiable bloody force, my arse. I'll show the little shit what unjustifiable bloody force looks like if I get my hands on him. Stan stopped him getting away, that's all. We told them: he hit his head on the pavement when Stan tackled him."

Yes, Sam remembers clearly. The man he now knows is called Stan tackled the driver of the Ford. The driver had struggled to get away. Stan had threatened to 'punch his lights out' - and delivered. The story about him hitting his head – it isn't true.

But this needs no thought! There was only one criminal that fateful day. No-one who went to the funeral could have any sympathy with him.

"Yes, I saw" says Sam. "Your husband tackled the driver. I ... I think you're right – he went down very hard." He says it loudly so that the neighbour will hear.

"There you go. The little sod banged his head. Stan never hit him – he banged his bloody head. Will you tell them that?"

"Yes, if they ask, that's what I'll say." The law might say that Stan assaulted the driver. But justice and common sense say he did the right thing. If it takes a lie to see justice done, Sam's up for that.

"You do that. You tell them." She turns to talk again to her neighbour.

It seems that Sam is no longer needed. Well, thanks again for asking how I am. He continues his walk home, seething with anger.

"*Hey – what's up?*"

"*Oh, hi, Ngozi. I didn't call you.*"

"*No. But something's up – I can feel it. Are you angry?*"

"*I'll say!*" Sam tells her what's happened.

"*You're joking!*"

"*Wish I was. He knows how to steal cars and how to drive like a bloody lunatic – sorry – and he knows his rights. He's probably got some don't-give-a-shit lawyer trying to get him off by generating sympathy for him.*"

"*No wonder you feel angry.*"

"Glad you understand. Anyhow, I'm home now. Oh, no – the police are here. Three guesses what they want. Speak to you later."

The net curtains twitch in the house next door. That will be the holier-than-thou witch Mrs. Jobson, checking what's going on - sticking her nose into other peoples' lives again. She'll be eaten up with curiosity about the police visiting Sam's house.

She is the only disadvantage of living in their road. Though she rarely leaves her home these days, when she does she is always ready to pass comment on everyone and everything and to proclaim her alleged religious values. Sam isn't in the mood. He scowls at the unwashed net curtains, intending that she will see.

His father is waiting at the door. He nods at the next room and says quietly: "Police. Some more questions about the accident."

"Great."

Two uniformed Officers are waiting in the lounge – Sam recognises them as the ones who took his statement in the hospital. They stand as Sam enters. They're sorry to disturb him again but could they clarify a couple of points?

"OK, but I told you everything."

"We were very grateful, Mr. Wright." The Officer is being very formal. "We're investigating an allegation made by the driver we arrested."

"Allegation?"

"Do you mind if we move straight to the questions?"

"No, I suppose not."

"Thank you, Sir." They pull out notebooks. "In your statement you said that you saw the driver of the Ford Focus exit it after the crash?"

"Yes. I told you last time. He tried to run away. He tried to leave the scene of the accident – isn't that an offence?"

"Yes, Sir, it is."

"I hope you charge him, then."

The Officer ignores this. "Where were you when he tried to get away?"

"Sitting on the kerb."

"Were you able to see clearly what happened after the driver left the crashed vehicle?"

"Yes. I told you. I saw it all."

"In your previous statement you referred to a man – you called him 'Rugby Man' because of the shirt he was wearing."

"That's right. He stopped the driver getting away."

"Do you know this man – the one who stopped the driver?"

"No. I mean, I've seen him before, but I don't know him. He lives down the road, I think."

"Have you spoken to him since the accident?"

"No." That's the truth. "I don't think I've ever spoken to him." That's true too.

The officers are visibly pleased.

"What, exactly, did you see after the driver left the crashed car?"

"What I told you before. The driver tried to run away. 'Rugby Man' stopped him."

"How exactly did he stop him?"

"He rugby-tackled him."

"And what happened then?"

This is the crunch question.

"What do you mean?"

"What happened after 'Rugby Man' tackled the driver?"

"Nothing. The driver lay still and 'Rugby Man' knelt over him. I think he must have hit his head. On the pavement. As he fell."

"Hit his head? Are you sure?"

"Pretty sure. He came down with a real thump – it was either that or he'd have got away. Why do you ask?"

Again his question is ignored. "After the rugby tackle, did you see 'Rugby Man' hit the driver?"

"No. Why would he?" Sam feels his heart racing as he lies, and hopes that the police can't tell.

The two officers look at each other. They nod. "That's very useful. We're grateful to you for sparing us your time and apologise for disturbing you again." They close their notebooks. Sam senses their pleasure: he has the distinct impression that those were exactly the answers they wanted to hear.

He decides to push the point: "Will Rugby-man get a reward? He should, I think."

"I doubt it."

"That's a shame. He helped you."

The Officer notes the implied criticism. There is an edge to his voice now: "Yes, Mr. Wright. Sometimes we don't like what we have to do any more than you do." Then he backs off. "But I'm sure everything will be OK. Thank you again for your help."

Sam's father sees the police to the door. When he returns he looks at his son quizzically.

"I know Stan. He's a big guy, and he knows how to handle himself. Did he hit him?"

Sam says nothing. He looks at the floor. He doesn't want to lie to his father as well.

"Ah. Forget it. I never asked that question." George Wright pauses. Then he smiles gently and puts his hand on Sam's shoulder. "Well done, son. I'm glad you see things so clearly."

It takes a few seconds for Sam to realise what his father actually means. He smiles. "Thanks Dad".

"I'll walk down to see Barbara – Stan's wife. I'll tell her what you said."

"She was pretty upset when I walked past."

"I'm not surprised."

"Before you do ..." Sam is going to tell his parents about the football match. But his phone is ringing. "No, it can wait – I'll tell you later."

He checks his phone. It's Maddy.

CHAPTER 10 – SPYING

Uh-oh, something's happened. Sam knows it instinctively. Yes, he's right: she sounds tense. He groans inwardly; he's pretty certain what it will be. He walks upstairs, listening.

"Thank goodness you're back. Dad's just had one of his mystery calls."

As he feared. "Isn't that earlier than normal?"

"Absolutely. I almost missed it. He'd only just got in from work. He answered his phone, took it straight into the other room and shut the door. He knew immediately who it was."

"Any clues?"

"No. He was talking really quietly but I could tell he was angry – really wound up - red in the face. He was pacing about. Now he's gone all quiet and later on he'll go out. That's what always happens. Sam, I'm worried. He's going to meet someone in secret who makes him angry."

"OK, I understand." Sam wants to reassure Maddy that he's there for her. He doesn't want her losing her rag with him again. "I'd be worried too. Phone me when he leaves, and I'll watch to see where he goes. I'm in my room now – I'll stay here till I hear from you."

"Thanks, Sam. I feel awful about this."

"I know." Sam crosses his fingers, hoping that he won't need to spy on a family friend. But with a heavy feeling in his heart, his mobile rings again a short time later. Maddy says simply: "He's just left".

Sam's bedroom is at the front of the house and the window overlooks the main road. "Right. I'm turning off the light." He crosses back to the window. "OK. I'm watching."

Outside, the road is in shadows. The street lights are already on, but their effect is to throw puddles of light rather than illuminate evenly. After a couple of minutes, Edward James walks into view, visible for a few moments, then hidden in the dark and then seen again under the next light.

"Maddy, I see him. He's heading this way. He could be going to his office. He's keeping to the inside of the pavement, like he's trying to avoid attention. He's going past our house now. He's gone by. Hold on: he's stopped - he's looking round. He's crossing the road. Damn – I'm going to lose him: he's going down the Crescent."

"The Crescent? We don't know anyone down there. Why's he going down there?"

"No idea."

Maddy's father has taken a side street about thirty yards to the left of Sam's bedroom window. He is already out of sight. "One thing's for sure, Maddy – he's NOT going to his office."

This is no good. Now Maddy will do nothing but worry about where her father has gone. For her sake, he'll have to find out more.

"OK, Maddy, I'm going to find him. See where he's gone. Got to hang up though – call you back later. Sorry."

"Sam ..."

Sam doesn't wait. If he talks it through for too long, he'll risk losing track of Edward James completely. As quietly as he can, he slips downstairs and out the front door, closing it gently behind him. He wants no questions from his parents.

Mrs. Jobson's curtains twitch again. Sam wonders they don't fall apart. He sticks his tongue out. Witch!

He pauses for a moment. Instead of turning left out of his house and following Edward's route, Sam turns right. He sprints to a road that he knows joins The Crescent. He walks cautiously in case he sees Maddy's father coming towards him or stopped, talking to someone.

No, no-one is walking towards him. Could Maddy's father have gone into one of the houses? If he has, Sam will have to find some unobtrusive to hide, waiting for him to come out again.

No, wait.

A white car is parked on the other side of The Crescent facing him, carefully positioned in a dark stretch between two street lights. Edward James is leaning on it, talking in low tones to the driver.

Sam drops to his knees behind a hedge and peers ahead, breathing shallowly, trying to make no noise. He strains to see the driver's face.

It's not possible. Just a vague, pale blur behind the windscreen. Neither can he hear what the two are saying, but whatever it is, Maddy's father is agitated. As they talk, he looks nervously up and down the street.

The conversation becomes more intense. Edward throws his head back and swears, then walks round the car and gets into the passenger seat. As the door opens, the interior light snaps on and Sam is able to catch a tantalisingly short glimpse of the driver: male, balding, about the same height as Maddy's father, a thick moustache. Chunky gold rings on his right hand, which is resting on the steering wheel. It's not much, but it's something.

The light goes out.

Sam thinks that Maddy is right to be worried; this looks all wrong. But what could cause someone like Edward James – an honest man - to keep secrets from his daughter and possibly his wife, to come out of his house at night and have a furtive meeting in a side street with a stranger in a white car?

Why can't whoever is driving the car come openly to the house? It's only a few minutes' walk away, after all.

Why are they arguing?

And what about?

Questions, questions – and no answers!

For five minutes more the two men talk. To Sam, crouching behind the hedge, it's like watching a scene from a silent movie, but with no captions to tell him what the actors are saying. Finally, Edward James takes an envelope from his inside pocket and slams it angrily onto the dashboard.

Money?

The handing over of the envelope marks the end of the conversation. Edward gets out of the car. He makes to slam the passenger door, but stops himself and closes it quietly instead. He is still doing everything possible to avoid attracting attention.

He starts to walk home, away from the point where Sam is hiding. Sam stays where he is: it's the driver of the white car who interests him now.

The man rests his forehead for a few minutes on the steering wheel, long enough for Sam to see the street light reflecting from his balding head. He too is acting as if he's upset. Interesting – for both of them to be angry. He takes the envelope from the dashboard and puts it in an inside pocket. Definitely money, thinks Sam.

There's no time to dwell on the implications: the car will move off soon. Sam takes his phone from his pocket. He'll try to get some pictures as it goes by.

The balding man wipes the misted-up inside of the windscreen with the back of his right hand. The rings glint again in the light. The engine starts and the car drives slowly towards Sam, who crouches back behind the hedge.

The car passes by him. The light is poor for taking photographs, but what the hell? Assuming they won't come out well, Sam holds his finger on the button and takes a series of shots whilst straining to get whatever view of the driver he can.

There's a final, tantalisingly brief glimpse of the balding man with the bushy moustache. On his right hand - gripping the steering wheel - Sam again sees two large rings that he assumes are gold. That is what reflected earlier, when he wiped the screen. In the back window is a Manchester United sticker.

The white car slides quietly by, disappearing unobtrusively into the distance: no fast acceleration, nothing that might attract attention. Only Sam gives it a second look. He makes a note of the car's number plate on his phone.

It's not much, but he hopes Maddy will find the information useful. She might be able to work something out. At least he's kept his promise to her. Now he needs to phone and tell her what he's seen. But not out in the street. This conversation needs to be private. He'll go back to his room and call her from there. He jogs home.

A car he doesn't recognise is parked outside the house. Not another visitor, surely? Once again, the curtains twitch next door as he arrives. Mrs. Jobson is having a busy night: she'll be able to construct a detailed conspiracy out of what she's seen today. Sam scowls again at her and taps his nose. She will see.

Good.

As he lets himself in through the front door, his father calls. "Ah, Sam – we were wondering where you were."

"I ..."

"No matter, tell me later. You're in demand tonight. You have another visitor."

"For God's sake!" Sam groans under his breath. Who on earth could want to see him at this time of night? He needs to phone Maddy.

Half fearing it will be the Police again, he steps into the lounge with a scowl on his face. Oh! His look changes to one of surprise and bewilderment. Not the Police but Dr. Rhodes, his Head Teacher, sitting talking to his parents, clutching a cup of tea. Sam senses the mood: they're happy – almost jovial.

"Ah. I'm glad I didn't miss you, Sam." Dr. Rhodes puts down his cup and stands up. "I've been telling your parents about your most commendable actions at the football match this afternoon. I gather, though, that you had not yet informed them?"

Sam's phone is ringing in his pocket. That'll be Maddy. Her father has returned and she'll be frantic to find out what Sam saw. He fumbles to switch it off. No choice – like it or not, she'll have to wait.

"Er ... no, not yet. I was going to. It's been a busy night. I haven't really had time yet." Sam wants to change the subject: "How is Squires?"

"He is well, I'm delighted to say, and that is wholly thanks to you. Which is why I'm here. I was just telling your parents: I do apologise again ... I wouldn't normally call late and unannounced, but I've been at the hospital where I spoke with Squires' mother. She told me that the doctors expect her son to suffer no lasting effects from today's incident. They'll keep him under observation for a while, of course, but they expect to allow him return home very soon."

"That's good." Sam's phone is ringing again. He hangs up for a second time without taking the call. He hates doing this to Maddy.

"It's more than good; it's remarkable. The medical staff told Mrs. Squires that, beyond any doubt, the outcome would have been catastrophically different had it not been for your excellent work, the last few minutes of which I witnessed for myself. You acted coolly and calmly in an emergency and your level-headedness is a credit to you."

Sam looks at the floor. This is embarrassing.

"Mrs. Squires has asked me to pass on her gratitude and on behalf of the school, I came round to thank you as well." Dr. Rhodes smiles and holds out his hand. Sam takes it. "That was very well done, young man. Very well done indeed."

"Thank you Sir."

"We will, of course, find a way of recognising your achievement more publicly."

"Please, no - I'd rather not." Sam groans inwardly; people already think he's arrogant and stuck-up. And now the telepathy thing – Ngozi keeps telling him to avoid any publicity.

"Nonsense. No time for false modesty. Now, I'd better get home" says Dr. Rhodes. "I've taken enough of your time and my wife will be starting to wonder what I look like." He lets go Sam's hand and looks towards the door.

Sam has never thought about Dr. Rhodes having a wife. Perhaps he has children as well?

"Thank you for the tea. You should be very proud of your son."

"We are. Thank you for coming."

It takes another twenty frustrating minutes of running over the story again and again before Sam can free himself from his parents' attention. They want to know how he knew what to do.

"I don't know – I just did. Must've read about it, sometime." What else can he say?

Sam can see they are pleased and proud ... but he needs to talk with Maddy. This is taking so long! Hell – he has homework to do as well tonight.

His parents look at each other as their son dashes upstairs. "What's all that about?" asks Helen. "You'd think he'd be bubbling over ..."

"I have no idea. He saves a boy's life, but he doesn't think it matters enough to tell us? And then there's something more important he has to do?"

"He's changing. There's something ... different about him lately."

"He's growing up fast."

"No" says Helen. "No, it's deeper than that ..." She shakes her head. "I can't put my finger on it. There's a mysterious side to him now ... secretive ... darker."

They sit in silence for a few moments.

"Hey ... our son saved a boy's life today. That doesn't seem dark to me."

Upstairs, Sam phones Maddy at last.

"For God's sake, Sam, where the hell have you been? I've been going spare trying to get through to you. Why didn't you answer?"

"Sorry. I wanted to. Couldn't. Dr. Rhodes came round and I had to talk to him and my parents. I ran back to phone you, but I couldn't get away."

This bombshell has no effect. "Dad got back half an hour ago. Half an hour, Sam! I've been going crazy here."

"I know. I'm sorry."

"Well ... did you see where he went?"

"Yes, and you were right - it wasn't the office."

"I know that! That's the last thing you said before you hung up on me. There's something so wrong! He's in trouble, I know it. He's going to get arrested! What shall I do, Sam?"

"Hey! Calm down! You don't know he's in trouble. I haven't even told you what happened yet!"

Maddy sniffs. "Get on with it then!"

"Right. Your Dad went down the Crescent. I knew you'd want to know what was happening, so I ran down the other road. He was there, talking to a man in a white car."

"White car? What sort? Who was in it?"

"Toyota. Don't know. I only got a glimpse of the driver's face. Anyhow, your Dad was really up tight. He didn't want to be seen and when they started arguing he got into the car ..."

"Arguing? What about?"

"Don't know. If I'd been close enough to hear, they'd have seen me. But your Dad got into the car and when the light came on I got a brief look at the other guy. About your father's height, bushy moustache, balding. They talked a few minutes more, then your Dad took an envelope from his inside pocket and threw it on the dashboard."

"How big an envelope?"

"Business letter. Looked like it might have been money. That's what I thought it was."

"Money? Oh, God."

Sam presses on. "Then your Dad got out and walked back. The white car started up and drove past me – and that's all, I'm afraid. I took some photographs and I've got the number – I doubt they'll come out well but I'll try to enhance them and e-mail them to you.

"But before you go off on one, that doesn't mean your Dad's in trouble. There's no law against meeting someone in a white car, you know."

Maddy sounds close to tears. "But going out at night and talking to this stranger! Arguing! Handing over money! That doesn't sound good, does it? Oh God - he's in real trouble - he's being blackmailed! That's the only explanation!"

That possibility had occurred to Sam too. But he needs to calm Maddy down. "Not necessarily, Maddy. Don't automatically think the worst. That's one explanation but not the only one. Obviously he knows the driver - it might even be a friend. Friends do argue. There you go - he might be helping a friend, or a relative."

It doesn't sound very convincing. Still, it gives Maddy something more positive to think about. "OK. It could be. Surely you saw something more of the driver – balding, bushy moustache – anything else? Something that might give me some clues as to who it was?"

"A bit. I didn't want him to see me, so it wasn't much. He had two big gold rings on his right hand."

"What sort of rings?"

"Like I said, big ones. Chunky. Are they significant? Does it sound like someone you know?"

"No. Yes; well, someone I used to know. Can you send me the photographs?"

"OK. If they've come out. It was pretty dark."

"I mean, now. Right now? Let me see them and I'll phone you back."

Intrigued, Sam does as he's been asked. The photos aren't brilliant, but he cleans up the three best ones and adjusts the colours. They're better than nothing, anyway. The first two show the balding man from side on, and the gold rings. The third shows the back of the car as it drives away.

After a few minutes, his phone rings again. Maddy says, speaking very quietly: "I got them."

"And ... is it someone you know?"

"Yes, but it can't be."

"What do you mean?"

"It's weird. The man in the car; he looks like my Uncle Frank – Dad's brother."

"I didn't know you had an Uncle."

"I haven't seen him for years. He was definitely going bald the last time I saw him. He had a moustache, not as bushy as in the picture but he could have grown it. The age looks right. But, it's the rings. That's pure Uncle Frank. He really liked his bling. That's who I'd have said it was."

"There you go. Your Dad was meeting his brother. Mystery solved."

"No. Mystery deepened. You see, it can't have been him."

"Why not?"

"It's a long story. We don't talk about it. Uncle Frank is what you'd call the black sheep of our family. A few years ago he was accused of helping to rob a bank in Reading – he worked there.

"They suspended him and launched an internal inquiry. He was told to stay away and not contact anyone. Two days later he left his house and never came back."

"He did a runner? He's on the run? He's a criminal?"

"Not exactly."

"But now you think the driver of the car could have been your Uncle Frank – he's come back?"

"It's the rings – I met Uncle Frank a few times and each time he was wearing two chunky gold rings on his right hand. He shook my hand once and they dug into my fingers and hurt."

"But there must be loads of people who wear gold rings."

"Yes, but how many of them know my father, and meet him secretly at night?"

"Good point. Could be him, then. Could be he's in hiding and your Dad's helping him. That would explain why he doesn't come to the house. Although, if he's on the run, that doesn't look good ... helping a fugitive who tried to rob a bank."

Maddy speaks very softly. "Yes, apart from one thing. Uncle Frank didn't do a runner as you put it. He was found. Or rather his body was. He killed himself. According to my parents, Dad's brother - my Uncle Frank - is dead."

Sam flops back onto his bed. His life has been taking some strange turns lately but this is the most extraordinary day so far.

He's saved a boy's life at school.

He's lied to the police.

He's spied on a family friend.

And now he's just photographed a dead man driving a white car.

CHAPTER 11 – SUICIDE

"They found Uncle Frank's body in the river near his house. According to Dad he couldn't live with the shame of it, even though he was innocent. He dreaded going to court and couldn't face seeing his photo plastered all over the papers. Even if he was acquitted he'd never be able to rebuild his career or completely recover his reputation. People would always be pointing at him and whispering behind his back: 'wasn't there something fishy about that guy?' So he took a fistful of painkillers, washed them down with a bottle of whisky and jumped off a bridge into the Thames."

"Bloody hell! He didn't do things by half. But surely if he wasn't involved and he had to be found innocent ...?"

"That's what I said, but Dad just shrugged his shoulders. He said you can't tell people what to think when they are facing pressure like that and public humiliation."

"It must have been terrible for your family."

"I guess so. They played it down – didn't make a big thing of it. To protect me from it, I suppose. I think Dad handled everything. Uncle Frank didn't have anyone else – he wasn't married or anything."

"What did your parents say afterwards?"

"Not much. Just that they always believed in him. He wouldn't have been involved in anything illegal. They talked about it a lot though – I could hear them downstairs at night."

"Were you close to him?"

"Not really. He came to see us sometimes, that's all. He sent cards for birthdays and Christmas. He brought presents when he visited."

"So, how old were you at the time – when he died, I mean?"

"Like I said, it was about three years ago."

"You've never said."

"It's not the sort of thing you talk about, is it? Your Uncle being a suspected bank robber and topping himself."

"I guess not. Did you go to the funeral?"

"No. Just Dad. It was very low key. I didn't really know what was going on – just that Mum and Dad were upset. I asked about it once. Dad said I should know that Uncle Frank would never do anything wrong and I should always think good of him. He said not to talk to anyone about it though, because it was sad and private."

"Then the guy in the car has to be someone else" says Sam.

"I'm not sure. I have this strange feeling."

"Why?"

Maddy pauses, collecting her thoughts. "I suppose it's ... well, now I think about it, and telling you about it: Mum and Dad never talk about him. They don't even mention him. Surely he should come up in conversation sometimes? You know, 'what a shame Frank's not here – he'd have enjoyed this' or 'it's the anniversary of the day Frank died.' And I've just realised - they never visit his grave. That's a bit weird isn't it?"

"Could be. Perhaps he was cremated. What are you suggesting?"

"Oh, I don't know. What if he's still alive, I suppose. What if the suicide story is a lie? What if he's still living and blackmailing Dad to give him money, and Dad will be in trouble if anyone finds out?"

Sam is shocked. What can he say? It's such a serious possibility and it fits in with what they know.

"Sam. You know I have to get to the bottom of this now, don't you? I have to know what's going on. If Dad's brother is still alive, and he's blackmailing him, I have to find out and make it stop."

"Yes, but how?"

Maddy pauses, thinking. "I suppose the obvious thing to do first is to check out the suicide story. Try and find out if he's really dead."

"How?"

"Let's think it through. What was his address? I know roughly where he lived, but not precisely. If I can find out exactly where, I can check if he's still there. If he is, that will prove that he didn't commit suicide and my parents lied about it.

"If he's not there, I can look for evidence of his death. There must have been an inquest – there always is if someone dies and it isn't natural causes."

"Inquest!" Sam exclaims. "You're right. I had to give evidence at the one after the accident. It was in the papers afterwards, remember? If the story your parents told you is true, it's even more likely to have made the papers. 'Suicide verdict for suspected bank robber' – that sort of thing. There'll be official records somewhere. You know - death certificates. Where do we start?"

"You'll help?"

"Of course I will!"

"Thanks. His house. We check his house."

"But you don't know the address?"

"No. It was outside Reading. Near the River Thames. I remember, because we went for a walk last time I was there and watched the boats."

"Any more?"

"No. I'll try to find out. Dad knows, obviously. He went there a few times afterwards, to clear the place out, he said. That's where that signed Manchester United team picture came from – the one in our hall."

"Could you ask your father for the address?"

"Hell no. That would give the game away. But I'll try to find their address book. And I'll see ..."

"Stop!" Sam interrupts.

"What?"

"What you just said."

"Address book?"

"No. Something about a picture in your hall?"

"The Man U signed photo. You must've seen it."

Sam remembers. Of course he's seen it. "That was your Uncle's? I didn't realise."

"God yes! His pride and joy. He was a huge fan. He'd go to all their away games when they were playing down this way. He won it in a competition."

Sam forces himself to stay calm. "Maddy, look at the third photo I sent you."

There is a pause. "OK. The back of the white car. What am I looking for?"

"In the rear window."

"It's a sticker" observes Maddy.

"Zoom in."

There's another pause. Then Sam hears Maddy gasp. "Holy shit, Sam! That just has to be a Man U sticker."

"No doubt about it – that's what it was. I saw it clearly."

"So, you mean ..."

"Oh yes. Maddy, there are too many co-incidences ... If someone looks like your Uncle, wears chunky rings like your Uncle, has a moustache like your Uncle and supports Man U like your Uncle, I'd bet anything that that's who your father met tonight."

"But that means Mum and Dad lied to me about him being dead. Why would they do that?"

"There's loads of possibilities. We've talked about one – a bad one. There'll be others. It could be ..."

"Damn. I'm sorry – Mum's calling: better go now. Sam ..."

"Yes?"

"Thanks. You're a good friend." She hangs up.

Sam looks at the phone for a while. What a strange thing to say! Of course he's a good friend. They've known each other for years. But, hey, it's better than being called a jerk.

As Sam and Maddy finish their conversation, fifty miles away a slightly built, innocuous looking, middle-aged man sits in an immaculately tidy room lit by a single small lamp. The room is poorly furnished: bare floorboards, a narrow bed in the corner, a wardrobe, a table and a chair.

He looks up from the newspaper he is studying. A supercilious smile plays around his lips. He takes a small black notebook from the inside pocket of the jacket hanging on his chair. He flicks through it with quick familiarity. Quietly he murmurs: "William Beaston, if you still work here, I do believe I know where you'll be next week."

With fastidious care he cuts an article from the paper. The headline reads "Reading braces for trouble." Underneath it says "All Police leave cancelled."

The man writes a few words in the book, folds the cutting and places it neatly inside. "William, I think it's time you and I met again."

He clasps his hands behind his head, leans back and smiles.

But not his eyes. His eyes don't smile.

The supermarket staff smile at the young lady in the red dress. She's a regular sight lately, doing her shopping late at night when the place is all but empty. They don't know whether it's because she works late or because she prefers to come when the shop is quiet and she can get round quickly.

Looking at her, they whisper that it's probably the latter reason: she looks a nervous person. Many people don't like supermarkets when they are crowded.

CHAPTER 12 – RULES

Contacting his telepathic partner tonight is easier: he knows he has to clear his mind of everything else and reach out for her. Ngozi asks straight away *"Hi Sam. How's your friend?"*

"Maddy? She's OK, thanks."

"Not Maddy! The one whose life you saved! Remember?"

"Oh. Right. Yes ... sorry. Good news. He's OK. Our Headmaster came round tonight to thank me. God, that was so embarrassing. Then I had to explain to my parents everything that happened. Three times. I didn't say anything about you and me, of course, but your instructions were brilliant. Thanks for your help."

"I'm glad." But Ngozi sounds distracted. She also has something on her mind. Lewis Squires is not her main concern right now, either. *"Sam, this is really important. You've used your telepathy for real now. You need to understand how dangerous that is."*

"Dangerous? No, really - nobody knows. I've not said anything. No-one has any idea that you were telling me what to do."

"And that's good. But think it through, Sam. Today you did something that you actually didn't know how to do. When you saved your friend's life, you did it because of our telepathy. Worst of all, it was very high profile – lots of people saw."

"So? Loads of people could have done what I did."

"No, Sam, they couldn't. That's the point. Very few people could have done what you did. Not that well, anyway. I take it that none of the others said 'stand back, I'll handle this, I know what to do'."

She's right, of course.

"*Because of us communicating like this, people saw a fourteen-year-old take control of a serious medical emergency, carry out skilled work and save someone's life. You did it in complete silence, like you knew exactly what you were doing.*"

OK. Where's this going?

"*You know what people will ask next: how come Sam Wright knows that stuff?*"

There is no denying that. "*My parents have already asked.*"

"*There you go. The first question people will ask.*"

"*But surely people won't get paranoid because I saved someone's life?*"

"*You reckon? A lot will say you did a fantastic thing and leave it at that. But – think how the authorities would react if they found out how you did it.*"

"*Wouldn't they be pleased too?*"

"*No, Sam, they wouldn't. They'd go ballistic.*"

"*Then they're crazy!*"

"*No, they're not crazy. They're frightened. Terrified out of their wits. They know about people like us and it scares them. They won't give a damn about the good you've done. All they'll care about is what else you could do. Bad things. Things that could embarrass them.*"

Sam is startled. "*Bad things? How?*"

He feels, rather than hears, Ngozi sigh.

"*This is very difficult*" she says slowly. "*OK. I'm going to tell you a story. Pay attention to this, Sam: it really happened.*"

"*Right?*"

"*Picture this scene: a workplace. A small internal office with half-glass walls, just the one door, a table and a chair. Nothing else. No external window, no telephone, no computer. A box with windows, basically.*"

As Ngozi talks, Sam imagines the scene as it unfolds. In the office is a man, sitting at a table. The door is locked and standing just inside the door, watching everything the man is doing, is a security guard.

The man is reading a document. Occasionally he writes a note in the margin. He's giving it a final check for accuracy - spelling mistakes, untidy presentation, figures that don't add up.

The man makes a few notes in the margins of the document and when he has finished, he puts it in an envelope, seals it and leaves it on the table. The guard opens the door for him, sees him out and locks the door again. A few minutes later someone else comes to collect the sealed envelope.

"*That must be an important document to be treated with such high security.*"

"Spot on. It's a bid."

Ngozi continues with the story. The company is competing for a major order. So the bid document is really important and very sensitive. It has prices in it and competitive information on how the company would handle the order if they were to be chosen. The management of the company has staked everything on this bid. They have to win. The future of the company and hundreds of jobs depend on it.

But the man in the office is no ordinary man. He's a telepath, like Ngozi and Sam. As he reads the tender, he is silently relaying its most crucial information to his telepathic partner. His partner writes it down and that evening sells the information to a rival company for a personal fortune.

The company that bought the stolen information worked overnight, changed its own bid, stole the good ideas and undercut the price of its rival. Needless to say it won the contract. The first company almost went out of business.

And the guy that did it – no-one could prove a thing against him. He wasn't even a suspect. He never moved from the office. He was watched all the time. He took no copies, he made no notes. He just read the document, suggested some improvements and left it on the desk. Job done.

It was the perfect industrial espionage crime. His partner lived in another part of the country and they'd never met. There was no way the two of them could be linked and nothing could ever be proved against them.

Sam is shocked. *"That's just ... wicked."*

"Yes. Now start to understand why governments get paranoid about people like us. You see, people like us could use telepathy to pass national secrets too."

"Real spying!"

"Exactly. If you or I had sensitive jobs in Government, everything we read or see could be half way round the world in an instant and nobody would know how on earth the secrets were being smuggled out."

"But how do you know all this?"

"The partner who received the information eventually felt so guilty about what they had done that she confessed - years later, mind you, and to us, not to the authorities. The man in the office turned out to be a complete head-case and eventually she shut herself off from him."

"She? His partner was a woman?"

"Yes."

"She told you this?"

"Not directly. You remember I told you I was in contact with another couple of people? One of them was appointed to advise me. He told me."

"Appointed?"

"Yes. Which brings me onto the next thing I need to tell you. The senior members in our community try to protect the interests of people like us. I've told them about you. As I'm your only telepathic contact, I am your mentor. I'll advise you on how to cope in a world where you are, let's say, different. I'll suggest ways for you to avoid being discovered. How to avoid misusing your telepathic ability. How to make sure no-one suspects what you can do. That means absolute secrecy and a huge amount of self-control."

"You make it sound like a secret society."

"A bit over the top. It's not really a society but, yes, it is very secret. We simply mustn't draw attention to ourselves and we mustn't abuse our powers. We have a code of behaviour, Sam."

Sam groans.

Ngozi senses Sam's disappointment. *"I know, I know. You get a new toy and then people say you can't play with it. But it's not like that. The rules are sensible but you must promise to obey them. If you don't, I may not be allowed to talk with you like this anymore."*

Whoa! Sam feels a stab of fear. He remembers how empty his life had been before he and Ngozi found each other. He won't go back to that! Even though it's been only a few days, the thought of being cut off from Ngozi fills him with dread.

"Yes, that makes you feel pretty awful. We get very close to our contacts. Our lives are incomplete if we lose them. Some people never recover from such a loss."

"I'd hate it."

"Me too. Hey – it won't come to that as long as we're both sensible. The rules aren't difficult. They're common sense really. First of all you must promise never to use your powers for personal gain."

"Well, that's easy!" Sam almost laughs out loud. *"Of course I won't."*

"Don't be too cocky, Sam. You've done it already."

"I have not!"

"Listen to me, Sam - yes, you have. Personal gain isn't just about money, you know. In saving that boy's life, I bet you've made yourself quite a celebrity. People are pleased with you. Your Headmaster came round to thank you personally. Your parents are bursting with pride and probably talking about their brilliant son right now. At school tomorrow, you'll be the centre of

attention. Won't it feel good to be the local hero? Won't you like being the must-know person?"

"But that's not fair. That's not why I did it. Getting praised - it never occurred to me."

"Of course it didn't. You did what you did because it was the right thing to do. I wouldn't have helped you otherwise. But now, like it or not, you're going to be Sam Wright, the hero. Do you understand now what I am saying about personal gain?"

"Suppose so. But it's harsh. If I hadn't done what I did, Squires would be dead."

"I know. I'm just saying – don't be tempted to use your telepathy for the wrong reasons: don't show off or make yourself look big in front of others. And remember – you already have one inexplicable event linked with you. Get too many and people will start to take an interest. The wrong people."

Sam forces himself to the control the anger welling up inside him. "OK. I understand. You'd better tell me the rest."

Ngozi continues: "You must never use your powers to help someone else achieve a personal gain."

"Like the spy?"

"Yes, but there's other ways ... "

"Like what?"

"Oh, there are hundreds of possibilities. Here's one - did you say you have exams soon?"

"That's right."

"So picture this: you're in the exam. I'm here in Nigeria but I have your text books in front of me. Or the relevant internet sites. You ask me questions. I read the answers to you - I help you to cheat. You get top grades. You can see that would be wrong, surely?"

"Wow - neat idea!" This time Sam does laugh. He pictures the scene as he writes the perfect answer in the exam.

"Sam! Not even as a joke! This is serious!"

"Sorry. Yes, of course I see that would be wrong." Ngozi has reprimanded him again and Sam is annoyed with himself. "Is that it?"

"Well ... no." Ngozi hesitates for a few moments. "This is more difficult. There's a third rule. A very rare one that we normally don't mention but I'm going to tell you anyway. You must never use your mental powers to control other people."

"Control other people? I can't ..." Sam stops himself. He's learning not to doubt Ngozi when she tells him something. "I mean - is that possible?"

"I'm afraid it is. In fact, you've already done it, though you didn't know."

"I have? How?"

"The day of your accident. When you screamed and I heard you. You were terrified. I felt that. I felt your fear."

"You dropped a tray."

"That's right. The feeling was horrible. Overpowering. It made me panicky, shaky. I wanted to run away but there was nowhere to go. It's difficult to describe but it was like having fear injected straight into my head."

"Wow." Sam shivers.

"My daughter thought I was ill. I told her I was OK, but I wasn't. I was like jelly inside. It took me hours to work out what had happened. That's why I spent so long trying to contact you."

"Oh" says Sam. *"I had no idea. Sorry."*

"No need to apologise. You couldn't know." Ngozi pauses. *"Thing is, you did it again today."*

"I did?"

"When you were walking home - remember? I contacted you to ask what was wrong. You were angry and I sensed it. It made me feel irritable myself and I didn't know why. What I was feeling was completely irrational."

Sam remembers. It happened when he was talking to Stan's wife.

"You did that, Sam. I sensed your emotions. Powerful things, emotions. And at least one person who has strong abilities like yours has used them deliberately – for his own ends. He's used his mind to create overwhelming, artificial feelings in others - fear, anger, hate, despair or contentment. He exercised control over them. He's actually killed people that way."

"Killed people? Really?"

"Oh yes. If someone makes you feel the deepest, blackest despair... it's deadly, Sam. It's possible that you could do that, I think. So you must promise never to do that - never to control other people. Don't even try. It's ... immoral."

Sam feels overwhelmed. So far his telepathic ability has seemed like just a means of communication. A telephone without a telephone. Now Ngozi is telling him that it might be more than that. It could even be a weapon. This is much more serious.

"Of course I won't do that." He pauses: *"can you do it?"*

"No. Absolutely not. Can't even get close. But I reckon you can, or you'll be able to soon. Your abilities are just developing. They're going to get stronger. I think you are going to be very powerful. Which means you'll have to be very strong in controlling yourself."

Sam is shocked. *"I had no idea. I've never even thought about this."*

"*Why should you?*" Ngozi continues: "*But now you know the code. Take it seriously. It's there to protect you – all of us, actually.*"

"*Yes, I understand.*" Sam wants to change the subject. "*Now, can I...?*"

Ngozi senses his impatience but won't be rushed. "*Not too fast, my friend. The rules. Do you give me your word that you'll obey them? Will you promise me that?*"

"*Yes, of course I do.*"

"*Good man. Now, before we get onto whatever you want to talk about, can you get hold of a good first aid book?*"

For the umpteenth time that day, Sam is caught off balance by this quick change of tack. "*A first aid book? Why?*"

"*Come on Sam. Work it out. Think it through.*"

Sam thinks. "*I suppose you want me to read up on what I did this afternoon?*"

"*Exactly. Then, if people ask how you knew what to do, you say you read it. You name the book. Simple as that. It's a boring answer, it makes you look geeky, but it's safe. I'd rather they think that you spend your spare time reading first aid books than they suspect the truth. If you don't have the right book at home, find one – or look it up on the internet, but have your story ready. Cover your tracks. You see where I'm coming from?*"

"*Yes, of course.*" Sam understands. "*This is quite frightening, you know. It's like I'm being sucked into something; like I'm not fully in control of my life anymore.*"

"*I understand. That's natural, Sam. But you'll be alright: I'll help you. This is a huge change for you but if you do as I say and keep your head down, you'll manage your way through this. You'll learn how to live with it.*"

Sam is so shocked at what he had just been told that for the rest of the night, the subject of Uncle Frank James and Maddy's father is completely pushed from his mind. But if he were to think about what he has heard tonight from Ngozi and Maddy, Sam just might be able to start putting two and two together.

CHAPTER 13 – A HERO!

Maddy is excited.
Sam is worried.
She has news to share before they reach school.
He is afraid of what will happen when they do.

On the bus, Maddy leans close to Sam so that nobody can hear: "after we spoke last night, I googled for newspaper stories about my Uncle Frank. I looked for reports about him going missing, being found dead or an inquest."

"And?"

"Nothing – I found nothing." Maddy pauses and looks at Sam meaningfully. He understands the implication.

Maddy misinterprets his silence. "Don't you see? I found absolutely nothing. Zilch. I tried every combination of words I could think of. Sam, there's no history of Frank James committing suicide. Nothing at all!"

"And if the story about his suicide was true, you'd expect to find something."

"Precisely." Maddy whispers forcefully. "I even looked at some of the family history sites to see if there was a death certificate for a Frank James in the Reading area. There isn't. Not the right age, anyway. There's nothing about him dying, Sam. Absolutely nothing."

"But?" Sam can tell from the tone in Maddy's voice that there is something else.

"But, I did find this." She takes two identical pieces of paper from her pocket and hands one to Sam. "A report from the internet from the internet. I printed it out. Read this."

Sam starts, but Maddy doesn't give him chance to finish. "It's from the 'Reading Chronicle', five years ago. Sam, this story says my Uncle was a hero. The robbery didn't take place three years ago, but five. And he wasn't part of it – he helped to stop it."

"So why was he accused? That doesn't make any sense."

"Exactly. None of it makes any sense. The other thing I did was look through my parents' photo album. It was buried away: everyone uses digital these days. Anyhow, I found this picture. Is this the man you saw in the white car?"

It's a typical family snapshot, slightly posed. A man in his mid-thirties is sitting at a table with Maddy's father, smiling into the camera. Neatly combed hair, receding at the front, small moustache ... kindly eyes.

"I don't know. I'd love to say 'yes' but I really can't say. Sorry. I only had a brief glimpse. The man in the car had less hair. And a bigger moustache. No, I'd love to answer you, but I really can't tell either way."

Maddy nods: "I expected that. Read the story, though. It's interesting".

The story is about a trial that had just finished, four years before.

CONVICTED ROBBER THREATENS REVENGE

A violent bank robber screamed revenge threats against everyone connected with his capture and conviction in Reading Crown Court. As he was being sentenced, a violent Donovan Chatsworth had to be restrained by court staff before being led away.

Chatsworth was sentenced to serve a minimum of twenty years in jail for armed robbery, grievous bodily harm and causing death by dangerous driving.

During the trial it emerged that Chatsworth masterminded a ruthless attack on Marshall's bank in Reading. The attack was foiled by the early arrival of police officers, following which the gang attempted to escape. A high-speed car chase ensued, which resulted in the death of Chatsworth's partner.

In what was a daring daylight raid, Chatsworth and two accomplices, armed with shotguns and disguised by Halloween masks, stormed into the bank. They ordered staff and customers to lie on the floor. Chatsworth shot and wounded a woman for moving too slowly.

The robbers demanded cash which they stuffed into rucksacks. But, unknown to them, a silent alarm had been activated by a quick-thinking member of staff, Chief Cashier Frank James. The brave employee risked his life by using the tip of an umbrella to press a hidden button as he lay on the floor. Praising Mr. James' bravery, the Judge expressed the opinion that he would surely have been shot had he been spotted.

Responding to the signal, armed Police arrived as the robbers were leaving. A high-speed car chase followed, through crowded streets, during which Chatsworth's car reached speeds of over 100 miles an hour. The desperate gang left a trail of damage in their wake, seriously injuring four people and writing off ten other vehicles.

The pursuit ended when the getaway car smashed into a brick wall on the London-bound A4, near Slough, narrowly missing a group of schoolchildren.

Chatsworth shot and wounded a Police Officer before being overpowered and arrested. One of the gang - a woman who was later identified as Chatsworth's girlfriend - was found unconscious in the wreck of the car and died from her injuries in hospital.

As Judge Ormorod Whetton delivered his sentence, Chatsworth screamed abuse across the court and vowed to kill him and the prosecuting solicitor. He also threatened the jury, the prosecution witnesses and his own legal team before being forcibly led away.

Sentencing Chatsworth to start his sentence in a secure psychiatric unit, the Judge told him: "At first appearances you present the façade of a quiet and mild-mannered citizen. But your behaviour in this court has demonstrated how false that image is. Under your innocuous exterior lies an extreme criminal mind, devoid of compassion, that conceived and almost succeeded in carrying out this ruthless robbery.

"Your callous shooting of an innocent woman, your complete disregard for the safety of others as you tried to escape and your violent conduct prior to arrest, coupled with your threats in this court add credence to the psychiatric reports I have received saying that you are a psychopathic criminal, from whom society needs to be protected. I note that you have shown no remorse for your crime or compassion for the people you hurt.

"I therefore have no hesitation in delivering the maximum sentence available allowed by the law."

"That's incredible".

"Glad you think so too" says Maddy grimly.

"So, five years ago your Uncle was a hero. But later, according to your parents, he's accused of being part of the robbery he actually helped to stop. That makes no sense."

Maddy nods. "Exactly. So what the hell is going on? This report is true – it has to be. I believe it. But the suicide story – there's no evidence – it doesn't make any sense. There's nothing about my Uncle having died and now – I simply can't believe it. So that means ..."

"Your parents have been lying to you."

Maddy looks miserable. "Yes, and I want to know why. I hate it. Sam, I've always trusted them ... now I don't know ..."

"There's something very strange going on. I'd say your father definitely knows all about it. And possibly your mother. Sorry, but that's how it looks."

"We have to find that address" whispers Maddy. "And I've had another thought. I can't expect you to recognise my Uncle. You've never seen him before. But I have. So I need to follow Dad next time. I'll take the chance: I have to see the driver of the white car for myself. I can't leave it all to you – not now."

"Okay".

"Will you do that with me?"

"Of course I will" whispers Sam. No question – he's caught up in this now.

The sound of giggling makes them both look up. They have been sitting close and talking in low tones for a long time – too close and too long. Some of the girls are looking at them and pointing. One starts making kissing noises. Sam scowls and shifts self-consciously away from Maddy. Those girls need to grow up.

The two friends sit almost silently for the rest of the journey. Sam wants to tell Maddy about Lewis Squires, but she's reading and re-reading the newspaper article in the hope of finding any tiny clue she missed before.

She's the lucky one, thinks Sam. There she is, pre-occupied with her secret but able to share it with him and here he is, burning up inside about the secret he desperately wants to share with her, but simply never can.

Dammit. Ngozi was right. As soon as he arrives at school, Sam is the centre of attention.

"Is it true – you saved Lewis Squires' life?"

"Kiss of life? But you hate each other!"

85

"OK, you saved him. I understand that. And I understand how. But why?" Sam pushes away the boy who asks him that one.

Someone passing behind him says deliberately loudly: "Bloody creep. He'll be even more of a cocky pain in the arse now."

Is that what people think of him? He hopes not. But ...

Maddy looks at Sam quizzically, but the bell rings and they go their separate ways.

At morning break, Sam does as Ngozi suggested and goes again to the library, this time in search of a book on first aid. The first he finds describes exactly the procedure that she'd talked him through. The library is virtually empty and, to be frank, Sam is again relieved to get away from people – this time to escape the incessant barrage of questions. He memorises the name and author.

As he is putting the book back on its shelf Tariq Alufi walks in. "Still doing your project?" he whispers.

"Yes" lies Sam.

"Need any help?" asks Tariq eagerly.

"Er, no thanks." Sam's refusal is almost automatic. Then he has a thought. "Actually ... yes ... you might be able to give me some advice."

Tariq beams. This is what he wants. "Shoot."

"I'm trying to trace someone ... a lost friend of the family. I want to find where he's living. I don't suppose you know ... is it possible to find out whether someone is still alive and where he might be?"

Tariq smiles. "Absolutely. Dead easy."

Sam is startled. "Really? How?"

"You know his name, I assume?" Sam nods. "And roughly where he lives?" Sam nods again. "Then look him up on the electoral register."

"The what?"

"The electoral register – it lists everyone in the country who's registered to vote. It's published every year. Available on CD. You can find pretty well anyone in the country – well, any adult - as long as they filled in the forms. And it's against the law not to fill them in."

"Where do I have to go?"

"Nowhere! There's a copy here on CD – probably an old one though."

"That's brilliant", says Sam, genuinely impressed. "So I can simply check on the computer whether the person I'm looking for is registered to vote, and that'll give me his address?"

"Exactly. If you know his name and have a rough idea of where he lives, you'll find him" says Tariq. "Over here - I'll show you." He leads

Sam to the other side of the room. "Here you go." Tariq pulls a CD from the shelf proudly proclaiming to list over forty million registered electors and their addresses. "Sorry, it's three years old."

"That's good enough." The bell sounds. "I'll check it later. Thanks for the steer."

Tariq smiles.

Sam makes a mental note: first chance, find Maddy and then they can search for where Frank James was living three years ago. He follows Tariq from the library and down the stairs.

"Shit." Tariq curses under his breath and flattens himself against the wall. In spite of this, a large boy that Sam knows only by sight barges into him. Tariq's books fly everywhere. The boy walks on as if he had neither seen Tariq nor felt anything. It was quite deliberate.

As Tariq stoops to pick up his books, Sam wheels round. But, kneeling on the stairs, Tariq hisses: "Sam! No! Say nothing. You'll make it worse.

"But ..."

"Stop! PLEASE. For my sake, SAM - leave it!!"

Unwillingly, Sam checks himself, taken aback by the intensity in Tariq's voice. He's never heard Tariq speak like that before - he's frightened.

Sam helps instead to pick up the scattered books. "What the hell was that all about?"

"Oh. It's nothing really. He doesn't like ... my family."

"What do you mean it's nothing? And not liking your family ... that's just ..." Sam stops. Racist - he doesn't want to say the word. "That's just no excuse. Does he do that all the time?"

"Yes ... well, only when we cross in the corridor like that. I try to avoid him. Keep away from trouble. It's better that way."

They walk on. Sam is about to say something else but Tariq ducks quickly into a classroom. "My lesson's here. Thanks for your help - see you later." His fear has been replaced by embarrassment.

Sam is left seething. Racist bullying? In his own school? Under his nose? And he's been blind to it? For how long?

Sam feels angry and ashamed and dirty even to have been a witness. He will talk to Tariq again, first chance he has.

But not at lunchtime. He has to find Maddy. She's with a group of friends but detaches herself when he signals to her.

"Is it true? Did you really save ..?"

"What? Oh, yes. That's why Dr. Rhodes came round and that's why I couldn't phone you when I got home last night. Tell you later. This is more important. I know how to find out where your Uncle lived."

That grabs Maddy's attention. "You do? That's fantastic. I've tried remembering. I'm certain it was near Newbury. On the way to Reading. Not a big house. A three-bed semi, with a path down to the front door. And, like I said, near the river. That's all I remember though."

"That should be enough. In the library there's a CD that lists every voter in the country. It's three years old but actually that's perfect. We can check whether there was a Frank James living in that and if there was, what his exact address was. Interested?"

"Of course. Then what?"

"I suppose we'll have to go there and check it out. Thing is, if we know his exact address we can look for other things like death certificates and obituaries and stories in the local papers. It's a starting point, at least."

"Come on, then!" Maddy is delighted to be doing something concrete to investigate the mystery.

Sam thinks ruefully that he hasn't spent so much time in the library in all his time at the school as he has in the past couple of weeks. The CD lists six people called Frank James living in the Reading area. Five have other family members listed – wives or grown-up children, presumably. But one is living alone.

Maddy points and whispers. "This one. It has to be. Uncle Frank never married. This is the only Frank James living alone with a Reading postcode. Purley."

"Where the hell's Purley?"

"No idea."

They look it up on Google Earth. "There you go – right where we want it to be." Maddy points at the screen. "Purley - just outside Reading on the Newbury side. Near the River Thames. Everything stacks up. That has to be the right address. Just has to be."

Sam prints the map.

The supervisor taps her pen meaningfully.

"Let's talk about this outside."

They walk out to the playing field.

"OK, so now we know where to go."

"And when we get there – then what?"

"Knock on the door, I suppose. If your Uncle answers – mystery half solved. Then you'll have to ask your parents why they've been lying to you."

"And if it's someone else?"

"We ask if there's a Frank James living there. If there is, and it's not your Uncle, then we're wrong – it's not the right place and we'll have to start again. If there isn't, we may be able to get some clues as to where your Uncle went or what happened to him. A forwarding address, perhaps."

"That's it?"

"Unless you have a better idea?"

Maddy shakes her head.

"That's the plan then."

"No wait – there's something else we can do while we're there. After we've been to the house we can find the Reading library or the newspaper offices and search the back copies of the local papers. Look for a story about my Uncle's death."

Sam nods. "Do you fancy a day in Reading then? It's the Easter holidays next week. We can get the train. We'll tell our parents that we're going to look round the shops and see what's on at the Hexagon."

"Good idea" agrees Maddy. "But let's go on Saturday. Now I'm actually doing something, I don't want to waste another day. For Dad's sake. Then we've got the rest of the holiday to follow up any leads we get."

But let's go on Saturday. Five fateful words.

And then Maddy adds: "Why didn't you tell me about Lewis Squires? It's all round the school. I'm the only one who didn't know."

Great! What chance has he had? She'd been on about her father and Uncle all the time!

CHAPTER 14 – THE HOUSE IN PURLEY

Douglas Bartles stands as Jane Baxter walks into his office. "Thanks for coming, Jane." He signals her to a chair. "I have a job for you. Have you seen this?" He holds out a newspaper cutting.

"The Times, London? Professor Stamford Harkness. No, I'm not familiar with this."

"Have you heard of him?"

"No." She reads the article. It is about a lecture the Professor gave to the Royal Society. "Is he serious? People developing telepathic powers? The human race evolving?"

"He's serious all right. He really believes this stuff."

"Then he's got a screw loose." Baxter looks at her boss quizzically. "Doesn't he?"

"That's the question. And you're going to find the answer for me. Thing is, what if he's right? Think what a couple of freaks like that could do: one here in Langley, or the Pentagon or the White House and the other in Russia or China. Nothing would be safe. No secret would be secure."

"What do want me to do?"

"We've set up a watch project. I want you to head it up. Project UltraGuard. Read into it and then start digging. Meet with this Professor. Find out what we should be looking for – if these people exist, how do we recognise them? If we find any ..."

"You want them eliminated?"

"Hell no. I want them working for us. We only eliminate them if they refuse."

Baxter looks at Bartles sharply. He isn't joking. "OK, Doug, I'm on it."

* * *

"You wouldn't think this was a main line."

Maddy nods. The train is clattering and swaying on the narrow line between Basingstoke and Reading.

Saturday has dawned fine and the two friends have planned their day carefully: from Reading Station they'll take a bus to Purley and find Uncle Frank's house. In the afternoon, they'll visit the main library to research past copies of the local newspapers.

The traffic is heavy in Reading, as always, and progress is slow as the bus winds its way out of the town centre. Once in Purley, however, it takes them no time at all to find that they are in Purley Rise, the main road through the village. A five minute walk brings them to the house where someone called Frank James was registered as an elector three years before.

Travelling many miles had been easy. Taking the last few steps is difficult. Nervously Sam and Maddy stand on the pavement looking at the front door.

The house is the left of a pair. Its window frames need painting and the grass hasn't been mown. Compared to its neighbour it looks run-down and neglected. Next door a woman is weeding the flower beds. She looks up curiously for a moment but seeing that Sam and Maddy are more interested in the next house, she resumes her gardening.

To complete the look of being uncared for, there's a 'To Let' sign leaning at an angle on a post in the garden.

"Does this look like the place you came to?"

"Could be. Semi – that's right. Steps down to the front door - I'm pretty sure. Thing is, it's years since I was here." Maddy points: "It's being rented out. That's interesting. I reckon that even if it is the right place, Uncle Frank almost certainly doesn't live here anymore. What now?"

"Nothing for it. Knock on the door. See who answers. If you're right and it's not your Uncle, we ask if we can speak with Frank James.

If he's not living there we can ask if there's a forwarding address or something like that."

"What excuse do we give?" asks Maddy nervously.

Sam feels his resolve weakening for a moment. "I don't know. We'll make it up as we go along. Come on. We haven't come this far to bottle out now."

Sam takes a deep breath and marches down the path. He knocks on the door. A man's voice with a South Wales accent comes booming from inside. "No, you go dammit – I'm busy."

A woman in her twenties opens the door. She looks puzzled to see two teenagers standing nervously on her doorstep.

"Hello? Can I help you?" She too has a lilting Welsh accent. Sam feels that she's annoyed at being disturbed.

Maddy speaks first: "we're sorry to disturb you, but we're looking for someone we think lives here. Frank James. Is this the right address please?"

"Frank James? Nope – can't say I've ever heard of a Frank James. Sorry luv, you must have the wrong address."

"Oh." Maddy is worried that the woman will shut the door, but she sees the disappointment in Maddy's face and relents. She pauses.

"Frank James, you say? No, I'm sorry. But we've only been here a year, like. But if you can hold on a minute, I'll see if my partner knows."

"Thank you."

The woman shouts through to the back of the house. "Ewan! Do you know anyone called Frank James? There's some people at the door who think he lives here."

The broad Welsh accent comes again from the back of the house. "Nope. Tell 'em I've never heard of him. They've got the wrong house. I'm busy."

The woman shakes her head. "That's what I thought. Not been 'ere long, you see. Moving on soon as well. Sorry, luv."

"Oh" says Maddy. She is clearly disappointed. "Thank you anyway. We're sorry to have disturbed you."

Sam and Maddy are half way back up the path, when the man's voice comes again, louder this time. "Hey, you two. Hang on a just a minute will you?" A stocky man in his mid-twenties has come to the door. He's holding a spanner in oily hands.

"James, was it? James? I might just be able to help you, thinking about it. We rent this place, you see, and the guy that owns it – I'm pretty sure his name is James." He looks at the woman expectantly: "it were James weren't it, on the rental agreement?"

She shrugs. "Don't ask me, luv! You handled all the legal stuff. I just signed where you said."

The man looks more eager. There's a point to be scored now. "James, you say?"

"Frank James" repeats Maddy, hopefully.

"You just wait there a mo. I'll get the papers. I know where they are."

Ewan disappears into the house. Sam and Maddy stand in uncomfortable silence half way up the path. Then Ewan's voice shouts "I knew it!" He reappears at the door. He is holding legal-looking documents which are already liberally marked with oily fingerprints. But he has a satisfied smile on his face.

"Told you so!" he says. "Knew I'd seen it. Never forget a name, you see. The bloke who rents this place to us is called James. You got the first name wrong though. It's not Frank James, don't you know. It's another guy - Edward James."

"Edward?" gasps Maddy. "Edward James?"

"That what it says, clear as you like." Ewan stabs the paper to emphasise the point. "Edward James - he lives in Winchester now. Strange that ..."

Maddy looks at Sam with wide eyes. "Dad?" she mouths at him.

"Begging your pardon?" asks Ewan.

"No – nothing", says Sam quickly. "This Edward James - does it give his address?"

"Hold on ... it does indeed. Edward James lives at..." Ewan reads out Maddy's address. "Here it is: electronic signature these days, you understand ..."

Maddy looks at the paper being held out for her and nods.

"... never met the gentleman though: wouldn't know him if I passed him in the street - did it all through the estate agents, you see. They found us this place, they did the papers. Still, it's a bit of a coincidence, don't you think? You thinking that a Frank James lives 'ere when actually it's an Edward James who owns it. Perhaps you got the two confused, like?"

"That must be it." Sam can see that Maddy is off balance. He adds quickly: "Look, you've been very helpful. We're sorry to have disturbed you. We got the names mixed up. Thank you for your time. Goodbye."

Sam takes Maddy's arm and guides her back to the pavement. "It definitely was the right house. But your Uncle Frank's not here anymore. So he's either dead, like your parents said, or he's moved out."

"That was Dad's name and address! His name was on that document. But he's never said anything about owning the house and renting it out." Maddy is stunned. "What the hell's going on, Sam?"

The woman next door looks up curiously again from her gardening. "I couldn't help but overhear ... do I take it you're looking for the man who used to live here?"

"Frank James" says Sam.

"Well, you didn't get it wrong: he definitely used to live here. If you see him, tell him best wishes from Cathy – that's me. He left one night without saying goodbye or anything. Very strange. If you see him, tell him Cathy hopes he's well."

"We will" smiles Maddy. "I wonder ... as you live next door, do you know if anything happened to him? I'd be very sad if ... you know ... he died or something."

"No, nothing like that; not that I know of anyway. He just left. Overnight. Disappeared. Never heard of him again. I must say I was a bit sad that he left without a goodbye or anything. But I'm sure I'd have picked it up if anything bad had happened to him. Him being my next door neighbour."

"That's a relief. Thank you for your help. If we find him, we'll give him your best wishes."

"You do that. Nice to meet you." Cathy resumes tending her garden.

Sam speaks quietly as they start walking back to the bus stop. "So he used to live here and he vanished overnight. It stacks up, you know. If something had happened to your Uncle and he had no other family, his closest relative, in this case your father - his brother – would inherit the house. We were talking about that in Citizenship a few weeks ago."

"OK" agrees Maddy "but that's another secretive thing Dad's done, along with the phone calls and meeting the man in the white car. Why would he keep it so quiet? And if Uncle Frank died, like he told me, why is there no evidence? His next door neighbour was sure she'd have heard about it and she hasn't. I believe even more now that he didn't die."

"Beats me. But we've found out what we wanted. Your Uncle Frank definitely used to live here, he's been gone at least a year and it happened overnight. Something HAS happened to him, and it was sudden. What we have to do now is find out what the hell it was."

He pauses. "Of course, we're right back with the two possibilities. He could be dead or he may have wanted to disappear – to do a runner. If he killed himself – that will be in the papers. If he did a runner to avoid being arrested – that should be in the papers too."

"But that would mean that Dad's helping someone who's wanted by the Police."

"It would explain why he's being so secretive."

"Oh God! It looks bad, isn't it?"

Sam thinks it better not to answer. But his silence speaks volumes.

"The library then?"

"Reckon so. Check the back copies. I know they keep them, because Mum told me – she does work for our local paper. She says that they keep the papers for a while scan them in a hold pictures or electronic images."

"But it could take hours, searching through thousands of old papers."

"We can narrow it down. We know the date of the trial. Your Uncle was alive then, 'cos he gave evidence. So whatever happened to him, it took place after the trial. Let's assume the story made the front page. Don't worry. If it's there, we'll find it."

They catch the bus back into Reading.

Sam checks the map on his phone as the bus pulls up. "I reckon the library's down there. Let's see what we can find."

They have a few hundred metres to walk.

They don't make it.

CHAPTER 15 - ENCOUNTER WITH EVIL

"Stop being such a bloody wimp. Hold yourself together." Sergeant William Beaston curses himself. OK, you're nervous. No, stop fooling yourself, you're frightened. Beaston wants to run, and he despises himself for his weakness.

Come on, do the exercises ... take a deep breath ... get these emotions under control. They're inside - people can't see what I'm feeling ... they're just in my head. OK, I feel panicky but it will pass. It won't kill me. Don't let it take me over.

He looks left and right. There, his fellow Officers are at his side. They stand together.

I'll be alright.

Won't let my friends down.

Won't let myself down.

Do what I always do - cope.

More than once Beaston has been offered desk duties but turned them down. He thinks wistfully of what Matt Lawson said to him many times: "I joined the Police to meet the public, to help people - not to be a bleedin' pen-pusher."

Poor Matt – he had hated paperwork with a vengeance. Sometimes he got so far behind he had to stay hours late to catch up. Then he'd say how depressed he was at letting his family down.

William misses his friend. But despite Matt's strange death, in the so-called 'Ghost Train mystery', he refuses to hide away, even though he knows who probably caused it. So today, here he is: with his colleagues, standing in full view of the public, working to control his fear and watching as a crowd of protesters moves slowly and noisily towards them.

"This is no problem", he tells himself. The crowd is good natured. Loud and boisterous, but that's good, certainly not against the law. The important thing is, it's not violent. Beaston expects it to stay like that. The organisers have been sensible. The rules have been agreed. Communications between Police and protesters have been good. As long as no-one does anything stupid ...

Sgt. Beaston's trained eyes automatically scan the sea of faces before him. He recognises a couple at the front as serial demonstrators. They won't cause any trouble. They are political idealists who don't mind lying down to block a road, or climbing trees to stop a development, but basically they are peaceful people, willing to break the law in a minor way to get their point across. They'll grow out of it. He sees more of the usual activists who like to march and demonstrate and then a sea of anonymous faces he doesn't recognise.

Except ...

What the hell ...?

Beaston's heart misses a beat and he does a double take. Has he just seen ...?

No! It can't be!

He looks again.

Yes it bloody well can!

Oh my God. Him! His worst nightmare! Matt's worst nightmare too.

That face – he recognises it.

What's more, the owner of the face recognises him too.

A slightly built, innocuous looking, middle-aged man is walking just behind the lead protesters. He is neither chanting like the rest of them, nor carrying a banner. Instead, he is staring fixedly, intently and deliberately at William Beaston. Staring ... waiting ... waiting ... staring ... until the inevitable moment when their eyes meet.

That moment has come.

He sees William Beaston give a start of recognition. He sees, rather than hears, Beaston shout.

The man smiles coldly and waggles his fingers in an insolent wave of acknowledgment. Without losing eye contact with the Police Sergeant he points at him with slow deliberation. With his other hand he makes a cutting gesture across his neck.

With his stare locked into the shocked face of the Sergeant, the man stops walking, allowing himself slowly to melt back into the noisy crowd.

He is gone.

Having been rooted to the ground in shock, William Beaston bursts into action. "Stop that man!" he screams, and lurches forward.

A voice from behind shouts. "Sarge! What the hell are you doing? Bill - come back!"

But William Beaston ignores the call. He runs into the crowd, pushing people aside, desperate to catch his quarry. This is important.

A barrage of noise greets Sam and Maddy as they leave the bus. Shouting, chanting, whistle-blowing and bashing drums, a crowd is heading towards them and blocking the way ahead. Hundreds of protesters are heading slowly down the road.

"Better stay back till they've passed." Sam has to shout; he points towards a shop doorway. He's not sure that Maddy can hear him but she understands the signal, and nods. The two of them duck into the shelter it offers.

Trapped for the time being as the march passes them by, they see one of the Police Officers break away from his colleagues and run at the demonstrators, pointing aggressively. It seems a provocative thing to do.

No, it's a stupid, irresponsible thing to do.

Sam feels irritated. Angry. No, more than that – he feels fighting mad.

He isn't alone. The demonstrators react the same way. They had been peaceful, obeying the agreed rules, doing things right and now this idiot has attacked them. It's another example of the irresponsibility of the Police. How dare he?

The tone of the demonstration changes in an instant. The controlled chanting and shouting turn to screams of rage. The marchers shout abuse at the Police. A hail of missiles starts to fly through the air - at first coins and drink cans, then stones and bottles.

In a few moments the peaceful demonstration has spiralled out of control. It's now a riot.

Extra police run forward from a side road where they'd been stationed out of sight. The newcomers look menacing with shields and truncheons at the ready. They form a line in front of their colleagues, facing the demonstrators. The noise of thrown missiles thudding off their shields adds a new, sinister element to the clash.

The police intentions are clear. The march has turned violent, so it will go no further.

Battle lines have been drawn.

Some of the demonstrators pull up paving stones, smash them on the ground and throw the jagged remnants at the Police line. Above the din comes a crash of breaking glass as a shop window shatters. Thousands of splinters cascade onto the pavement.

Pandemonium!

In the middle of the mayhem, William Beaston finds himself isolated and surrounded. He has lost sight of the man he was chasing.

He curses his stupidity. Because of it he is now alone and defenceless, separated from his colleagues and at the mercy of an angry mob. They are shouting abuse at him and spitting in his face.

He draws his truncheon to defend himself.

The rioters take it as a threat. In their fury they turn on him.

"Bastard!" A protester punches William Beaston in the face. The punch doesn't so much hurt him as cause him to lose his balance. He stumbles and falls backwards. He lands heavily on the road. He struggles unsuccessfully to get to his feet, a trickle of blood running from his nose.

The angry crowd shows no compassion to the defenceless man. "You beat up my mother!" screams one, aiming a kick at Beaston's ribs. He grunts in pain and curls into a foetal position to try to protect himself.

Watching from the shop doorway, Sam feels the mounting sense of fury being displayed by the demonstrators. To them the Sergeant symbolises the vicious police who are stopping innocent people using the streets. He deserves his fate!

But hang on ...

As if in slow motion, Sam turns his head to look at Maddy. She too is affected by the scene unfolding in front of her. She has picked up the chant from the crowd and is screaming with the demonstrators. "He murdered my Uncle Frank. Kill him! Kill the pig!" Her face is contorted with anger.

Sam is stunned. Killed her Uncle? Maddy doesn't even know that he's dead! He probably isn't. This is nonsense! Kill the pig? It's crazy – Maddy has a temper but she isn't like this. What is going on to make her behave like this?

Sam shakes his head to clear it and forces himself to control the anger that is threatening to take him over too. What's happening to him? Why has a peaceful demonstration suddenly turned so violent?

Why does he feel such hatred towards a man he's never even seen before? Why is Maddy shouting like that? Why is she getting involved at all? In fact, why do either of them care? It's nothing to do with them, visitors as they are in a strange town.

These questions flash through Sam's head in an instant and he can answer none of them. But all around him he can see furious faces as people scream their hate.

One thing he does know for certain: a man's life is at risk. There is a ring of people looking down at something – or someone – in the road. He can only assume it's the man who ran into the crowd. It looks like he's at the mercy of the mob and taking a bad beating.

To add to Sam's horror, Maddy is walking forward to join in. He has to stop her! Sam steps in front of her, grabs her arms and pushes her back towards the shop doorway. "What are you doing?" he screams. He can only just make himself heard above the barrage of noise.

"Let me go. I hate that man! He killed my Uncle."

"Don't be stupid." Sam has to shout at the top of his voice to get Maddy to hear him. "You don't even know he's dead. Snap out of it, Maddy. This is wrong. Don't get involved."

Maddy struggles to free herself. "Get your hands off me! Why are you siding with him?"

Sam doesn't want to fight with Maddy. He forces himself to stay calm, hoping she will respond. He drops his hands but blocks her way into the crowd. He forces his voice low and speaks soothingly: "Maddy! Relax! Take a deep breath. Let it go. Calm down."

"But ..."

Sam tries use body language that will project a feeling of calm. "Maddy. Calm down. Relax."

Maddy nods blankly. She looks confused.

Slowly, gently, Sam takes her hand. "That's it. Let it go. It's nothing to do with us." He tries to make clear, through his voice and body language that his friend needs to relax and get the negative emotions out of her head.

"OK, Sam. I'm alright."

As Maddy calms herself, the noise from the crowd starts to reduce as well. The feeling of fury in Sam's head is under control. He is driving the violent emotions out and forcing himself to stay calm, for Maddy's sake.

The demonstrators kicking the Police Sergeant stop. Like Maddy they look puzzled, confused, guilty - embarrassed at what they've been doing. Awkwardly, they back away. A gap develops round the fallen man, whose face is swollen and bleeding. Weakly, he lifts himself onto his hands and knees.

A couple watches him with their hands to their mouths, horrified and scarcely believing what they have just been doing.

As the rain of stones and drink cans subsides, four of William Beaston's colleagues run forward to rescue their injured Sergeant. The crowd parts to let them pass. Without ceremony they pick him up and carry him away.

Through swollen and bleeding lips the Sergeant mumbles. "He's here. I saw him. I saw him." His mouth is too swollen for anyone to make out the words. They are simply thankful that he's still alive, the bloody fool.

Maddy is shaking. "Oh God! Sam - what happened? That was so frightening. That poor man! The way they turned on him - and I wanted to join them. Sam, I wanted them to kill him! I'd have been over there with them if you hadn't stopped me. I'm so ashamed." She buries her head in his shoulder and starts crying.

Awkwardly, Sam puts his hands round her shoulders. "Don't beat yourself up. You didn't do anything."

"But I wanted to. I would have if you hadn't stopped me. What happened to me?"

"I don't know. But you weren't the only one. Everyone was caught up in it."

Maddy wipes her eyes. "I didn't know what was happening to me. All those weird feelings going through my head. I couldn't control them. I felt like I was out of control - like I hated him – like I knew him and really hated him. Then you held me back and spoke quietly and the next minute it was gone and I didn't know why I'd been behaving like that." The words are tumbling out of her. "Sam, I'm scared. What happened to me?" She puts her head back on his shoulder. He can feel her shaking.

But Sam says nothing. He hears what Maddy is saying, but he is still feeling strange emotions. After the feeling of anger, he is now experiencing something different - a sense of puzzlement.

Not his puzzlement though - someone else's.

What had Ngozi told him? *You must never attempt to control other people by using your powers.* Is that what just happened? Was someone manipulating that crowd? Is that what he and Maddy felt? Is there someone here who created the anger – intentionally, generating and feeding the violence? Deliberately inflaming the demonstrators?

If somebody was goading them to attack, he wanted them to kill the police Sergeant. But why?

Sam shivers. He is in the presence of something malevolent.

He senses it.

It's ... evil.

With a sense of profound shock, Sam realises that he just witnessed an attempted murder. Somewhere nearby is a ruthless person who just manipulated hundreds of people, a person who tried to cause the death of an innocent man.

Maddy has taken a step back. She's looking at him with alarm. "Are you alright? You've gone white as a sheet." Her green eyes, still glistening with tears, are now wide with concern for her friend.

With difficulty, Sam drags his attention back to her. No, he realises, he's not alright. He feels as if he is going to throw up. Everything he looks at seems distorted. His head is thumping. His legs are buckling under him. He's ill.

"Feel really bad ... sick ... headache ... just came on" he mumbles. "Need to rest." Sam staggers back against the shop window. He feels it bend from his weight. His legs give way and he slides down the glass to the ground. His heart is thumping heavily. His head is pounding, throbbing to each beat. He closes his eyes and puts his head on the cold, hard pavement. He thinks he will pass out. The cold helps.

Sam kneels motionless, trying to blank out the sounds around him. He's never felt as ill as this before and he's frightened. He feels Maddy touching his hand. Thank goodness she's here: without her he'd be even more scared, ill and miles from home.

Should he go to hospital? What's happening to him? He thinks about contacting Ngozi, but this is no place to have a conversation with her and his head is swimming too much anyway for him to be able to concentrate on anything.

There is nothing for it. Stay still. Do nothing. Hope it will pass.

Maddy helps him to a sitting position. She holds his hand, wanting to help, concerned for him. "Are you feeling better? I think your colour's coming back a bit."

"Give me ... couple of minutes." Sam can only mumble the words. His speech is slurred.

Slowly, painfully slowly, the weakness passes. But not the thumping agony in his head. With Maddy's help, Sam lifts himself gingerly to his feet and stands, swaying slightly. The effort is a torture as a stabbing pain behind his right eye knifes through his head. He retches but doesn't throw up. He must get moving – he needs to go home. He puts his hand to his temples and can feel his heartbeat pulsing through the veins there. His vision is affected – like he's in a tunnel.

Across the road, someone is taking pictures. Each flash from the camera is a needle that pierces Sam's brain. He's stands unsteadily, with his right eye closed.

"We should go" says Maddy. "Forget the library – you need to get home. And I don't like it here – it's scary." Sam lets Maddy take his arm and guide him gently away.

As the crowd disperses, the two friends head slowly towards the railway station. The short walk seems like miles. Once there, Maddy sits Sam down in the cafe while she buys two drinks. He flops forward and rests his head on his arms. Nearby, a child throws a tantrum and the noise makes Sam wince with pain.

Maddy is thinking clearly: she phones her parents to let them know that they are OK and on their way back. Sam slowly sips at the drink but can't finish it; he's still afraid he will throw up. Maddy leads him to the platform; thank goodness she's there to take control: his eyes won't focus on the signs. Their train is already waiting: with difficulty he climbs the steps and lowers himself heavily into a vacant seat.

Every jolt of the train sends more stabbing pains through Sam's head. He closes his eyes, not to sleep, but to block out the lights of the carriage. He tries to stop himself thinking about the events of the afternoon, but fails. He keeps returning to the certainty that someone had deliberately inflamed the demonstrators.

Sam pictures the scene. A man is standing in the crowd. Sam can't see his face. But he can imagine the man talking quietly. "You feel anger. You feel hate. That man is your enemy. Hate him! Be revenged on him!"

And as the unseen man whispers the words, the crowd reacts with violence.

Sam knows he has encountered something evil – something beyond his comprehension. A mad and malevolent mind.

But who?

And there is another emotion that Sam sensed. An awful base emotion that makes him shudder.

Revenge!

A cold-blooded, ruthless, heartless, madness-driven lust for vengeance.

Retribution without pity or conscience.

Revenge without limits.

Till today Sam's new powers have been interesting, exciting. But now as the train clatters slowly, taking him back home, Sam is ill, terrified and chilled to his very soul. He feels, instinctively, that his life has just taken another step on a journey where he has no idea of the destination.

What has he gotten himself into?

CHAPTER 16 – IDENTIFIED

"Sam, Dad's over there."

"Thank goodness … couldn't do a bus: I'd throw up. Could I have the window open on the way back?"

It seems a curious irony that Maddy's father has met them at Winchester station, given that his mysterious behaviour was the secret reason behind their journey in the first place.

Sam wants to talk to Ngozi – he needs her advice. But first he must find out what is wrong with him and do something to get rid of this awful throbbing headache and the sickness he's feeling.

"Sam!" When he walks in, his mother rushes forward and throws her arms round him. The sudden movement makes him groan: it feels as if his head is going to explode. She stands back. "Oh my, you're white as a sheet."

Sam feels worse than before the car journey. "Feel really ill … head thumping … pain behind my right eye … flashing lights … feel sick … can't focus properly … need to go to bed."

She looks closely into her son's ashen face, into his eyes.

"Migraine. I get them. Your first one. Poor you. I hoped you'd escape them. You've gone grey, just like my father used to. Sure sign. Hold on." Sam leans against the wall as his mother bustles into the kitchen and returns with a glass of water and couple of tablets. "Take these. They'll help. They work for me."

Normally Sam tries to avoid taking tablets but he has no energy to argue. He's done with trying to control situations. If his mother reckons it's a migraine, that'll do for now. He heaves himself slowly upstairs to his room, kicks off his shoes and lowers himself gently onto the bed.

His father draws the curtains. "I'm putting all the lights out. The dark helps your Mum when she gets a migraine. Try to sleep – let the tablets work."

Sleep! That's easier said than done. Sam can hear Maddy and her father downstairs, talking with his parents. She'll be telling them about the riot. Why do they have to talk so loudly?

He struggles to find a comfortable position on the bed: most make his head thump even more. After what seems an age, he finds one. He listens to the blood pulsing through his head but is comfortable at last.

He wakes at midnight. Gingerly he rolls over and sits up. His head stays on. That's good. He's hungry – that seems a good sign too. Sam can hear low voices and the television from downstairs. He pads down slowly. His parents are still up.

"Feeling better?" asks Helen.

"Think so. I've been asleep. Why are you still up?"

"Good ... best thing for a migraine, sleep. We're watching the news. That riot in Reading, it was awful. That poor policeman."

"It's been on?"

"Virtually non-stop. It's the main story. It's the first major incident in Reading for years. There are calls for a public enquiry into how the Police handled it. And you and Maddy had to be there today of all days!"

"We kept out of it. We could see what was going on but we sheltered in a shop doorway."

"Yes. Maddy told us. And we saw you."

"You did?"

"Briefly. There were a couple of shots with you in. You were talking to Maddy – holding her arms."

Sam feels a quiver of fear. If his parents have spotted him, who else might? "Have they said how it started, and how it finished?"

"Not really. Both sides are blaming the other. The organisers say the police attacked them and that provoked the violence. The police say the demonstrators planned it."

Sam says very carefully: "But from where I was, it looked like the whole crowd was getting ugly, not just a few people."

"Oh, I don't know" says his mother. She turns back to the TV. "Hold on: it's coming on again." She turns up the volume.

The pictures are low quality, having been taken mainly on mobile phones by people watching from office windows. But one has been able to focus in tight on the rioting and show the very worst of it. Even though he'd been there, Sam is shocked to see how suddenly the violence started and the viciousness of the attack.

And there he is, briefly, with Maddy. His father freezes the picture.

"That's when I was trying to get her to calm down" thinks Sam.

It's only a fleeting shot, but it worries him. Of all the people there, he and Maddy are the only ones not joining in the violence. If the crowd WAS being manipulated by someone, will that someone see these pictures too? Will he be able to single out Sam as the person who resisted him– the only one not affected?

"I thought so." Sam's mother has been studying the screen as intently as Sam. "You're holding Maddy's arms. Where was she going?"

Sam has to think quickly. "She was frightened. She wanted to run over and stop them. I told her she was safer sheltering in the doorway till the trouble passed." It's not the truth, but it will do.

"Quite right. Well done."

The report continues: "Breaking news ... in the last half hour Thames Valley Police have released the name of the injured Officer. He is Sergeant William Beaston who is married and has two children. His injuries are serious but not thought to be life threatening. He is in a stable condition."

Does Sam imagine it? Did his mother just let out a small cry of shock? He looks round. She is busily picking up newspapers from the chairs in the lounge.

"What's up?"

"Nothing. Nothing at all. I just don't like watching those pictures." The reply is quick – too quick. Hurriedly, she leaves the room. Sam looks quizzically after her. She's scared: he feels it. He's sure she recognised the name of the injured Police Sergeant. But how come?

His father is staring fixedly at the television. There is no flicker of recognition or emotion on his face. No clues there.

This whole episode is getting more bizarre by the hour.

Sam makes himself toast and takes it to his room. He is hungry but can't face anything that requires effort to eat. Not just that - he needs to talk with Ngozi. He feels very sombre and scared as he goes through his mental routine in the hope that she will answer.

She responds straight away.

Ngozi hears Sam out in silence until she has heard the whole story. *"You know this is potentially very serious – not just for you but for all of us?"*

"Yes. I knew it straight away."

"I'm so sorry - I know you're feeling washed out, but I need to ask you some questions."

Sam swallows hard. He can tell by the way Ngozi listened to him so intently that she has taken in every word and is now considering their implications.

"Let's check a few things first. Did you know what the demonstration was about?"

"No."

"Did you know anyone there?

"No. Well, Maddy, of course."

"Yes, yes. Did you know the Police Officer who was attacked?"

"No. Not at all."

"That's what I thought. So you knew nothing about what was going on."

"That's right."

"But even though you had no connection at all with the demonstration or the Police Sergeant, you felt anger against him?"

"Yes. I felt angry inside and, I suppose because he was the focus of the attack, I thought I was angry with him. Does that make sense?"

"I'll tell you later. Carry on ..."

"I felt like I hated this guy, even though I didn't know him. And Maddy felt it too. She got it worse than me. She shouted that he'd killed her Uncle. That was crazy because ..."

"So you both felt it − this anger?"

"Yes."

"Did that feeling come on at the same time for both of you?"

"I think so."

"What made you stop feeling like that?"

"I forced myself to calm down. I had to stop Maddy joining in. I didn't want her getting into trouble. I told her to calm down − take a deep breath and let it go. I tried to show her that I was staying calm. If I'd shouted at her it would have made things worse so I let go of her, put my hands down at my side and spoke softly."

"Maddy didn't know anything about the demonstration either?"

"No."

"But she reacted to the anger and violence?"

"Yes. Like I said, she's not normally like that."

"And you calmed her down?"

"I think so."

"How?"

"Well, like I said, I forced myself to fight the anger and spoke to her softly."

"And that worked?"

"I think so. But perhaps the moment had passed: it all started to quieten down then anyway."

Ngozi pauses.

"You still there?" asks Sam.

"Still here" says Ngozi. *"Thinking."*

There follows another period of silence. Finally Ngozi's thoughts come to Sam again. *"Sam, this is bad, this is very bad. I'm really sorry. I feel awful about what I have to tell you now, because you're having to learn too much in such a short time. But I don't see how I can avoid it."*

"Tell me. Please. I need to know what's happening to me."

Ngozi speaks slowly and carefully: *"I don't believe that demonstration turned violent because of a group of trouble-makers. Neither do you."*

"No."

"That crowd was being manipulated."

"Yes. But how?"

"I think this was the work of an Emotist."

"A what?"

"An Emotist. He's one of us - a telepath. But his powers are much stronger. He can do more than exchange thoughts with another person, as we are doing now. An Emotist can also transfer emotions. He can make people feel happiness, fear, joy, anger, despair, hatred … any feeling he chooses. That's what our last rule is about. Remember?"

"Yes." This time he isn't going to question what Ngozi is saying. Incredible though it is, he knows it is the truth. He's experienced it. *"That's exactly how it felt. Like I had someone else's feelings being injected into my head. I wouldn't have believed it was possible. But it was so strong. We both felt it."*

Ngozi continues: *"You remember I told you how I sensed your presence the day you fell off your bike? I didn't just hear your voice – I also felt your fear?"*

"Yes, but you're telepathic."

"That's explains why I heard your voice. It doesn't explain why I felt your emotion."

"Oh."

"An Emotist is so powerful he can make ordinary people feel his emotions. That's why he's so dangerous. Maddy isn't telepathic, but she reacted. The people in the crowd weren't telepathic, but they reacted too."

"That's incredible" says Sam.

Ngozi continues: *"On this scale, it is. But not on a small scale. That happens all the time. You see, people are sensitive to emotions – to feelings.*

More sensitive than they realise. Ever walked into a room and felt – an atmosphere?"

"Loads of times."

"That's right. We all have. Perhaps we pick it up through body language. But perhaps we just sense it - that people are annoyed, or sad, or happy. Mainly it's the negative emotions that you notice most strongly.

"So it's quite common for people to react to other peoples' emotions, without knowing for certain how they picked them up. What is very, very rare, thank goodness, is for people to be able project those emotions deliberately, to manipulate others. That takes something special."

"And that's what I felt today?"

"Yes. It confirms our worst fears. There have been stories in the community for months now."

"Stories?"

"Things have been happening, Sam. Bad things. People are dying. Some of us don't want to admit it. But I believe it."

"You believe this is a – what do you call it – Emotist?"

"I do. There were ancient stories – legends really – and no-one really knew whether they were fact or exaggeration. But then things started happening a few years ago - real-life incidents. This is another one. It's the only possible explanation. Sam - someone was manipulating that crowd."

"But why? Why would anyone do that?"

"You tell me. You were there. I only know what you've told me."

Sam pauses. He needs to choose his next words carefully, to be absolutely accurate. *"I – I think it might have been an attempted murder. Whoever it was wanted the Police Sergeant dead."*

"Why do you say that?"

"Ngozi … there was another feeling…."

"Yes?"

How can he put this? How can he describe into words what he sensed? *"Revenge, Ngozi. I sensed revenge."*

"Oh."

"That's bad too, isn't it?"

"As bad as it gets. An Emotist on the loose, but on a mission. Wanting to use his mental powers, trying to kill people. Oh Sam, this is awful."

Sam's head is spinning. *"Hold on a minute though: you said that you had heard of other real-life incidents. Where?"*

There is a pause. Then Ngozi replies: *"In your country as well. Over the last two or three years. But all in your country. That's what's so suspicious."*

"What happened? Could the events be linked?"

"Maybe. Look, give me some time. I need to check the facts. I may be jumping to wrong conclusions. I'll come back to you. We'll talk again tomorrow. By the way, how did you feel after the demonstration?"

This question surprises Sam. *"Awful. Exhausted. I had to lie on the pavement. My legs turned to jelly and I felt really weak. I was close to throwing up all the way home. I'd have never made it without Maddy. Mum said I had a migraine."*

"Feeling better now?"

"Yes, thanks. She gave me some tablets and I went to bed. They worked."

"Good. But ask yourself, why do you think you felt like that? Think about that, Sam...."

Sam stays awake, thinking about what Ngozi has just told him. He knows immediately why she asked that last question, and he recognises what it means.

He shudders.

Too fast - this is all moving too fast.

Eventually he drifts off to sleep again and dreams of uniformed men called 'Thought Monitors' arresting anyone who laughs or looks happy.

As Sam sleeps, fifty miles away a man is sitting in his scrupulously neat room watching and re-watching the recordings he made of that evening's news broadcasts.

Through the night, frame by frame, he pages through the video of the demonstration in Reading. He examines each frame in turn with minute attention before moving to the next. It is painstaking work. Obsessive.

As dawn approaches and light starts to filter across the sky, he stiffens and leans forward, staring intently at the screen.

"There. I see you. That's interesting. Very interesting indeed. I really must find out who you are and why you weren't joining my little party."

He zooms into the image of a shop doorway, saves the frame he has selected and prints it. He circles the images of two young people. Two people who are acting differently – not behaving as all those around them are.

"But finding you won't be easy, I fear."

Carefully the man folds the picture and places it neatly inside a small black notebook that he keeps in his jacket.

Fifty miles away, Sam Wright turns over in his exhausted sleep, unaware of the evil that now stalks him.

CHAPTER 17 - FIFTEEN MINUTES OF FAME

Blearily, Sam fumbles for his phone on the floor beside his bed. "Hello?"

"Hi. Feeling better?" It's Maddy.

"Think so. You woke me up."

"Really?"

"Yeah." Sam yawns. "What's the time?"

"Twelve-thirty. Do you want me to call back?"

So late? He hadn't realised. "No. I'm awake now. Better get up, I suppose."

"Are you sure you're alright? I was so worried about you yesterday."

"Think so."

"Good. Can we talk about Uncle Frank?"

"Twenty minutes?"

"OK. I'll meet you at the swings." This means Maddy wants a private conversation, with no risk of being overheard.

Five minutes from Sam's house is an open field and a playground that has seen better days. It was an important part of Sam and Maddy's childhood and they still use it as a meeting place.

Maddy is sitting on the bench waiting for him. "You look better. You went really grey yesterday. Horrible."

"I felt grey. Thanks so much for looking after me – I'd never have made it home without your help. I'd have ended up in hospital or something."

Maddy smiles. "I was hardly going to leave you there, was I? Especially after you stopped me from getting mixed up in that violence. God, that was so weird! I've never felt anything like that before."

"But it's gone now?"

"Think so."

"Good." Time to change the subject. "You want to talk about your Uncle?"

"Yes. Here's the question: do you think I should tell Dad that we went to Uncle Frank's house?"

"Oh. That's difficult. I assumed you wouldn't." Sam thinks for a moment. "You know, I don't think you should. What good would it do? It won't change anything. If your Dad's telling the truth about your uncle killing himself, there's nothing different he can say and he'll not thank you for raking over sad memories. He'll just wonder why you're checking up on him.

"But if he's lying, you'll tell him that you suspect something and then he'll just clam up even more. You'll find it even harder to find out what's going on."

"But he might say 'as you've found out, here's the story. You need to know'. I hate keeping things from my parents."

"I know. It's difficult." Sam says that with feeling. "What are the chances of that, do you think? They've been keeping a lot more from you."

"I don't know. I suppose if he wanted to tell me, he would have done by now." Maddy looks depressed. "We didn't achieve much, did we?"

"We know a few things now that we didn't before. First, we have your uncle's old address.

"Second, we know he's definitely not there anymore.

"Third, we know that he disappeared overnight. His neighbour knew nothing about it and,

"Fourth and most importantly, she's a person who would have picked up on it if he really had committed suicide. She had no idea that he might have died."

"So ...?"

"If you want my opinion, I reckon your uncle is still alive."

"I agree. Which means that Dad's been lying to me."

"So the real question now is: why doesn't he want you to know?"

"Because he's mixed up in something bad." Maddy looks miserable.

"I know it looks that way..." Sam takes Maddy's hand "... but I don't believe it. I would trust your Dad with my life. Whatever's going on, he's not involved in anything wrong. He wouldn't be."

"Oh, Sam." Maddy's eyes are glistening with tears. "Thank you for saying that. So what do we do now?"

"Go back to Reading some time, I suppose. Try to get to the library again. But the most important thing is - next time your Dad goes out to meet the man in the white car we'll both follow, like you said. It's the only way to find out what's really going on. And we must keep our eyes and ears open for more clues that your Uncle is still alive."

Maddy nods: "Thanks for coming with me yesterday. And thanks for believing in Dad. You're such a good friend." She kisses him lightly on the cheek.

Sam is puzzled. That's the second time she's said that in two days!

Rain is pouring down on the Monday morning after half term. The bus to school is packed solid: much more crowded than normal and with their usual seats taken, Sam and Maddy have to stand for the whole journey. Crammed in with so many other people, it makes it difficult to talk.

It's Maddy's turn to have dark rings under her eyes. "I lay awake for hours again last night. I feel so guilty about ... you know."

"I understand - it's difficult to have secrets that you can't share" Sam murmurs and he means every word.

Maddy nods miserably. The bus stops and they run, head down, into school.

As Dr. Rhodes enters morning assembly, he is accompanied by a stranger: a large man in a crumpled suit. Sam and Maddy look at each other. "What's going on?"

"Dunno." Sam shakes his head.

Then the blood drains from his face when the Head says: "Could Samuel Wright please come forward?"

"Oh shit, Maddy."

"Well, go on." She nudges him.

There is a buzz of conversation as all heads turn to look at Sam. He shrugs his confusion to Maddy. With heart pounding and his face burning hot with embarrassment and nervousness, he walks slowly to the front of the hall. Everyone's staring at him. What has he done?

"It is with great pleasure that I welcome an important guest to our assembly" announces Dr. Rhodes. "Councillor Phillip Seymour is the Executive Member responsible for Education on Hampshire County Council. He is here to present an award to Samuel Wright. This certificate honours Wright for saving the life of his friend, Lewis Squires who, I am delighted to see, is back with us today."

A murmur goes round the Hall and there are a few sniggers: everyone knows that Wright and Squires are not friends at all. They hate each other.

"No doubt this story has been passed round the school and exaggerated in the telling, although I have to say that exaggeration is scarcely possible in this case. I shall read the citation ..."

There is a buzz of chatter at this. So it IS true! Dr. Rhodes holds up his hand indicating silence.

"In addition, I have received a letter from the ambulance staff who described Wright's actions" – here he rustles a piece of paper and reads from it - "as 'faultless. Your pupil's cool head and exemplary actions under pressure were of the standards that might be expected from a fully trained and experienced paramedic.' I am sure you will agree that that is praise indeed. They go on to say that, even though they arrived as quickly as they could, they are certain that, without Wright's intervention, they would not have been in time. As it was, Squires was fully conscious when taken into the ambulance."

The collected pupils applaud. Sam looks down at the floor. This is awful. It is publicity and he doesn't want it. But there's no escape. He's trapped. Dr. Rhodes thinks he is doing him an honour.

Now the large Councillor is speaking. "... this young man's calmness under pressure is an example to us all of the importance of learning the correct actions to take in an emergency. His efficient work saved his friend's life and prevented a tragedy. It is so easy to criticise young people today, but Samuel Wright's achievement shows ..."

Sam groans inwardly. Please, make it stop! He'll never live this down. There are enough people already who regard him as a stuck-up creep.

"Sam ... are you there?"

Sam jumps. *"Ngozi?"*

"I need to talk to you. It's important."

"What? Yes, of course. But I can't right now … I'll have to come back to you."

"Please."

"… and so it is my pleasure to present this certificate of commendation to Samuel Wright."

What could Ngozi want? She'd sounded agitated.

Sam becomes vaguely aware that the large Councillor has stopped speaking and is looking at him expectantly. He is holding out his hand, as if it should be shaken. Headmaster Rhodes is signalling urgently for Sam to step forward.

Reluctantly, Sam does as he's bidden. He has no choice. "Thank you." He glances quickly at the certificate which is in a glass frame. He wants to get off the stage. He is more interested in finding out what Ngozi wants.

No such luck. The Councillor pulls him back. "Not so quick, please! We need to record this important moment." Two cameras flash as the large man pummels his hand again. Unwillingly, Sam has to pose for more photographs, holding the certificate, smiling at the Councillor, shaking hands again. They're not for his benefit – but the Councillor will get his picture in the papers.

The papers! Oh shit!

Dr. Rhodes is smiling again. "As you will gather, I have allowed members of the local newspapers to record this proud moment. It just remains for me to close this small presentation by saying thank you, Wright, and well done. Your quick thinking and correct actions were a credit to you and to our school."

As Sam steps off the stage, at last, to another embarrassing round of applause, a reporter stand in his way. "Can I have a word please?" he asks. "Outside perhaps?"

"Better not", whispers Sam. "The assembly …" He glances up at the stage. He will use it as an excuse to avoid giving an interview.

"Wright, on this occasion, you are excused from the rest of assembly" says Dr. Rhodes. "Perhaps you will take our guest outside. Mr. Masterson will accompany you." He beams again as if he is doing Sam a favour.

Damn! It gets worse. Sam groans under his breath. With his unwanted certificate under his arm, he leads the two reporters out to the entrance hall.

The journalist is a middle-aged man, thin with greying hair, and a bored look of cynical world-weariness etched into his face. Sam is wary of him.

"Sam. My name's Chris Moss. Why don't you tell me in your own words, what happened?"

"Nothing much to add really. You just heard. When Squires – I mean Lewis – collided with Mr. Masterson, they knocked each other out. I helped Lewis", explains Sam, feeling that even this is too much.

Mr. Masterson supports Sam: "That's quite right. I was unconscious but when I came to, I saw what he was doing. Everything that happened is down to Wright here."

In the background Sam hears the assembly singing "There is a green hill far away". He wishes he was on it.

"So you and Lewis Squires are good friends?"

"Er, no, not really. We know each other through the football, I suppose."

"But he must be forever in your debt now?"

"Debt? No. I don't think of it like that. He'd do the same for me."

"Ah, but would he? Would he do the same for you? More to the point – even if he wanted to, *could* he do the same for you? The thing is – you knew what to do. Most people don't. I don't. But you did. I take it you have been trained in what to do in an emergency?"

Ngozi had warned him about this question.

"No. Not a course or anything like that." Sam remembers his friend's advice. "I read about it in a book, that's all." This comes across as such a boring answer; he can see and feel the reporters' disappointment. Their hero has become a geek, in a single sentence. And then he has a brainwave.

"And I saw it on 'Casualty'. I suppose I remembered it from there as well."

Chris Moss whistles through his teeth. "Now that's a great angle!" he says excitedly. "TV drama helps boy hero to save friend's life. That should make the nationals!"

Sam gulps. "No, please not. I don't want any publicity. Really."

"Hey, don't play it down. Your modesty does you credit" beams Cathy. "You deserve your 15 minutes of fame."

My God, Sam says to himself, what have I done now? Why couldn't I just tell the boring story like Ngozi said? Why did I have to dress it up?

Silently, he curses himself. As well he should.

The doors to the school hall crash open. Assembly has ended. Dozens of inquisitive people crowd round, eager to see Sam's certificate.

Sam is depressed at being the centre of attention again. After an eternity of showing the certificate and listening to their congratulations, the crowd around him goes quiet and parts. Lewis Squires has moved to the front. What will happen?

Squires looks self-conscious. Stiffly, he holds out his hand. "Thanks, Wright."

"Good to see you back" says Sam safely, shaking the offered hand, painfully aware that a hundred people are watching and hanging on their every word.

Lewis looks as awkward as Sam feels. "I ... I hope ... you get picked for the school team. You deserve it."

Sam beams. "Thanks." He means it. "You too." For the first time that either can remember, they smile at each other. The cameras flash again.

Hurriedly Sam lets go of Lewis Squires' hand. The moment is over. Squires merges back into the crowd and the reporter waves goodbye as he hurries away to file the story.

To Sam's dismay the bell rings: time for his first lesson. He hasn't been able to speak to Ngozi and find out what is so important. In frustration and anger, Sam pushes the newly-presented certificate into his locker and slams the door.

He walks to the classroom with friends congratulating him and others pointing as he goes by. But being the centre of attention is the last thing he wants. He dreads the publicity that is coming.

In the middle of what everyone else sees as his moment of triumph, Sam is desperately anxious. There are too many changes happening in his life. What will be the effects of today's events?

What is he turning into?

Why can't people just leave him alone?

CHAPTER 18 – TESTS

I t's lunchtime before Sam gets a chance to talk to Ngozi. Once again, but this time to avoid the crush of attention, he escapes to the relative peace and quiet of the school library. He nods at Tariq, who beams back and mouths the word "Project?"

"More research" lies Sam as he walks past. Without looking to see what it is, he chooses the largest book he can find and takes it to the back of the room where, hopefully, no-one will disturb him. He pretends to read, occasionally turning a page for good effect.

"Are you there?"

There is a pause.

"Ngozi?"

"Yes I'm here, Sam. Hold on - I'm talking to someone ... be right with you ... I'll just say goodbye ..."

Another pause.

"Right. Sam, thanks for coming back to me. I have something important to tell you."

"I'm sorry I couldn't speak to you earlier. Things were happening here."

"OK – tell me later. Now, don't worry about what I'm about to say ... the thing is, you need to be tested. Actually, we both do."

"Tested?"

"Your telepathic powers are exceptionally strong, Sam. Phenomenal actually. I hear you much better than my other contacts. And much more understandable."

"Understandable?"

"Yes. You speak my native language very well."

"What language? I only speak English. And you speak English too."

"No. Well, yes, I can speak English, but it's not my first language. My family's language is Ibo. That's what we use at home. And when we talk, like we are now, I hear you in Ibo. A very well spoken young man you are as well, if I may say so."

"That's not possible!" Sam immediately regrets the words. Ngozi doesn't like to be contradicted. *"I mean ..."*

Too late. *"Sam, you must stop saying that every time I tell you something new. Of course it's possible. It's possible because I am telling you – that's what's happening. And you might as well know that when I talk to you I use Ibo. I am doing that now. But I'll bet you're hearing me in English?"*

Sam is shocked. *"Well, yes, I am. I didn't think about that ..."*

"And why should you? I also predict that when you hear me, not only am I coming across to you in English, but also without any trace of an accent?"

"Well, yes. You sound like – someone who reads the news on television."

"Hmmm, I think there's a compliment hiding in there somewhere. I can tell you, though, that when I speak English out loud, I don't sound like that. I'm told that I speak it with a broad accent, because it's only my second language."

"Oh." Sam can't think of anything better so say.

"Telepathy is about exchanging thoughts, Sam, not words. People like us exchange thoughts. Our brains translate them into words – in your case you hear English and in my case I hear Ibo.

"But sorry, that's taken us off the point. My fault. I told the senior members about you and how powerfully we communicate. They want to learn more about you and how much we can do. They want to send someone to meet you. It's voluntary, of course. But I think it's important."

"Why?"

"Because you're causing quite a stir. It's not every day that someone is discovered with a gift as powerful as yours. That's why they want us to take the tests. They're not difficult. Will you do it?"

"I suppose so. Where? When?"

"That's up to you. You suggest a time and a place. You can't do them at home, obviously, not without letting a complete stranger into the house and having your parents asking what's going on. And we can't ask you to meet someone unknown to you in a place where the two of you would be alone. That would be irresponsible. Can you suggest a public place, but quiet, near where you live?"

"Does it have to be indoors?"

"I don't suppose so."

"Then how about the park? There are seats there, and there's shelter if it rains. People are always milling about there."

"Is it easy to find?"

"Not too bad." Sam gives her directions.

"That sounds perfect, Sam.

"Then how about ten-o-clock on Saturday morning?"

"I'll pass that on. The person you will meet is French – Monsieur Emmanuel Cabrieres. He's our senior mentor: he travels wherever necessary to give advice to people like us. It's quite an honour to meet him, you know."

"How will I recognise him?"

Ngozi chuckles. *"Don't worry, you'll recognise him. Saturday, 10-o-clock, park. I'm free that morning as well, so that's perfect."*

The bell rings for the next lesson. Sam has been concentrating so hard on his conversation with Ngozi that he has forgotten to turn the pages. Neither has he noticed Tariq now standing next to him. He shuts the book he has been pretending to read and replaces it on the shelf.

Tariq makes a mental note to ask Sam what is so important that he has stared intently at the same page for the last five minutes. What project, Tariq wonders, makes Sam Wright so interested in the gay community of San Francisco?

"OK, Doug. I'm off to England next week. It took some doing but I've got me a meeting with your Professor Harkness." Jane Baxter waves her passport at Doug Bartles.

"Your cover? You're not telling him you're CIA, I hope?"

Baxter looks at him, offended. "I'm not an amateur! Nope, I'm going as a researcher for NBC. Interested in doing a programme about evolution: you know, Darwin, Origin of the Species. But we thought it would be a really interesting ending to include a look into the future. We've learnt about his theories on telepathy and how the human race might evolve and that might be just the finishing flourish we need. We'd like to call the episode 'The Destination of the Species' – it's a phrase he used so we need his permission."

"Brilliant. If there's one thing that academics can't resist, it's being an expert on television. You'll ask him how we might recognise a freak if we see one?"

"That term has really stuck, hasn't it? Yes, I will. That's the whole point."

On Saturday, one look tells Sam that this is the man he has come to meet. Emmanuel Cabrieres is nothing if not distinctive. Sixty years old or thereabouts, tall, tanned and well built, his silvery-grey moustache wraps round his mouth on both sides and matches an impressive mane of silver hair which is brushed back and adds to his height and stature. He is dressed impeccably in a light grey suit, a darker grey silk handkerchief flopping from its top pocket and matching the tie and, to complete the image, he carries a silver-topped cane.

Sam almost laughs – it's like something from an old film. And yet, there is an air about this man, a bearing that speaks of authority, a person at ease with himself, someone in control of his life. A leader. Yes, Emmanuel Cabrieres looks every inch the remarkable man that Ngozi described.

Sam approaches him nervously.

"Excuse me, Sir, my name is Sam Wright."

The stranger smiles and bows slightly. He speaks in a deep voice and without a trace of an accent: "And I am Emmanuel Cabrieres. I thank you for meeting with me. I have heard a lot about you."

Sam is surprised. He had been expecting a pronounced French accent. Instead, M Cabrieres speaks impeccable English – a second language that he speaks better than many English people.

Sam takes the Frenchman's outstretched hand as confidently as he can, but inside he feels intimidated. "Pleased to meet you, Sir." He instinctively shows this man the respect that he shows his teachers at school.

"Please – no! You must not call me 'Sir'! I should like you to call me Emmanuel. As I say, Madame Agalaba has passed to me a great deal of information about you and your new-found abilities. You are causing much interest among my colleagues on the Council. If just part of what we have been told about you is true, I expect some excitement today."

Sam smiles weakly.

"Mr. Wright – or may I call you Sam?"

"Please." Sam nods. Perhaps he should have said that immediately. He feels this is going badly.

"Good. Sam it is." Emmanuel drops his voice and speaks now quite quietly. "We must be – discreet – in this public place? Shall we walk a little?"

It is less of a question, more an instruction. The two of them take a path that curves lazily through the park, Sam wheeling the new bicycle he bought with the money his parents gave him for his birthday.

"I understand you have a very clear telepathic contact with Ngozi?"

Sam smiles at the mention of his friend's name. "Clear? Yes, though I have nothing to compare it with. She says it is. It's like talking to someone in the same room."

"So I understand. And you can sense her presence all the time? You sense her now?"

"Yes. It's ... like having a TV tuned in to a station: even if it's not broadcasting, you know it's there. It's like having someone who is always there for me."

"Quite so. I understand exactly what you mean. Could you please tell me about this from the very beginning?"

Sam describes the events from the moment of the accident. M Cabrieres already knows about the events at the football match, and purses his lips when Sam explains he was receiving advice from Ngozi when he saved Lewis Squires' life.

"What you did - that is very good. The publicity - that is very bad. I must advise you to give no further interviews. None at all. Say you are embarrassed. You do not want publicity. Then the story will be forgotten. A fire will die if no-one adds fuel to it, yes?"

Sam nods.

"And what is done is done. We shall say nothing more of this."

Sam senses his companion becoming apprehensive. M. Cabrieres continues: "Will you tell me about the feelings you experienced at Reading?"

Sam recounts, in a soft voice, how he had felt an irrational anger, how Maddy had felt it too, and how he had fought against it and calmed her down.

"I hope you're not disappointed at that" asks Sam as he finishes.

M Cabrieres shakes his head. "No, of course not. You did nothing wrong – you remained sane while everyone round you went mad. You did well. But I ask myself, how was it that you – and you alone – were able to maintain your self-control? This is an interesting question that we must consider in due course. But my priority now, if you will permit this, is to ensure you receive the support you need to live with these new abilities of yours."

"Ngozi said something about an ... Emotist? She felt that the violence might have been caused deliberately by someone controlling the crowd?"

Emmanuel pauses. "Ah. Your friend has moved quickly. You must forgive me, however, if I make progress one step at a time. For now, let us concentrate on the matter in hand, and that is the tests."

Sam nods and makes a mental note to return to this.

"So, to business. I have in my pocket the tests we use. Do not worry: they are very simple and they involve no danger or stress to you." He points. "Shall we sit at those benches over there?"

He nods at two empty bench seats, behind which a group of children is playing football, their coats on the grass acting as goalposts. A steady stream of people is walking past.

"Sam, if you will please sit there, I will sit on the other bench, here. You can lean your bicycle against the arm."

Sam, sitting where he has been told, nods nervously: "Ready. What do you want me to do?"

"First, I ask you make contact with Ngozi."

"*Ngozi. Are you there? I have Monsieur Cabrieres with me.*"

"*Yes, I'm here, Sam. Tell him I have a gentleman called Abdul Ahmed with me.*"

"Yes, she's there. She has a gentleman named Abdul with her."

"My goodness; that was quick! Is it so easy every time?"

"Yes. Once I learnt how. It seems like second nature now."

"Very good." M Cabrieres reaches into his jacket pocket for a notepad and pen. He scribbles a few words and then, from another pocket, produces what looks like a pack of cards.

"Monsieur Ahmed, who is with Ngozi, is a colleague of mine on the Council. He is my telepathic partner and will observe the tests at the other end. Now, I want you to look at these cards one at a time, and describe to Ngozi what you see. Please describe each card accurately, because Ngozi is going to draw what you describe."

For a few minutes they sit in silence. Sam leafs through the cards, each of which is numbered to ensure he keeps them in sequence. He studies them and describes what he sees to Ngozi.

A circle.

A square.

A triangle with two wavy lines underneath.

A circle with a diamond shape inside it.

A square with its top half black and its bottom half white.

A rectangle inside a circle.

An upward pointing arrow.

The symbols carry no meaning so far as Sam can tell.

After working his way through the cards Ngozi says to Sam: *"Mr. Ahmed is looking at the drawings now. Ah, he says we have done well."*

"You and Ngozi have done well."

Sam smiles: "Ngozi said."

"Sam, we are now going to do the same exercise in reverse. I describe and you draw."

"OK, I'll ask M Cabrieres for some paper and a pen ....oh." He is already holding out a notebook and pencil for Sam to use.

Sam draws the shapes that Ngozi describes ... a circle with a diagonal cross in it, an oval on top of a rectangle, a square inside a circle; all abstract, all capable of being described precisely, all easy to draw.

There are three more similar tests with the imagery getting more complex each time. After fifteen minutes M Cabrieres calls a halt.

"Enough, I think. Thank you for your attention. I suggest that you and Ngozi rest for a while. Then I have some pictures to show you."

"OK, I'm going to make a 'phone call." Ngozi sounds relieved.

M Cabrieres walks to the flower beds and studies the plants. Sam leans back on the bench. The tests were easy. At first he'd been nervous but now he is, if anything, bored. He fidgets with his shirt and flicks a piece of mud from his bike. He looks impatiently in the Frenchman's direction.

Nothing.

Sam checks his watch. He wants this to be over. He has better things to do on a Saturday than sit on a park bench, wasting his time. But the Frenchman has his back to him and is apparently totally absorbed, studying the flower bed with great interest.

After many minutes sitting in silence, being ignored, Sam feels impatience building inside him. He doesn't like being treated as if he isn't there. It's, well, rude. He's given up his morning to meet this man. It wasn't his idea to waste all that time doing stupid tests.

"Ngozi, anything happening at your end?"

No answer. Presumably she is still on the phone.

Sam coughs, hoping to attract the Frenchman's attention. No effect.

He waits a little longer, drumming his fingers on the arm of the bench. Then he decides that the Frenchman must have forgotten him. He walks over: "Excuse me. Was there something else you wanted me to do?"

M Cabrieres looks up, half distracted. "Ah, yes. I forgot you were here. My - but you have the impatience of youth, I fear. I expect you will learn."

Patronising, arrogant git! Forgot he was here? Impatience of youth? Now Sam is angry. Aren't these tests meant to be important? Has he really given up his morning to be – forgotten?

M Cabrieres continues. "Take these back to the bench and study them." No 'please' or 'thank you'. The Frenchman reaches absent-mindedly into his inside pocket again and produces an envelope. "Let me know what you think."

Sam bridles more. That was hardly polite. He is taking a dislike to this arrogant mentor with his perfect appearance. He feels like saying something but there are too many people walking through the park now. Better not to make a scene and risk attracting attention.

Sam snatches the envelope and stalks back to the bench. This meeting is not turning out at all as he expected. He has a mind not to do as he's been asked. But he does: of course he does. Everything to do with his telepathy is new to him and he can't turn down the opportunity to learn more about it.

Angrily, he takes the papers from the envelope.

What? WHAT?

He has in his hands a montage of photographs and they make him feel sick.

Sam recognises the first pictures as a 2nd World War concentration camp. Hundreds starved and naked bodies lie on the ground where they fell, unattended, disrespected. Emaciated, naked survivors are holding out their hands, pleading for food. Human beings stripped of all dignity: no clothes, barely alive, their heads shaved, their rib-cages showing and their arms and legs as thin as matchsticks. Behind them, a trailer contains a mound of corpses, piled carelessly like dead animals. A heap of discarded meat that was once real people.

Bloody hell!

Sam feels repulsed. Before looking at these pictures he had already been irritated by the Frenchman's rudeness. But if that wasn't enough, now - this. He feels furious at being ignored, appalled by the images and outraged at the way he is being treated by this supposed new friend.

How dare he? What possible reason can he have for asking Sam to look at pictures like these?

What sort of behaviour is this?

Who the blazes does this man think he is?

Sam stands to tell M Cabrieres what he thinks of him. But the grey-haired stranger is still standing with his back him, his hands in his pockets, still gazing at the flowers and apparently deep in thought.

Sam is distracted as a young boy in a pushchair throws a tantrum, screaming and hurling a toy across the path. His mother picks it up and snaps at him to be quiet. The boy's protests grow louder till they echo round the park.

The moment to speak with the Frenchman is gone. Sam sits again and turns back to the papers.

The next sheets of photographs are as violent as the first. With a title "Attack on Hiroshima" they show pictures of a mushroom cloud, as created by an atomic bomb. There are graphic images of the devastated city.

Desperately injured children are having horrific burns bandaged. Others lie in pain on the ground. A child's tricycle, lies scorched and twisted, its owner gone. On a blackened wall is etched the outline of a person killed in an instant: the only remaining record of the life he led.

Finally there is a line of survivors with their eyes bandaged, blinded by the flash of the explosion, being led through the wreckage of their devastated homes.

This is too much! Sam feels even angrier than before. He is aware – who isn't – of the horrors of the last War, but why on earth is he being asked to look at these terrible pictures?

"Ngozi" he calls, *"this man is sick...."*

No answer. She'd said she was going to make a phone call. Just his luck - when he really wants to sound off to her, she's busy doing something else.

Angrily Sam screws up the photographs. He throws them venomously at the litter bin. They miss.

A passing stranger snaps: "That's it, mess the place up."

The woman with him is angry: "For God's sake, Jim, don't start another row! There's no need for that."

"There you go again, always siding with them - never standing up for what is right. Bloody hooligans. What's happened to standards?"

The two of them walk on, arguing furiously.

Hooligan? Me?

Bloody hell!

Sam retrieves the papers, though, and puts them more carefully into the bin. As he does, he sees that the boys' football match behind him has disintegrated into a fight. There is a furious dispute about whether the ball had crossed the non-existent goal line. A boy is threatening to take his ball home and end the game altogether if the goal doesn't stand.

The third and last bundle of photos is better. It shows a mother feeding her baby. It shows a young child laughing and an old lady smiling in gratitude at a man as he helps to pick up the shopping she has dropped. These images are soothing, and Sam feels better. But what is this all about?

At last! M Cabrieres is returning now to the bench. "The flowers – they are very beautiful, I think."

Sam makes to answer, but M. Cabrieres holds up his hand to demand silence. "Monsieur Wright – Sam. Before you say anything, I offer you my apology. I ignored you most rudely. I spoke impolitely. And those photographs – they are very bad, no? They deserve to be thrown into the bin, which I see is what you have done. This was all deliberate. Now I must explain to you what this last test was about."

"This was a test too?"

"But of course! Please do not think for a moment that I carry such awful things around with me. I assure you that I do not. Neither do I make a habit of behaving like this."

That's a relief.

"This test was of a different nature. I was impolite to you. I turned my back. I ignored you. I spoke rudely. This made you angry, and rightly so. Then those horrible pictures: they made you angry and sick - how could they not, given what they were?

"When you were looking at them, I was standing with my back to you. I wondered whether I might feel your emotions, Sam. Would you, I wondered, make me experience your anger and your disgust?"

"Oh. And did I?"

"Oh yes, most certainly! There is no doubt about it."

Sam looks down. He doesn't like this.

The Frenchman continues. "I felt it most strongly. I was shocked at how powerful the feelings were. It is a most disturbing sensation, to be so affected by someone else's emotions. I found it almost impossible to resist. I had to place my hands in my pockets so that you would not see them trembling. It was like I was not in control of myself."

"That's how Maddy and I felt in Reading."

"Quite so, but please allow me to finish. Do not rely on me telling you how I felt. I am but one person and I am telepathic. Use the evidence of your own eyes. Think of the people around us and how they behaved.

Did you see the effect your anger had on them? The young boy cried for no reason and his mother scolded him. You remember this?"

Sam nods. He hates where this is going.

"And on a fine summer day, two lovers suddenly quarrelled. A man shouted at you and his lady told him to stop. That is the truth, is it not?"

Sam nods again.

"And the football match – it turned into a fight, did it not?"

"Yes." The word catches in Sam's throat. A cold sense of dread is creeping over him.

"These things all happened when you were angry, Sam. More than that: they happened because you were angry. You made many people feel what you were feeling. It was horrible for them. They did not know what was happening. They could not control it.

"You probably did not know what you were doing. But I knew. I felt it. I recognised it for what it was.

"Then the anger was replaced by softer emotions and, after a while, happiness. You did that, Sam. You did all that with your mind."

Sam says nothing. What can he say?

"By the way, did you try to contact Ngozi?"

"Yes, I did. She was busy, on a phone call, I think."

"Not so. She did not answer because she had been instructed not to, as part of the test. We did not want you sharing your experience with anyone else – that would have diluted the trial. She will answer again now."

"Ngozi, are you there now?"

"Yes, I'm here. What happened at your end? You made me feel quite shaky!"

"You felt it too? Emmanuel Cabrieres showed me some horrible pictures."

"Well, please warn me if you ever decide to look at them again! And tell him to behave himself!"

Sam ignores the second part of what Ngozi has just said. He doesn't yet feel confident enough with this slightly sinister Frenchman to pass on a message like that. "Ngozi felt it too. So what does this all mean?"

M Cabrieres sits down again and sighs. "Sadly, my friend, you already know what it means. Ngozi warned you. It means that you definitely are, as she suspected, capable of making ordinary people - non-telepathic people - feel your emotions. She became concerned about this on the day you were angry about your neighbour being arrested. She felt there was something wrong and called you. You remember this?"

Sam nods. He hadn't thought twice about it at the time, but yes, Ngozi had called him and asked him what the matter was.

Emmanuel Cabrieres continues: "You affected many people as they walked through the park – a most wise choice of location, by the way.

"Young man, I have no doubt now that you possess a rare and dangerous power. So far you have used it, I think, four times without knowing."

"Four times? That's not possible!"

"But hear me out and consider what I tell you before saying anything. The first time was how Ngozi found you – I understand you screamed when you had your accident. She heard you and she felt your fear."

Sam nods.

"The second time was when you were walking home and your neighbour's wife made you angry. And the third time - in my opinion, you calmed the demonstration in Reading and, in doing so, you saved a police officer's life.

"And today was the fourth."

Sam leans back and tries to keep calm. It's the truth – he knows it. He also knows with dread certainty that his life can never be the same after this. "I'm frightened now. I don't know what to do with this. Please – I need you to help me. Tell me what to do."

"You are right to be frightened. You must learn to control this." Emmanuel shakes his head sadly. "You have such difficult lessons to learn and you must do so very quickly. You will need advice on how to avoid using this power. For the rest of your life you will need to control your emotions in case you affect the people around you. At the same time you must try to live as normally as you can. This will be difficult for you, I am afraid, doubly so because you will not be able to turn to your family and friends for advice. But if you wish, I shall help you as much as I can and you must not hesitate to turn to Ngozi."

The Frenchman smiles, without humour. "And you have to know - the power you have is exceptionally strong. For you to calm a riot, you must have affected hundreds of people. That is truly remarkable. You are a uniquely talented young man."

"You really think I calmed the riot in Reading?"

"I do. You were focussing on your girlfriend, to be sure, but your calming emotions affected everyone. So yes, in my opinion you stopped that riot. Which means you saved a man's life." He stands up. "Now, I think that I have taken up enough of your time for one day."

Sam shakes his head: "But please, I have another question. In Reading the crowd became violent because someone was controlling them. I felt it. That means there's another person who can do this."

"Yes, there is."

"You said you would tell me more. Do you know who it is? This other person?"

M Cabrieres looks grim and sits again. A look of great sadness passes over his face as he replies. "Yes, I believe I do." He looks closely at Sam. "It is a long story. It has caused a major crisis in our community. My colleagues do not want me to tell you. But I believe I shall. Not now though. You already have enough to think about."

Sam wants to know why the Frenchman looks so sad. But he doesn't have the confidence to press the point – not yet.

Sam looks grim. "I don't like this. I'm going to need someone to help me. I will need to talk you again."

"Of course. That is my wish too. Shall we meet here again next Saturday? Then, I shall most certainly tell you about the other person. And we shall review how you are coming to terms with your ability. Madame Agalaba and I will attempt to offer you the advice and support that normally would come from your parents."

Sam nods his thanks.

"But now I shall take no more of your time and you must enjoy the rest of this fine day with your friends. You must not let this discovery stop you living your life."

Yeah right! Sam's mind is whirling.

Emmanuel holds out his hand: "Sam, it has been a privilege to meet you. One final thing: each one of your drawings was correct in every detail."

"That's good."

"It is more than that, young man. You completed the tests in a record time. You and your friend Ngozi beat even the most powerful members of our community. This has been a most interesting morning."

And with that, Emmanuel Cabrieres shakes Sam's hand, smiles and walks away, his cane tapping on the pavement as he goes.

"Abdul?"

"Emmanuel: I have been waiting."

"I am alone now."

"Then tell me ... is he ... you know?" M Cabrieres' partner is anxious.

"Yes, Abdul. No doubt about it. And powerful too."

"So now there's two of them. Will you kill him?"

"No, of course not. He's just a boy. He is overwhelmed by what is happening to him. He is looking for help and advice."

"Then what? You surely cannot take the risk of two of those monsters loose in the world?"

"I shall. I must. I do not execute innocent teenagers."

"You know what will happen if this gets out: more Government agents: more deaths among our people. More disappearances. You will put us all in danger. The Council won't like this."

"It's a chance I must take. The news must not get out."

"But if he goes bad ..."

"I don't think he will. I have met him."

"But if he does? The other one did."

"That would change everything, certainly. But I liked him. I have spoken with him and am confident it won't come to that. For what it is worth, that is what Madame Agalaba thinks too. She says he is just a normal fourteen old boy with an exceptional talent."

"Very well, if we allow him to live, do you think he could take care of the other one?"

"Set them against each other? No. Well, possibly, in time. But certainly not yet. He's only a boy, confused and struggling to come to terms with it all. I am going to counsel him. Help him."

"Counsel him? One of those ... obscenities? I hope you know what you're doing, Emmanuel, for all our sakes."

"As do I."

"Very well, my friend. But at the first sign of him turning bad ..."

"I know. I know. Do not lecture me, Abdul. I know my duty."

The Frenchman walks from the park.

Unaware that his very existence is being discussed, Sam stands for a few minutes watching the children playing their resumed game of football. Their fight has ended, their argument is forgotten. They won't remember it – such disagreements happen all the time. It is difficult to believe that he, Sam Wright, had started it.

He sighs and then, picking up his bike, rides slowly away. Not really aware of what he is doing, he cycles to the cemetery. There he pauses by the grave of the mother and baby whose burial he watched a few weeks before.

So much has happened since that day. It's not just that two innocent people died. His naïve and uncomplicated childhood ended that day too.

He pictures the simple teddy bear lying on the hard coffin in the cold earth in front of him. At least he, Sam, is still alive. Alive, yes – but what sort of life can he now expect?

Everything is different now. He possesses powers that frighten him. Will he be able to cope with them? Without help? He has no-one to advise him except a woman in Nigeria he has never met and a slightly sinister, eccentric-looking Frenchman he's not sure he trusts yet.

He hasn't asked for this.

He doesn't want it.

Sam Wright allows a couple of tears to run down his cheeks - one for the mother and her child, the other for himself and his lost childhood.

It's alright, he tells himself, to show emotion here. He's in a cemetery.

People are allowed to be sad here.

CHAPTER 19 – ATTACKED

Normally Sam Wright finds newsagents inoffensive. As far as he can remember, none has ever made him swear before. Deep in thought though he is as he rides his bike home, the screaming headline on the billboard makes him skid to a halt.

"Oh, shit!"

Had he said that out loud? A couple of passers-by look at him curiously for a moment and then hurry on. Clearly he had.

The headline reads: 'Local boy hero - exclusive interview'. Nervously Sam walks into the shop. His photograph is on the front page of the local weekly paper.

"Schoolboy hero honoured."

"I saw it on TV says life-saver" screams a sub-headline.

The man at the till looks up idly. Then he picks up the paper: "Hey – aren't you ..."

"No, I'm not. Sorry, changed my mind." Sam hurries out. More publicity; the last thing he wants. He pulls up the hood on his top and cycles home, head down.

Quickly.

Don't be seen, don't be seen! Get home. Don't be seen!

God! What will people say about him at school after this? He'll be even more the stuck-up cocky bastard.

At home the phone rings constantly. Friends of Sam's parents call with their congratulations. A local television station phones three times asking for an interview and each time Sam refuses, much to his parents' disappointment. They'll send a car to bring Sam to the studio, if that's a problem. OK, they'll send a camera team to Sam's home. On the third call they even offer money.

"You should be proud of what you did, son. We are" smiles his father. Sam feels good about that – of course he does. But the advice he's received couldn't be clearer. No more publicity, full stop. That's how it will be.

"Thanks. But no. I don't want to."

"But why not? You did a great thing, saving that boy's life."

"I just hate the publicity. I don't want to be on television. It's bad enough being in the papers." He goes upstairs to his room to prevent any more discussion.

His parents look at each other in disappointment and shrug. "You know, Helen, not so long ago he'd have done it, especially if we were encouraging him."

"I know. Now all we get is a flat 'no'. And he's so intense about it: it's not worth trying to change his mind. It doesn't matter what we say, he's not going to do it, and that's that."

"Shame."

"We can't make him."

"Absolutely: it's his decision. But I've not seen him like this before. He's made his mind up and there's absolutely nothing we can do about it."

Helen Wright looks meaningfully at her husband. He nods in agreement at her unspoken comment: he sees it now. There is definitely something different about their son these days – something darker, something deeper. He's changing. But they can't put their fingers on it.

"Oh no." Sam stares in disgust at his computer screen. "It's on the internet now." The local paper has put the story on its website.

And the trolls are piling in, offering their poisonous comments. "Shud get out more insted of waching TV all the time" says one anonymous spelling expert.

"Some people will do anything for publicity" says another.

"Faked, just to make money. How much is he being paid by the crooked press?"

And "Why can't he beat up an immigrant, like normal teenagers do?"

Two days later, as Sam is starting to hope that the furore has died down, two of the national dailies copy the story and the requests for interviews start all over again, but even worse. One of the tabloids runs a trail on its front page and inside prints the photograph of Lewis Squires shaking Sam's hand with the caption 'The Wright Stuff'. Squires has given an interview in which he is complimentary about Sam. The rest is cobbled together from quotes given by so-called 'best friends', though some of them are people Sam hardly knows and one is a name he doesn't recognise at all.

Sam fumes but there is nothing he can do. And to rub salt in the wound, he knows that he helped to make things this bad. He should have kept his mouth shut.

Far from being anonymous, Sam now sees people pointing at him and whispering. He finds himself being engaged in conversation by people he hardly knows. More and more he takes to wearing his hoodie to hide his face.

So it is a relief when a genuine contact seeks him out – someone who was friendly before all the publicity. Sam senses that Tariq Alufi is nervous. "I was wondering, Sam – well hoping - would you like to come round my house tomorrow? After school."

"Oh. Well ... OK." Sam is caught off balance. Although he and Tariq have been talking more often, this is unexpected. Tariq isn't known for inviting friends home. The common view is that his parents are pernickety and obsessed with him doing well with his schoolwork. "Anything special?"

"Yes. No. Well not really -" Tariq is tongue-tied. "OK, if you must know, it's my birthday. We don't do big parties or that sort of thing – well, we do inside the family, but not normally outside - but my mother says I can invite someone for tea after school. I was hoping; would YOU would like to come?"

Sam senses how tense Tariq is. He can hardly refuse. "Thank you. That's ... well, yes, of course, it sounds great. Thanks for asking." He smiles at the look of relief on Tariq's face.

On the way home, Sam and Maddy choose a card and a DVD as a present. Maddy is amused that Sam has been invited home by Tariq of all people, but when Sam reminds her who showed them how to find her Uncle's address, she lays off.

Tariq Alufi's home is in a street of semi-detached houses, all built to the same basic design. Nevertheless, it stands out.

The front garden is the best tended in the road. The small lawn is the most carefully mown.

The low hedge is the most neatly cut. The colourful flowers stand to attention in military precision.

The shining white window frames are recently painted. The brick path is swept. Even the red doorstep is freshly stained and clean.

Sam knows before he sets foot in it that the house will be as faultless inside as it is on the outside.

Tariq's mother is tall, thin and elegant with jet black hair, cut short and very, well, neat. She meets the boys at the door and greets Sam like royalty.

"Sam Wright! I recognise you from your picture in the paper. I was so pleased when Tariq told me who was coming, having read so much about you."

Sam smiles uncomfortably.

"When he told me whom he had invited I said to Tariq: this is definitely the type of friend you should have. This shows that you are mixing with the right people. I tell him; mix with the right people and your life will progress in the right direction as well."

"Mum!" says Tariq, embarrassed. "Don't start!"

"Don't start, he says...."

Before she can discomfit him further, Tariq takes Sam's arm: "got something to show you" and they go upstairs.

"Happy Birthday." Sam holds out the card and present. "I got you these." And he adds "Maddy helped choose it. She says 'Happy Birthday' too."

"You're so lucky."

"Sorry?"

"Having a girlfriend like that. I mean, she's so hot."

"She's ..." Sam stops. This is the second time he's been on the point of denying that Maddy is his girlfriend. Perhaps she is? Everyone seems to think so. Perhaps he's missing something obvious.

"... great." It feels good saying that.

Tariq's pride and joy is his new mobile phone – a gift from his parents that morning. Sam whistles. It's only just been released, and to rave reviews.

Not only is it a phone, Tariq's mother explains over tea, it is also a music player, a camera, a personal organiser and global positioning system. "With a machine such as this, you can keep in touch with your family and be organised at the same time. To be successful as a man, you must be organised."

"And mix with the right people."

"Yes, and mix ..." she stops and looks sternly at her son. Tariq is making fun of her. Sam stifles a smile, keeps his head down and concentrates on eating. Not difficult: the food is good.

Really good.

Tariq's mother has baked a cake: it has a single, lit candle. Carefully Tariq removes the candle and places it in a lamp on the table. Seeing Sam watching with interest, Tariq explains "We don't blow out a ceremonial candle: for us it's important to let it continue to throw its light."

Interesting how different parts of the community do things differently.

The tea enthusiastically eaten, Mrs. Alufi asks meaningfully. "Now boys, I expect you have homework? Even on a special day essential tasks must be done." Sam takes this as a signal that the event is over. He thanks Mrs. Alufi and makes to leave.

"I'll walk some of the way with you" offers Tariq.

The evening is drawing in and the houses on the other side of the road are silhouetted against the setting sun. The pavements are virtually deserted. The only noise to disturb the silence is the drone of an electric mower from the next street. A noise of the approaching summer: an evening for relaxing.

Tariq and Sam amble slowly, enjoying the opportunity to unwind for a few more minutes. "Sorry about my Mum. She's never used a smart phone. Explaining it all like that."

The path takes them past a piece of scrubland and they step briefly into the road to avoid bushes that are hanging over the pavement. As they do, two men appear from behind the drooping branches. They are deliberately blocking the way.

The taller man has an ugly scar on his right cheek. His dark brown hair is long, unwashed and greasy, and his clothes are holed and stained. The shorter man keeps looking around, nervously. He is wearing smart, expensive trainers that are out of place with the rest of his clothes. "Stolen, probably", thinks Sam to himself. The two men's features look oddly similar ... familiar somehow.

"Why, if it ain't the local nerd!" The taller man sneers cynically and bows. "We are honoured indeed."

Tariq and Sam stop. "Hello George ... Tom." says Tariq. "Good to see you."

Sam looks at his friend quizzically. 'Good' is the last word he would have used. There's trouble brewing here.

"Sam, this is George Warren and his brother Tom. They used to go to our school. You met their brother Nathan with me on the stairs the other day."

The penny drops. That's why they look familiar. These are the brothers of the racist bully.

Tariq is being formally polite, hoping to avoid trouble. As he introduces them, he quietly slips his new phone into his pocket.

Not quickly enough.

The two men exchange a glance and a nod. Each takes a pace away from the other.

Without warning, the shorter one – Tom - punches Tariq in the stomach, a vicious and unprovoked blow that leaves him winded. As he doubles over, gasping for breath, George grabs the phone from Tariq's pocket. The two men run off as Tariq falls to his knees, struggling to breathe.

A few seconds, that's all. Mugged!

If it isn't bad enough that Tariq is being racially abused at school, now he's been robbed. And by members of the same family.

Without pausing to think, Sam sprints after the two men. He is fitter than they are and quickly closes the gap. They hear his footsteps. At a fork in the road, George goes to the left and Tom to the right. Sam runs after George – the one with the phone.

Idiot! He should have seen it coming. Sam curses himself as he realises what the Warren brothers have done. With the smoothness of frequent practice, they have laid a trap for him. George stops and turns to face Sam, grinning insolently. No wonder. Sam hears running footsteps approaching from behind. That's Tom. Sam is between the two of them. Trapped.

Sam looks round anxiously for help. There's no-one. Apart from the three of them, this part of the street is deserted. It will do no good to shout. There's no escape.

"Well now, you really are the friggin' superhero, an' no mistake!" sneers George.

"But pretty stupid" adds Tom.

"You bastards – give that phone back."

"Phone? What phone? Know what 'e's talking about, Tom?"

"Nope."

"You hear that? No phone."

"Cut the crap. You just took it from my friend. Give it back."

"I do believe you ain't listening. No phone." George holds his hands out.

"In your pocket."

George pokes Sam in the chest. "You deaf? No ... friggin' ... phone."

Sam is forced to step backwards. George pushes him again, and again, and again till Sam loses his balance and falls awkwardly into the road. He is lying defenceless on the ground. Tom is shaping to kick him.

Sam feels in his pocket for his own phone, wondering whether he can dial 999. No, that's a useless idea. Not enough time.

Now Sam knows how the police sergeant must have felt in Reading. He's going to take a beating. He fears what is about to happen. He's afraid.

To his surprise, the kick that Tom is shaping to deliver never comes. "What's 'e got in his pocket?" he hisses.

"How should I know?"

Fear!

The Warrens are afraid! They are feeling HIS fear. Just as at Reading with Maddy and in the park with Emmanuel Cabrieres, he is transmitting his emotion to them.

It's his way out. He can save himself.

Sam keeps his hand in his pocket. "Yes, be afraid." Now he projects his fear at them deliberately, thinking to himself: 'I'm afraid, I'm scared' – forcing himself to keep the emotions flowing.

"'e's got a knife!" shouts the taller man.

"Or a shooter!"

With slow deliberation Sam stands up. He speaks calmly. "It could be either. Which of you wants to be the first to find out?"

"He's a psycho! Jeez!"

"Just give me the phone and we can all walk away from this with no harm done. Don't push me though – I don't want to use this." Sam keeps his hand on the phone in his pocket.

Be afraid!

George and Tom swear and take a step back.

"I do know how to use this, in case you are wondering."

That's true enough. It's a phone.

"OK, OK." With exaggerated care, George Warren puts Tariq's phone on the kerb and raises his hands. "Look, we don't want no shooting trouble. Friggin' hell, the nerd knows 'ow to choose 'is friends."

With his free hand, Sam picks up Tariq's phone and inspects it. "Now, what should I do with you two parasites?" he asks out loud.

Tom looks at George and hisses. "What'd 'e say? What's a parasite?"

"Init what you wear when you jump out an airplane?"

Sam rolls his eyes.

The two men are rooted to the spot. The fear that Sam is projecting at them has sapped their will to do anything.

"For Christ's sake ... you've got the friggin' phone back. Leave us alone." George Warren is pleading, his hands clasped together. He's pale. There are beads of sweat on his forehead.

"In a moment. Just stand there while I check you haven't done any damage" says Sam. He makes a show of inspecting Tariq's phone, holding it up to the light to make sure.

"Please. Just let us go. We won't do this again." Tom Warren is pleading, pitifully.

Sam smiles: "You can count yourself lucky. It looks like it's OK. I suggest ...", and here he grins at the two thugs, "... that you piss off now."

Sam can't resist saying out loud: "Boo!"

The two men yelp and turn and run. Sam laughs.

Not for long.

"Sam. What on Earth is going on?" Ngozi's voice in his head makes him jump. She sounds annoyed.

"Everything's alright. A friend and I were attacked."

"Are you alright?"

"I'm OK. They hit my friend and stole his phone. I got it back."

"How?"

"I chased them ... I frightened them."

"You did what?" Ngozi pauses. *"You frightened them? You frightened them? Sam - please tell me, after all we've said, after all the advice you've been given - you didn't use your Emotist powers?"*

"No. Well, yes. Sort of. Not on purpose. I mean, I think I did but I didn't mean to. I didn't realise it was happening - didn't even know I was doing it. They trapped me and I fell. I felt frightened. They picked that up and backed off. That's all. They thought I had a knife!"

"And you're sure that's all?"

"Yes." It isn't the whole truth, but Sam isn't going to admit everything. *"Like I said, I didn't realise I was doing it."*

"Then you are a very lucky young man. And it looks as if you are even more powerful than any of us thought."

"It was quite easy."

"Sam. You must ... no, let's talk later. How's your friend?"

"He's up the road: I left him when I chased after the muggers."

"Then hadn't you better see how he is?"

Sam pauses for a minute: he's recorded the exchange with the Warren brothers. He mails it to his phone and then deletes it from Tariq's. Then he runs back to where he and Tariq had been attacked. He wants to intercept him before he gets home and has to face his parents.

Tariq is gone.

Sam runs on towards his friend's house. Ahead of him, his friend is walking home dejectedly, head bowed.

"Tariq! Tariq – hold on."

Tariq turns and stops and waits for Sam to catch up.

"Are you OK?" asks Sam.

Tariq sniffs. "Yes, I'm on top of the world, thank you. I've been mugged and had my phone stolen but apart from that ..."

"Sorry, it was a stupid question, but..."

"My parents will kill me when I tell them. It was expensive. And I've gone and got it nicked on the first day! A great birthday this has turned out to be!"

"You didn't go and do anything. You're the victim, remember that. Anyhow, relax." Sam holds out his hand, with Tariq's phone in it. "I got it back."

"Bloody hell!" Tariq grabs the phone in delight and turns it over in his hand, inspecting it. "Sam, those were the Warren brothers! They're complete nutters. Nobody crosses them and lives to talk about it! When you ran after them ... I couldn't believe it. How'd you do that?"

"Let's just say I - persuaded them. But do me a favour; don't say anything about this, eh? I've had enough publicity to last me a lifetime. I'm sick of it. Tariq, you have to promise; it's important to me ... keep this to yourself. Not a word to anyone." He has a great thought: "That way, there's no risk of your parents hearing about it either."

Tariq nods. He's in no state to argue and the last thing he wants is for his parents to know.

Sam sits on a garden wall and signals for Tariq to do the same. "You'd better tell me what's going on with the Warrens. Why do they treat you like that? The way Nathan behaved at school ..."

Tariq looks disconsolately at the pavement. "You know what it is. You don't need me to spell it out."

No, of course he doesn't. Another stupid question. He's not doing well tonight. "It's disgusting. How long has it been going on?"

"Ages. Years. Sam, this goes on all the time. It's a way of life for some people. I try to avoid them. They don't like – people like me."

"Just because you're ..." Sam doesn't know how to finish the sentence.

"Not white? A Paki? Not one of you lot? That's right." Tariq spits out the words. "Sorry ... I don't mean you. Look, I try not to let it get to me but sometimes it does. Tonight it has." He turns to Sam angrily. "You know, I was born here, I've lived here all my life. I'm as British as you are - but to them I'm just a ..."

"Tariq, they're scum." Sam feels ashamed. "But not everyone's like them."

"I know that. There's enough though. More than you'd think. People you'd expect to know better – you'd be surprised, honest. The Warrens are just one example."

Tariq takes a deep breath, as if he's decided to say something that's difficult. "They weren't violent when I was younger. At first I thought it was something I'd done that made them not like me. I blamed myself. As I grew older I started to understand the race thing. I realised it wasn't anything I'd done: it was the way I looked and the way they were brought up. So I learnt to ignore them and they acted cold towards me and that was it. Then they moved on from name calling and shouting across the road to the more physical stuff."

"You shouldn't have to put up with that crap. No-one should."

Tariq snorts. "That's easy for you to say. Who's going to stop it? The police?"

Sam tries not to nod.

"Don't make me laugh! Some of them are just as bad." Tariq continues in a rush: "Look, this shit's a fact of life for me. You've seen it twice and you're shocked, but for us it's an everyday thing. I could show you a dozen families in this area like the Warrens. Anyhow, verbals - I can cope with that. You kind of get used to it and learn not to let it get to you. And most of them are so thick that you don't have to take them seriously anyway.

"Then Nathan decided he really didn't like me. A little thing. He said something stupid in class – can't even remember what it was now - and the idiot teacher sneered at him. If that wasn't bad enough, he asked me to give the correct answer and like a fool, I did. From then on, in Warren's eyes, I was a swot, deliberately putting him down. Knowing stuff is a bad thing, as far as he's concerned. It shows him up. He takes it personally."

"But you can't act stupid, just because he's in the same class."

"That's exactly what I should have done. Others do. I should have played dumb. Anyhow, that's when he started to get physical and winding up the others to have a go at me."

"So you've been avoiding them?"

"Yes." Tariq sniffs to hide how upset he is. "It's all I can do really – just try to keep out of their way. That's why I go to the library so much. They wouldn't be seen dead in there. It's supervised too. I feel safe there."

"Oh. I thought ..."

"Yes, I know. You assumed I was there to study hard and please my pushy parents. I know what people say about me. Yes, I want to do well and yes, I am working hard and yes, my parents are pushy as hell.

"But do you think I want to be holed up in the bloody library by myself day after day? I can get the grades I need without doing that, thank you very much. I'd love to be outside with you lot."

"But that's awful. And if you were with us – real friends, I mean – we'd stick up for you." Sam pauses. "How long has this been going on?"

"Last term and this – about six months, I suppose. He and his brothers took money from me a couple of times and gave me a kicking when I refused to give them any more. Nathan nicked some of my coursework and I got a detention for not handing it in on time. Detention! Me!"

"Have you told the school or your parents?"

Tariq snorts. "I tried explaining at school about the coursework. They asked who took it and I wouldn't say. So they wouldn't do anything about it. I'd put a lot of effort into it. It was good stuff. But Phillpotts wasn't interested. All the weaker teachers care about is keeping the disruptors under control: no time left for those who really want to get on."

"And your parents?"

"They're the last people I'd tell! Dad would go mental. He's got a real temper: he's quite capable of doing something stupid like confronting the Warrens or marching into school to complain. We'd end up with a full-scale family feud on our hands. Then I wouldn't put it past the Warrens to do something really stupid."

Sam feels his blood boiling. "So you've had to handle all this with no-one to turn to? That's not right."

"Welcome to my world, mate."

Handling a problem with no-one to turn to: Sam knows what that's like. It's lonely.

"It has to stop. Right now. I'll help."

Tariq shakes his head. "You can't. Look Sam; thanks, but there's nothing you can do. It means a lot that you care and I'm grateful, I really am. And it's fantastic that you got my phone back. Amazing, actually. But you can't do anything else – you mustn't. You'll just make things worse for me, and for you too if you get involved: these people are head cases. They only know one way to behave."

Sam makes to speak. Tariq puts up his hand to stop him. "Sam, this is something I have to handle myself. Believe me; I've lived with it all my life. I don't mean this nastily or anything but you've only just realised what's been going on.

"I'm hoping they'll get bored with picking on me. If they don't – well, in a couple of years I'll be going to sixth-form college and Nathan Warren sure as hell won't get there. Till then, if I keep my head down and don't react, with a bit of luck they'll find another way of getting their entertainment. So I'll just keep going to the library and stay out of their way."

Sam shakes his head. "No. That's not fair. And you're wrong about them getting bored. They think they're hard. But they're not – they're just bullies. Bullies carry on forever unless someone faces them down. And they'll try to get their revenge for today."

"Please ... don't get involved".

"Sorry, Tariq; after this I am involved. I just made a couple of enemies."

"Look, I'd better get in or my mother will ask me what I've been doing. Sam - thanks for caring. I ... I've never been able to talk to anyone about this before. It makes a difference." Tariq walks up the path to his door.

Sam calls after him. "Happy birthday, anyway."

"Yeah, right."

As Sam walks home, a plan is forming in his mind – a plan that will take a few minutes work on his computer and a conversation tomorrow with Nathan Warren.

That night Sam sits at his computer and prepares for the following day with a feeling of grim determination. Despite Tariq's plea not to get involved, he won't let the Warrens' racist bullying continue. Not if he can do anything about it.

As Sam makes his plans, fifty miles away a man sits in a dimly lit room leafing through a stack of newspapers on the table in front of him. As he does every night, he quickly scans each page. Once he is finished with a paper, he refolds it precisely and places it onto a neat pile on the floor.

Tonight, his body stiffens and he inspects a page closely.

The photograph of a boy hero peers out from one of the tabloids – a trail on the front page pointing to a story inside. The man takes his black notebook from his jacket pocket. He unfolds the picture that he printed from the television news on the day of the riot in Reading and he compares the two.

No question, they are the same person.

"My, but you ARE a resourceful young man. But you should have avoided publicity. And your name is ... here it is ... Samuel Wright. From Winchester. And you go to Queen's School. I must take steps to meet you, young man."

He logs into the internet. There – the same Sam Wright featured in the local papers. Good photographs too. He prints a couple.

He reaches for his phone. "It's me. I have a job for you." He gives precise instructions. "Yes, I know it's a risk but I need to speak to him." He hangs up.

The man writes a brief entry in his notebook and then, with great care and precision, cuts the article from the paper, folds it with the previous picture and those he's just printed and places them inside the book.

"Soon, Samuel Wright. Soon."

The man's mouth twists into a smile.

But not the eyes.

His eyes never smile.

CHAPTER 20 – LEAVE MY FRIEND ALONE

"Any idea where I can find Nathan Warren?"

Richard Hartson grimaces. "Jeez: why would you want to talk to him? Well, if you must, he's on the wall behind the gym. Listen for the abuse: his current entertainment is to insult people as they walk past."

"Creep alert, Creep alert." Warren is indeed sitting on the wall with a group of hangers-on. They watch curiously as Sam walks towards them. This is unexpected. What's going on?

Speaking slowly and carefully to hide his nervousness Sam says the lines he's rehearsed: "Nathan. Sorry to interrupt. Could I have a word with you, please?" Very polite – deliberately so. Overdone? Hopefully not.

No. Overdone. "Oh my, don't we speak rather awfully well!" Warren is as surprised as everyone at Sam's approach and attempts to take control immediately. He'll play along but he needs to be cautious.

Encouraged by the sniggers his response provokes, he continues: "Mr. Wonderful! I am truly honoured to be spoken to by such a high and mighty person." He places his hands in a prayer position and bows. His friends laugh. Nathan sure knows how to deal with people like this.

OK, that's enough. "What you want, creep?"

"Nathan, I need to talk with you – alone, please."

"Anything you got to say, you say it here."

Warren's friends lean forward, expectantly. This is shaping up for a fight. They hope it is. Nathan will smash him.

"No, I don't think so. It's private - between you and me. If it's not convenient now, perhaps another time?"

That pushes Nathan Warren into a corner. He'll lose face if he refuses to talk now. Carefully he lowers himself from the wall. He stands close to Sam and stares belligerently into his face. "This had better be important."

Sam stands his ground. "It is." Up close, Sam sees that Warren is two inches taller than he is. And heavier. He hopes he can avoid a fight.

More people are gathering ... there's something going down, surely? There's no history of trouble between these two, but thinking about it ...

Sam points to the playing field. "Over there. Where no-one will hear us." He turns to the watching group. "You stay here, please. This really is very private."

The group looks to Nathan for guidance. He nods. He doesn't like being out-manoeuvred by the creep, but he has no choice. And he can take him down if it comes to a fight. His friends will still be able to see everything and they'll welcome seeing him given a lesson he won't forget.

When they are out of earshot, Nathan Warren stops. "Right. Far enough. Say what you've got to say ... one minute. This had better be worth it – I don't like it when people waste my time. Understood?"

"Understood. Here it is: I want you and your brothers to leave my friend Tariq alone."

"Piss off." Nathan snorts. "We don't take orders from you."

"Seriously. Leave him alone."

"And I said piss off. Who the hell do you think you are?" Warren clenches his fist. "When did this become your business?"

"Last night. Look, I'm saying this politely, but I don't like the way you, or your family, treat Tariq."

"And I don't give a toss what you like or don't like. It's got nothing to do with you. We'll treat the Paki how we want, whether or not he's the friend of God-Almighty Sam Tosser Wright. If that's all you have to say, you go stick your head up your arse. Better still, I'll do it for you."

Sam feels the anger building up inside him at the racist insult. He forces it down. "I apologise: I've failed to make myself clear. I'm not asking you to lay off Tariq - I'm telling you. You and your brothers are to leave my friend alone."

Fighting talk! "And why should we do that? What you gonna do – pull your knife on us? Yes, I heard about your stunt last night. You're a psycho, carrying one of them things."

"I don't have a knife. Or any other type of weapon. I've no idea where your brothers got that idea. But I do have something else and I'm prepared to use it."

"Yeah? What?"

"I'll show you. I've got it here." Sam takes a step back and slowly, so that Nathan Warren can see clearly, takes a sheet of paper from his inside pocket. He holds it out.

"What's this?"

"Take it: open it: it's yours to keep."

Warren looks suspiciously at what he is being offered. It looks like a piece of paper: nothing more. He snatches it from Sam's hand.

"A photograph?"

"That's right." The picture is from the night before. It shows Nathan Warren's older brothers, each looking terrified, one with his hands in the air and the other as if he is praying.

Last night Sam selected one of the frames to print, adding a caption: "The Warren brothers plead for mercy."

Nathan Warren's face turns an angry shade of red. "You bastard. You took this?"

"Got it in one, Nathan. Last night. It's come out very well, I think, even if I say so myself. The two local hard cases pleading for mercy. Captures the spirit of the moment quite nicely, wouldn't you say?"

"You show this to anyone and we'll tear you apart."

"No, you won't. I know that's your usual answer to everything, but not this time. Listen very carefully, 'cos this matters – to you, more than me. This picture is part of a video. With sound. I think your brothers' exact words were 'For Christ's sake ... you've got the friggin' phone back. Leave us alone'. But my favourite is 'Please. Just let us go. We won't do this again.' I found that bit particularly touching."

Sam has mimicked the Warren brothers' voices. He continues: "As I say, I'm pretty sure those were the exact words. But if you think I've got them wrong I can check, if you like. It all comes out really clearly, you know. On the video. I've got it here on my phone if you want to check now."

Nathan still looks blank. Sam sighs. He'll have to spell this out. "Nathan, I'm talking about the video I made last night. The video that's now on my PC at home."

Nathan Warren has been slow on the uptake, but now he understands. He looks more cautious. "OK, so you've got a video on your PC. So what?"

"Ah well - we've got broadband at home."

"As I say, so what?"

"Here's the so what ... I want you to take that picture home. I'll print another if I need to. In fact, thinking about it, I can print hundreds if I need to. I want you to show it to your brothers. Ask them how they'd like it if the video found its way onto YouTube. Or Facebook. Or Twitter."

"You do that and we'll kill you."

"No, you won't. But even if you tried you wouldn't be able to stop hundreds of people seeing it. Everyone who knows your brothers will wet themselves laughing."

"You're gonna do that, then?"

"No. I am proposing NOT to do that."

Once again Nathan Warren looks confused, so Sam explains. "It's your lucky day, Nathan. I'm making you and your brothers an offer you can't refuse. I'm offering to do nothing with the picture or the video. I think the only people who should know about them are you, your brothers and me. Even Tariq doesn't know."

Warren looks suspicious. "You're gonna do nothing with them? How does that work?"

This guy is awesomely thick! Sam speaks slowly.

"It works like this. That video stays on my computer. I give you my word that no-one else will ever see it, for as long as you and your brothers keep away from my friend Tariq and me.

"But if you do anything to Tariq - barge into him again like you did on the stairs the other day, or dish out any more of your racist crap, or if your brothers lay a finger on him, or me, I promise you that thousands of people will see it. I'll post it on YouTube and then send the link to the people I know.

"You know what will happen then? It'll be round the school in a day. It'll be round the City in two days. Everyone you know will see it or hear about it.

"Your brothers will never be able to show their faces in public again. They'll be the cowards who pleaded for mercy when one guy half their size stood up to them. People will laugh out loud when they see them in the street."

"You can't do that! That's blackmail."

"No, I don't think so. I'm not asking for anything from you. I just want you and your brothers to behave - better."

"It IS – it's friggin' blackmail! There's laws against that!"

"And there's laws against nicking peoples' phones, you idiot. But call it what you like – that's how it is. If you and your brothers behave, I'll show my appreciation. But if you or they step out of line, lay a finger on my friend or insult him again, in or out of school, you know what will happen.

"So now it's for you and your brothers to decide, Nathan. I've told you the deal. You can take it or leave it. It's your choice."

Sam places his hand on Nathan Warren's shoulder in a companionable way. "It's been good to talk. See you." He turns his back and walks slowly away, tensing himself for an attack from behind. It doesn't come. He allows himself a smile. "Yes!" he hisses to himself. That felt good!

Slowly, Nathan Warren returns to his friends. "What the hell was that all about?" No fight. They're disappointed.

"The creep apologised for being rude to me and my brothers yesterday." It's a pretty good lie for the spur of the moment.

"Apologised? That's not what it looked like."

"Well he did. What a wimp!"

"What'd he give you?"

Nathan Warren pauses. He needs another plausible answer. "You know, he's actually written them a letter of apology! Wants me to give it to them."

"Let's see."

"No!" He's not showing that paper to anyone!

His friends look startled.

"No ... he's done the right thing so I'll keep it private. They'd have been waiting for him otherwise. Now, there's no need to soil their hands on him."

The group laughs. The incident is over. They don't know what happened yesterday but faced with the Warrens, the Wright creep has backed down. As everyone would expect.

As they laugh, Nathan Warren looks thoughtfully at the departing figure of Sam Wright. That guy had a certain self-confidence about him ... not seen it before ... unexpected.

He needs to talk with his brothers.

That afternoon, Sam feels like laughing too. The school team for the game against Fairbrother Hill has been posted and, thank goodness, his name is there. He breathes a sigh of relief. After his appalling performance last time, he'd all but given up hope

Sam walks home with Maddy with a spring in his step.

He is relieved to hear that her father has had no more mystery calls.

He is pleased with what he has done to help Tariq.
He is delighted at being chosen for the school team.
Life is better today.
At least, that's how it seems.

That evening, a chance meeting takes place. Well, it looks like chance. The supermarket staff nudge each other as the young lady who is in the habit of doing her shopping late at night stops in the aisle in smiling conversation with a man.

He looks a little old for her but other than that he's unremarkable – innocuous looking, really. He comes in late each night and collects copies of the daily papers. Always pays cash. They put the papers aside for him and he rarely misses a night.

Lots of people meet whilst out shopping. And these two seem to be enjoying each other's company. It was only a matter of time before they came in separately but left together, and tonight is the night.

It's quite sweet really. They'll watch these two with interest.

CHAPTER 21 – SELF-CONTROL AND MATURITY

On Saturday morning Emmanuel Cabrieres is waiting in the park, pacing up and down. As soon as he spots Sam he walks to meet him. No pleasantries this time – exactly what happened that evening with Tariq?

Sam isn't sure he likes answering to this man. Does he really have the right to interrogate him like this? But as this is one of only two sources of advice available to him, and the only person to whom he can speak face-to-face, Sam controls his feelings and resentfully repeats the story.

Emmanuel is exasperated. "Once again, you acted with good intentions, Sam. But again, you risked giving away your secret – the one thing you must not do. You must control yourself better!"

"It was self-defence."

"Rubbish! It was not self-defence. You chased them! Chasing people is not self-defence. Running away is self-defence. By your own action you put yourself in danger. Had you not run after them there would have been no confrontation, is that not so?"

"Yes, but Tariq ..."

"Ah yes, Tariq." M Cabrieres snaps back the words. "Let us consider your friend. He must think you are quite the most remarkable person. Even now he marvels at your courage and wonders how you recovered his phone from two people who have tormented him for years.

Have you learnt karate? Judo? Perhaps you work out in secret? In between your first aid lessons, maybe?"

Sam winces.

"Tariq will tell the story. Others will pass it on. It will be exaggerated. In a week you will be superman. And then the Government will get to hear about you and ..."

"No. It won't be like that." Sam interrupts angrily. "I'm not stupid. I made Tariq promise not to say anything – I told him I was sick of publicity. He'll keep quiet. For a start he doesn't want his parents to know what happened. His Dad would go mental."

"I pray you are right. If so, you are luckier than you deserve. You may not have to regret your foolhardy action."

Sam feels anger welling up inside him. "Foolhardy? For God's sake ... I can't do anything right, can I? I stopped a crime, didn't I? I helped someone who's having his life wrecked by a family of racists and who had his new phone nicked within hours of being given it. When did stopping a crime become the wrong thing to do? It may be where you come from but I think it's an OK thing to do here."

Emmanuel sighs: "Sam, my friend ... I feel your anger. I am to control it." He pauses as Sam takes a deep breath and forces himself to calm down. "That is better, thank you."

The Frenchman touches Sam's shoulder, gently. "I am sorry. I did not come here to make you feel bad. I am cautious for you – perhaps too much so. But please believe that it is for your sake that I say these things. I am scared for you. I fear that people will notice what you do. This power of yours – it is a phenomenon. For you to learn to live with it, without giving yourself away; it will be very hard. You will need to calm your emotions, suppress your feelings, act against your instincts – and that is not easy for a young man.

"But if you attract attention, then people who fear us will come and your life will be in danger. And not just you - other members of our community too. You understand? I say these things for your safety."

"I suppose."

"To protect your secrecy will take great discipline – self-control and maturity."

Sam is depressed now. He had been so pleased after he dealt with the Warren brothers. And yes, he had felt, well, cocky. Like the people at school said. "So I should have let them take Tariq's phone? I should have done nothing?"

"Oh - probably not." Emmanuel shrugs his shoulders as only the French can. "You know the difference between right and wrong. There are too many crimes such as these. The Police – they cannot be everywhere: they cannot protect people as they should. These days, always it is the criminal who has rights. Always it is the victim who is forgotten. Had you done nothing, a wrong would have been done. If you had stood by, when you could have helped, you would now be disgusted with yourself, I am sure."

"That's right." Sam feels better, hearing these words. "And I didn't know I could help. It was just instinct to chase after them."

"Make no mistake, my friend, I am impressed with what you did. I am torn between scolding you and shaking your hand to congratulate you. But it is my responsibility to teach you that each time you use this ability of yours, you increase your risk. You understand what I am saying?"

"Yes, I understand."

"And why I say it?"

"Yes."

"Good. Then we have spent too much time on this already and I fear I was too harsh. So let us talk of better things. Tell me what else is happening in your life."

Relieved that the lecture is over, Sam retells enthusiastically his conversation with Nathan Warren.

Emmanuel Cabrieres laughs. "And will these horrible people now do as you say?"

"I think so. They can't afford the loss of face."

"That is good, because you must know that you can never deliver on your threat. You can never post that video. It would publicise how you came to make it."

Sam swears under his breath. "I hadn't thought of that." He pauses. "But they don't know that, do they?"

"No, they do not."

"Then I've called their bluff."

"Yes. In a way it is a game of poker you are playing."

"OK, I'm good with that." Sam changes the subject: "the best bit of news is that I'm in the school team for the Fairbrother Hill game. I had pretty well given up hope of being picked because I was playing so cra – sorry, so badly, when I wasn't sleeping. I'm better now, but I've never been so nervous. I just hope I deliver!"

Emmanuel Cabrieres smiles – these are the issues that a fourteen-year-old should really have on his mind. "I wish you luck, my friend. Next time, you must tell me how you did."

The four days to the match drag by. Each evening, Sam changes into his football kit and takes a ball to the field by the swings to practice taking free kicks. He concentrates on curling the ball round an obstacle – mainly a long-suffering and patient Maddy - and into the goal, the posts for which are two trees.

Wednesday arrives clear and bright. In vain Sam tries to stay calm. On the bus, Maddy smiles as she hears - for the two-hundred and thirty-second time – how worried he had been that he might not be selected and how he hopes his form has returned. "Don't worry, you'll do well" she whispers.

"Do you think so? Really? Last time I missed an open goal. I thought ..."

"Sam!" Maddy cuts him short, but smiles to remove any offence. "Sam ... just calm down. You've earned your place. But if you carry on and on about it ... I won't come to watch."

Sam stares at her, mortified. Maddy rolls her eyes. "For God's sake, dumbo." She squeezes his hand. Of course she'll be there. She's almost as nervous as he is.

The entire school is allowed to miss the last two lessons of the day to support their team, so there is an excited crowd as the twenty-two players run onto the pitch. Sam looks around, soaking up the atmosphere. Maddy waves. Even Tariq is there, sitting by a corner flag with a pile of books. His time won't be completely wasted.

"Ngozi, we're kicking off! I'm petrified!"

"Don't be. Just relax and honour your ability."

"Sorry?"

"It's a saying in my family: honour your ability: do the best you can."

"OK. Here goes."

From the opening whistle the Fairbrother Hill players crowd forward aggressively, passing the ball quickly, moving immediately into new positions. Their plan is clear: take control, dominate their opponents, score early and then force Queen's to come at them. It's going to be tough.

A deflected shot; a corner to Fairbrother. Scrambled nervously away.

Another attack. Boot it anywhere – straight to a Fairbrother player – an immediate shot. Deflected! Another corner. The home crowd is quiet: this constant pressure looks bad.

A short corner: taken into the penalty area – a shot, deflected. Yet another corner kick.

This time the corner is taken long – a fierce shot from the edge of the penalty area – deflected - it's going in! No, Richard Hartson lunges despairingly. The ball cannons off his foot with a thud that echoes round the field.

It could go anywhere.

It rockets out to Sam, standing almost alone half way to the centre line.

Sam controls the ball and looks up. He is far ahead of his team-mates who have all been forced back into defence. He has two choices: be cautious, hold the ball and wait for the others to come forward and join him, or try for goal himself.

The Fairbrother Hill defence is out of position. "Honour your ability" was Ngozi's advice. "Honour your ability." He will do that for her – and for himself after his last debacle.

With the ball at his feet, Sam sprints forward. He crosses the half way line without a challenge. A Fairbrother midfielder attempts a sliding tackle – it's clumsy and badly timed. He misses the ball and Sam leaps over his flailing legs to avoid being fouled. The crowd cheers.

Encouraged, Sam continues his run. The crowd is urging him on. They can see the potential – but is Wright up to it?

Sam is now deep into the Fairbrother half. Three defenders are racing back but not closing him down as they should. They've just seen one of their team commit to a losing tackle, only to be left behind. They won't take the same risk.

Except that is what they should be doing.

Sam cuts inside the first defender, forcing him to lose balance. The crowd cheers louder. He is now at the edge of the penalty area. The next nearest defender is now racing towards him; too late and too far away.

The Fairbrother goalkeeper is doing the right thing – running from his line to narrow Sam's shooting angle. In a few more strides he'll have done that.

Now, Sam! Now, or never.

For Sam the rest of the world ceases to exist. The noise of the crowd disappears. All that matters is this shot. He side-foots the ball firmly.

Damn! He's put the ball too close to the advancing keeper! He'll stop it!

No, despite an athletic dive, the goalkeeper can't get down quickly enough. His outstretched hand misses the ball by a fingertip.

Sam has hit the shot cleanly. In what seems like slow motion the ball clips the inside of the post and rolls into the Fairbrother goal.

Sam stands rooted to the spot, scarcely able to believe what he has done. He double-checks that the ball is in the back of the net.

Oh yes! There it is!

Elation? No. Sam's overwhelming emotion is relief. Relief that he's put his last appalling game behind him. Relief that, at the start of the most important match he's ever played, he hasn't let himself or the team down.

Now he can relax!

These thoughts take an instant to flash through Sam's mind. Then he becomes aware of the referee's whistle and the roar from the home crowd. He turns to walk back to his own half. Before he can take more than three steps he is mobbed by his team-mates.

"Bloody well done" beams Stephen Kettler. "That's more like it!" That matters, coming from the guy who had been so critical of Sam's last performance.

"Sam Wright! Sam Wright!" The home crowd is cheering his name! This has to be the best feeling ever!

The Fairbrother goalkeeper and defenders are arguing furiously. Their coach is shouting instructions from the touchline. "Calm down. Remember your training. Get those tackles in! Close them down! That one's fast and you gave him too much room."

Standing at the back of the line of spectators, an unkempt man in dirty jeans and a blue and white striped shirt is watching with interest. "Who's that – the guy who just scored?"

Maddy looks round. She doesn't recognise the stranger. He must be with the Fairbrother Hill visitors. There are many unknown faces in the school this afternoon.

"Sam Wright."

"He did very well."

"Brilliantly."

The man moves away. He's using his 'phone to call someone. Maddy doesn't give him a second thought as the game restarts.

Buoyed by the early goal, Queen's are now able to settle down. The defenders are tackling confidently, their passes are accurate. Players are helping each other by running into easy positions to receive the ball. As the end of the half approaches, the ball is crossed from the right wing and Stephen Kettler heads a second goal.

At half time, Sam sees the Fairbrother Hill coach lecturing his team. He looks furious. He jabs his finger at the defenders who had failed to tackle Sam. He sees them looking in his direction and nodding. Then Mr. Masterson calls the team together for their own instructions for the second half.

When play restarts, the opposition makes a substitution. "Jeez – look at that lump!" groans Stephen Kettler. "He's got to be seven foot tall and he's built like a bloody tank."

It quickly becomes clear that the bloody tank has just one instruction – to man-mark Sam and take him out of the game. And he'll do it by fair means or foul.

The new player has no great skill, neither is he quick. But he has strength and weight and he knows how to use them.

Now, if the ball is passed to Sam, he is tackled – sometimes quickly if the new defender is close, otherwise late and illegally. The pattern of the game changes as the fouls rain in and the referee whistles for one free kick after another.

The home crowd reacts, booing every foul. Twice, the referee takes the new defender aside to warn him. He ignores the shouts of 'Off, Off, Off' from the partisan crowd; at this level of the game he doesn't want to book a player or send him off.

For Sam the euphoria of the first half is forgotten. It is now an endurance test. Worst of all, he feels his anger mounting each time he picks himself off the ground.

Control it, Sam. You have to!

That's easier thought than done. Sam knows his patience is wearing thin. It doesn't help that the violence is accompanied by comments designed to rile him. Not only is the Fairbrother Hill defender trying to injure him, he also wants to goad Sam into retaliating. If he does, the referee will have no option but to send him off. Then the day will be remembered not for the dream start, but for Sam Wright letting the side down, leaving his other ten team-mates to struggle on, a player light - and possibly lose after starting so well.

Ten minutes from the end of the game, Sam runs into space on the left of the Fairbrother Hill penalty area, with a pass coming towards him. Before he has time to gather the ball and turn, a searing pain on the back of his left knee tells him he's been fouled again. He crumples to the ground. It was a jarring high tackle from behind; a cynical and dangerous foul with no attempt to play the ball. It could have broken Sam's leg.

It's the last straw.

Angrily, Sam pounds the turf with his fists. Then he painfully raises himself to his feet and faces his tormentor.

"Come on" crows the Fairbrother Hill defender. "What you gonna do about that then? Hit me? You ain't got the bottle." He sticks out his chin, inviting Sam to take a swing. It is tempting – surely everyone would understand?

Sam clenches his fists.

On the touchline Maddy whispers: "No, Sam. Don't!"

Sam faces his tormentor. He thinks: "If you knew what I could do, you would be so afraid." A look of fear crosses the other boy's eyes and he takes a step back.

No! Sam is mortified. "You're doing it again" he tells himself, "in full view of the whole school ... you can't ... you mustn't ... don't go down this road."

Calm down. Take a deep breath. You can control this!

Sam lowers his hands to his side. He unclenches his fists. He concentrates with all his might on not sharing his emotions with his opponent.

He says nothing.

He does nothing.

Instead, Sam looks the other player from head to toe with as much disdain as he can muster and then turns his back and limps away, shaking his head in disgust.

As a tactic it works far better than any other.

Angry with himself for having backed away and not understanding why he showed such weakness, the Fairbrother defender reacts. From behind, Sam hears a snarled curse and staggers forward as he takes a blow between the shoulder-blades. He hears a scuffle as the other Fairbrother Hill players haul their defender back. Their coach runs onto the field to calm the situation.

Sitting on the ground, Sam watches as, to a huge cheer, the referee finally orders his attacker from the pitch.

Without asking permission, Sam picks up the ball. He places it carefully and deliberately where he had been fouled. This free kick is his to take and his alone – he's earned it.

No-one argues.

On the touchline by the Fairbrother goal, the man in the dirty jeans and striped shirt walks unobtrusively behind the rows of spectators. Positioning himself to get a clear view of the coming free kick, he readies his phone to take a picture.

No-one pays him a second look – all eyes are focussed on the pitch. This is a potential scoring position. The question is: does Sam Wright know how to curl a free kick round the wall of four defenders that has now formed?

Does he! This is what he has been practicing for weeks.

Sam has heard many times "let your actions do the talking". He hasn't reacted to the constant goading. He controlled his emotions. And now he has just one objective left in this game … one last act … if he can just do now what he has been practicing every night.

The crowd falls silent. There is a sense of expectation. Will justice be done? Maddy has her hands together, as if praying. Tariq looks up from his book.

Hush.

Sam has practiced this kick hundreds of times. With grim determination, he takes three steps forward and hits the ball hard with the inside of his foot.

The man in the striped shirt clicks the shutter and holds it down. The phone takes twenty shots in rapid succession. He checks the screen. Not bad. Not bad at all - good pictures of the boy, even if he says so himself. Action shots too.

It is a cold and clinical and ruthless strike.

It feels right.

The ball swings up and round the wall of defenders. They twist round to watch. It's going to miss. No, perhaps not: it's curling in the air.

The ball curves towards the right goalpost and dips cleanly into the top corner of the net. The Fairbrother 'keeper doesn't move. There was no way he could reach it.

Sam punches the air: "Yes!"

The home crowd erupts. 3-0! And, more importantly, justice!

The dismissed Fairbrother defender glowers from the touchline. Then, for the second time in the game, Sam collapses under the weight of his delighted team-mates.

As a result of the treatment he has received and most especially the last foul, Sam is limping. He's learnt his lesson about playing on when he isn't fit. He signals that he needs to be substituted.

He acknowledges the cheer he receives as he leaves the pitch. Tomorrow he'll be stiff as a board, but this feeling is worth it ... and to think how worried he'd been about letting himself down!

Sam watches the final minutes of the game from the side-line, but sitting on the bench now feels completely different. At the final whistle he is surrounded by people congratulating him. Maddy catches his eye and smiles. She indicates that she will wait, and walk home with him, as usual.

The players are heading happily back to the changing rooms when a familiar voice says "A word, Wright, if you please."

Sam turns: it's the Headmaster. Dr. Rhodes has Mr. Masterson with him. What could they want with him, now?

"I seem to be spending a large proportion of my time commenting on your – ah, exploits – on the football pitch" says Dr. Rhodes. "I just want to congratulate you on your performance today."

Sam blinks. "Thank you, Sir."

"By which I don't just mean the two goals you scored, admirable though they were. The best thing you did today was to soak up that most regrettable and, I have to say, unsportsmanlike treatment without retaliating. I shall be having words with my opposite number about that. In particular, you did well to walk away from that last foul, which I considered quite disgraceful. I hope that you are not badly hurt?"

"Bruised, Sir. It'll ache tomorrow."

"I'm sure it will." Dr. Rhodes nods. "You showed self-control and a great deal of maturity there, qualities from which many of our country's Premiership players would benefit. You did well, Sam, both for yourself and for the team."

Sam mumbles his thanks but inside he is elated. It is unheard of for the Headmaster to address pupils by their first name at school! But even more, he's delighted by the compliment: self-control and maturity!

This means he can control his emotions. He really can live with his new-found powers.

Self-control! Maturity!

Ha! He can't wait to tell Emmanuel Cabrieres.

An excited gaggle of friends walks home with Sam and Maddy that evening. Maddy is overjoyed at how the game went - as relieved as Sam, knowing how important it was to him. Tariq is bubbling over. "That first goal – man, I've never seen anything like it. You must have run the length of the pitch!"

Ashley Jones adds "That gorilla they put on – I thought you were going to punch him."

"I prayed you wouldn't" adds Maddy.

"Bloody hell – think what his parents must look like. Godzilla meets the bearded lady."

Tariq phones his parents to tell them the news. He passes his phone to Sam so that his mother can congratulate him. That subdues the party atmosphere for a while as Sam waves at his friends to keep the noise down.

As the young people joke and laugh, happily reliving the match, no-one notices the unkempt man in the dirty jeans and blue-striped shirt following at a discrete distance. As Sam reaches home, the man once again takes his phone from his pocket.

"Boss? It's me. Did you get the photo?"

Pause.

"Good. And that's definitely him?"

Another pause.

"Thought so."

He listens.

"No – too easy, if anything. Hundreds of people shouting his name for me. Very obliging of them. Your mate's a bit of star on the football pitch, you know. Took a good free kick."

A pause.

"Yes, I'll have his address in a minute. And his girlfriend's. Pretty thing."

Another wait.

"No. No idea at all. They're too busy celebrating to notice little ole me."

He nods.

"OK. I'll find that out. Yes, I understand: do nothing. Not till you say."

Fifty miles away a man sits in a small dimly lit room. He switches off his phone and mutters to himself as he peers at the latest photographs.

"You really ought to be more careful, Sam Wright. I've found out who you are, and now I know where you are. Next I need to find out what you are.

"For that I need to meet you. Let's choose a date ... sometime soon, I think. In a place of my choosing ..."

This evening the man has company. A woman walks over to him from the bed on which she has been lying. Her red dress is hung over the edge. "Have you finished now? You work so hard."

The man turns to her. "Of course, my dear."

She stands behind him and puts her arms round his neck. "I'd forgotten what it feels like to be this happy" she smiles.

CHAPTER 22 – THE BMX TRACK

Sam's parents are delighted. Maddy happily gives them a blow-by-blow account of the game and they lap up the exaggerations. No doubt about it, Sam is one step away from his England shirt.

In Sam's room later, she leafs through the copy of the local newspaper with Sam's photograph on the front page. "It's been quite a couple of weeks for you, hasn't it?" She taps it.

Sam controls a scowl. "Why'd you bring that up with you? I hate it. I want Mum and Dad to bin it, but they won't."

"Of course they won't. They'll keep it forever."

"Can I ask you something?" Sam looks worried. He points at the paper. "I overheard someone saying I'm too cocky – that I'll be a right pain in the arse after this. Do you think I'm like that? Is that how people see me?"

"No, of course not."

"Are you sure?"

"Sam, they're jealous. If anything you're being too quiet about it."

"But you would tell me?"

"Course I would. You don't think I'd be up here now, in your room, if that's what I thought of you?"

"Oh." Is there a message there? He's too nervous to pursue it.

Maddy pages through the rest of the paper. "Did you see this? I think it's just terrible."

"No. I don't often read the papers. I don't want to look at the front page, let alone the other stuff."

"Well you should." She taps the page she has open. "It's the Vincent Stewart case."

"Who?"

"Sam! You must have heard of Vincent Stewart?"

"No."

"Oh my God - where have you been? It's all over the television news as well as the papers. It's a major court case. Here in Winchester."

Sam has had other things on his mind. "Nope. Tell me."

"Wow." She shakes her head. "OK - a year ago this guy Vincent Stewart was injured at work and he's been unconscious ever since. He's in a coma and on life support. The doctors say he's brain-dead and they want to switch the machines off. His family says 'no'; they believe he's still alive inside his body. So there's this huge court case to decide whether the hospital can switch the machines off anyway, against the family's wishes."

"Will the family win?"

"They should, but they're losing. Listen." Maddy reads the report out loud:

The Hospital Trust's solicitor told the court that since the accident, Vincent Stewart has been in a coma in the Royal Hampshire Hospital, kept alive for a year only by life support machines.

Medical experts described Mr. Stewart's condition to the court as 'persistent vegetative state'. Three leading specialists testified that there are no signs of brain activity, leading them to believe that he has no chance of emerging from the coma. In their opinion, therefore, it is time to switch off the machines and let Mr. Stewart pass away quietly and with dignity.

Mr. Stewart's parents are seeking an injunction to require the hospital to maintain their son's life support. The family is keeping a 24 hour vigil at his bedside, talking to him and playing his favourite music. They are sure that their son knows they are there and that he is still alive and will eventually recover.

The Judge reserved his judgement and will deliver his decision next week.

"That's a tough call".

"No, Sam, it's really easy." Maddy is vehement. "It's the family's opinion that matters, or at least it should be - not the bean-counters at the hospital. To them Vincent Stewart is an expense, not a person. He's blocking a bed and costing them money. That's what this boils down to – money. He's interfering with their targets."

"But he's hardly likely to recover now, is he?" says Sam. "Not after so long."

"You don't know that! No-one does! People have been in a coma for years and then suddenly" – Maddy snaps her fingers - "they wake up. That's the point: the doctors aren't always right. They make these life and death decisions but they shouldn't be allowed to go against the family's wishes."

Sam nods. But the conversation is interrupted ... his mobile phone is ringing: it's Ashley Jones saying 'well done' and asking how his leg is.

The moment is gone. Maddy doesn't mention Vincent Stewart again and the issue slips to the back of Sam's mind.

He should remember.

Two Sundays later, Sam takes another phone call from his friend Ashley. Does he want to go to the BMX track? Sam's footballing bruises have faded. Yes, of course – see you there in half an hour.

From the open front door, Sam shouts: "Mum ... going to the BMX track."

"OK. Be back for six."

As usual, Mrs. Jobson's curtains twitch. She is even more blatant these days in the way she spies on him. Stupid bag – doesn't she have anything better to do?

Ashley Jones is a long-standing friend: they met at primary school but see less of each other now they are in different sets at Queen's. Like Sam, Ashley is fourteen: a few inches taller but unmistakable because of his long fair hair and pale skin.

They are pleased with the track they have taken over in the woods near the park. No-one knows who started it, but successive generations of young riders have risen to the responsibility of maintaining and improving it. Many hours of work with borrowed garden spades and scavenged planks of wood have increased the slopes and improved the jumps and landing areas.

The unofficial facility is appreciated by others as well; there is often a small group of younger boys there, watching wistfully and looking forward to the day when they are old enough to use it and take over its maintenance.

"Saw you in the paper" says Ashley.

"That was weeks ago!" Why can't people forget about that?

"Bet your parents were dead pleased when you showed them the certificate."

"They haven't seen it yet."

"No? Why not?"

"Keep forgetting to take it home."

"Bloody hell! Mum would go spare if I did that. So they've read about it in the paper but haven't seen it?"

"Yep." Sam has no choice but to sound nonchalant. He'd meant to take it home. But it's a symbol of the publicity he wants to avoid. Besides, he's had other things on his mind. "They've mentioned it. I'll do it next week. Come on ..."

For a while they are joined in their riding by a couple of others who leave early. Later, three adults stop to watch, one of them a man in dirty jeans and a blue and white striped shirt, whom Sam hasn't seen before. Twice this man uses his mobile phone but he never takes his eyes off Sam and Ashley.

Sam feels uncomfortable. He's used to adult spectators, but usually they're parents accompanying younger children. Why would three grown men want to watch a couple of fourteen year old boys riding their bikes?

"Let's get out of here" says Sam quietly.

"Already?"

"Don't look, but those guys behind me - they've been watching us for too long. They haven't got any kids with them. They're talking about us. They're trouble, I reckon. After our bikes, maybe. Well, yours."

That strikes home. If there is one thing guaranteed to motivate Ashley, it's his bike. By common consent it's the best among their circle of friends: all his spare money goes into improving it. So many components have been upgraded that there's precious little of the original left. It's Ashley's pride and joy and he won't risk anything happening to it.

"OK; make like we're going for the jumps again, but at the end carry straight on – over the ditch and onto the pavement before they know it. Then fast away."

"Right."

Ashley goes first. He takes the jumps and clears the ditch. He skids his bike to a stop on the pavement and waits for Sam to join him.

Perhaps he's tense. Or distracted, thinking about the watching men. Or perhaps he's not yet used to his new bike. Whatever the reason, Sam misjudges a jump that he clears 99 times out of 100. He lands in a tangled heap of arms, legs and bike.

Shit! He scrambles quickly to his feet. He has to get away.

Too late! Another two men step from the trees. Five of them now. This is bad.

"Ashley - go" shouts Sam. "Get out of here."

"Without you? No way." Ashley returns to help his friend.

"Run! Get help" screams Sam, struggling with his bike. Dammit - the chain is off. Escape is impossible now. He throws the bike down.

One of the men lunges for Sam and another for his bike. Sam hits out at his attackers and kicks one in the groin. The man collapses to the ground, swearing.

For a moment Sam thinks he might be able to dash to safety. He'll sacrifice his new bike if he has to. But strong hands grab him from behind and pin his arms to his side. Sam struggles to free himself, but the person holding him is strong.

Ashley crashes his bike into one of the men, who screams in pain and crumples into a heap. Ashley is off his bike now. He runs towards Sam shouting "let him go!" But he too is caught and wrestled roughly to the ground. Even so, he manages to swing a foot at his attacker, catching him on the shin.

Sam squirms and twists, desperate to free himself. He fails. He tries head-butting the person behind him, but misses. "Let me go."

"Keep still you little bastard."

Ashley struggles to his feet and once more tries to reach his friend. To Sam's horror, the man that Ashley kicked – the one in the jeans and striped shirt - picks up a fallen branch and swings it.

"Look out!" screams Sam, but there's nothing Ashley can do. With a sickening thud the branch connects with the back of Ashley's head. The wood breaks from the force of the blow, and Sam's friend crumples in a heap.

"You bloody fool, you'll kill him" snarls the man holding Sam.

"Serve him right. Little shit almost broke my leg."

"He can identify us. Bring him. The boss will decide what to do."

Sam stops struggling. Ashley is unconscious. "Right" he thinks, "it's time for you to feel what it's like to be afraid."

Fear!

Immediately he sees one of the men take a step back, a look of horror on his face. He feels the grip on his arms slackening. It's working!

But then someone puts a strange-smelling cloth over his face and everything goes dark.

Sam is dreaming. He's walking through a town he's never seen before. He's looking for something. He searches and searches - and finds nothing. He keeps looking in places he knows will be empty. Searching ... searching ...

As he comes to, Sam realises what is happening. Ngozi is trying to contact him.

"Ngozi?"

"Thank goodness, Sam. I was getting worried. Are you alright?"

"My head's thumping something chronic." Gingerly Sam opens his eyes and tries to sit up. *"Oh shit!"*

"What's wrong?"

Sam is lying on a concrete floor. His hands are tied behind him with what feels like packing tape. His feet are taped too. And his mouth.

"I'm definitely not alright! I'm in trouble. I'm in a cellar and I'm tied up. Ngozi, I've been kidnapped."

CHAPTER 23 – THE CELLAR

"Useful trip?" Douglas Bartles welcomes Jane Baxter into his office.

"Yes. At first Professor Harkness wasn't in the mood to be helpful. Or he's naturally a git. I sat in on one of his lectures. Interesting but nothing he hadn't said before. I hung around afterwards to get a word with him. I asked him if there might be any ways in which we could recognise freaks – sorry: people with telepathic abilities. He said 'yes'."

"That's good. Tell me more."

"He said to look out for people with two heads, who glow in the dark."

"Ah. A joker."

"He enjoyed taking the piss. 'Why should they look any different?' he said. 'If that's the way the human race is going to evolve, they'll be ordinary people who can communicate in a new way, that's all.' He said we won't recognise them by their looks but by their actions."

"Actions?"

"Yes. He reckons it's a huge secret to control. Some won't be able to manage it: they'll talk about it. Then they'll get referred to doctors and psychiatrists. And that's where we'll pick them up: from the shrinks."

"Does he know of any?"

"He says no. He says he's had hundreds of people contact him claiming to be telepathic, but he reckons they're all cranks or nutcases. He's devised a test for them and when he tells them about it, they back away. So he's met no-one yet that he would trust as being genuine."

"So?"

"So we need to keep our eyes and ears open for interesting medical cases. That's what I propose to do."

"OK, we'll add that to our list of tasks. It wasn't a totally wasted journey, but welcome back." Douglas Bartles turns back to the pile of papers on his desk.

"Kidnapped? Tell me, quickly!"

Sam's head is fuzzy. As best he can he describes what he remembers – the BMX track, Ashley, three – no five - men, a fight. A strange-smelling cloth.

Ashley! They hit him so hard! How is he? Sam struggles to sit up and look round, trying to get his blurry eyes to focus. He wants to rub them, but his hands are tied.

The cellar has a single, small horizontal window, high up. A stream of sunlight throws a dusty beam onto the opposite wall. Even so, it's cold. Against the far wall Sam can see what looks like a dark bundle of clothes. Is that his friend?

He shuffles over as quickly as he can with his arms and feet tied. Yes, it's Ashley. There is a large, dark patch of blood on the back of his head, staining his fair hair red and then black. Sam doesn't like the look of it – there's too much fresh, shiny blood. It looks like the wound is still seeping. But he's breathing – that's a relief.

"We have to get you out of there."

"I'd like that very much - all ideas gratefully received. I've no idea where we are. Ashley's in here with me and he looks in a bad way."

"The first thing we need to work out is where you are. I need clues from you. What time were you attacked?"

Instinctively Sam tries to look at his watch. He winces as the packing tape burns his wrists. *"It must have been about 5-o-clock. Can't see what time it is now."*

"OK. I don't think there's much time difference between us. So ... it's coming up to 6-o-clock now. You were unconscious for about an hour. That's how long I wasn't been able to sense you or contact you. So, it sounds right that you were attacked around 5-o-clock."

Sam knows what Ngozi means. Even when they're not talking, he's aware of her just being there.

Ngozi continues. *"Let's think through what must have happened after you were attacked. No-one is going to carry two unconscious boys through a built-up area in broad daylight. So, your kidnappers had a car or a van close by. In an hour they might have taken you, say, fifty kilometres – thirty miles. So I'd say you're thirty miles maximum from the BMX track – probably less. Make sense?"*

"Suppose so. I'm not thinking well at the moment."

"If you tell me exactly where the track is, I'll print out a copy of the map and draw a circle round it with a thirty mile radius, and you'll be somewhere inside it. Now let's get to work on other clues. Tell me what you can see."

"Nothing. A cellar. Concrete block walls, not bricks."

"A door?"

"Yes."

"Locked?"

Sam looks. *"There's no keyhole. It could be bolted from the other side though."*

"Can you get to it?"

Sam shuffles across the room. *"Can't reach the handle. Hold on."* Forcing himself to ignore his aching head, Sam manoeuvres himself until his back is against the wall and levers himself into a standing position. Now he can reach the door handle. It turns. The door is heavy but it opens.

Inwards!

"Shit." Sam twists sideways as he topples onto the concrete floor. With his hands tied behind him he can't cushion the fall and hits his head. He swears again.

"Sorry, Ngozi. Banged my head."

The open door reveals a flight of stone steps. At the top is another door. That one does have a keyhole.

"The door's not locked, but there's a flight of eight – nine - ten stone steps and then another door. I bet that one's locked."

"OK. Stone steps are good. You can use one to rub through the tape on your wrists. Any other clues?"

"No. I'll take a proper look round when my hands and feet are free but there's nothing obvious."

"Can you smell anything?

"Smell?"

"Yes. Any information will help. Can you smell anything that has been stored in the cellar? It might give us a lead."

"Nothing I can make out."

"Shame. You say there's a window? Can you reach it?"

"Not a hope. It's only small and too high to see out."

"Oh dear, this isn't easy. You can't see anything, you can't smell anything. OK, can you hear anything?"

Sam stands silently. *"Yes."* He strains his ears. *"I can hear.... a train! There's a train going by!"*

"*Good clue. Far away or close?*"

"*Difficult to tell. Some way off, I reckon.*"

"*Good information. I'll look inside the circle for a railway line that passes through it. Anything else?*"

Sam listens again. The sounds of the train fade. "*Yes: there's a noise – a crack – I know that sound. I can't place it.*"

A few minutes later – crack! "*There it is again! And people clapping.*"

"*What sort of crack? Shooting? A gun?*"

"*No. But I know it. Damn, I know it … what is it?*" The noise is out of context – he can't work it out.

Sam listens again. "*There's a bird outside – but the other noise has gone away…*"

Crack!

Applause.

"*Got it! Cricket!*"

"*What's that?*" queries Ngozi.

Sam guesses this is a thought that doesn't translate easily if Ngozi is unaware of the game. "*It's a sport we play in England. Wooden bat, leather ball.*" He spells the word. "*The point is – someone's playing cricket out there. And cricket is played on specially prepared pitches. That means I'm near a sports ground. If you're looking at an aerial photo, it will be visible even if the picture was taken in the winter. The cricket square gets roped off and protected to keep it smooth and level.*"

"*OK. That's really good. Go on.*"

"*Hold on.*" Ashley has started to stir. He tries to say something but his mouth is taped too. "*Ashley's coming round.*"

"*Right. Look, you concentrate on getting yourself free. See to your friend. I'll get onto the computer and set to work. I'm looking for a building with a cellar, no more than thirty miles from the BMX track, near a sports pitch and with a railway line in the distance. I'll find the railway and look along it till I find a sports field. That'll get us in the right area. God, Sam, it all happens to you, doesn't it?*"

Sam hops to where Ashley is lying and kneels so his friend can see him. Ashley's eyes widen with fear when he sees that Sam is tied and gagged as well. He struggles to free himself, but gives up immediately. He's weak. Sam shakes his head as a signal for Ashley not to try that again.

Another train goes by in the distance. The cricket match has gone quiet, or has finished. A helicopter rattles overhead. And then - another sound!

"Ngozi! A really good clue! I hear a church clock!" Sam feels elated. *"Quite close. It's chiming like Big Ben, and it's one – two – three – four – five - six- o clock. You were right about the time."*

"Well done. Railway, sports field, church clock. That should do it. Leave it with me. In the meantime, don't rely on me getting you out. Start looking for ways yourself."

Awkwardly, Sam hobbles back to the stone steps. Bracing himself against the bottom one, he rubs the tapes tying his wrists against the rough and cold stone.

It takes a good five minutes to free his hands, by which time his wrists are bleeding where he's grazed them. Gingerly he pulls the tapes from his mouth – that hurts too - and sets about unpeeling the ones round his ankles. Then he crawls over to Ashley as the circulation returns painfully to his hands and feet.

Gently, Sam frees his friend. Even in the dim light he can see that he is deathly pale. Sam puts his hand up to tell him to save his energy.

"Remember those guys who attacked us at the BMX track? One knocked you out. They tied us up and we're in a cellar." He sees Ashley struggling to move. "No, don't. You need to stay still. You're hurt."

Ashley winces. "My head! Don't feel good." His speech is faint and slurred.

"You're lucky to be alive, Ash. He swung a huge tree branch at you. I was afraid he'd killed you."

"Who are they?"

"No idea. I think they're after me, for some reason. They brought you along because you could have identified them."

"What do they want?"

"No idea. Personally, I don't want to hang around to find out. Whatever it is, it won't be good. I've got to find a way to get us out before they come back."

Gingerly, Ashley tries again to sit up, propping himself against the cold wall. "I feel terrible. What will you do? Shout for help?"

"No, there's probably no-one to hear us. Waste of breath. You rest and I'll ..."

But Ashley isn't listening. The effort of sitting up has been too much. He groans and slumps sideways. Sam dashes forward to stop his friend's head hitting the hard concrete. His hand comes away wet: blood is still oozing slowly from the wound on Ashley's head. That means it has been bleeding for over an hour – far too long.

"*Ngozi. I've got the tapes off. Ashley's in a bad way. He's passed out again. I'm going to try the top door now.*"

But before he can move, he hears a key rattle and a bolt slide. The door swings open.

"*Ngozi, that's fantastic, you've got people here already!*"

And then Sam's heart falls. The man is wearing dirty jeans and a blue and white striped shirt.

"*Oh no! It's one of kidnappers! It's too late!*"

CHAPTER 24 – A COLD NIGHT

Ngozi is efficiently calm. "Alright. Now, Sam, this is important … you have one job now and one job only: to stay alive. For now, do whatever they say. These are obviously dangerous men. Don't antagonise them. Don't argue. Don't shout. Don't try to attack them. Buy me some time to work out where you are. We'll find you, I promise, but it will take time. I've spread word via the network."

"Network?"

"Later…"

The man in the striped shirt pauses at the top of the steps, taking stock of the situation and allowing his eyes to adjust to the gloom. "Thought you'd be awake by now." He smiles, sneeringly: "and you've rubbed through the tapes – well done. I won't need this, then – not yet, anyway."

He has taken a long-bladed knife from his belt and passes it from hand to hand, grinning; showing off. Sam takes a step back. The message is clear: this man carries a deadly weapon and, what's more, he knows how to use it. More than that, he enjoys using it and will have no hesitation in doing so if he gets the chance.

Worse still - he wants to use it.

"Well boys, you're in luck. I've brought something for you. Here's a bucket. There's food and water in it. Make the most of them."

"Thank you."

"Oh, very polite." The man places the items on the top step.

"What's the bucket for?"

"Work it out." He laughs.

"Why have you brought us here?"

"A friend of ours wants to meet you."

"Who? Why?"

"You'll find out tomorrow."

"What happens when he gets here?"

"Not for me to say - he'll decide."

"Are you going to kill us?"

The man looks Sam up and down as if sizing him up. "Might do." He says this without a trace of conscience or doubt. "Killed better people than you. Depends what the boss says. He's very anxious to talk to you."

"Why?"

"Can't say."

"OK then, when?"

"He'll be here in the morning."

Sam points to his friend. "But if we're here all night, I don't know that Ashley can survive. He's passed out – he's not breathing well. His head is bleeding. He needs a doctor. Can't you take him to hospital? Please? It's me that your friend wants to meet, isn't it?"

The man at the top of the stairs peers into the cellar. "And have him talk? Don't be stupid. Tell you what - if he stops breathing, give him the kiss of life. I understand you're good at that."

Damn! The Lewis Squires publicity. They know about him through that. Ngozi and Emanuel were right.

The man slams the door. Sam hears the key turn in the lock and a bolt being rammed home. He hates those sounds – they make him feel caged, like an animal. What's worse, the man laughs at his own joke as he walks away, his feet crunching on the gravel outside.

"Bastard" Sam mutters.

Sam listens as two cars start up and drive away. He hears the noise of their engines fading into the distance. Strangely, he wants them not to go. He will feel less alone if there are people outside. Even bad people.

Then silence. A lonely, eerie absence of noise.

Isolated.

Trapped.

These people know too much about him. And the man coming tomorrow – will he order Sam to be killed? Stop: there's no sense in dwelling on that. His top priorities are Ashley and getting away.

Collecting the bucket from the top of the stairs Sam finds two rounds of sandwiches wrapped in transparent triangular packaging and two bottles of water. Sam runs to his friend, opens one and, cradling Ashley's head in his arms, holds it to his friend's lips.

"Ashley. Water. Can you take few sips?" Ashley is limp in his arms.

Sam splashes a few drops onto his unconscious friend's lips. Ashley moans weakly and licks them, instinctively. At least he's still alive, if only just. Sam offers him a little more water. This time Ashley sips at it and some runs down the side of his face. He whispers. "Feel - cold." His voice is hoarse.

"You've lost a lot of blood." Taking off his top, Sam places it under Ashley to cushion him from the floor. He rubs his friend's hands and wrists in the hope that it will restore their circulation. He offers him some more water.

Perhaps Ashley can eat something? Sam investigates the sandwiches. In the bottom of the bag is a small piece of paper. He seizes on it, eagerly.

"*Ngozi? The man's gone.*"

"*Good. Nothing to report yet. Give me time.*"

"*I'm not chasing you. But I have more information for you. Someone's coming tomorrow who wants to meet me. I don't like the sound of that ...*"

"*Neither do I. Did they say who?*"

"*No, he wouldn't tell me.*"

"*Or why?*"

"*No.*"

"*This is bad. You've obviously come to the attention of someone. All that publicity. Now perhaps you'll understand why we're so paranoid about it.*"

"*You're right. Sorry.*"

"*No good speculating. It means we have tonight to work out where you are and get you out of there.*"

"*Please do! Depending on what this man says, they may kill us.*"

"*They said that?*"

"*Good as. The better news is that he's left us some sandwiches and water. But that's given me more clues. The sandwiches are labelled 'Spar' – that's a chain of shops here - and they left the receipt in the bag. The stuff was bought at the Ripley Road Service Station, at 5.47 this afternoon. That must be near here because it was only half an hour ago. It's probably a petrol station with a Spar shop attached to it.*"

"*That's a fantastic bit of information. It narrows down the search area again. Anything else?*"

"Just that the door at the top of the stairs is an outside door. He locked and bolted it from the outside. When he left he was walking on gravel. I heard two cars leave and they were driving on gravel too."

"Well done Sam. This is good stuff." Ngozi asks him to spell 'Ripley'. *"So, I've drawn a circle thirty miles round the BMX track. Now hold on. Yes: Ripley Road. It's not long. Now I'll draw a circle about fifteen miles round that. Where those two circles coincide is where you should be, near a sports field and a church and a railway line. Leave it with me. We've got to be able to work it out with all that information."*

The changing angle of the sun's rays through the window shows that the evening is drawing in. Three more trains pass. The light from the window gradually turns to orange, then red. Sam looks at it longingly, yearning for it not to fade completely. But inevitably it does. Sam finds a light switch, but there is no bulb in the holder. The cellar is dark and dank and getting colder. Exactly what Ashley doesn't need.

The church clock strikes ten. He's now four hours late – his parents will be frantic.

Time drags. Ashley sleeps most of the time, sometimes mumbling. Sam can't make out what he is saying other than 'leave ... bike."

Three times Sam tests the door at the top of the stairs. There is no hope of breaking it down.

He searches his pockets and the floor of the cellar for something he might use to pick the lock – not that he knows how. There's nothing. His pockets have been emptied and the cellar is bare. And even if he succeeded, the door is bolted on the outside as well. He heard it.

Sam tries turning the bucket upside down and standing on it, but he can't get anywhere near to seeing out of the window. He tries jumping, but the bucket is moulded from weak plastic and he only succeeds in bending it out of shape as he lands on it. He topples off. If he carries on, the most likely outcome is that he will break his ankle.

He looks for footholds to climb the wall, but there are none. The cellar has been well chosen for its purpose. It's an effective prison.

Sam offers his friend some more water and is relieved to see that he's resting better now. Perhaps the water is helping. He shivers. Without his top he is in for a miserable and uncomfortable night. But Ashley needs it more than he does.

"Ngozi? Any news?"

"Still working on it, Sam. There's a couple of places that could be where you are. Get some sleep if you can. You're there for the night. How's your friend?"

"Still breathing. He's unconscious or sleeping most of the time. The back of his head is caked in blood. Can't tell whether it's still bleeding – it's too dark to see. I've given him some water."

"Keep doing that. Little and often. Prop his head up if you can. Eat a sandwich. Keep your own strength up."

The hours tick slowly by. Eerie silver-blue moonlight takes the edge off the darkness for a while. Then either the moon sets or clouds obscure it, and the cellar is pitch black again.

It's impossible to get comfortable on the hard concrete floor. Sam spends most of the night pacing up and down in the dark, rubbing his hands and beating his arms to keep warm. He speaks with Ngozi regularly in an attempt to keep his spirits up. Without her he would be completely isolated. God, how do people survive solitary confinement?

As dawn approaches, light starts to seep in again through the window. The sound of birdsong echoes strangely loudly into the cellar. A helicopter clatters overhead.

Ashley stirs. "Bloody hell, Sam … look awful. Need shave." His words are mumbled and slurred.

"You can talk! How're you feeling?"

"Dizzy. Head swimming. Can't feel … legs. Numb." Ashley tries unsuccessfully to lift himself. "Want to get up".

"Not a good idea. You've lost a lot of blood."

"Need to change position." Ashley struggles to stand. Against his better judgement, Sam helps him to his feet. Ashley's frozen legs collapse under him straight away. Taking his weight, Sam helps his friend to stumble slowly round the cellar, trying to restore his circulation.

"Bloody hell, that hurts!" Ashley winces as his blood starts to circulate again.

"Have some more water. Fancy a sandwich?"

Leaning on Sam, Ashley takes the water and sips at it. He turns away from the sandwich with distaste. Sam considers eating it himself but decides Ashley is right: Tuna and sweet corn with mayonnaise doesn't seem a good idea first thing in the morning.

Ashley sits down again and closes his eyes. The exercise has drained him.

Soon after the church clock strikes eight, two cars crunch over the gravel and stop outside. Sam hears voices but can't make out what is being said. Then laughter.

A key rattles in the lock. The bolt slides back and the door opens. A figure stands silhouetted in the morning sun. The same man as yesterday.

"You two alright? Had a pleasant night?"

"No. But we're still here if that's what you mean. My friend needs a doctor. Please."

"We'll see. Perhaps he won't need one at all."

Sam ignores that. "When's the man coming – the one who wants to meet me?"

"We're going to get him now."

"Can't you tell me who he is?"

"You'll find out soon enough." The man is giving nothing away. He locks and bolts the door again.

Footsteps. Two car doors open and slam. The car's engine starts and Sam hears the wheels scrunching across the gravel.

Two people are going to collect ... someone unknown.

He tells Ngozi.

He and Ashley are alone again and still trapped. Sam sits down next to Ashley and waits for the unknown person to arrive. Will it be the last person he ever meets?

The church clock strikes nine.

* * *

The station clock clicks onto 09.15. Also waiting for someone to arrive, an innocuous looking man is standing outside Winchester railway station. He wears a wide-brimmed hat, pulled low over his eyes. He has chosen a position where the CCTV cameras won't track him. He holds a bottle of water and, strangely, whenever someone walks past, he finds it necessary to take a drink.

Nobody sees his face.

But equally, nobody spares him a second glance. Just an anonymous man, waiting at the railway station, causing no-one any problem. Many anonymous people wait at stations.

For the tenth time he checks his watch. He glances impatiently at the clock. Whoever he is waiting for is late.

After another ten minutes, he makes a phone call. "It's me. Where are they?" he snaps. "I'm standing out here in full view of everyone, for God's sake."

He listens.

"No. I'm not waiting any longer. Something's gone wrong. I'm going back."

He listens again.

"No. It looks as if I'm obliged to forego the pleasure of meeting Mr. Wright. You know what to do."

Pause.

"Yes. Of course the other one as well. Can't risk you or the place being identified. Take care of them both. And let me know why the others haven't picked me up. They'd better have a good reason."

Unperturbed by the death sentence he has just delivered, he walks back to the platform and boards the next train heading north.

CHAPTER 25 – LET'S GET THIS OVER WITH

mprisoned in the cellar, Sam listens intently for clues from outside. Since the car left, everything has been quiet. Ashley is conscious, groaning occasionally.

"Sam. Are you there?"

"Yes."

"Right. We're pretty sure we've worked out where you are – a farm between Romsey and Winchester. We've told the police."

"How?"

"I'll tell you later. They should be there any time now. Listen out for them."

"Thank goodness. Ashley needs a doctor."

"Sam, pay attention now. You don't need me to tell you how much danger you're in. Your kidnappers will most probably react violently when they realise the Police have found you. They may try to kill you to stop you giving evidence. So, do whatever you have to do to save yourself and your friend. You understand what I mean?"

"Yes – are you sure? I thought I mustn't do that."

"Sam, we're not messing about here – this is your life we're talking about. You have the means of defending yourself. Do it."

"Jeez." Sam is uneasy. Attack someone deliberately? *"I'll try to avoid that. I don't like the idea of attacking someone like that."*

"Normally you'd be right Sam. But when it comes down to life or death – your life, your death – don't let that get in the way. You have to survive whatever's going to happen in the next few minutes. Do what you have to do."

Sam has no time to discuss it any further. *"Hold on – something's happening now. I hear a car."*

"OK. Let's hope it's the Police. Sam – I'm serious. Do whatever it takes. If you have to - just do it."

"OK."

Sam listens as the car draws closer. Its wheels crunch over the gravel. It stops.

"A car door's opened – no, two – no, three, four doors. Two people left earlier: I reckon at least four have just arrived."

"It could be the Police. Or it could be the person who wants to meet you. Protect yourself if you have to."

"Yes, OK. Hold on, something's happening out there."

A cracking noise.

A shout! Sam can't make it out.

Sounds of people running on gravel.

Another cracking noise.

A scream of pain.

A thump.

Another crack.

Shooting? Guns?

Men are fighting, that's for sure.

"Ngozi. There's shooting out there. Someone's been hurt by the sounds of it."

"It has to be the Police. Now, when the door opens, be very careful. If it is the Police, you have no idea how they found you. You're just delighted that they have."

"OK. And if it isn't?"

"If it's not the Police – I've already told you what to do."

The noises of the struggle outside stop.

Sam runs up the stairs to the top door. "Help! We're locked in here!" He bangs on the door.

Footsteps. Two sets of feet crunching over the gravel. They stop outside the door.

"That trigger-happy fool. He's blown it this time. If he's killed them ..."

"We've gotta get out of here."

"Ready for this?"

No! It's the kidnappers – Sam recognises the voices. What is going on?

"How did the bastards find us?"

"Dunno. Don't care. We'll get the boss to work it out later. Let's get this over with and then get the hell out of here."

The second voice is the man with the knife.

The one who said he might kill them.

Sam has no doubt what their intentions are.

"Ngozi – it's bad! It's not the Police- it's the people who brought us here. One's just said 'let's get this over with'. They're planning to kill us."

"That means something's gone wrong. In that case - it's down to you now. Save yourself and your friend."

The key rattles in the lock. Sam bounds down the stairs. Leaving the bottom door wide open, he stands behind it.

He hears the footsteps of the two men coming down the stone steps. As they draw closer he watches through the gap left by the door hinges. The first man is clutching a cloth and a bottle.

The second has his knife ready.

Do they intend to kill Sam and Ashley in the cellar? Or drug them and take them somewhere else?

Sam waits until the first man is at the bottom of the steps. Bracing himself against the wall, he kicks the heavy door as hard as he can.

The kidnappers are not expecting an attack. The door swings hard into the leading man's face, leaving him no time even to raise his hands to protect himself. He grunts in pain as the force of the blow throws him back heavily onto the steps. Instinctively he raises his hand to his broken nose. The anaesthetic on the cloth completes the process and he slumps unconscious.

The second man swears and kicks the door back open, intending to do to Sam what Sam has just done to his accomplice.

But Sam has moved. The door handle smashes loudly against the bare wall, making a hollow-sounding thud, its handle splintering away a shard of stone that falls to the floor.

Sam runs to the other end of the cellar. He backs himself against the far wall. "Keep away from me."

"Don't be stupid. You can identify us. And now you've really pissed me off."

"What about your friend who wanted to talk to me?"

"Plans change. He doesn't want to talk to you anymore and he doesn't want you talking to anyone else either. Neither of you. Now, we can do this the hard way or the easy way. I've got the knock-out stuff over there. If you let me use it on you, you won't feel a thing. It'll be painless, like."

"No bloody way."

"Then we'll do it the hard way. First you, then your friend."

Instinctively Sam looks at Ashley, half conscious on the hard floor. Mistake! As Sam is distracted, the man lunges at him with the knife. It's a cowardly attack. Sam dodges away at the last moment.

The door at the top of the stairs is still open!

Can he make it? No, not yet. He isn't going to run: Ashley came back for him at the track; he isn't going to leave his friend at the mercy of this ruthless killer.

The man with the knife keeps his eyes on Sam. "Pete. You there?" Pete is lying at the bottom of the stairs. "Still got the cloth?"

Pete doesn't respond. He's dazed, drugged and covered in blood from his broken nose and a cut on his forehead.

The knifeman passes his weapon from hand to hand. Sam watches it fearfully - from which direction will the next attack come? Keep watching the knife!

The man's mouth twists into a sneering grin. He's enjoying himself. He's toying with his victim. Bastard!

With the knife in his left hand now, he makes another lunge for Sam, aiming high this time, towards his neck. It's an awkward movement to avoid. Sam drops to the floor to save himself.

The man hisses. "Well done lad, but that leaves you nowhere to go."

Sam kneels on the floor and says quietly: "you'll be very sad if you kill me."

The man falters. Sam is affecting him. Deliberately.

"You feel so scared."

The man backs away. "What's happening?"

Sam stands up. "You feel afraid. Drop the knife."

The would-be killer stands rooted to the spot. He can't cope with these unaccustomed emotions running through his mind.

"Fear. You feel great fear." Sam projects the emotion. The man called Pete whimpers in his drugged sleep. So does Ashley.

"Drop the knife. You're scared what might happen to you." Sam projects the raw emotion at the man, as he had with the Warren brothers. But this time it is intentional – he's fighting for his life, using the only weapon he has.

Unable to control the forces swirling in his head, the knifeman obeys. The blade clatters to the floor. Sam kicks it away. He faces his would-be killer. How he hates this man! Sam clenches his fist and hits him on the chin with all his might and pent-up anger. "That's for Ashley, you bastard."

The man grunts and, for a moment, holds his mouth.

But Sam has made a mistake.

The fear has gone. Now Sam is projecting anger. His opponent knows all about anger. In a rage generated by the blow and amplified by Sam, he roars his fury. Instinctively Sam steps away as the low, animal noise takes him aback.

The man grabs Sam violently by the throat, intent on throttling the life out of him. He digs his knuckles roughly into both sides of Sam's neck. "No-one – no-one does that to me and lives. You hit the wrong man, you little shit."

Sam tries to scream but the sound comes out as a weak groan. He feels the life being throttled out of him. Unable to breathe, he drops to his knees. Uselessly he tries breaking the man's grip. He's not strong enough.

The man carries on squeezing. "No-one - hits - me – like – that – and – lives – to - talk – about - it." Sam's attacker hesitates between each word as if to emphasise every one as he throttles the life out of Sam.

The room is spinning. Sam can't concentrate enough to use his mental powers again. "It's over" he thinks. "I've failed." The room swims. His vision is blurred. Soon, blackness.

Someone screams. What's happening?

The pressure eases.

But why?

The man topples forward on top of Sam, holding his back. A bloodstain is spreading down his striped shirt and onto his jeans.

Gasping for breath, Sam crawls out from underneath his attacker. Ashley is lying there with the knife in his hand. It has blood on it.

"I was having this awful nightmare that something frightening was happening ... it woke me up." Ashley is slurring his words and his eyelids are drooping.

Sam had affected Ashley too, in his sleep.

"Saw him with his hands round your throat. Your eyes looked like they were going to pop out of your head. The knife was right by me. I ... I stabbed him."

"You saved my life" says Sam, simply.

The man is cursing. He tries to stand but groans in pain from the deep wound in his back.

Sam thinks quickly. His kidnappers are temporarily incapacitated. He has to get away: get Ashley to hospital. Grabbing the cloth from the man called Pete, Sam splashes some of the anaesthetic on it and holds it over each man's face in turn. They lie limp, drugged as Sam had been yesterday when they brought him here.

"They won't go anywhere for a few hours. Let's get out of here" says Sam, stooping to help Ashley up.

"Can't - don't feel well ..." The knife clatters to the floor as Ashley collapses again. He'd recovered just long enough to save Sam's life. But can Sam now save him?

Sam catches his friend as he falls. Using the anaesthetic rag he wipes the knife handle clean to remove Ashley's fingerprints, and drops it. Then he picks up his friend and, with some difficulty, carries him up the stairs and out of the cellar.

Sam blinks in the bright morning sunlight.

They are out!

But now he has to get Ashley to a hospital, or he'll die.

CHAPTER 26 – BAD DRIVING

After the gloom of the cellar, the daylight hurts Sam's eyes. Screwing them almost shut, he steps back into the shade and stands at the top of the stairs looking out onto a yard surrounded by farm buildings. Above the door from which he has just emerged is an open barn. To his right and behind him, at the other end of the barn, is a black pick-up. To his left is a disused farmhouse, its windows boarded up. Facing him is a low terrace of stables. A road leads from the yard beside them.

Two cars are standing in the yard, one with its engine still running and all four doors gaping open. Four people are lying ominously still on the gravel. Police? Perhaps - they're not in uniform though. Are they dead? He can't tell.

"Ngozi. We're out."

"Thank goodness. You ... you took care of the kidnappers?"

"With some help ... fill you in later."

"I felt that something was going on. Get away as quickly as you can."

"I'm going to. Ashley's in a bad way. I have to get him to hospital. There are bodies in the yard here. That was the shooting I heard."

"Then get out of there! Whoever did the shooting must still be there!"

Damn. He should have thought of that.

Sam leaves the cover of the doorway and, carrying Ashley, staggers as quickly as he can to the car that has its engine running. With difficulty he lays his friend across the back seat. He bends to lift Ashley's feet into the car.

Above him, the door window shatters. The bullet intended for him went through it as he stooped.

"Bloody hell!" Sam throws himself to the ground and rolls under the car. He drags himself to the rear and peers round. A man is walking from the barn, holding his gun in two hands in front of him. Sam recognises him as the fifth person at the BMX track.

"Where are the others? What've you done to them?" the man snarls. He walks warily towards the car looking for an opportunity to shoot again.

Sam edges backwards round the car, away from the gunman, struggling for cover.

"Why aren't they with you?"

Sam stays silent. He doesn't want to give away his position.

The man is edging his way round the yard, trying to get Sam in his sights. "I don't know what you did down there, but you're not going anywhere." He fires and the bullet ricochets off a stone by Sam's left foot. Frantically Sam drags himself away and crouches behind the back of the car, desperate for the limited cover it gives him. But it can only be a matter of time ...

"You don't want to kill me."

"Try me."

"You can't carry on killing people." Despair! "You know it's wrong."

The gunman shakes his head. He feels strange. He doesn't know what's happening to him.

Sam has him. Nothing for it now: he has to trust in his power to control people. Conscious that he is taking his life in his hands, Sam stands and walks towards the gunman.

"There's been enough killing today. Your gun is no use now. Throw it over here. You don't want to kill any more people. Especially a fourteen-year-old boy. You'll be running for the rest of your life."

Despair.

The gun falls with a dull thud onto the gravel. Sam doesn't pick it up.

Despair changes to fear.

The man is standing rigid, unable to cope with the emotions pouring through his head. Sam says quietly: "you're sick of all this killing. The only place you'll be safe is with your friends down there."

Fear.

With a look of dread on his face the man backs away towards the cellar. Sam walks slowly forward, shocked at how easily he can control another person. But he feels no pity – there are people lying dead in the yard and this man killed them. He just tried to end Sam's life too.

This time Sam won't make the mistake of releasing the pressure too soon. That almost cost him his life a few minutes ago. "You're so sick of all this violence. You need to join your friends."

The man is at the top of the stairs now.

"Go down. You'll be safe down there."

"Not sure. There could be spiders." The man wavers at the top of the stairs, facing Sam.

Spiders? A murderer scared of spiders? For pity's sake! No ... that's not it ... he'd be scared of anything under Sam's emotional onslaught.

Sam has no time to waste. He pushes the killer through the doorway. The man curses as he tumbles painfully down the stone stairs. Sam slams the cellar door, locks it and rams home the bolt. A few moments later there is a barrage of swearing and angry banging on the door from inside.

Sam nods grimly. There's no way out of that cellar - he knows that from bitter experience. Three of his five kidnappers are now locked in there. The other two, he reasons, left earlier in the morning. In case they return, Sam takes the key from the locked door and puts it in his pocket.

Now to get Ashley to hospital.

No, wait! A noise. He looks round. One of the men lying in the yard has just groaned and is moving his head.

"Help me. I'm shot. Police." With difficulty he raises an arm.

Sam runs over. The man is in a bad way. His front is covered in blood. "I need to get you to hospital. Can you make it to the car if I help you?"

"Try."

Walking backwards, Sam drags the injured Officer to the car and manoeuvres him into the front passenger seat. The Officer grunts in pain as Sam swings his legs round and belts him in. Sam checks the other three men lying in the yard. They're not breathing. There's nothing he can do for them.

He finishes placing Ashley on the back seat, closes the passenger doors and sprints round to the driver's seat.

Sam has never driven before. He knows roughly what to do from watching his parents. The driver's seat is set back and he can't find how to move it forward. He can barely reach the pedals.

"Ashley ... hang in there. I'm taking you to hospital" says Sam. "If I can ..." he murmurs more quietly.

Almost sliding off the seat in the process, Sam pushes down the clutch pedal and rams the gear lever forward. He winces as the gears grate. Push the clutch pedal further! Don't stall it!

He revs the engine. Too much! The engine screams and the car shakes but doesn't move.

"The hand brake, you idiot! Let off the bloody brake!" Sam curses himself.

Sam releases the brake and lets up the clutch pedal again. The car jerks forward. It would have stalled on a normal surface: as it is, its wheels spin on the gravel, firing a shower of small stones backwards as it starts to move. Sam risks sliding off the seat to change gear. The car slews to the right as he forces it into second. "Won't do that again".

With the engine screaming, he swings the car round and careers down the track at the side of the stables, swerving from side to side as he gets used to steering. Sam knows he is breaking a hundred different laws, but this is no time to think about that. He has two passengers whose lives depend on him getting them to the hospital.

"Ngozi. I'm out."

"Thank goodness. Did ..."

"Sorry, can't explain now. I'm driving the car with Ashley and an injured policeman in it. I need to get to Winchester City Centre − the hospital. Do you have any idea where I am?"

"If we're right, you're at Stumbles Farm."

"Can you direct me?"

"Yes. I have the map on the internet here. Tell me what you see."

"I'm going down a farm track to a T-junction."

"OK. At the bottom, turn left."

The car slides across the road − it has mud on its wheels and Sam has taken the corner far too fast. He wrenches the wheel back.

"Shit."

"Sorry?"

"Nothing. Fighting with the car."

"Do you see anything? Tell me what you see, so that I can check that you're where I think you are."

"No ... yes! On the right ... a church tower. With a clock. That must be the one I heard."

"That confirms it. Good man! I can see where you are. The road's going to bend to the left and then to the right. In about a mile there'll be a junction on your right. You need to take it."

Locked in the low gear, Sam tortures the engine. The noise echoes off the trees at the side of the road and back into the car through the shattered window.

Desperately Sam peers over the wheel hoping to see a familiar landmark or road-sign. He doesn't know this area at all. Worse, the road is narrow and it takes all his concentration to negotiate the bends and keep the car from crashing into the ditch.

There!

He's onto the junction before he knows it. The sign saying 'Winchester' is partially obscured by bushes. A white van is coming towards him. The van has right of way – he expects Sam to wait. Sorry. He can't stop, even if he wanted to.

Sam wrenches the wheel to the right, cutting across the path of the van. The injured policeman groans, hurt by the violent movement. Behind him Sam hears the blare of a horn and tyres screeching. Then a crunch. The van has crashed.

Sam isn't stopping to see what has happened. He has to get to the hospital. Ashley, lying across the back seat, is ominously silent. Sam glances round anxiously.

Mistake! When he looks forward again he's heading for a ditch. The car judders as it half mounts the grass verge. Desperately Sam pulls it back to the right. He'll keep his eyes on the road from now on.

"Sorry Ash. We're on the way. Hang in there."

No answer. The injured policeman is silent too.

"I took the turning you said."

"Good. Next you'll come to a T-junction. Turn left. It's a main road. It will take you into the City."

In the low gear, Sam can't get the car to do more than 40 miles an hour. That will do – he isn't confident of staying on the road if he goes any faster.

God! How far to go now?

There's the T-junction! A large green road-sign. Winchester to the left. Romsey to the right.

The major road means a new danger. Traffic.

Lots of it.

Keeping the car on the road in a deserted country lane was one thing. Driving in traffic is going to be completely different.

Sam swerves onto the main road. More screeching brakes and another blaring horn. Sam ignores them.

"Ngozi, I know where I am now. I can find my way to the hospital from here."

"Well done. Good luck."

Sam grips the steering wheel.

A petrol station.

Oh hell! A roundabout.

A queue of cars.

Sam daren't stop. He can't.

With one hand on the horn and the engine screaming in protest, Sam heads down the outside of the queue and cuts across the car at its head. A motorcyclist on the roundabout turns his bike sideways to avoid him.

Sorry. Can't stop!

The road narrows. Sam forces his way in front of a red Mini. More angry hooting. There's a long downhill stretch now. The car is accelerating, the tortured engine vibrating. Is that steam coming from under the bonnet? There's a smell of burning. He's wrecking the engine.

Traffic lights.

Red!

Sam grips the wheel and prays. "Change, please change."

They stay red.

Sam swerves onto the wrong side of the road to avoid a van that has stopped at the lights and then wrenches the wheel back to miss a car stopped on the other side.

More horns blast. He is not the most popular driver on the road.

The hospital will be on the right, down the hill. Sam tries braking again.

Too hard! The whole vehicle shudders as the engine tries to keep it moving against the brakes slowing it down. The Police Officer groans. Sam takes his foot off the brake. The car accelerates again down the steep hill.

The hospital - on the other side of the road. An entrance.

Can he make it?

Sam stamps on the brakes again and pulls the car over to the right. The screaming engine struggles for a moment and then stalls. Immediately the steering goes heavy and it's impossible for Sam to turn the wheel. Power steering - gone! Sam hadn't reckoned on that. He's going to miss the entrance.

OK, just stop! You'll have to carry Ashley in.

Sam can't get enough pressure on the brake pedal. He pulls hard on the hand brake instead. The rear wheels lock. The car hits the kerb hard and a tyre explodes with a bang that makes pedestrians flinch. The car judders to a halt, half blocking the road and the pavement, steam billowing from under the bonnet.

That'll have to do. Get Ashley!

Sam throws open the door and jumps out

"What the hell do you think you're playing at?" A middle-aged man is standing on the pavement, shouting. Sam ignores him and runs to the rear door. The last thing he needs is interference from a bystander.

The man gawps at the sight of a young teenager getting out of the driver's seat. "You can't leave that there" he shouts, emboldened now he knows he is dealing with someone unlikely to shout back.

"Please, help me. This is an emergency. There's an injured man in the front seat. We need a doctor."

"I said ..."

"The man in the front seat - he needs your help. He's been shot. We need to find a doctor."

"Shot? What sort of drugs are you on today, sonny?"

"Oh, for God's sake, you bloody moron. If you won't help, just piss off."

The man stalks away, content that the insult gives him the excuse he needs not to get involved.

Idiot.

Sam lifts his friend from the car and half runs, half staggers, towards the hospital entrance. People stare, but still no-one offers to help. Can't they see that this is serious and he needs them?

"Help me!" Sam screams at the top of his voice. "Help!"

At last someone in uniform comes over: a male nurse.

"My friend's badly hurt. There's another man in the car. He's been shot."

The nurse stares for a moment and then runs inside. He re-emerges half a minute later with more people in uniform and a trolley. They help Sam lay Ashley on it.

"He's been hit on the head. He's been unconscious for most of the night."

Medical staff surround the trolley. They take Ashley's pulse and blood pressure. They hook up a drip.

"Who is he?"

"Ashley Jones."

"Who are you?"

"Sam Wright."

"Relative?"

"No, friend."

"How did he get this injury?"

"Someone hit him with a lump of wood."

"You?"

"No, of course not."

"You should have brought him in before."

Sam lets that go. "Will he be alright?" he asks anxiously

"He's in a bad way. Blood pressure's very low. Dangerous." The medics wheel the trolley away.

"Can I go with him?"

"No. Stay here, we'll send someone to take details from you."

More hospital staff wheel in a trolley on which they have laid the Police Officer from the car. He's unconscious.

"He's been shot" explains Sam.

"We can see that. Out of the way, please ... we need to get him to surgery. And stay here. The Police will need to talk to you about this."

Too right! Sam has no intention of going anywhere. "Yes, please call them."

"Ngozi: I've made it to the hospital. What should I do now?"

"Phone your parents of course. They must be frantic with worry."

Instinctively Sam reaches in his pocket for his phone. He doesn't have it. There's a payphone in the hospital entrance. He places a reverse charge call.

His father answers.

"Dad?"

"Sam? Is that you?" He hears his mother scream his name in the background.

"Yes, Dad. Listen. I'm all right but I'm at the hospital. Ashley's badly hurt. Can you tell his Mum and come straight away please? And the Police – you'd better ring them."

"They're here already. What's happened?"

"We were kidnapped. You'd better get here quick." Outside, horns are sounding and a crowd of people is standing round the abandoned car. "It may take you a while. I've caused a traffic jam."

Outside the hospital, Philip Styles stares in disbelief at the car left stupidly half across the pavement, half in the road with three of its doors gaping open and the key still in the ignition. It never ceases to amaze him how idiotic some drivers can be. He sees many examples of gross irresponsibility every day, but this - this is a humdinger. He'll have to act on this one. Oh yes! The numbskull driver of this car won't forget this day in a hurry, not once Philip Styles has finished with him.

A slight man with a thin pinched face and close trimmed moustache, Philip Styles is not a happy person at the best of times. Suffering from a chronic case of short-man syndrome, for which he knows there will never be a cure, he has never been able to command respect through strength of character. He finds contentment only when able to assert himself through the authority of a uniform.

It is therefore with some relish that Styles fills in the details of the abandoned vehicle on his hand-held ticketing machine, photographs it and prints a fixed penalty notice. He places the paper with a flourish on the windscreen, the gesture being for the benefit of the small knot of people milling around and watching.

"Bloody brilliant. Well done."

Styles wheels round, his insecurity pricked immediately. "I beg your pardon?"

"Bloody brilliant. There's probably a medical emergency: the guy's inside having a crisis and you stick a ticket on his car."

Philip Styles is trained not to react angrily. "Sir, this vehicle is causing an obstruction and it's a danger to the public. Is it your car, Sir?"

"No, of course not."

"Then I cannot discuss the matter further with you." Nevertheless, that was a good point: the driver of the vehicle could well be inside. Notebook out, Styles marches into the hospital. Yes, he will get to the bottom of this. It's his duty. Already he is being abused simply for doing his job.

There are only four people, other than staff, in the reception area.

"Is the driver of the silver car in here?"

Nobody answers.

"The silver car out there: is anyone in here responsible for it?"

Sam groans inwardly. If he responds, he'll get involved with loads of questions he doesn't want. He needs to keep his head down and hope the police arrive soon. He'll tell them everything.

"The driver of the silver car …"

The reception staff look in the direction of a young man sitting at the end of a row of plastic chairs, deliberately looking down, clearly hiding his face. Styles walks over.

"Sir, are you the driver of that car outside?"

Head down, the young man ignores him.

"Excuse me. Did you drive that car here?"

Still no reply.

Despite his training, Styles feels anger welling inside him. He raises his voice.

"If you're the driver of that car, you have to move it. Immediately."

Briefly Sam looks up. Styles is shocked to see that he is just a teenager, and a young one at that. Surely not old enough to hold a licence?

"You have no right to be driving at your age. Have you any idea what you've done? That car can't be left there. It's causing an obstruction."

Sam looks down again, determined to ignore him.

"Look sonny, I'm speaking to you." Styles pokes Sam on the shoulder.

For the first time the young man reacts. He takes Styles' wrist and forces his hand away. His eyes bore into the warden's face.

"Don't touch me again" he hisses.

"You're in deep trouble, sonny."

There is no reaction. Sam is looking down again and ignoring him.

"You'd better give me your name and address."

No reaction.

"Right." Styles feels angry. More angry than he had ever felt before on this job. Strange. This young hooligan – who the hell does he think he is? Despite his training, Styles grabs the young man and pulls him to his feet. "Answer my questions you little…"

"Get your hands off me and leave me alone." Sam has given up trying to control his anger. After everything else that's happened …

"Give me your bloody name." Styles screams into the face of the young man. Then he recoils as if he's been hit. Suddenly he feels desperately, morbidly afraid of this teenager. He's never felt anything like it. Suppressing a whimper, Styles backs slowly to the other side of the room where he continues to watch the young man with shock in his eyes. What the hell happened?

Outside a siren wails. The Police will be here soon. Still keeping his distance, the warden shouts across the room "Hear that? It's the Police. You won't be able to ignore them. I don't know what you've been smoking today sonny, but you're in big trouble now."

Sam has sat down again. The scene with the warden was the last thing he wanted. He'd not been able to control his anger and had affected the official – he's sure of that. But forcing him to back away – that had been deliberate and he shouldn't have done it. Now he feels tired: washed out.

A car is outside, its blue lights flashing. A man in plain clothes runs in followed by three uniformed Officers. Sam recognises one of them as the man who took his statement after the accident. He whispers to the detective.

"Mr. Wright ..."

Styles steps forward, emboldened by the arrival of a potential ally. He will strike the first blow. "Officer, you must arrest this hooligan ..."

The Officer shows his warrant card and says in a low voice. "Detective Inspector Ian Murphy. Thank you, but I'll handle this from here."

Styles stands in his way. "Good. Inspector, I demand that you arrest that lout. Look at the state of him ..."

Sam looks at his clothes. Styles has a point – they're filthy after the night in the cellar.

"... he stole that car – must have. He's under age; that means he's been driving without insurance or a licence. He's mounted the pavement and he's ..." His voice tails off. He can't very well complain about Sam sitting there.

"And you are?"

"Philip Styles." The warden puffs out his chest.

"Thank you for your assistance, Mr. Styles. You may go now. As I say, I will handle this now."

"Don't you want my statement?"

"No, Mr. Styles. Mr. Wright will tell me what happened."

"So, you know him. I might have guessed. I tried to take his name and address. He refused to tell me. He's on drugs, I'll vouch for it, you mark my ..."

Murphy raises a hand, gesturing for silence. "Mr. Styles." The Detective Inspector looks down to make eye contact with the warden. "You will leave this to me, now, please. If I need a statement from you, I will contact you through the usual channels."

The warden opens his mouth but Murphy stands close and murmurs quietly: "And if you say one more word I'll have you arrested for obstructing the work of the Police."

Styles stalks away. The world has gone mad.

Detective Inspector Murphy sits on the chair next to Sam. "Mr. Wright - Sam. I don't think we've spoken before but Constable Giles here met you after your road accident."

"Yes, I recognise him."

"I also read about how you saved the life of your friend at school."

"Oh."

"I mention these things only to explain that I am jumping to no conclusions as to how you come to be here: I am prepared to believe that whatever you have done has been for good reasons. But I do need to understand what they are." He looks round. "This is a bad place – too many people." The Inspector beckons to a member of the hospital staff. "Can you find us a room where we can talk in private, please?"

The woman looks curiously at Sam and the detective. She wants to know what's going on.

"As quickly as possible, please?" Murphy looks pointedly at the woman, irritated at her failure to react. She scowls and scuttles off.

"Good." He turns back to Sam. "Do you have the keys to the car?"

"No. I left them in it."

Inspector Murphy issues more orders quietly to a colleague who runs out.

"We'll take care of it. Tell me ..." he says quietly, "... were you kidnapped yesterday?"

"Yes."

"And held in a cellar in a farm?"

"Yes."

The Inspector shakes his head. "Unbelievable." He recovers. "How come you were you driving the car?"

"I escaped. Ashley – my friend – was injured. I had to get him here. They hit him when they kidnapped us. He's very ill. I'm afraid he might die. And the other man."

"Another man? Who?"

"One of yours. He was shot. In the stomach. I brought him here too."

"Oh, my God."

"I'm sorry - there were people on the ground at the farm when I left. I'm sorry – I think they were dead."

The Inspector goes pale. "How many?"

"Three."

"Where were you?"

Sam thinks quickly. He only knows the name of the farm through Ngozi. "I don't know. It was near a church. I came out on the Romsey Road."

"Excuse me."

Murphy beckons to two Officers and rapidly issues more instructions. One of them runs to find information about his injured colleague. The other goes outside to speak on the radio.

"That confirms what we thought. We were at the right place. We'll have more men there soon. Do your parents know you're here?"

"I phoned them."

"Good. While we wait, I suggest I get you a drink. When they arrive I'll need you to tell me everything that happened."

Sam is impressed. This man is icily calm, in spite of the awful news he has just heard.

CHAPTER 27 – BACK TO THE FARM

"There he is. Sam!"

Sam's parents sprint into the hospital with Ashley's mother. Helen throws her arms round her son. "I've been so worried about you. Are you alright?"

"Where's Ashley?"

Sam points. "They took him that way. He's badly hurt ... his head ... I'm worried ..."

"Hurt? How?"

"They hit him with a lump of wood. Back of the head."

Ashley's mother hurries away to find her son.

"Are you alright, Son?"

Sam nods to his father. "No damage. Just tired."

"How did you get here?"

"The car outside - blocking the road – I drove it."

Helen Wright looks at her son, wide-eyed. "You can't drive!"

"I know. Had no choice."

"You could have crashed. You could have been killed!"

"I know. But I had to get Ashley here. And the Officer."

Inspector Murphy interrupts. "Now you're here, Mr. and Mrs. Wright, it's important I hear the story from start to finish. Are you up for that, Sam?"

Sam nods.

"At this stage, I'm not arresting you or cautioning you. If my understanding of the situation is right, that would be inappropriate. But do please tell me everything. There have been some serious crimes committed." The Inspector beckons. A uniformed lady constable joins them. "PC Grantham will take notes and she has a tape recorder with her." He calls to the hospital receptionist. "Did you find us that room?"

"That one, over there." She points, sullenly.

"Ngozi, I'm at the hospital with my parents and the Police. They want me to tell them everything."

"Not everything, Sam. Nothing to do with how we worked out where you were. And if the Police say anything that surprises you, believe it."

"What's he going to say?"

"Better you don't know. That way you can be genuinely surprised."

Sitting at a plastic-topped table and sipping on a Coke, Sam recounts the events: being attacked and how Ashley came back to help him. Being drugged. Waking in the cellar. He describes how the kidnappers brought a bucket with water and sandwiches. The Inspector shakes his head in disbelief.

"Just out of interest, did you see anything else in the bucket? Apart from the water and sandwiches?"

Of course he had. The receipt. If he mentions it, that will be a clue that he was in contact with someone outside. He has to keep that secret. For the same reason Sam misses out all the details about the church clock, the cricket match and the railway.

"No, that's all they brought for us." He plays dumb and changes the subject: "We really could have done with something hot and a blanket to help Ashley during the night. I used my jacket to cushion his head but he was cold, lying on the floor."

The Inspector nods.

"Did they say why they took you?"

"They said there was someone who wanted to meet me. They called him 'boss'."

"Did they say who that was?"

"No. I asked but they wouldn't tell me."

"They wanted money" says Sam's mother.

"Oh?" Sam is startled.

"It was horrible. When you didn't come home by six, we were getting worried and as time went on we were desperate. We thought something terrible had happened to you – we thought you might have come off your bike and been injured at the track. We tried your mobile but it went to answerphone straight away. Ashley's did the same. Dad went to the track to look for you. I phoned Ashley's mum He hadn't come home either. We tried some of the other boys who use the track. They said you'd definitely been there, but they'd left before you."

"That's right."

"We phoned Maddy but she hadn't seen you. The hospital said they had no record of you coming in. We tried the Police but all they said was to call back if you weren't home in a couple of hours more. They said it's not unusual for teenagers to go off and not tell anyone. I told them you wouldn't do that and neither would Ashley and there was something wrong, but they wouldn't listen. They just told us to wait."

Helen Wright shakes her head. "But then they called us back to ask if you were home yet. Apparently someone had reported seeing you attacked at the BMX track - they recognised you from the picture in the paper."

Very clever, Ngozi! Sam is sure that no-one was there to see them being kidnapped.

"... and then this lady detective – Jones I think - came round and we had to let her in through the back door in case the house was being watched, and we stayed up all night waiting for news."

No wonder she looks exhausted.

"Then this morning there was a phone call asking ... demanding money."

Helen's words have been tumbling from her in a continuous stream but now she stops, overcome with emotion and relief. George takes her hand and continues: "they demanded ten thousand pounds or we'd never see you again. They said they had you both and one of you was badly hurt but they wouldn't tell us which it was. They said they would phone back later with instructions."

Sam shakes his head in disbelief. "The bastards. That was so harsh. I asked them to let Ashley go – to get him to a doctor - but they refused. He could have died. He still might."

Sam is puzzled now. Up to this moment he believed the story that someone wanted to meet him. Now it seems that he and Ashley were being held for ransom. No – that's not the whole story, surely?

His father continues: "This morning Detective Jones was on the radio for a long time talking about farm buildings, cellars, church clocks, sandwiches and trains. It sounded gibberish really. Then she announced that they had a good idea where you were, and they were going to investigate."

Sam asks: "How on earth did you find out? I thought there was no way." It's a dangerous question, but it seems the natural thing to ask and it might seem strange if he didn't.

Inspector Murphy looks slightly awkward but not at all surprised by the question. "It's a bit confused, but we received a series of phone calls from a man claiming to be a medium ..."

Sam's thoughts race. A man? Not Ngozi? Then he realises what Ngozi had done. She used one of the other people she can talk to telepathically. "A medium?" he says in disbelief. "But they're nutters!" And he adds for effect: "Aren't they?"

"That's what we thought. We get them all the time. But this one – it was uncanny. He told us he had a vision of two boys with bicycles being kidnapped and locked in a cellar. Our first reaction was to ignore him. But when we saw that your parents had reported you missing ... weird, though ... I've never believed in that sort of stuff, but this guy had amazing details of what was going on. The most incredible thing was the sandwiches..."

"The sandwiches?" asks Sam.

"He said he had an image of you eating sandwiches, bought at a petrol station. He even named it – Rapley or Rupley. There's no such place, but then we thought of Ripley Road."

Very clever again, Ngozi!

"So we checked at the filling station but the assistant who'd been on duty had gone home by that time. We phoned him and yes, he remembered two men buying petrol, a bucket, sandwiches and bottles of water. The garage's CCTV gave us the car's make and number. It was the one you drove here.

"Then we looked at the other clues – near a church and cricket pitch. And when we put up the helicopter this morning to check out local farms..."

"I heard it" murmurs Sam.

"... we sent a van to watch from the bottom of the lane. We still didn't know whether to believe it all." The Inspector looks thoughtful. "Now ... you haven't yet told us what happened this morning."

"OK. About eight-o-clock I heard two men walk to the car."

"How do you know it was two?"

"Two sets of footsteps on the gravel. Two car doors opened and shut. The car drove away. Later it came back and all four doors opened."

"That stacks up. The people who drove the car away were two of your kidnappers, and the ones who drove it back were four of my people."

Murphy explains that the officers waited at the bottom of the lane to intercept any movements in or out. When the car left the farm, they stopped it and detained the two men. Two of them took the arrested men to the police station in the van. The four who remained decided to drive into the farm in the car, hoping to take the rest of the kidnappers by surprise.

"It sounds like the plan didn't work."

"No, it didn't."

"So what happened?"

Sam continues the story: "I heard the car arrive. I heard all four doors open. Then there was a fight. Shooting. Lots of shouting. People screaming. Then two of the kidnappers came to kill us."

"Sam!" Helen Wright gasps.

Inspector Murphy looks shocked. "Explain. How do you know that was their intention?"

"I was listening at the door. I knew one of them had a knife – he'd taken great pleasure in showing it to me. He was talking about 'getting it over with'."

"And then?"

"I managed to get away."

"And how did you do that?"

Sam has to be very careful now. "I knocked one of them out by kicking the cellar door into his face as he came down the stairs. Then the other one attacked me. I used the anaesthetic rag on him."

"Rag?"

"They were going to knock us out with it."

"Carry on."

"I carried Ashley upstairs and put him in the car. Then a third guy shot at me, but I persuaded him to stop."

"What do you mean, you persuaded him?"

"I told him there had been enough killing."

"And that worked?"

Sam nods. He's on dangerous territory now.

"Then I drove Ashley and the injured policeman here."

"There's lots more information we need. But what I want now is for you to show us. We need to go back to the farm. Are you up for that?"

Sam nods.

"I'm sorry, Mr. and Mrs. Wright. It will be a crime scene. I can't let you go there. You'll have to stay outside the cordon."

Inspector Murphy opens the door and signals to a colleague. "Bring a car round the back. There are too many people out front now. We need to go back to the farm."

Back at the farm, Sam feels detached from reality. It's as if he'd watched everything on film – it all happened to someone else and not to him.

A Police line is in place: tapes to stop anyone driving into the farm. Leaving his parents in the car, Sam and Inspector Murphy walk the length of the track. As they arrive, Sam sees three shapes on the gravel, covered by blankets. An Officer approaches.

"How bad?"

"Bird, Wilkinson and Franski, Sir. Shot, all three of them."

"Dead?"

"Yes Sir."

Murphy swears. "They were good men."

"Yes, Sir. Sorry. No sign of Winters though."

"He's injured but at the hospital, thanks to Mr. Wright here." Inspector Murphy looks round. "Evidence?"

"Lots, Sir. A box of bullets in the back of that pick-up. A gun over there." He points.

"That's the murder weapon" says Sam. "He dropped it."

"Two pedal cycles in the pick-up. Two mobile phones on one of the seats."

"They'll be ours. That pick-up must be how they brought us here."

"Any sign of the people that did this? We have two at the station; we think there should be three more."

"No Sir. As far as we can make out, the farm is worked by two brothers who live a couple of miles down the road. They don't use these buildings any more: not for a couple of years. Apparently the brothers want to redevelop the site but are having trouble getting permission from the Council. In the meantime they're renting the barn and the cellar to a company that uses them for storage. The old house, as you can see Sir, is boarded up. We've searched it: nothing.

"The brothers were over the other side of the fields this morning, milking the cows, at the time the shooting took place. Didn't hear anything. They say the two cars and the pick-up have been here before. Didn't think anything of it. They know nothing about two young men being brought here."

"You believe them?"

"They sound genuine, Sir. Very nervous. Anxious to help. They'll be in the new house if you want to talk to them."

"Later. Apart from the two farmers – no other witnesses?"

"No Sir. Looks like they've got away."

"No, they haven't."

The Inspector looks at Sam quizzically.

"The other three - they're in there." Sam points. "That's the door to the cellar where they kept us last night."

"We've not been able to get in there, Sir. Substantial door. Bolted and locked. No key."

Sam takes the key from his pocket and holds it up. "This is it."

"Young man" asks Inspector Murphy. "If we open that door, exactly what are we going to find behind it?"

"Ten steps down. Stone. Heavy metal door at the bottom. A cellar. Single window, high up. The other three men. The one who injured Ashley has a stab wound in his back. The one who drugged me has a broken nose. The third is OK. He had the gun. The first two should be unconscious."

"Unconscious?"

"From the anaesthetic. And there'll be a bucket, a sandwich and water."

"My, you have been busy. Shall we go and see?"

As Murphy places the key in the lock, fifty miles away, a man is sitting once again in his immaculate room.

"So, Mr. Wright" he murmurs to himself. "I didn't get to meet you after all. And I have to assume that my friends are captured or worse, otherwise they would have called me by now.

"But that tells me all I need to know about you. We will meet, be assured. As you have apparently caused the capture of my friends. I think a change of tactics is required."

Sam watches as Inspector Murphy turns the key. He shivers as the door to the cellar opens. The men he attacked will be in there: he has no wish to meet them again.

He needn't have worried.

In the cellar are four wooden packing cases, three racks of wine bottles and twenty sacks of flour, all stacked against the wall.

Apart from that, the cellar is empty.

CHAPTER 28 - THE SPIDER

Empty? That's not possible!

Two men drugged, one of whom was injured, and the man who Sam had pushed down the stairs – how can they have disappeared? The door had still been locked and bolted from the outside, and Sam had had the key with him all the time.

How could they have escaped? And where did the packing cases, wine and flour come from?

The unexpected scene makes him look like a complete liar.

"I don't understand" says Sam.

"Strange, indeed."

"Those things weren't there before."

"Even stranger. But this is definitely the cellar in which you were held?"

"Absolutely. Ashley and I were down there all night and there was none of this stuff. I would have used the crates to stand on and look out the window."

"Continue the story, anyway. What happened after the shooting?"

Sam forces himself to speak calmly. They'll think he's a fantasist or something if he's not careful. "After the fight in the yard, I heard two men outside this door, about where we are now. They were talking about killing us. When they came down the steps, I stood behind the bottom door – see, the one down there - it was wide open and I kicked it into the first man. It broke his nose. Then the other came at me with a knife. I dodged it."

Inspector Murphy looks sceptical: "Let me get this straight - a man with a knife attacked you?"

"Yes."

"Can you describe him?"

"About your height: short dark brown hair: wiry build. Mean looking. Jeans. Blue and white striped shirt."

"Taller than you, then. Heavier too?"

"Yes."

"And you escaped from him?"

Sam doesn't like the tone of that question. Now he has no evidence to back it up, his story sounds too far-fetched. Added to which, he's holding back information: he can't tell the whole truth about what actually happened.

"I was lucky, I guess. He came at me and I dodged him. He dropped the knife. Then he tried to strangle me. Ashley stabbed him."

"Your friend? I thought he was unconscious?"

"I thought so too. But he came to, for a few minutes. Lucky for me he did."

"Very lucky indeed - just at the right time too. So, then what?"

"They'd brought the drug they used to knock us out, so I used it on them. Then I carried Ashley up the stairs – he was too ill to walk."

"And the last man?"

"The one with the gun. He was in the barn, by the pick-up over there. I reckon he was there when your men came, and he ambushed them. He shot at me while I was putting Ashley in the car. That's how the side window got smashed."

"Yes, we saw it was broken. So then, having dealt with the man with the knife, presumably the one with the gun dropped his weapon and you shot him?"

"No." Sam is very worried now. It's clear that the Inspector thinks he is making it up. "I locked him in the cellar."

"How did you do that?"

"I hid behind the car. When he came round looking for me, I persuaded him that there had been enough killing."

"You persuaded him? That's the second time you've said that."

"I don't know how else to say it. Then I put him into the cellar with the other two and locked the door. I bolted it too, in case they had a spare key."

"And then you drove the car to the hospital?"

"Not straight away. I helped the injured man to the car first."

212

"That much we know to be true." The Inspector calls one of his men across. "Was this door still locked and bolted when you arrived?"

"Yes Sir."

"Has anyone opened it?"

"Definitely not, Sir."

"So no-one has gone in and no-one has come out?"

"Not since we've been here, Sir. We'd have seen them."

"Certain?"

"Yes, Sir."

"Very good. Thank you."

The Inspector turns to Sam. "So, we have something of a mystery on our hands. You were at this farm overnight. That I believe. You were in this cellar – I believe that too. Your description before we opened the door was entirely accurate. And otherwise why would you have the key to it in your pocket? You drove from here to the hospital – that's clear enough. But where are the three men you claim to have - ah - bettered?"

"I don't know."

"If your story is correct, I would expect to see not just three men, but also a bucket, water bottles and an uneaten sandwich. I don't see them, Mr. Wright. I see packing cases, wine and flour – quite normal for a cellar, I think."

"They must have put them somewhere. They must be hiding."

"Where, Sam? There's nowhere to put them."

Sam feels his face reddening. "If you don't believe me, there will be other evidence as well."

"Like what?"

"Bloodstains. They couldn't have cleaned them up."

"Williams!" Murphy calls to a man who has been inspecting the barn. "Take a look down there, if you please. We're looking for bloodstains." He sees that Sam is puzzled. "Forensics."

Sam nods.

Williams walks down the steps to the empty cellar and shouts back up. "The floor is covered with a layer of white dust. I'd say this place hasn't been used for weeks."

"Ngozi. I'm back at the farm. I locked three men in the cellar. But they're gone. There's packing cases and stuff that wasn't there before."

"That's strange."

"I know. It's all different."

"There are only two possible explanations, Sam. Either there's another way out of that place, or they're still there. If they didn't use the door you locked, there has to be another one."

"Where?"

"I don't know! Look for it. Look carefully. That's all I can suggest – sorry."

"I don't see any blood."

"Look at the bottom step." Sam shouts down.

"Yes, could be. There are definite marks."

"I cut my wrists rubbing through the tapes they used to tie us. That's my blood." Sam holds up his grazed wrists as proof.

Murphy shouts down. "We're still looking for three men."

Williams peers curiously into the packing cases. Empty: no clues there. He moves them with his foot to make doubly sure, and jumps back as a spider darts out and runs towards the wall. The spider scuttles to safety under the wall.

"I found a spider."

"Not unusual for a cellar" shouts Murphy.

"No. But it disappeared under the wall, Sir."

Williams inspects the wall. Where the wall meets the floor there is a small gap. Possibly some mortar has come loose? He rips a label from the packing case, pushes it into the gap and runs it from left to right and back again. For a distance of a metre it encounters no resistance.

"Could be onto something here."

Williams knocks on the wall. It sounds hollow. He walks the length of the wall, knocking. The hollow sound comes only from the centre section, where the spider had run.

"Sir, there could be a tunnel or a room behind there."

"Then there must be a catch or a lever of some sort." Murphy looks at Sam. "Did you see anything when you were down there?"

Sam shakes his head. "No. Never occurred to me. Why should it?"

"OK. Williams, keep looking please."

For a few minutes Williams runs his hand over the vertical surface of the wall. "Ah – here we are. It's brilliantly done. If you're not looking for it, you'll never see it. Very well made."

The Inspector calls across the yard. "Sergeant!"

"Sir."

"Two armed men at the top of these steps, at the double. With torches."

"Yes Sir."

Two uniformed Officers run into position.

"Both of you armed?"

They nod.

"Weapons at the ready then. Sam, stand over there if you please." The two men stand apart, holding their guns with both hands in front of them, pointing into the cellar.

Williams presses the brick. A section of the wall swings towards them and stops. He pulls it fully open, revealing an opening large enough for a man to stoop and pass through.

"Looks like there's a room there, Sir."

"They must be in there. Warn them."

Williams calls "This is the Police. Whoever is in there will come out immediately. We are armed."

No answer.

Murphy shouts down the stairs. "Come out now ... we can wait here as long as it takes. You can't hide in there for as long as we can keep watch out here. And I believe that at least one of you is in need of medical attention."

A disembodied voice curses. A man crawls through the opening. Williams points for him to leave the cellar.

Murphy asks Sam: "Do you recognise this man?"

"Yes. He's the one who shot at me. His prints will be on the gun upstairs."

The man scowls. "Don't know what you're talking about. Never seen this boy before."

"I am arresting you for suspected murder, attempted murder, kidnapping and assault. Sergeant, read this man his rights and take him up to the car."

"Williams ... if you would be so kind as to tell me what you see in there." Stooping low Williams crawls into the hidden room. "See anything?"

Williams' disembodied voice comes back. "They had a battery light. Long room, just high enough to stand. Hold on ... yes. There are two people in here, unconscious. I see an article of clothing, a bucket ..."

"What's in the bucket?"

"Some used wrapping tape, an unopened sandwich, an empty sandwich wrapper and two bottles of water, one opened."

Sam looks meaningfully at the Inspector.

"Fingerprint disciplines".

"Yes Sir. There's a back section of the room." There is a pause. "Bloody hell". The voice comes from deep within the secret room.

"What is it?" snaps Inspector Murphy.

"There's loads of stuff in here, Sir. Ten – Fifteen - Twenty games consoles – latest ones, tablet computers, phones ... Inspector, there's thousands of pounds worth here."

"OK ... out. I want photographs and fingerprints - the works."

Williams returns. "This lot's been active, Sir. It's a treasure trove in there."

"Right then, I think we can piece together what happened here. When Sam locked them down here, the last man dragged the others into the hidden room and removed the evidence. He moved the packing cases and other stuff out of the hidden room and into the cellar. He then covered the floor with flour to disguise what happened last night. Clever.

"Their only hope was to persuade us that they had escaped, somehow. Then they would wait for hope for someone to rescue them."

"OK Williams, do your stuff. Tell me when we can remove the two men." He turns to Sam. "I'll need you to identify them."

Sam nods.

Inspector Murphy holds his hand out. "I can't imagine what it must have been like last night in this place. I have to admit that when you claimed to have captured three men, I was finding it difficult to believe. But somehow you did, and we have them and a significant amount of probably stolen property to boot."

"As far as I am concerned three of your men died today and another was injured trying to rescue us. I have a friend in hospital who could be dying for all I know. I know you are being kind, Inspector, but I don't think this has been a good day."

Inspector Murphy swallows hard. "Thank you for saying that. Later on, I'll have to visit the families of the dead men. One of them has a partner who's just had a baby."

"Oh."

Silence. What can he say?

"Can I go home now?"

"Yes. We'll need statements, of course, but we can take them later. I suggest you get some rest."

"I want to find out how Ashley is."

"We'll phone the hospital."

Wearily Sam trudges down the farm track to rejoin his parents. He's been dragged, against his will, into more danger and has seen more innocent people killed. More worrying, he knows that out there, somewhere, is a mystery person who originally intended to meet him, but then ordered him to be killed.

This episode might be over but Sam knows, with a dread foreboding, that it won't be the end of this frightening chapter in his life. Whoever it is out there is not going to give up.

No matter how hard he tries to avoid it, Sam is being sucked into a world he doesn't understand, a world he doesn't want to know, a place of crime and danger and murder.

It's a place he doesn't want to go.

CHAPTER 29 – THE HOSPITAL

There is a knock on Sam's bedroom door.

"Sam?"

"Hi Dad."

George Wright comes in and sits on his son's bed. He looks concerned. "Look, I don't think there's any polite way to ask this so I'll come straight out with it, and I'm sorry if it seems, you know, as if we're prying but ... we're worried, your Mum and I. There's been so much happening round you and to you lately. We ask ourselves: why? Why you all the time?"

It's a good question. What can he say? Not the truth, that's for sure. And he's too tired to think up a plausible answer.

"I've no idea. I wish I did. All I can think of is that the publicity I got over saving Lewis Squires brought the nutters out. That's why I didn't want to do any interviews. I had a bad feeling about it: that's why I refused to do any."

"You were right about that. Kidnapping you and holding you for ransom just because you'd saved someone's life? Who'd have thought that? But are you sure that's it? Nutters? Criminals after a fast buck?"

"No, I can't be sure. But these days with all the crap you see on the social media: I think it brings them out. What else can it be?"

"I've no idea, son, that's why I'm asking. I ... I wouldn't have thought a common-or-garden nutcase would be up to organising a kidnapping like that."

There is an awkward silence.

"Sam ... is there anything you want to tell us? Anything we should know? We care about you. And all this bad stuff - it just doesn't seem right."

Of course there's something he wants to tell them! He'd like nothing better than to be able to share his secret. But he can't. "Thanks Dad, but no. There's nothing. I expect things will quieten down now."

Telling lies is becoming second nature now.

No sooner has his father left than Sam's phone rings. It's Maddy. She's concerned. Is it true ...?

"Afraid so."

"But Sam ... what the hell's going on? Mum and Dad said your parents were frantic. I couldn't sleep."

"I know. Look, do you want to meet at the swings? I'll tell you everything that happened last night. But you have to promise to keep it secret. Three people were ... no I'd better not, not over the 'phone. And there's stuff that won't be made public."

"Sam?"

"Not over the phone Maddy. See you at the swings. Ten minutes?" He'll tell her what he can. He'll tell her it was a ransom attempt.

At the swings Maddy listens, dumbstruck, as Sam relates the story. "That's so frightening. Are you sure you're alright?"

"I'm fine."

"I'm so glad." Maddy rests her head on his shoulder and he puts his arm round her. "It must have been so awful for you."

Damn, the moment is spoilt by Sam's phone ringing. But it's good news. Ashley's mother. The doctors say he lost a lot of blood and is still very weak but they've stabilised him, given him a transfusion, and after some rest they expect him to recover. They want to run tests to check that he's suffered no brain damage, but they're optimistic. Is Sam OK? She is so grateful to him for saving her son's life. Driving the car like that ...

Sam feels uncomfortable at this: it was Ashley who turned back to help him at the cycle track, when he could have got away. And it was Ashley who saved his life down in the cellar.

Relieved, Sam hangs up the call. Maddy looks at him and smiles. "I heard most of that. You saved his life."

"He came back for me when he could have got away."

Sam makes time to tell Ngozi everything that has happened and to thank her again. *"The idea of the medium was brilliant. The Police have no idea at all..."*

"Let's hope not. It's not an original idea ... we use it in emergencies. Sometimes people get suspicious about it, but if we're careful they have to take it at face value, because there's no other possible explanation...."

"The Police said a man phoned."

"That's right. My other regular partner – remember I told you? I told him what to say and how precise he needed to be. I thought of asking Emmanuel Cabrieres to make the calls, but he's been seen with you and that would have been too risky."

"It's a huge comfort to know that I have this as a back-up."

"You don't. Not anymore."

"Sorry?"

"We can't do this more than once for any member of our community. Imagine what would happen if you were in trouble again and were saved for a second time by the intervention of a so-called 'medium'."

"Hell, you're right. From what you've told me I'd get every Government official interested in telepaths crawling all over me. I might as well wear a sign round my neck saying 'Dangerous. Lock up and throw away key.'"

"Somewhat flowery language, Sam, but that's about it. This is a card we can play once and only once. For you... never again."

Sam spends the following afternoon identifying the men who kidnapped him, giving statements to the Police and going over, in minute detail, the events of the previous two days. They confirm that the full story will not be told publicly – Sam wants no publicity and they'll respect that. Instead they will report the arrest of members of an alleged criminal gang involved in dealing high-value consumer electronics.

Following a tip-off, a suspected storage facility was raided. Three Officers were killed and one badly injured in the operation. Five men have been arrested in connection with the investigations. A sixth is thought to have escaped.

On Wednesday, Sam insists on visiting Ashley in the hospital. He finds him in a single room, a bandage round his head and drips connected to both arms.

Sam is shocked; his friend is still ashen-faced and looks desperately ill.

Ashley's mother is sitting at his bedside. She beams when she sees Sam and hugs him. She thanks him over and over again for helping her son when they were in the cellar and for getting him to the hospital. That must have been so frightening!

Sam plays it down - he hadn't really done anything. In fact, Ashley was the brave one – coming back to help Sam when he could have escaped. He's a good friend.

Tears well up in her eyes when he says this and she turns away, wiping them.

Ashley opens his eyes at the sound of the voices. His voice is a hoarse whisper. "You're a bloody awful driver, you know."

Sam nods. "Must learn how to change gear sometime. How're you feeling?"

"OK, I suppose. Want to go home. I'm fed up. Bored."

"You'll stay as long as the doctors say." Ashley's mother is firm.

Ashley rolls his eyes.

"Good news – they found our bikes."

Ashley's smiles weakly. "Good." His eyes close and Sam thinks he has fallen asleep. Then they open again. "The bike - not damaged?" He's more worried about that than his injured head.

"I didn't get a chance to check, but I reckon they just chucked them in the back of a pick-up. Should be OK."

"Glad." Ashley's eyes are closing again. With slurred speech he asks "How did they find us?"

Sam pauses before answering, conscious that Ashley's mother is listening. "Dunno really. The Police worked it out. Better ask them." This seems the safest reply he can give.

"You're a crap driver ..." Ashley's voice fades away.

"I'll have to ask you to leave now. We can only allow short visits – Ashley's still very weak." A nurse gestures towards the door.

Sam nods. "He's going to be alright?"

"The doctor is optimistic. Ashley's had a bad time, but he'll be fine, as long as he gets his rest."

That is a relief. "See you again soon, Ash. Bye, Mrs. Jones."

Ashley's mother isn't listening. She is holding her son's hand and wiping his forehead. Ashley is asleep.

Sam is relieved to be closing the door on another strange episode in his life.

He has no idea how much more bizarre it is about to become.

"Aargh." Walking away from Ashley's room, Sam groans, staggers and almost collapses. A searing pain is shooting through his head. He clamps his hands to it instinctively. It feels as if a red-hot poker has been stuck into his skull. No matter which way he turns, the pain stays with him. The building spins. He thinks he's going to pass out.

Sam feels the nurse's hands on his arm, steadying him. "Are you alright?"

The world is whirling. "Pain ... head. Room ... spinning." It's an effort to say even those few words. Gratefully, he leans against the nurse to stop himself collapsing. He hears her calling for assistance.

Sam's knees buckle. The corridor has gone dark now. He can't see. There's a loud buzzing in his head.

"... Kill. Me. No!" Like a muffled conversation heard through a bedroom wall, Sam senses someone shouting - anguished words he feels as much as hears.

Ngozi?

No, it isn't Ngozi. It's a man's voice.

Tentatively Sam opens his eyes. His vision is blurred but he can see again. The corridor has stopped spinning. The nurse is looking at him with concern.

"Are you alright?" She's staring into his eyes, her face lined with worry.

Mumbling, Sam tries to respond, "Feel weird. Head hurts. Hot ... need fresh air."

With an effort he pushes himself upright and shuffles towards the lift. The corridor seems endless – getting longer with every step he takes. The nurse holds his arm. They stop at a water dispenser and she hands Sam a cup. His shaking hands spill most of it down his front.

Sam's head feels again as if it will explode. The buzzing returns and he screams again. Everything goes dark and he slumps to his knees, hitting his chin against the plastic container.

"... no ... here ..." Distorted, muffled words again, rasping through Sam's throbbing head.

A second nurse runs to him with a trolley. The two of them lift Sam bodily onto it and he is rushed down the corridor to an examination room. In a daze Sam feels his pulse and his blood pressure being taken. A doctor peers into his eyes and Sam cries out as the bright light sends another searing pain stabbing through his head.

"Can you speak?" asks the doctor. "Can you tell us what's wrong?"

"Head ... hurts." It is all Sam can do to mumble the minimum words.

"Whereabouts? Can you point?"

But Sam groans again as another wave of pain stabs his head. *"Help ... no ... still ..."* More muffled words that he can only just make out.

The pain is unbearable.

It intensifies. There is a red hot skewer in his brain and someone is slowly twisting it. Sam groans. He's never known anything like it.

"No ... still ... here ... Noooooo!"

Sam doesn't scream again. Blackness envelopes him.

The tunnel through which Sam is passing is long and spirals up and down. At breakneck speed he travels, sensing rather than seeing the cold, black walls rushing past him. He holds his hands to his side, not daring to reach out and touch anything, seeking to protect himself from the friction burns he must surely suffer should he make contact.

There is no sound to accompany his journey. Just the faint "Noooooo!" that he heard before. Eventually that becomes a distant echo and fades.

Something's wrong. Where is this? Why isn't his head hurting?

The walls rush past. Where is he going? Is he – dead? That must be it. Oh, that's such a shame: I've died.

A new sound.

Groaning.

A different voice.

A woman.

A dot of light appears at the end of the tunnel. It grows and grows, becoming brighter and brighter until Sam has to screw his eyes shut against it. He raises a hand to shield himself from the glare.

Abruptly the tunnel ends. Sam is standing in hot sunshine outside a rough mud house. He walks in. A woman is lying on a rush mat. She is giving birth. That explains the cries of pain. Older women are gathered round, helping the mother-to-be.

The outline of another man is standing next to Sam. A young, white man – someone Sam has never seen before. As the baby boy is born, he steps forward and takes the baby's hand. His image fades until it disappears.

The baby turns its head towards Sam. *"Go away. You shouldn't be here. It is not your time. Leave."*

The baby? Communicating with him? Sam doesn't understand, but he knows it is true. He shouldn't be here. He turns and leaves.

Behind him the baby takes his first breath and cries.

Gingerly Sam opens his eyes. The lights of the hospital ceiling swim into view.

He's still on the trolley. He's alive. Yes, definitely alive. The buzzing is gone. Gingerly he lifts his head. It's OK. He's bathed in sweat, but the pain is gone.

The doctor and nurse are talking. Are they aware that he passed out? Possibly not. Sam looks round.

No woman. No baby. No mud house. So what was that all about?

There's a clock on the wall. 3.32. He must have been unconscious for a few seconds, that's all.

"Sam, what on earth is happening?"

"Ngozi?"

"Yes. What's going on? You've been screaming. Has someone been hurting you?"

"You weren't trying to contact me, were you?"

"No. For goodness sake tell me what's been happening."

"Huge pain in my head ... heard muffled words ... a man's voice."

"Where are you?"

"In the hospital ... came to visit Ashley. Something happened ... I heard words but not clearly. I think I passed out. I saw a baby being born ... I shouldn't have been there."

"A baby being born? In the hospital?"

"No. In a mud house."

"You've been hallucinating ..."

"Don't think so. There was another man there. He joined with the baby."

"You've definitely been hallucinating. How're you feeling now?"

"Bit better. The buzzing's gone."

"What sort of words did you hear?"

"Difficult to make out. Things like 'no ... still ... here' .and 'help'. Didn't recognise the voice. It's gone now."

"And the hallucination?"

"Gone."

"Lie back. Take it easy. It's a good job you're in the hospital. You've been through a lot, you know. Could be the after-effects of your kidnapping. They drugged you, after all. You can get after-effects from anaesthetics."

"I don't think it's that..."

After half an hour Sam is feeling embarrassed still to be the subject of attention. Seriously, I'm feeling better now. No, please, don't phone my parents - they'll only worry. The pain is gone. Whatever caused it, it has passed.

The doctors find nothing wrong with him. They want to keep him in overnight, possibly do a scan and an EEG, but Sam refuses. He's had enough of having his life disrupted. What's more, they can observe him and scan him as much as they like ... he can never tell them what happened ... the voice ... the baby. He needs to get home, away from prying questions, and try to work it out for himself.

Reluctantly they agree to let him go. They advise Sam to go straight to bed when he gets home and to stay there.

As if he would do anything else.

As he lies in his room, Maddy sends him a text. "Put on the news."

Wearily Sam flicks on the television. As he listens, tears stream down his face.

"... and so at 3.30 this afternoon, the life support machines were switched off and Vincent Stewart passed away peacefully, with his family at his bedside. After a drawn out battle to persuade the hospital to keep their son alive, his family's last hope was a court injunction. When the court sided with the hospital they had to accept that Mr. Stewart was indeed beyond further hope."

The programme switches to an interview outside the hospital with the family's solicitor, who reads a statement on their behalf.

Sam pounds his bed with his fist. 3.30? Today? That's when he suffered the buzzing, heard the muffled voice and passed out with the pain in his head. *No ... still ... here ... help!!*

Sam groans. Now he knows what happened. Vincent Stewart had indeed been alive, as his family believed. Despite being in a coma, he was aware of what was going on around him. He knew what was about to happen. He couldn't move. He couldn't speak. But he didn't want to die.

Vincent Stewart had been silently screaming, pleading for the doctors not to switch off his life. But no-one could hear him.

Only Sam.

Sam had heard the young man's last frantic pleas to be kept alive. But he hadn't known what they meant. He hadn't understood.

Sam buries his head in his pillow. He'd heard a cry for help and hadn't done anything; hadn't been able to do anything. Sam was Vincent

Stewart's last hope – and he failed him, just like he failed the mother and her baby in the car crash.

'No', he tells himself. 'Don't think like that. Even if I had realised what the voice meant, what could I have done? Nothing.' Even so, he can't shake the sense of guilt, as if he'd been party to a killing.

He tells Ngozi what he has learnt. *"It's a tragedy, Sam. Our telepathy is not always easy to handle or to bear. I agree - it must have been Vincent Stewart you heard."*

"But how ...?"

"The human mind ... it's a mystery. No-one really knows how it works."

"But if I'd realised ..."

"It would have made no difference. There was nothing you could have done. Even if you had realised what was happening, and I don't see how you could, how could you have found the ward in time? You couldn't even walk. And what could you possibly have said to make them believe you?"

"But I thought being telepathic was a gift and that it would be good."

"And in the main it is. But special people often have to bear the downside of being different. Artists, composers, sportsmen – just think how many times you hear of them suffering because of their special talents. You have to be strong, Sam."

"I don't feel strong right now."

"No, of course not. But don't beat yourself up over something you couldn't control. You've coped so well with everything. Just keep telling yourself there was nothing you could have done. We must talk about this again if it troubles you, and with Emmanuel Cabrieres if you wish."

"But I didn't ask for any of this. I've been kidnapped, people who come to rescue me get killed, I hear dying people screaming for help. I don't want this, Ngozi, I really don't want this."

"I understand ..."

"Do you? Do you really? Ngozi, I can't even lose my temper now in case I start a riot. Now I can't go to a hospital in case I hear ... voices. Right now, Ngozi, I want out."

"Sam. I do understand. And I'm so sorry, but there is no way out. You can't switch it off. You have no choice but to learn to cope. You can do it; I know you can. I believe in you, Sam. You're a very gifted person, and you're strong. You're handling all this stuff – you're managing it. Stay brave, Sam. You'll get through this."

Sam hopes this is right but that night, for the first time since he was a child, he cries as he falls asleep. His remarkable power ... at first it had seemed a fascinating addition to his life. Tonight it seems more of a burden than a blessing.

And when Sam's parents come upstairs themselves, they hear him murmuring in his sleep 'still alive ... don't kill me" and they look at each other with concern. They assume he is dreaming about the kidnapping.

Their son has had too much happen to him in too short a period. They are worried about him.

But neither they nor Sam himself have any idea how worried they should really be.

CHAPTER 30 – A WALK IN THE PARK

Sam's priority is to get some rest and, thankfully, that's what everyone else thinks too. Gratefully, therefore, he stays indoors as much as possible. His sister Rachel is put under strict instructions to keep her noise down – a partially successful exercise, as ever.

Ashley leaves hospital on Friday and the Police guard is removed from the Wrights' home.

Tariq phones. "Missed you at school."

"I've had 'flu. Thanks for phoning."

"Actually you haven't missed much. School's been winding down all week. No homework –Dad's really suspicious. But something weird has happened. Three times I passed Nathan Warren in the corridor – couldn't avoid him. I expected the usual crap – you know, insults or him barging into me. But ... nothing!"

Sam grins but keeps his voice calm. "Really? That's interesting."

"Nothing at all! He walked past like I wasn't there – ignored me completely. Couldn't believe it."

"That's great, Tariq. Looks like he's going to lay off you. I'm glad."

"You're glad? If this keeps up, I'll be over the moon! I'll be able to do normal stuff again. What the hell did you say to him?"

"Nothing really."

"Come on ... "

"Just that he was letting himself down and people expect better of him and his family. You know – the usual. Seems he understood."

"BULL. SHIT!" scoffs Tariq in capital letters. "You're telling me that the Warrens respond to reason? That's crap and you know it!"

"Apparently not. Seems there's a good side to everyone" says Sam happily. "You just have to find it."

"Sam, you're hiding something."

"Like what?"

"I don't know. But you are. Tell me."

"Well, when you decide what it is, you let me know. I'd be interested in what you come up with."

Tariq pauses. "One other thing you missed."

"Oh?"

"Assembly - the Football cup was shown and Masterson reported on the game. People cheered when you were mentioned."

The football cup – that seems an age ago! But Sam is sorry to have missed that.

On Saturday Sam leaves the house for the first time in days to keep his appointment in the park with Emmanuel Cabrieres. They sit on the same benches where Sam took the tests.

Emmanuel leads the conversation: "I know, of course, about the events of this week, and how Ngozi helped the Police to find you."

"It was brilliant, the way she handled things."

"She did well. Very well indeed. The story has been passed to me on our network – Ngozi told you about this?"

"Not really. She mentioned it. Is there something I need to know?"

"Not much. It is simply what it says. Some of us have more than one partner so we can take a message from one person and pass it to the other. I have taken it on myself to make a map, as it were, of the network ... it is on my computer, though I am nervous about it even existing. Be that as it may, one of Ngozi's partners is in Mexico and he has another: Mr. Ahmed, who is also my contact. So the information came to me through Ngozi, a man in Mexico and Mr. Ahmed."

"So can I get a message to you any time?"

"Always, just as I arranged to meet you here. It might take a few hours, depending on what the members of the network are doing. They have been known to sleep, you know!"

The fact that he can contact Emmanuel is comforting.

The Frenchman looks thoughtful: "Now, I understand that you had a most difficult experience – a very sad one - at the hospital? Ngozi did not tell me all the details but said you might wish to talk about it. She felt it had distressed you."

Sam is grateful to be able to talk to someone face-to-face. He's had to keep this experience bottled up inside him. He retells what happened and his belief that Vincent Stewart had been alive when his life support was switched off.

M Cabrieres is genuinely shocked. "This is a most upsetting story and an awful experience for you. It is quite natural that you feel bad."

"It doesn't matter how I feel – it's the poor family. They tried to stop it happening. They believed he was still alive. They were right – and I know they were."

M Cabrieres places his hand on Sam's shoulder and speaks quietly. "Yes. Sadly, you know they were right. You and you alone know this. They must never be told, of course. Not only would it reveal your telepathy, my friend, it would also break their hearts. This secret must stay with you, Ngozi and me."

"I know. I won't say anything."

"Good. In time, they will come to accept that the doctors were right. Till then, they have the comfort that they did everything they could. We will do nothing to take that comfort away from them. You agree?"

Sam nods, miserably.

"But, Sam, my friend, this is another mystery. This Monsieur Stewart – he was not a member of our community, I think. But you heard his voice, in your head. That is most unusual. Have you heard other people too - people who are not telepathic like us?"

"No. The only answer I can think of is that Vincent Stewart was telepathic, but he'd never found a partner. Perhaps his ability was only weak, so he never discovered it. He was telepathic but he didn't know."

"Yes. That is possible." Emmanuel looks relieved. "Then I expect this experience to be a one-off. The circumstances – they were exceptional after all."

Sam looks at him quizzically. The Frenchman is speaking very cautiously. He senses an unease. Does M Cabrieres think Sam's telepathic abilities are developing still further? In another direction?

His friend is still speaking "... can you come to terms with this sad event? Do you wish to talk more about it?"

"No. I'll cope. I have to. But I'll never forget it. The screams ... the poor man was terrified. I've never known such a feeling of fear, panic, hopelessness. It's too sad for words ..."

"I understand."

Sam punches the wooden arm of the bench angrily. "No, you bloody well don't understand! You can't! You can't imagine what it's like to hear terror like that pumping into your head. Dammit, I didn't want to know he was still alive. I didn't ask to be involved."

"No, of course not. I said a foolish thing: I cannot understand what it was like. I wanted only to offer some sympathy."

"You know, I'm sick to death with all this. I'm fed up thinking about it, going over and over it, again and again and again. It's too much. It's not fair!"

Emmanuel looks at Sam with concern. Is the boy breaking under the strain? Goodness knows, no-one should be surprised. He speaks gently: "It is natural that you should feel this way. Of course it is. In your place, I should feel just the same."

"I told Ngozi that I want out of all this."

"Do you still feel like that?"

"Pretty much."

"You wish me to go?"

Sam pauses. "No. Sorry. You're the only person I can talk to face-to-face. I just ... need things to be less difficult. I want to be normal again."

"I'm afraid that is not possible, Sam. You are not normal. You can never go back to how you were. I am sorry, but that is the truth."

They sit in silence for some minutes.

"OK. I'm not normal and I never will be." Sam sighs. "Weren't you going to give me some information ... about the Emotist?"

M Cabrieres nods. "Indeed, I came here intending to. But perhaps this is not the right time? So much has happened to you, and the story I was planning to tell you – it is very serious. You have enough on your mind already."

Sam shakes his head wearily. "No, go on. You'll have to tell me some time. It might as well be now."

"You are sure?"

"Yes. Otherwise it will be another thing for me to worry about. Tell me and let's get it over with. Hah! That's what the guy with the knife said – let's get this over with."

"Very well. Then let me start by saying that this is a true story about one of our community who went – how do you say – off the rails. You understand? What I am about to tell you - it really happened."

Sam nods.

"Very well." M Cabrieres leans close. "I shall illustrate it with a tale that is impossible, but nevertheless true. I want you to imagine a scene. Three years ago, a criminal in this country ... a very clever person but an evil man, was being taken from one prison to another.

"This man looked normal but inside he was quite mad ... a psychopath who would kill without remorse. In the twisted mind of such a man, everything revolves around him. He is never wrong: it is the world that is out of step. If someone slights him, he can justify to himself the most outrageous revenge. And that revenge – it is what drove this man.

"Now you must prepare to be shocked, Sam. He was in a van designed for transporting dangerous people securely. The most likely time for a criminal to escape is when he is already outside the prison. So these vehicles – they are very strong."

Sam nods. This seems obvious. "I've seen them, from the outside at least. There's a prison here in Winchester."

"Very well. Then you understand." Emmanuel Cabrieres continues: "Here is a picture I took from the internet." He passes a diagram to Sam. "It shows the inside of one of these vehicles."

Sam studies the picture. The prisoner sits in a cell with room only for one person. There is a small square window. He is handcuffed to a rail inside the cell. The cell door is locked. Outside sit three guards. In extreme cases the guards will be armed, and they will shoot if the prisoner tries to escape. In the front are a driver and a navigator. They have a radio to tell the Police where they are and to call for help if they require it.

Emmanuel pauses, meaningfully. "So we have one prisoner, handcuffed and locked in a small cell and five trained and experienced men to guard him and drive the van. It is impossible that anyone could escape from this, is it not?"

Sam is not in the mood for rhetorical questions. He just wants the facts, short and simple. "And?" he snaps impatiently.

"And ... he escaped, of course." M Cabrieres shrugs.

"An ambush? A crash?"

"No, he acted alone."

"I don't understand."

"The van - it never arrived at its destination. The radio – the guards never used it.

"When the van failed to arrive, a search was started. But it was not on its expected route. It was only discovered the following day. It had been driven off a country lane and parked under trees where it would not be seen. The prisoner was gone. The five Officers were in the back of the van ..."

"Dead?" breathes Sam, as they walk slowly. "He killed them?"

"No, not dead ... worse than that."

Sam looks startled.

"Oh, yes – be shocked, my friend. What was done to them - it was worse than death." M Cabrieres shakes his head, sadly. "They were locked in the van. There was no mark on them. They were handcuffed together and they were weeping."

"Crying? Grown men? Because their prisoner escaped?"

"No. They did not weep because they had lost their prisoner. They wept because they had lost their minds."

Sam gasps and looks with horror at the Frenchman.

"You start to understand. Shall I continue?"

Sam nods but as the scene unfolds his interest turns to fear.

Each of the guards had suffered a complete mental breakdown. Their minds, their very souls, were destroyed. Their prisoner had used his powerful mental ability to torture them, to fill their heads with fear and despair and such intolerable sadness; more misery and despair than any man could bear. He bombarded their senses with the most powerful and destructive emotions till their minds could cope no longer, and they broke."

Sam feels a cold chill run down his spine. M Cabrieres looks at him sombrely. "You understand the horror of this, I think. To this day not one of these poor wretches has recovered, nor will they ever. Their lives are wrecked, their families ripped apart. These men are alive, though 'existing' would be a better word, only because they are heavily drugged. Each has attempted to kill himself, some more than once.

"You understand why I say it is worse than death? At least if they had died, their families could have grieved and rebuilt their lives. These poor creatures are alive but with destroyed minds in healthy bodies. What has been done to them – it is a permanent torture."

"That's – terrifying!"

"Yes, it is. 'Terrifying' is a good description. But not just that – it is utterly, utterly wicked. Evil. So evil that I shudder at the thought of it. He could have killed them, of course, but instead he chose to destroy their minds and leave them to live out decades of suffering and mental agony."

M Cabrieres takes Sam's arm again. "Can you imagine the viciousness of a person who would do such a thing? The cold-blooded ruthlessness of such a man? Such a vile creature is, in my opinion, the most dangerous person in the world and certainly the most evil.

"Understand, my friend. This man can kill without striking a blow. He can destroy a person using no physical force. He leaves no mark, no evidence. His mind is the weapon and with it he devastates his victims."

"But why didn't you warn the Police about him?" asks Sam. "Those five men - they never stood a chance ..."

M Cabrieres looks sad. "A good question. Alas, at the time of his escape we did not yet know that he could do this. Had we known, we would have found a way to warn the authorities; of course we would – we are not irresponsible. But before his escape, before the killings started, no-one had any idea of what was to come. When he was convicted, we knew him only as a member of our community who had tried to rob a bank. We had no idea he would develop this other ability. That happened in prison."

He looks intensely at Sam. "Have you seen inside a prison, my friend?"

Sam shakes his head.

"Believe me, it is not a good place to be. Men are locked in their cells and spend long hours each day with nothing to do. They have much time to think, to plot. Some plan for how they will live better lives when they are released. Some plan their escape. Other plan for revenge. This man used the time to develop his mental power.

"As he learnt what he could do, he practiced on the other prisoners. Sometimes he generated fights, another time a riot. But each time these things happened, the culprit was sitting in his cell or watching from the landing above, apparently playing no part. The prison staff had no idea what he was doing. He was too clever to attract suspicion to himself. They thought he was a model prisoner and they even downgraded his security status.

"For two years this man developed his power until he judged it was powerful enough to enable him to escape. His plan was simple: he needed the authorities to take him outside the walls. As soon as that happened, he would be as good as free. Therefore, he made people believe he was a reformed character. The Governor authorised him to be moved to a lower security prison. To move him they put him in a van and drove him out. That was all he wanted; all he needed.

"Through the window in the van, he watched to see where they were. In a quiet country area, he used his mental power to disable the driver and the guards. He broke their minds.

"As broken men they did as he told them. The driver stopped the van. The guards unlocked his cell and freed him from his handcuffs. They let him go. He then put the driver and navigator in the back and used the guards' own handcuffs to bind them together.

"He drove the van well off its planned routes and found a deserted country lane where he left it out of sight. After making a big show of thanking the guards for the lift, mocking them, he looked into the back of the van simply to torture their minds one last time. Then he walked away. When the van was found the following day, the guards were still in it, sobbing in despair. The keys were never found."

"He just walked away?"

"He just walked away. It was completely – how do you say – hushed up of course."

"Difficult to explain five people having mental breakdowns at the same time".

"Quite."

"But if it was hushed up, how come you know about it?" asks Sam.

"Because he is one of us. This evil man – he had a telepathic partner just as you and I do. Although she was not talking to him, he boasted to her about what he had done. That is how we know."

"Where did this happen?" asks Sam.

"Close by. He was being taken from a prison on your - White Island?"

"Isle of Wight?"

"That is it. Those are the facts of this matter, my friend. For two years, there has been an evil madman on the loose, a criminal who controls peoples' emotions – a psychopath with no conscience about destroying peoples' minds by using his mental power."

"And that could be what I felt during that demonstration in Reading?"

"What do you think?" asks M Cabrieres.

The question needs no answer.

"But why was he directing the crowd against that Police Sergeant in Reading?"

"Ah. Another good question. You felt another emotion that day, I think?"

"Revenge."

"Yes. Revenge. That is it. It consumes him – he will avenge himself against everyone who played a part, no matter how small, in his capture. The Sergeant was one of the men who arrested him."

"Oh."

"Quite."

"That's incredible."

"Reading was the first time this man had been sighted in two years – but the Sergeant recognised him straight away. That is why he ran into the crowd and was so nearly killed. But the Sergeant was lucky. He is the first and only person ever to survive such an attack."

"He's killed other people?"

"Oh yes. The Sergeant's partner in the car that chased this man – his was a most bizarre death. He died on a fairground ride; a ghost train. We think the Emotist joined him in the dark. The poor man died of fright – literally scared to death on a fairground ride, in front of his two young daughters. Terrible. Terrible." Emmanuel shakes his head.

"I saw that on the news."

"Indeed. And the Judge that sentenced him apparently fell, or jumped, or was pushed from a motorway bridge. If the fall didn't kill him, the two lorries that hit him certainly did."

Sam winces.

"Your Police advised everyone else associated with the case to go into hiding, to keep this evil man from finding and killing them too. Even so, more have died - three members of the jury and one of his defence team. In Reading there would have been another victim to add to the list, but you were there."

Sam says softly: "But at the end of the demonstration, I felt a different feeling – one of surprise – of puzzlement."

M Cabrieres' eyes cloud over and he looks desperately sad. "Yes, Sam. When you told me this I felt a sense of horror. I fear for you. I fear that this evil man is now certain that you exist – another person with Emotist powers – someone with the same ability that he possesses.

"In Reading, he was puzzled that, for the first time, someone had defied him. He had never failed before. The puzzlement you felt was this man wondering who could resist him. So now I must tell you, though it grieves me to do so – he will be looking for you, too."

"Oh shit..."

"I warn you, Sam; now he knows you exist, this man will not rest till he finds you."

"And then?"

"He will most certainly try to kill you."

Though Sam expected that answer, the brutal truth still shocks him to the core. He forces himself not to react. His mind is whirling: his pulse is racing: his heart is beating like a hammer. Suddenly he can put together the strands of everything he has learnt over the past few weeks.

"This prisoner who escaped." he asks quietly. "Is his name Donovan Chatsworth?"

"Mon Dieu!" M Cabrieres takes three paces backwards and collapses onto a bench as if he had been pole-axed. "How could you know this?"

"You mentioned he was in a failed bank robbery." Sam relates the contents of the newspaper article that Maddy found. The bank robbery. The chase. The threat Chatsworth made in court.

"Then yes. This is the truth. The man I described is Donovan Chatsworth." He stands and grabs Sam's shoulders: "For God's sake, Sam - tell me you have not been trying to find him. Tell me that is not why you were in Reading!"

"No. Nothing like that. I want nothing to do with him."

The Frenchman breathes a sigh of relief.

Sam explains why they were investigating Maddy's Uncle Frank. "And now that you have told me about Donovan Chatsworth, what I think is this: Maddy's Uncle, Frank James, genuinely did help to foil the robbery. He gave evidence at the trial. When Chatsworth escaped and the killings started, the Police warned him that he was in danger. He would be on Chatsworth's list. They advised him to go into hiding.

"So, the story about him committing suicide is a lie. But a well-intentioned lie - it's a cover story. Frank James is alive and well, but he's in hiding – trying to avoid a man who is determined to kill him and who could do it in an instant. Maddy's father has rented out the house in Purley and when he meets his brother, he's handing over money for him to live on."

M Cabrieres looks thoughtful. "I cannot say whether this is true or not, but it is a theory that fits all the facts. The prisoner was, as you say, Donovan Chatsworth. His obsession is to track down everyone who was connected with his capture. He is quite, quite mad."

"Prison did that to him?"

"Alas no." M Cabrieres looks sad. "I fear that I did that to hm."

"You?"

"Yes, it was I and not the prison that turned him mad, bad though prison was. You see, Chatsworth never worried about being jailed. He had no fear about being locked away – even solitary confinement held no terror for him. He was a telepath, you understand. He thought he would never be alone, not even in prison. When you were locked in your prison; the cellar; you had Ngozi, no?"

Sam nods. Talking to her had been a huge comfort. "But what could you do to make him go mad?"

Again M Cabrieres looks weary. This is difficult for him. "What turned him mad was that his telepathic partner refused to talk with him. On my instructions. He could feel her presence but not talk. You can understand how this was a terrible punishment?"

Sam nods.

"Try to imagine your life now without Ngozi. Your telepathic partner is always there for you. Because of Ngozi, you will never experience loneliness, Sam."

Sam nods again.

M Cabrieres looks wistful. "Never to be lonely ... I think that is the greatest blessing for which a person can hope. I have seen many lonely people, Sam. They are so sad – so desolate – so lost. They crave the attention of others and when it does not come, each day they retreat a little more into themselves until they become shut off, isolated, bitter and so, so unhappy. Eventually they are not able to deal with company even when they are offered it. Loneliness – it is an awful thing.

"But Donovan Chatsworth did not fear loneliness - he thought he would survive the long days locked in a cell, because he could talk with his telepathic partner. On my instructions that comfort was taken away. For the first time in years, he was truly alone. He was not prepared for it. Caged and isolated, he experienced a loneliness far greater than any other man has ever endured. In his solitude and his anger, he reached out with his mind trying to find others. But he failed."

Sam feels a shudder of horror as he imagines what this must have been like. The loneliness. The desolation. He pictures Donovan Chatsworth lying in his cell, desperately trying to communicate with someone ... anyone ... alone ... lonely, so lonely ... in despair.

The Frenchman has continued: "...and the more he reached out with his powerful mind for someone new, the more he developed his other power. He found that when he was angry, which was often, fights would start around him. When he was sad, people near him became depressed also. And if he was happy, people would laugh and joke. But mostly, he was angry and he was sad.

"Chatsworth turned into an evil madman with a special power, and with regret I confess that my decision helped make him that way. Each day since I have asked myself if I did wrong."

"How many other people have this power?" asks Sam.

"In the world – only one other living person, as far as I know."

"Me?"

"You. And I give thanks that you are not evil like him. You use your powers to help people. He uses them to kill and destroy."

A cold shiver of fear runs through Sam. "So what happens next?"

"Chatsworth is growing bolder. He has risked being seen in public. I must watch for him. He must be caught and kept away from any other living person for the rest of his life sedated so that he never again uses his power."

"Will the courts do that?"

"No, not the courts. No court can try him for his crimes, because the truth is too difficult – it can never be made public. Besides, he must not be allowed in a public place like a courtroom. Think what he might do. And who would believe the truth of this matter anyway? A man that kills people with his mind? No, our community must do it. For the protection of the world, we must catch this man ourselves."

"We? You want me to help?"

"Mais non!" M Cabrieres lapses into French again and almost shouts the words. He looks anxiously around. Has he attracted attention? No. He adds more quietly: "No, Sam. I do not want your help. The very opposite - I forbid it! I cannot and will not involve you. Oh, there are some of my colleagues who have asked if you are the person to rid us of this evil madman. But I say no. I will not risk the life of a fourteen-year-old. Your future lies before you and I will not jeopardise it. If you met this man, he would not think twice before killing you – or worse, and you now know what that means.

"My instruction to you is not to get involved. Stay away. I do not often ask this, my friend, but on this I want your word; I need you to promise that you will do as I say."

Sam is relieved. He has no wish to get involved. He nods. "Yes, of course."

Emmanuel Cabrieres continues: "Thank you. In any event, you do not know that you can match him. You surprised him in Reading. You will not do that again. He is strong – he has been using his power for years but you are only just discovering yours. In a contest between the two of you, I am certain that he would prevail – in short, he would end your life. Believe that, my friend.

"So I shall find a way to control Chatsworth that does not involve you. We cannot and will not risk you. You must not interfere. You promise me this, yes?"

"Absolutely."

"Good. I will not allow further debate, Sam. On this I am unanimous."

Sam smiles.

Emmanuel continues: "You must go home and live your life as normally as you can. You will not tell your parents or your friend Maddy or her family about this. You must be silent about these things."

More secrets!

"Do we know where Chatsworth is living? Reading isn't far away, after all."

"No we don't. But you are right: he may be there."

Sam looks the Frenchman in the eye "After what you've just told me, isn't it likely that Donovan Chatsworth was the person coming to see me when Ashley and I were kidnapped?"

"I pray you are wrong, but I fear you are right."

"Then he already knows who I am and where I live."

"Possibly. Probably."

"That's bad. But I can't go into hiding, can I? Not without telling everyone about ... this stuff."

"No. We must find a way to protect you."

"And I have another question – how did Chatsworth know that I would be at the BMX track last Sunday?"

"That is a mystery. Perhaps they are watching your house?"

"Haven't seen anyone."

"Then I do not know. But you must be careful; look out for strangers who may be watching you. From now on, if you go out, do not go alone. Always let Ngozi know where you are going. Sam, my friend, if what we fear is true, you are in danger. Mortal danger."

"I know. I've felt what he can do."

"Then you understand why you must take great care and not seek out this evil man."

Sam knows only too well. But though he has promised not to get involved, he has a cold dread that the Frenchman will never be able to capture or control Donovan Chatsworth.

Sam will avoid it for as long as he can, but he knows that one day he will have to face Chatsworth down.

Till that day he can never be truly free again.

CHAPTER 31 – THE WHITE CAR

nspector Murphy sits on the train with Detective Jones. She whispers: "I thought MI5 was in Legoland?"

"Six."

"Sorry?"

"MI6. MI5 is Thames House in Millbank. It used to be offices for Imperial Chemical Industries."

"The security! I've never seen anything like it."

"Not surprised given what goes on in there."

"The guy that briefed us – John Smith?"

"Yeah, right."

"But what he said. It's unbelievable!"

"Until Chatsworth escaped I would have agreed with you. But the reason I asked for today's meeting is that I helped to investigate the trail of human wreckage he left in his wake, God help me. I met the prison guards whose minds he destroyed. That was one of the most disturbing experiences of my life. Couldn't sleep for days." He shakes his head sadly. "No, I'm afraid it's all too real. I asked for you to work with me."

"And the boy. Another?"

"Christ, no. At least, I hope not."

"I understand now why we have to report things like the intervention of a medium. I'm glad they're watching out for stuff like that."

"Me too. I'll believe the stuff about Chatsworth. But the boy – I can't believe that. I don't even want to think about it."

"Me neither. But our orders are clear: watch him like a hawk."

He's seen it many times, but the film Sam is half-watching is a favourite and its easy familiarity helps to put recent events out of his mind. It is Sunday evening and Sam is determined to spend it relaxing - doing nothing. Or as near to nothing as he can manage. So, he passes most of the evening lying on his bed.

Rachel has taken possession of one of the house phones and is sitting on the stairs, talking. Sam can't help but hear snippets of the conversation - how do young girls manage to spend so long saying so little?

Eventually their mother loses patience too. After signals that are at first subtle and then not-so-subtle, tapping of watches and annoyed glances, she shouts. "Rachel – you've got a mobile – why don't you use that?"

Rachel puts her hand over the phone. "I'm out of credit. This is important. One of my friends has a problem."

"Out of credit already? Then get her to call you back on your mobile. But get off that phone right now. And check whether anyone has been trying to get us."

"M-uu-um."

"Off - now."

Silence.

"Well, did anyone phone?"

With bad grace Rachel mumbles "Maddy."

"Sam! Maddy phoned." His mother calls up the stairs.

Sam falls off his bed in a tangle of arms and legs. "When?"

"Don't know. Rachel was on the phone a long time."

Shit! Sam's mobile is downstairs in his jacket. That was stupid ... if this call is what he fears it is, Maddy will have tried to get him on that as well. He runs down.

Dammit, Maddy had called twice. She left two messages.

"Sam." Maddy whispers intensely in the first. "There's been one of those calls, you know what I mean? First time on a Sunday. Ring back please. If you don't answer, I'll have to go out by myself. I'm going to try your house phone now."

The second message is shorter, but very clear. "Sam, where the hell are you? Your house phone is engaged and you're not answering your mobile. I'm going out the back door. Call me back. Please." That was ten minutes ago.

Sam curses. He's angry: surely Rachel must have heard the beeps of someone trying to get through? He kicks on his trainers. Not waiting for a response, he shouts "going to see Maddy" and dashes out the front door and down the road. He rings Maddy's mobile as he runs. No answer.

Sam swears again. Rain is lashing down and in his rush he didn't bring a coat. His shirt is soaked through in seconds. Well, he's not going back: his Mum will try to get him to change and he doesn't have time.

The white car isn't in the street where he watched it last time. Of course it isn't – if their objective is secrecy, they'll change the location each time. That's just great – the rain is tipping down and they could be anywhere within walking distance of Maddy's house. Sam runs further up the main road towards Mr. James' office, checking the side streets as he goes. The white car is nowhere to be seen. Neither is Maddy. Nor her father.

That was a waste of time!

OK, think it through. In this weather, they're likely to choose somewhere closer to Maddy's house rather than further away. Shivering now, Sam retraces his steps and heads in the other direction.

Two cars drive past, but neither is white. Curious faces stare at the young man in the wet shirt. Heaven knows what they make of him. There is no sign of the white car parked at the side of the road, nor Maddy nor her father.

He jogs on, in the direction of Maddy's house, checking the side roads as he goes. He runs past.

Still nothing.

This is useless. He can't check every road in the neighbourhood. He's soaked to the skin. His hair is plastered to his face. It's senseless to keep looking. He stands in the middle of the road and wipes the rain from his eyes. Maddy's father and the mystery man could be anywhere. His chances of finding them are too low. He turns back. He'll dry off indoors and apologise to Maddy later. What other choice does he have?

But as he trudges back, past Maddy's house, suddenly, there it is! Turning a corner comes the white car, moving slowly towards him. A few seconds later Maddy runs from the same street, sprinting as fast as she can after the car. She sees Sam and screams.

"Sam! That car ... stop it ... Dad's in it!"

There is only one way to do as Maddy wants. Sam steps in front of the white car and holds out his arms. It makes to move to the other side of the road and drive round him, but there's a van coming in the opposite direction.

The driver has two choices. He can mow Sam down, or he can stop. He stops.

Sam doesn't move. He puts his hands on the car bonnet, as much in relief as anything else. This situation is for Maddy to handle – it's her father in the car, after all. It takes a minute for her to catch up. She arrives, gasping heavily from sprinting down the road. Like Sam, she has no coat and is wet through, her blonde hair sticking to her face and darkened by the rain. Breathlessly, she pulls open the passenger door.

"Hi Dad" she pants. And turning to the driver: "good to see you again, Uncle Frank."

"God dammit!" Frank James bangs his head on the steering wheel. "Curse my stupidity. Frank James, you're a fool. You were right, Ted. I should have listened to you."

Edward James is furious: "Oh, you two, you've no idea what damage you've just caused or the danger we're all in now. You are meddling in things you don't understand. Get in quickly; let's stop attracting attention to ourselves."

Sam is about to do as he's been told when he hears footsteps approaching. It's his father sheltering under a huge umbrella. "Sam, what the hell are you doing dashing out on a night like this without a coat?" Then he sees who's in the car. "Oh."

"Oh, indeed" says Edward James.

Recovering his composure, Sam's father speaks through the car door. "Evening, Frank. Good to see you again. How are you keeping?"

Sam looks at his father, wide eyed. His father has known, all along?

Frank James says wearily: "You'd better get in as well, George. In fact, why don't we invite the whole bloody street to join us?"

As Sam and his father get into the car, a voice in his head says "Sam? Are you alright?"

"Hi Ngozi. Yes, no problem."

"What's going on? Fallen in front of another bus?"

"No. I stepped in front of a car. It stopped."

"I knew something was happening. Stepping in front of a car sounds pretty stupid. Any particular reason? Tired of living?"

"Maddy's Uncle Frank was driving it."

"Ah." Ngozi pauses. "Well, that answers one of your questions. Now you should get a load more answered. Speak soon? This'll be interesting."

"Sure. Later."

Maddy sits in the back of the car with Sam and his father. "Where to, now?" says Frank James, drumming his fingers angrily on the steering wheel. His gold rings glint in the light.

"You were taking me home. Back there, I suppose" mutters Maddy's father. "You'd better come too" he says to Sam and his father. "Maddy and Sam – you two have meddled in something you know nothing about and now you've caused a real problem."

"Don't be too hard on them. I took the risk" interrupts Frank. "It's my fault. But it will be good to see Jan again. It's been a long time."

Edward James runs into the house and switches off the hall lights. Only then does his brother hurry after him, head down. Jan James's eyes widen and fill with tears when she sees her brother-in-law. She hugs him: "Frank! It's been so long! How are you?"

"Not so good, but better for seeing you, Jan. I've been pretty low, actually. These last two years have got me down."

"I know, Ted told me. It must be horrible."

"I don't know how much more I can take. But these two" - he points at Maddy and Sam – "these two interfering young busybodies must have been spying on Ted, and they followed him. So here I am ..."

Frank James looks at Maddy. "Aren't you surprised to see me? What's it like, talking to a dead man?"

Maddy shakes her head: "Sam and I worked weeks ago that you weren't dead. I'm so pleased."

Her parents are shocked, but her Uncle stays calm. "Ah. And how, pray, do you know that?"

"There was nothing in the papers. And we saw you a few weeks ago – or rather Sam did. He described you - there's not many men with, sorry, a bald head, a Manchester United sticker in the car and chunky gold rings on their right hands, you know, who meet Dad on street corners at night."

"Do you have the slightest idea what's been going on these last couple of years?"

"No. Not really. At first I had believed that you were well, dead, because that's what Mum and Dad told me. But then I found out that you're not and I'm glad. But no, I don't really know what's been going on."

"And you, Sam. Do you have any idea what's been happening – what you're meddling in?"

"Yes" says Sam simply, and Maddy looks at him, wide eyed.

"Yes? This should be good. Tell us then?"

"You're hiding from Donovan Chatsworth."

"For God's sake, Sam. How do you know that?" It isn't often that his father loses it. George Wright takes a deep breath to calm himself. "Sorry. I assure you, Ted, Frank, Jan – Helen and I have said nothing. Not a word" He turns back to Sam: "You'd better tell us what you've been up to."

Maddy looks at Sam, quizzically.

Sam takes a deep breath. "OK, here's what we know ..."

"You've been to my house?"

"Yes."

"Frank, I assure you, we had no idea."

"Anyhow, you've been in hiding till Chatsworth is caught. Mr. James has been renting out your house in Purley and he's been meeting you to give you the money so you can live under cover. You've been phoning on nights when you can meet him."

"For God's sake Sam ... how the hell do you know all that? It's private." Sam has never heard Edward James so angry before.

"You'd better tell us everything you've been up to" demands Frank.

So Sam and Maddy tell their families about the real reason for their trip to Reading, how they spoke to the tenants of the house in Purley and how they know the house is being rented out by Edward James. Maddy shows the newspaper article about Donovan Chatsworth. The more they speak, the more everyone looks at the two young people in astonishment.

"Good grief" mutters Maddy's father. "I thought our plan for hiding you was fool-proof. How wrong I was!"

"It was fool-proof. But it wasn't idiot proof" sighs Frank James. "And I'm the idiot. I let my loneliness get the better of me. I thought that if I phoned at different times and we met just briefly, I could keep in touch at least a little. I was going stir crazy with no-one to talk to. I needed to see a friendly face, at least for a few minutes, or I'd have gone mad. I've been so lonely, you see."

Sam winces. That's what Emmanuel Cabrieres said. Loneliness – it is an awful thing.

Frank James continues: "Ted was angry with me: he said it was dangerous for me to come here and meet him and I shouldn't take risks like that ..."

That explains why the two seemed to be arguing.

"... and he was right, of course. And Maddy, he wanted to protect you. He didn't want Donovan Chatsworth taking a shot at me and including you as collateral damage."

Maddy gasps. The lie her father told was to protect her as well as his brother.

"I can see now that I was wrong. It was selfish and I've put you all in danger. So, I have to go away again - and this time, Ted, I'll keep to the rules we originally agreed."

When Maddy protests, her Uncle continues: "Maddy, you have no idea how much danger I'm in. The man who is after me is evil. He kills without even thinking about it. Would I do all this, otherwise?"

Maddy shakes her head glumly.

Sam thinks grimly how necessary it is for Frank James to hide. He's felt the effects of having his mind touched by Chatsworth. So has Maddy, though she doesn't know it. Her Uncle Frank really has no alternative. He will have to disappear again. It's desperately sad and utterly unjust. Once again, the innocent suffer while the guilty walk free. But this is how it must be.

Frank James shakes his head slowly: "It's been wonderful to see you all again, but I can't risk involving you anymore." He turns to Sam's father: "George. My thanks to you and Helen for keeping my secret. But these two worked it out. And if they can work it out, so can others."

The last piece of the jigsaw slots into place. Of course; his parents have known all along. That explains why Sam's mother gasped when she heard the name of the Sergeant who was almost killed in Reading.

Maddy's uncle turns to his niece: "Maddy, you're no longer a little girl. You're old enough now to know the truth and handle it. Support your Dad. You know he'd never do anything wrong. He's been helping me and risking himself. You should be proud of him."

Maddy hangs her head. "I am proud of him." She takes her father's hand. "I was worried for you. I thought ..." She stops. "Oh, Dad, I'm so sorry."

Her father places his arms round her and holds her close.

"Now that you all know my secret, for my sake, please keep it that way. My life depends on it. If anyone asks you about me, please tell them I'm dead. As far as you're concerned, I committed suicide. If you stick to that story you'll help to protect me. Please."

Sam nods. "Of course." They have solved the mystery – but this isn't like a story book where everyone then lives happily ever after. Now he feels more guilt than satisfaction. Maddy nods too, and Sam sees a tear running down her cheek.

Jan James looks close to tears as well. "You couldn't ... just stay tonight? I'll make up the spare room."

"Better not, Jan. But thanks."

"But stay and have something to eat, surely?"

"I'd love to but no." Frank James is firm. "This rain – while it lasts - it's security. If anyone is taking an interest in me, I trust they won't be out there tonight – not in that lot. But I'd better go before it stops."

Jan doesn't argue. She nods sadly. Maddy's father sees his brother to the front door. Frank smiles when as he passes the Manchester United photograph: "I'm pleased to see you're taking proper care of my treasure!"

"Till you take it back again, when this is all over." Edward James hugs his brother. "God, I hope they catch that bastard soon. I swear, if I ever lay my hands on him ..."

"Ted ... if you get within a mile of him, run."

A blast of wind and rain whistles into the house as Maddy's father switches out the light and opens the door. Then Frank James is gone – his head bowed as he sprints through the rain to his white car. Jan and Maddy James are both standing with tissues to their eyes.

Frank James drives slowly away and Sam watches the tail lights fade into the distance. It will be a long time before they see him again – if ever.

CHAPTER 32 – CARNAGE!

"I don't understand." Sam's father is irritated more than puzzled. "I thought you'd answered all their questions. What do they want now?"

"No idea."

"Unless it's something new I'm going to tell them this is the end. It's bad enough that you had to live through that experience without having to go over it again and again."

"Ngozi: I'm going with Dad to the Guildhall." It is a routine now for Sam to report where he is going. *"The police want to meet me there."*

"OK. Let me know that everything is OK."

Mrs. Jobson's curtains twitch, as always, as they leave the house.

"If you must know, we're going to the Guildhall." Sam shouts. "I'm going to be arrested and thrown into jail. Do me a favour ... don't visit."

Old bag!

"Sam, let her be. She's just a harmless eccentric."

"She's not. She's a witch. She eats toads and I've seen her broomstick."

"Sam! Leave it."

The Guildhall is in the centre of Winchester, a City famous as the one-time capital of England. Sam's father parks near the imposing Cathedral, the site of the marriage of Queen Mary I with Philip of Spain. They walk round, past the statue of King Alfred, put there in 1901 to commemorate the ancient King of Wessex who laid down one of the first codes of law in Britain. Alfred stands proud with his sword aloft in the wide road that passes in front of the Guildhall.

In the meeting room they are met by Detective Jones. "Thank you for coming. We won't keep you long."

"What's it about?"

"Just routine."

Sam doesn't believe her. He senses something: she's tense. He sits, as directed, at a table opposite Detective Jones. She wants to hear again how Sam overcame the man with the gun and locked him in the cellar. He repeats the story, conscious that he's adding nothing to what he said before. Detective Jones, having completed her notes, excuses herself and leaves the room. When she returns she has two people with her – a lady and a man in a wheelchair.

"Mr. Wright – Sam - this is Graham Winters. Do you recognise him?"

The name sounds familiar. That's all though. Sam shakes the hand of the man in the wheelchair who introduces the lady as his wife. "Sorry, no. Have we met?"

"Yes, once. You don't remember?"

The face looks familiar, but no.

"I was at the farm. You drove me to the hospital. I'd been shot."

The injured policeman!

"Oh, right. How are you?" Sam bites his tongue. Stupid question - the man is in a wheelchair. "Sorry, I ..."

"Recovering, thank you." Winters points to the chair. "The doctors say I won't be in this for too much longer. Back to work in three months."

"Six" says his wife.

"Thing is, I asked to see you. I wanted to thank you. If you hadn't got me to the hospital when you did, I would have died. I'm only here today because of you."

"I'm sorry there was nothing I could do for the others."

"Yes, me too." Winters pauses. "I also want to say that what you did that day was the bravest thing I've ever seen."

"Sorry?"

Detective Jones looks serious. "Sam, Graham was listening to your explanation just now. We have reason to believe that you haven't been telling us the whole truth about what happened in the yard after you came out of the cellar."

Sam feels clammy and cold. Damn! He thought he'd constructed a cast iron story.

"You told us that after the man shot at you, you persuaded him that there had been enough killings and then locked him in the cellar."

"Yes."

"It seemed unlikely, I have to say." She looks at her colleague. "Graham?"

"That's sort of the truth but not really. Not the whole truth, you might say."

"Were you conscious?" asks Sam's father.

"Yes. I saw everything."

Oh no!

Winters looks at Sam's father. "What actually happened was that the gunman fired at your son. Sam rolled under the car for cover. Then, as the gunman walked round to get a clear shot, your son stood up and, totally unarmed, walked towards him. I was scared stiff: more frightened than I think I've ever felt in my life. Sam walked towards this killer and told him to drop the gun. There'd been enough killing that day, he said.

"In short, Sam faced him down - just walked towards a man who had already killed three people and injured me - almost daring him to shoot again."

He turns to Sam. "I couldn't believe what you were doing. I was terrified. I was sure you'd be killed."

Sam knows why Graham Winters was terrified. It was because Sam had been projecting powerful emotions at the gunman. But Winters couldn't know that.

Sam's father looks stunned. "Is this true?"

Sam nods glumly.

"What happened then?"

Winters continues. "The man dropped the gun. I suppose he was just, well, overawed by Sam's bravery and couldn't bring himself to shoot him in cold blood. Then Sam pushed him down the cellar stairs and locked the door. I have never seen such courage in all my life."

Sam tries to play it down. "Look, I'm just glad it worked out."

"Is this the real truth then?" asks Detective Jones. "You didn't simply talk like you said? You walked towards him and faced him down? An armed man who had killed already?"

"Yes. Look, call it what you like … it's like I said; we talked … he threw the gun down. I'm sorry …"

"You're sorry? You deserve a bloody medal."

"No!" Sam almost shouts. "I mean" he continues more quietly. "I really don't want any publicity - nothing like that."

"Is that why you played down what you did?"

"Suppose so, yes. Yes, that's why."

Graham Winters smiles: "I'd heard that about you. That's why I wanted to see you personally, privately, to say 'thank you'. Away from the Police Station. That's why we got you down here." Winters holds out his hand and Sam takes it.

His wife comes round and kisses Sam on the cheek. "Thank you so much" she says. "I've just found out I'm pregnant. Thanks to you, our baby will know its father."

Winters turns to Sam's father. "You didn't know? He didn't even tell you what really happened?"

"No. First I've heard of it."

The four adults look at Sam in a mixture of puzzlement and admiration.

Sam says: "Can I go now? Have you embarrassed me enough?"

In the entrance area, Sam stops dead in his tracks. His eye is drawn to a poster.

"Have you seen this man?" it reads.

Beneath the bold letters is a photograph of an innocuous looking man - white, in his forties, his hair brushed back severely. A supercilious smirk plays around his lips. But the eyes! The eyes are cold, small, dark and deep. They burn into the observer with a fearsome intensity, even from a photograph.

Below are these words. "This man is extremely dangerous. Do not approach him. If sighted, report immediately and seek armed assistance."

The name of the wanted man is Donovan Chatsworth.

And this is what he looks like! So ... ordinary!

"Do you recognise this person?" Detective Jones is interested in Sam's reaction.

"No. I know the name. But it's the first time I've seen his picture. Any idea where he is?"

"No. How come you know his name?"

George Wright steps in. "We're friends with the James family. Frank James is one of those who's had to go into hiding. Sam knows about that."

"Ah. Then you know that this man is very dangerous. You mustn't approach him." She looks at Sam quizzically. "Have you seen him? If you have, you need to tell us."

"No – I've never seen him." That's the absolute truth.

Sam debates whether to tell Detective Jones that Chatsworth had been in Reading. But how could he, without giving himself away? There's no way to explain. Besides, they will know it by now, through the Police Sergeant who was attacked.

Somehow it's comforting to know what his enemy looks like. But he wants never to hear his name again.

Detective Jones thanks Sam for his time and sees him to the door. As she comes back in, Inspector Murphy is watching.

"That was interesting. Did he recognise the picture?"

"I don't think so, but he knew the name, Sir."

"Doesn't prove anything."

"No it doesn't. His family is friends with one of Chatsworth's targets."

"But we believe that Chatsworth was the person coming to meet the Wright boy. There's CCTV footage of him getting off a train in Winchester and then getting back onto one twenty minutes later. Why is that? What interest could Chatsworth possibly have in Samuel Wright?"

"Wish I knew." Jones pauses. "You're not going to tell his parents, Sir? You're letting them think it was a ransom attempt? If Chatsworth has added Sam Wright to his target list, the boy's as good as dead. You must know that."

"Yes, I know that and no, I'm not going to tell them." He's sees Jones looking quizzically at him. "I know, I know. I'm taking an awful chance. But for some reason Chatsworth is interested enough in Sam Wright to break cover and risk travelling to Winchester to meet him. He didn't want to kill Sam Wright outright – he wanted to talk to him first. What could they possibly have in common that would make Chatsworth want to talk to a fourteen-year-old boy he's never met?"

"No idea. Have you?"

"No ..."

"You have, haven't you?"

"Well, think about what you just heard ... a fourteen-year-old boy with the sheer courage to face down a killer, who gets him to drop his gun?"

"Oh hell: you're starting to think that he's another Chatsworth."

"No. Well, perhaps. Hell, I don't know. But why else would Chatsworth would be so interested in meeting him and having him killed? But that makes Sam Wright our best chance of getting to him."

"You're going to use a fourteen-year-old boy as bait?"

"No choice. There's something strange happening here. I feel it. I mean, think about how we knew where he was. A medium? Really? There's something about Sam Wright we don't know yet. And after that briefing you and I went to in London ..." His voice tails away.

Jones purses her lips. She's glad she's not having to make this decision.

Outside, Sam asks his father: "So, had you seen pictures of him before?"

"Yes."

"And he's the man that forced Maddy's uncle into hiding."

"Yes. Do you understand how dangerous he is?"

"Yes, I know. Don't worry, Dad, I have no intention of going anywhere near him."

George Wright had parked their car near the Wessex Hotel. It is a few minutes' walk round the building they have just left to get there.

They don't make it.

"Oh hell!" In the Broadway, Sam's mind feels as if it is exploding with rage. He staggers as if he's been punched.

Chatsworth!

No matter that Sam has no intention of going anywhere near him: Chatsworth has found him instead! How the hell did he know that Sam was going to be here?

No time to think about that.

As in Reading, everyone is affected. A group of young people, who a few minutes before had been talking and laughing, come together in an ugly brawl. Two women with pushchairs scream abuse at each other. Their babies' wails add to the noise.

Sam feels the anger: it's an artificial emotion. He fights it. The madman is using his mental powers to generate an anger that must surely be turned on him and his father very soon should they in any way make themselves the centre of attention. He has to keep control of himself and get his father away.

George shouts above the noise: "Bloody idiots. Why can't young people behave these days?"

"Dad, let's go back in." Sam tugs at his father's sleeve. If his father does anything to draw attention to the two of them, he and Sam are as good as dead.

And he doesn't want to die.

"Don't you tell me what to do!" His father walks away from the safety of the Guildhall. "Someone should sort those people out. No-one's interested in proper standards these days."

"Dad, please don't get involved." Sam grabs his father's arm. He forcibly makes his father turn round.

"Don't you dare manhandle me! Show some bloody respect." Sam's father is shouting at him. It's not his normal behaviour.

The feeling of rage intensifies. Sam tries to block it from his mind. He knows it's a false emotion, but no-one else does.

From the corner of his eye Sam sees a car swerve from the road and head straight for them. He pushes his father hard into the wall and flattens himself against it.

The car misses them by inches, scrapes the wall and swerves back onto the road. There are screams of fear and then pain as it hits two of the young people who were brawling and therefore not watching. It leaves them lying in the road and careers on without stopping.

"Bloody hell! That lunatic could have killed us" shouts George Wright above the noise. "He'd have had me if you hadn't seen him coming. Idiot!" He shakes his fist.

"Dad. We MUST get away. It's too dangerous here."

He takes his father's arm and together they run down the road.

"Sam - freeze!"

This is the instruction Sam's parents used when he was a child if he was in danger. A petrol tanker has pounded over the roundabout and smashed two cars aside. Travelling absurdly fast it hits the circular kerb surrounding the statue of King Alfred and launches into the air.

The old King has stood for over a century, but is gone in an instant. With a thud that is felt as much as heard, the tanker plunges into the statue. There is a loud crack from the stone plinth and then a screeching of torn metal as King Alfred topples, twisted and mangled by the impact.

The tanker falls off the plinth onto its side and slides along the road towards Sam and his father, destroying the cars parked in the middle of the street. It comes to rest opposite the steps to the Guildhall. Flames lick around it as petrol spills from the wrecked cars and ignites.

"Right, let's go." His father grabs Sam's arm. "If that thing's full, it'll blow." They run into Colebrook Street at the side of the Guildhall.

The flames round the crashed tanker are strong now.

"Ngozi - Chatsworth's here!"

"Where?"

"*Here - Winchester – the City Centre. He tried to kill us after we left the Guildhall. Everyone's going mad - turning violent.*"

"*He must have been waiting for you!*"

"*That's right. How the hell did he know I was here?*"

"*Work it out later. Right now, run! Get away. Leave immediately. He's found you and he means to kill you. Get away from him.*"

"*That's what we're doing, but my father's affected.*"

"*Leave him if you have to.*"

"*I can't do that!*"

"*No, sorry, of course you can't. You must both run for your lives.*"

Sam and his father sprint up Colebrook Street in the direction of the Wessex Hotel and the car park. The Guildhall is now between them and the burning tanker. Almost immediately he feels the waves of anger grow weaker. Have they run out of Chatsworth's sight? They slow to catch their breath.

And then Sam feels again – puzzlement. Just like at Reading. The waves of anger stop.

"What the blazes is going on?" asks Sam's father.

"No idea" lies Sam. "But we need to get away. That tanker will explode soon."

"*Sam!*" It is Ngozi again. "*M Cabrieres agrees. Under no circumstances are you to try to engage with Donovan Chatsworth!*"

"*Believe me; I have no intention of doing that! I'm not a fool. I want nothing to do with him.*"

Sam turns to his father. "There's the car. Let's get the hell out of here."

"*Sam. Emmanuel is coming to help you if he can. Where are you?*"

"*At the car park by the Cathedral – opposite the Wessex Hotel.*"

"*Is Chatsworth following you?*"

"*No... I don't think so ... oh hell, yes! I can't see him, but I can feel him again.*"

Sam has felt a sudden stab of fear – irrational fear. He recognises the false emotion planted in his head by Chatsworth. Sam's father feels it too. It has the effect on him that Chatsworth wants. "I don't think we should use the car. There's something wrong down there." He stops moving, rooted to the spot.

People run past them in blind panic. Guests are pouring from the hotel. A baby screams. People are shouting "Run! Get away!" The street is filled with terrified people running in all directions.

Sam glances hurriedly over his shoulder. Is that Donovan Chatsworth on the other side of the road? No. That man in the track suit? Or that one hiding between the parked cars? No and no. No-one matches the photograph.

Sam's father is scared. "What's going on down there?"

"A false alarm, I expect" lies Sam.

"Don't think so, there's something bad happening. I think ..."

A huge blast comes from the direction of the Guildhall. The fuel tanker has exploded. Father and son duck, sheltering their faces. A fireball rolls towards them down Colebrook Street and dissipates before it reaches them. People who had run towards the Broadway are caught in the flames and fall to the ground, their clothes ablaze.

A shock-wave of hot air rolls up the road and knocks Sam and his father to the ground. Windows shatter and shards of glass fly down. Dozens of burglar alarms trigger and fill the air with a cacophony of sirens and bells.

From the other side of the Guildhall a pillar of smoke is rising, at first mushroom-shaped, like an atomic explosion.

As they straighten, Sam sees that his father has been cut on the head by a splinter of flying glass. A thin line of blood is running slowly down the side of his face.

Sirens blaring, two police cars, race down the street by the side of the hotel and screech to a halt. Chatsworth's influence fades - he is disengaging. He doesn't want to be seen – not yet. Not by the Police.

"*Sam, are you alright?*"

"*Yes. Chatsworth tried again. He failed. He's caused a major panic in the City Centre though. A fuel tanker just exploded. People have been killed in the explosion. Survivors are running all over the place. I dread to think what the main street looks like. I expect it's wrecked. But Chatsworth is backing off.*"

"*Emmanuel Cabrieres is about fifty metres behind you.*"

Sam glances round. The Frenchman is there, with a small, dark lady he hasn't seen before.

"*I see him. What can he do?*"

"*Not much, I'm afraid. He'll watch you and your father back to the car and make sure you're not followed.*"

"Dad, the car! Come on!" Grabbing the keys from his father's hand, Sam forces him to sprint the last few steps. He throws himself into the passenger seat. His father is less fit and follows, panting from the sudden exercise. Sam hands him the key and he fumbles clumsily to get it into the ignition. Eventually he succeeds, crashes the car into gear and speeds down the side street by the Cathedral. They turn right into Bridge Street just as the Police start to block off all the roads.

Sam catches a glimpse of the Broadway as they race away. Flames from the tanker engulf the road. Cars are burning and a thick pall of black smoke is polluting the sky. Some of the historic timber-framed buildings are on fire.

On the way home, Sam is conscious of a car following them. He uses the mirror on the passenger's sun visor to see who it is: thank goodness, it's Emmanuel Cabrieres.

As they pull away from a junction, the car behind apparently stalls. His father thinks nothing of it, even if he notices, but Sam knows – the mistake is deliberate. No-one is following them now.

Back home, the calm of the day is broken by the rattle of helicopters circling the City Centre and the sounds of sirens from the emergency vehicles. The dark cloud of black smoke rising from the burning buildings hangs ominously and then trails away slowly in the wind – a sullen black gash across the blue sky, twisting itself into improbable shapes as if to emphasise the pain of the City below. People stand in their front gardens and watch in disbelieving horror.

Mrs. Jobson is standing outside her front door, telling anyone who will listen that it's the work of teenage hooligans, many of them foreign – people who should never have been allowed into the country. And helped by local people who should know better. She looks pointedly at Sam.

"No, it's a petrol tanker – it crashed."

The old witch snaps at Sam: "And I suppose you know, given all the dealings you've been having with the police lately?"

"Sorry?"

"Oh, don't think I don't know." She turns to George Wright. "Questioned by them again. He must be such a disappointment to you, George."

"No, we were there – we saw what happened. It's just as Sam said. And if Sam tells you something, I expect you to believe it. Didn't you see him in the local papers after saving his friend's life at school?"

"Papers? No – I don't need the words of man. People lie. They do cruel things. The truth I need comes from the Good Book. And let me tell you: there are many people deeply concerned at how your son is bringing down the reputation of our neighbourhood. The Reverend Sherwood and I pray each day that he may find the right path before it is too late."

"Stupid bigot. What brings down the reputation of a neighbourhood is a bitter and twisted old hag who sticks her hooked nose into other peoples' business."

"Sam, leave it. Go in." His father is firm.

Mrs. Jobson smiles thinly. "I do the Lord's work. We who follow the true path are used to being insulted. It's a hazard of the life we have chosen, as the Disciples knew and all the blessed Martyrs. Tonight I shall phone Rev Sherwood again and we will pray that both of you may see the error of your ways and be brought to the true path of salvation. 'I say unto you, that likewise joy shall be in heaven over one sinner that repenteth, more than over ninety and nine just persons, which need no repentance.'" Mrs. Jobson turns on her heels and stalks indoors.

"Bonkers. Completely nuts." George Wright shakes his head.

Sam has stamped upstairs, depressed and angry.

He hasn't asked for any of this.

He never asked to be the centre of this attention. Now he has a madman trying to kill him and a stupid witch of a neighbour passing judgement on him.

All he wants is to be left alone.

Regular television programmes are interrupted to show Winchester City Centre in flames. The news channels cover the disaster almost without stop. Their cameras have a morbid fascination with the twisted and wrecked statue of King Alfred. The exploding tanker destroyed scores of buildings and a jagged hole gapes in the front wall of the Guildhall where Sam and his father had been earlier.

Curtains and the remnants of blinds flutter idly out of smashed windows. The force of the blast has lifted a car bodily and thrown it against the wall of the old building. It lies twisted and unrecognisable on the pavement. Buses have been crushed against each other and burnt. Their blackened frames are all that are left.

The journalists report morbidly that there are casualties: they have witnessed bodies being lifted into ambulances. It is not yet known how many have been killed and injured: they must wait for official word on that but a journalist at the scene estimates at least ten fatalities.

Though there is no explanation yet as to what caused the tanker to crash, the incident is not thought to be terrorist action. The driver of the crashed tanker was its regular one. He has been rescued unconscious from his cab but it has not yet been possible to interview him. He is critically injured and may not survive.

The Wright family sits in stunned silence as they watch the TV pictures of the carnage on the streets of their historic City. It is a tragic sight.

"Oh, look at this" Helen Wright has been paging through Twitter. "There are already people saying it was probably someone who shouldn't have been driving: didn't declare his medical condition. They're just jumping to conclusions."

"Trolls" says Sam. "Idiots."

"How do you feel now, Sam?" Ngozi is concerned.

"Sick to death of all this." Sam feels a sense of bitter fury welling up inside him. *"I'm trying to avoid all this, I really am. But I have an enemy and it's just my luck that it's the person Emmanuel Cabrieres kindly described to me as the most dangerous person in the world. Looks like he's determined to kill me. And he doesn't care how many innocent people are destroyed in the process."*

Today, Donovan Chatsworth has turned the centre of Winchester into a war zone. He has shown again his complete and ruthless disregard for human life.

Frightened, Sam asks himself why HE had been chosen to have telepathic powers - and more. He didn't ask for this. Ever since his first contact with Ngozi, he has been sucked deeper and deeper into events he doesn't understand and towards a person who wants to kill him.

His life is out of control. Despite what Emmanuel Cabrieres said about not getting involved, he is being drawn into Donovan Chatsworth's evil world and there is nothing he can do about it.

Sam realises that one day, somewhere, Donovan Chatsworth will catch up with him again. When that happens will he, a teenage boy, have the physical and mental strength that he needs to survive?

How can he?

He knows he won't be strong enough. Sam knows his own weakness. He's just a fourteen-year-old boy from a comfortable home in a prosperous city. He's lived a sheltered life, at least until recently. He doesn't know how to mix with, let alone fight, a callous criminal. In his short life Sam has been protected from 'ordinary' criminals let alone a madman who can rationalise any action and any crime, no matter how evil.

Sam knows he can't afford a confrontation – he's neither prepared for it, nor strong enough, nor does he have the self-belief that he will need.

He needs help, but there is no-one who can give it. There is no-one in the world who can stand with him.

Sam Wright is alone.

And he's frightened.

CHAPTER 33 – MESSAGE RECEIVED

Maddy and Sam are sitting on the bench at the playground. "Dad and I were lucky. We were on the other side of the Guildhall when the tanker exploded. Otherwise ..." Sam leaves the sentence unfinished. "We saw it crash and just ran for it. When it went up there was glass everywhere."

Maddy puts her hand on Sam's. "Eight people dead. You could have been killed too. I can't bear to think about it."

"Well, we weren't." Then he adds, more softly. "I was scared though."

"Not surprised. What do you think caused it?"

"No idea. Nothing makes sense." Sam avoids the question. "I expect someone'll work it out eventually. The driver must have been affected by something. Heart attack perhaps. Last I heard he was still unconscious."

Maddy groans. "Oh no, not another person lying unconscious in hospital!" She takes his hand. "Sam, I want you to promise me something. Something really serious."

"Yes?"

"Those reports in the paper about Vincent Stewart - how the family lost the court case and the doctors went ahead and switched off his life support machines even though the family said 'no' ..."

Sam's heart misses a beat. Surely Maddy can't have any idea of what he knows from that tragic day? "Yes. I remember what you said. You thought it was so wrong."

"I still think it was. Sam, I hope – I really hope – that if anything ever happened to me, my parents and you would fight for me like Vincent Stewart's family did. Fight and fight and fight. Don't let anyone else decide - I want to know that the people who care about me will do everything they can and not let the medics give up on me."

"Oh Maddy, of course I would. So would your Mum and Dad. What happened to that poor man was completely wrong." Sam is able to say that with bitter conviction. "I promise you … I'd never let that happen to you. Not without a fight."

Maddy squeezes his hand. "Thank you Sam. You'd do everything you could, I know that."

"Of course I would. I promise."

"Not that I expect it to come to that."

Detective Inspector Ian Murphy scowls as he is interrupted by the phone ringing. Unwillingly he flicks the button.

"I thought I said I wasn't to be disturbed?"

"Yes Sir. Sorry, Sir. But I thought you'd want to take this. It's a man saying he knows about the incident in the City Centre yesterday …"

"Another crank …"

"I don't think so, Sir. He says his name is Donovan Chatsworth."

Murphy leaps from his chair and in two bounds is at the door to his office. In his wake, the papers on which he has been working scatter onto the floor. He shouts to the outer office: "this call – trace it. Get Jones! Tell her to drop what she's doing and get in here now. Right now." He strides back to his desk and switches on the digital recorder and speakerphone so that his colleague can hear.

"Hello, who is this?"

"Good afternoon Inspector Murphy. You know who this is." A soft voice. Silky smooth. "I believe you investigated my liberation."

"Please identify yourself."

Detective Jones hurries in and Murphy points for her to shut the door.

"Stop playing games, Murphy and listen. You'll be trying to trace this call. Don't bother. To save you the time and effort, let me tell you that I am no longer in Winchester and I am making this call from a mobile. After I have said what I require you to hear, I shall destroy it."

"How do I know you're Donovan Chatsworth?"

Detective Jones' eyes widen as she realises who the caller is.

"We wouldn't be talking now if you didn't believe it."

"What do you want?"

"Ah now, that's much better. I am calling to give you your instructions."

"I don't take instructions from madmen."

"Mad, Inspector? How very rude. Still, there's a fine line between madness and genius, so people say."

"Don't kid yourself that you're a genius. You're just another arrogant, cold-blooded murderer with a screw loose."

"I have much about which I can be arrogant, Murphy. That is the difference between us. However, I didn't call to discuss your shortcomings - I'd be here all day. Before I tell you what is to happen next, I expect you're wondering whether it was I who destroyed your City Centre yesterday."

"How could you do that?"

"Now you're trying my patience. You know, through your involvement with investigating my escape, exactly what I can do. You are one of a select few who understands me."

"Very well. Are you admitting that you caused it?"

"Of course. Even if I say so myself I'm rather proud of the - ah - excitement in Winchester yesterday. I tell you this because I want you to understand the seriousness of your situation. You realise, I trust, that what I did to Winchester I could do elsewhere? Places even more crowded. Perhaps even somewhere indoors. Think about that, Inspector. Wouldn't that be fun? Do I make myself clear?"

"Crystal clear" says Murphy through clenched teeth. "Why are you doing this? I thought you were interested in the people involved with your trial. You caused the deaths of eight innocent people with that stunt yesterday, Chatsworth."

"Stunt? Such a trivial word for such a momentous event. No matter. I'll tell you why I'm doing this. Something has changed, Inspector. You have five friends of mine in custody and that makes me feel - very sad."

"Who do you mean?"

There is silence at the end of the line.

"OK, OK. Let's assume that we do have friends of yours in custody. They are charged with murder, attempted murder, assault, possession of an unlicenced weapon and handling of stolen property."

"Quite so. Serious crimes Inspector, serious indeed..."

"And?"

"I am instructing you to free them. I will never allow you to bring them to trial, Inspector. Surely you realise that?"

"You want me to let them go, just like that? Drop the charges and release them? After killing three of my men and injuring another? Go to hell."

"That's the reaction I expected, Inspector. It's your instinct to refuse. You can't help yourself. But that's because you haven't taken time to think it through. Once you have, you'll see the error of your ways."

"Never."

"Cone now. You'll do as I'm telling you because if you don't I shall cause another disaster, and then another, and then another and I'll carry on causing them until you see that you have no choice. How many people are you prepared let die, Inspector? A hundred? A thousand? A hundred thousand? How many avoidable deaths can your conscience take, Inspector, before you can't sleep at night? I bet it's less than mine. Nothing stops me sleeping, Inspector."

Murphy clenches his fist. "Is that it?"

"No. There is one more thing. You have a young man working with you. The one who visited you yesterday. You know who I mean?"

"The one your friends assaulted and kidnapped."

"Very good, Inspector."

"He has no connection with your imprisonment. What is your interest in him?"

"You're right that he had nothing to do with my imprisonment. But he can identify my friends – the only credible witness given that the other boy was unconscious most of the time. I promise you, Inspector - that young man will die before you get him anywhere near a witness box. And as he is your only reliable witness and I promise you he will never testify, the case against my friends will collapse. You'll have no choice but to drop the charges against them and let them go."

"You're wrong. We don't need to involve him. We have forensic evidence, we have the murder weapon and we recovered stolen goods. We also have the testimony of the man who was injured but survived."

"One injured man and one teenage boy. Without them your case collapses, Inspector. I have therefore added the boy to my list along with your man in the wheelchair. If I have to kill them - and please have no doubt that I will do that if I judge it necessary - I assure you that many more people will die with them. Their deaths will be particularly unpleasant. You'll have another major spectacle on your hands. And when it gets out that hundreds of people died and it all could have been avoided, you and your superiors are going to be ever so unpopular. You'll be the people who were too stubborn, or too stupid, to make the right decision ... oh dear, Inspector, I wouldn't like to be in your shoes. I do hope your pension plan is up to date."

"What is your interest in the boy?"

"He's a witness who can implicate my friends. That's all. If you want him to live, you will release them. Do you understand?"

"You're mad."

Chatsworth ignores the insult. "Inspector, do you understand?"

"Yes." Murphy spits out the word. "Of course I bloody well understand."

"I'm glad. I give you a clear choice. Release my friends, and I will not repeat what I did yesterday."

"And if I refuse?"

"Oh - that would be so very, very unwise. I know you are capable of monumental idiocy, Inspector, but please consider that you will be sentencing the boy to a quite horrible death and hundreds of others with him. And all for nothing. Either way, Inspector, my friends will not come to trial. So which is it to be?"

Murphy puts his head in his hands. This is an impossible situation. "Do I have your word that you will never repeat what you did yesterday?"

"If you release my friends."

"It will take time. You know it won't be my decision."

"I quite understand. I have complete confidence, Inspector, in your powers of persuasion. You need a little time ... very well, I shall delay further action for a few weeks during which you can prove to me that you are a man of your word.

"I shall concentrate instead on my original targets, though many of them seem to have disappeared. But I am sure you would like to know ... I have selected my next execution. I shall attend to it very soon."

"You madman ..."

"Don't insult me again, Murphy. Oh look, you've made me angry." There's an edge to Chatsworth's voice. Sounds of people screaming and shouting come over the phone. "Oh dear, I seem to have started a fight. That's your fault."

"If it's the last thing I do, I'll get you, Chatsworth ..."

"Oh please. You sound like an old B movie. If you try to 'get me', as you so quaintly put it, it certainly will be the last thing you do. But do what you will, Inspector. I will swat you as I would a fly.

"I inhabit a world where you can't even think of going: I see and do things that are too difficult for your regimented little mind to understand. My advice to you is - don't try. Just do as I tell you. You have your instruction – obey them."

"But ..."

"One more thing, Inspector. I have a message for you. If you check outside your building, you should find a young lady standing there. She'll have been there for about thirty minutes now so she must be getting cold. She needs your help. I have no further use for her. Go and introduce yourself personally. Goodbye Murphy."

The line goes dead.

Murphy curses and leaps from his seat. He shouts to the outer office. "Where was he calling from?"

"It was a mobile, Sir. Near Woking Station."

"Woking? What the hell was he doing there? Find it. Find the phone. And get me CCTV records. I want to see exactly where he was."

"Yes Sir."

"And check downstairs. Is there a woman there? Outside?"

"Sir?"

"Do you have problems understanding English?"

"No Sir. I'll check straight away."

Murphy looks at his colleague and shakes his head, wearily.

"Will you release them?" asks Jones.

"Not my decision. I'll have to refer this up. But I don't see I have a choice. I'll recommend 'yes'."

"But that means Chatsworth wins."

"Can you offer me a different way?"

"No, dammit." Jones looks glum.

"The thing is – the Chief won't release them. Not in a month of Sundays. Three of our men are dead. Would you release their killer? We have stolen goods with matching prints all over them. Would you give Chatsworth the satisfaction of knowing that he is, in effect, above the law?"

"But surely ...?"

"They won't understand. They'll play it by the book. They'll make the wrong decision and sign the death warrants of thousands of people including a boy whose only crime, as far as I can make out, is to save peoples' lives." He pauses and shakes his head sadly: "I'd better report this conversation. Try to persuade them."

Wearily, Murphy picks up the phone. "Get me Mr. Smith in London."

"Sir. You'd better come downstairs."

"Cancel that." Murphy's normally calm face is pale and drawn. He has aged five years in as many minutes.

Outside is a young woman. Wearing only a thin red dress, she is standing in the rain, her black hair plastered to her pale, drawn face. She looks neither left not right, her wide staring eyes fixed ahead of her, unseeing.

"She doesn't respond, Sir." A female constable speaks softly. "There's no identity on her. She's just standing here, to attention like, fists clenched. We can't get her to tell us who she is or how she got here. Can't get her to respond at all."

"Try again."

"OK." She turns to the young woman. "Come on love. Why don't you tell us your name? I'm Sandra. Come inside and I'll make you a cup of tea. Warm you up."

The woman in the red dress stares straight ahead and doesn't move.

"You're with friends. We want to help you. You must be very cold. Why don't you come indoors?"

Still no reaction.

Murphy speaks softly. "Young lady, please let us help you. My name is Inspector Murphy and I want ..."

At the sound of his name, the young woman unclenches her fists and screams. With her fingernails outstretched like claws she runs at Murphy and rakes them down his face. He staggers back, blood running from three long scratches on each side. The woman resumes her stance. Sandra pins her arms to her side, not that there is any resistance.

A piece of paper fell to the floor when she unclenched her fists. Murphy picks it up. It is already soaked but he can make out two letters.

"D C."

"Is that all, Sir? What does it mean?"

Murphy dabs his bleeding face with a handkerchief. "Don't worry, I know what it means."

He passes the slip of paper to Jones. "Chatsworth is showing off – demonstrating what he can do. OK, message received."

He shakes his head wearily. "Call an ambulance. Not that anyone will be able to help her, poor kid. Her mind's gone."

CHAPTER 34 – ANOTHER VICTIM

Harkness repeats 'human evolution' claim

Professor Stamford Harkness, the controversial exponent of telepathic and mental powers, has once again courted controversy with his theories on human evolution.

Speaking to the Washington Post he said "Yes, I've been contacted by many people claiming to be telepaths and most of them I was able immediately to dismiss as fraudulent.

"But I have heard from one whose story I found more credible: this person didn't sound triumphalist about possibly representing the future direction of the human race. This person – and please note I am being careful not even to say if it was a man or a woman – was, frankly, scared. And that strikes me as the sensible position to take.

"This person told me that people with this ability live by rules designed to hide their powers and not exploit them. This person tells me that telepaths live in constant fear of being discovered by the authorities and either killed or subjected to enforced medical treatment designed to beat their capabilities out of them.

"This person persuades me that the theory I have been espousing is, in fact, the truth. Man is evolving. And in an age when a significant proportion of our population is still violently hostile to people who are gay, disabled or somehow 'different', it is no wonder if they live in constant fear."

It is the nature of life that even after a major disaster, everyday activities continue as best they can. They have to. In Winchester City Centre workers, shoppers and tourists go about their daily business, some sadly shaking their heads at the damage, others grumbling about how they are being inconvenienced.

"The buses are all over the place. And the heap of junk they used this morning ... must have come from the Ark."

"I heard they lost dozens in the explosion. They've probably had to bring in spare vehicles from other companies. I think they're doing well to put on any services at all after what happened."

"I'm late now, because of the extra walk."

"It looks so bare without the statue. It's such a shame."

For Sam's sister Rachel, normality includes school and her dancing classes. And it is her dancing that causes the next major excitement in the Wright household.

A fortnight after the City Centre was wrecked, Rachel runs into the house, enthusiastically waving a letter. Her dance teacher has been asked to supply four dancers to perform a children's ballet in an opera – Verdi's Aida. Could Rachel be one of them? It will mean extra lessons and rehearsals to learn the routine, but at the end they will perform for two nights at the Royal Albert Hall, no less, in London.

Rachel is beside herself with excitement. "Mum, please! I'll never get another chance like this! You know I love being on stage – and the Royal Albert Hall! PLEEEEEAASE."

Sam rolls his eyes – he hates it when his sister whines liked that. But he has to agree - what an opportunity! Surely his mother will be keen too?

"I don't know. It's a huge thing, and there are so many risks these days in going to London, what with the terrorist attacks and everything ... look what happened here."

"We'll be safe. Miss Grimes is arranging a supervisor for us."

"Someone we don't know! What if something happens?"

Eventually their father prevails: "Look, we really can't let her miss this chance. We can't order our lives by running away from danger all the time. Tell you what - I'll go with her – be with her on the journeys up and back. We could all go to one of the performances. We don't get out enough anyway and I'm owed some time off."

"But the underground ..."

"If you are worried about the tube, we'll get a taxi from Waterloo."

Helen Wright backs down. Yes, Rachel will go and her father will accompany her on both days. For the first performance the family will make it a day out, and invite Edward, Jan and Maddy James too. It's not every day your daughter performs at the Royal Albert Hall, after all.

Sam is delighted that Maddy and her parents are invited. They mark the date in their diaries: September 5th.

For the next four weekends, Rachel stays late each Saturday morning at her dance school, learning and rehearsing her ballet routine. At all other times the house echoes to the thump, bump, thump of her practicing in her bedroom, over and over again.

The dance school issues a press release, proudly publicising its success in having four of its pupils selected for the honour of performing at the most prestigious arts location in London. The local paper prints the story with their photographs. Rachel cuts it out to show her friends. Though Sam is pleased for her, he curses the extra publicity for the Wright family name.

Even though the threat from Donovan Chatsworth seems to have receded, Sam is constantly on edge in case he senses him. He stays away from the City Centre now. He tries not to go out alone. Even though he resents having to restrict his life, it seems that his caution is working and, as the weeks of the summer holidays pass and the memories of his kidnapping fade, he allows himself to relax a little.

Sam and his friends spend many hours on their bikes. Ashley is with them again now, fully recovered from the kidnap. Sam's parents take the two of them for a day to the indoor BMX facility in Newport, South Wales, as a 'thank you' to Ashley. The shared experience has made them closer than before – each knows that he has a friend on whom he can rely for loyalty and support, even in the most desperate of situations.

Maddy is happier now that she has solved the mystery of her father's strange phone calls and evening meetings.

"We talked about Uncle Frank last night." Maddy is sitting with Sam on their regular bench at the swings.

"Is your Dad all right about it now? He was furious that night ..."

"And yours. I've never heard him swear like that. But yes, he's being really kind. He says he understands why I was worried and he should have known that I would spot something. He says he should have told me the truth months ago and it's a relief really, now that I know. He's really impressed at how you and I worked everything out." Maddy looks quizzically at Sam again.

He smiles and says nothing. He can't.

Sam and his family spend a few days at the beach – their favourite holiday break. Sam relaxes whilst he's away from home – surely Donovan Chatsworth can't track him here?

Even so, he finds himself looking at the world through new eyes – valuing properly the sights and sounds he had taken for granted before and wondering whether he will live to see them again next year. The noise of the breaking waves, the sandcastles, the shells, the smell of the seaweed and the happy shouts of the children playing – these things are special now, where before he hadn't given them a second thought.

Wherever he goes, Sam tells Ngozi what he is doing and who he is with: he dreads to imagine what his life would be like without her. He meets Emmanuel Cabrieres most weekends in the park. They discuss how best Sam can keep secret his extraordinary powers and what to do if he senses the presence of Donovan Chatsworth. They review his progress in keeping himself out of the limelight and Emmanuel is pleased.

The official inquiry into the Winchester City Centre disaster publishes a draft report. It finds that the event was a series of tragic co-incidences and accidents. Mechanical failure in the tanker's steering coupled with the driver's previously undiagnosed heart condition caused it to slew off course and the driver to lose control and black out. There is no question of a terrorist involvement, no suggestion of a political motive. And the driver is not at fault.

The report is greeted with relief by local people. It's the explanation they wanted to hear; the one they want to believe.

But it's a cover-up and Sam knows it. There is no mention of Donovan Chatsworth, and as the summer wears on without further excitement, Sam allows himself to hope that his wish never to encounter him again has been granted.

No, that cannot be. He is not in control of his future.

Inspector Murphy looks miserably at Detective Jones. "As I predicted – they've overruled me. They're refusing to release Chatsworth's men. Point blank, no further discussion. Sufficient evidence exists, including or excluding the testimony of the eye witnesses, to obtain a conviction. Proceed as usual to prepare the pack for the Crown Prosecution Service, they say."

"But that means ..."

"I know, I know. But they don't understand what they're dealing with."

"So we do nothing?"

"No. The good news is that our security people have instructions to shoot to kill if they see Chatsworth and they're investigating why he's so interested in Samuel Wright. 'Mr. Smith' as we know him is taking personal charge of that."

Jones shakes her head. "So the upshot is that an innocent teenager is being stalked by the Intelligence Services while no-one knows where Chatsworth is. Sam Wright is being watched but the real criminal is walking free. Chatsworth's the one that's caused all this. He's the one they need to find. It's unjust. It stinks."

"That's about it."

"The fools ... they're watching the wrong person whilst you and I set him up for ... well, death."

"Tell me about it. There are times when I hate this job."

As August draws to an end and the nights start to close again, Sam comes downstairs to see his parents concentrating on the television. The TV news is dominated by a breaking story ...

"... the death of Jonathan Coombray, one of the South's most charismatic MPs. Mr. Coombray was seen as a rising star, whom many were tipping for early promotion and even as a possible future leader."

"You should watch this" says his father, pointing at the television.

The news report continues. "Mystery surrounds his death here in Woking Station, which is now shut. All trains through Woking have been stopped and that's a lot. For people trying to get into and out of London, this mean major disruption. No-one is being allowed into the scene of the tragedy until the on-the-spot investigation is completed.

"No official statement has yet been issued but we understand from passengers that this afternoon Mr. Coombray caught the 14:17 service out of London Waterloo. At Woking, which is not his usual stop, he left the train. Eye-witnesses who saw him on the platform reported that he appeared to be in a highly emotional state and in some distress."

The reporter turns to a man standing next to him. "Patrick Orde - you were on the platform – what did you see?"

"I saw this man staggering towards me. I didn't know who he was, but I asked him if he was alright. He pushed past me and told me to leave him alone. He was obviously upset about something. I let him go – I had no idea he was gonna do anything stupid."

"Did he give you any clues as to why he was upset?"

"No. Nothing. Next thing I know, he'd jumped onto the line."

"Thank you." The camera swings back to the reporter. Also with me is Mary Roker. Mrs. Roker: we have heard that Mr. Coombray appeared upset. What did you see?"

"Well, I was on the platform at the back of the train. Mr. Coombray was staggering and when he reached the back of the train he quite deliberately jumped down onto the track. Deliberately! Then he stepped onto the electrified third rail. There was this huge bang. It was horrible."

The reporter continues. "The power had to be switched off before the body could be recovered and when it was, Mr. Coombray was certified dead at the scene. The power flowing through the third rail is immense at 750 volts DC and almost always fatal if someone comes into contact with it.

"Police are appealing for witnesses. They are asking anyone who may have seen Mr. Coombray at London Waterloo, or on the train, or who witnessed the events at Woking, please to contact them. In particular they are asking anyone who may have seen him on the train to make themselves known."

The report switches back to the studio. "The reasons for this tragedy are shrouded in mystery. Why did Jonathan Coombray leave the train at Woking, which is not his normal stop? Had he planned to meet someone there? Did something happen on the train to cause his apparent distress? Why did he walk onto the tracks, a most dangerous and almost always fatal, thing to do? Were his actions deliberate or was this some kind of tragic accident?

"Joining us now from Mr. Coombray's constituency is his Association Chairman, Peter Russell. Mr. Russell, this death must come as a great shock?"

"A complete shock, yes. I am shocked and desperately sad. Jonathan was a brilliant man. Before he became an MP, he had built a formidable reputation as a lawyer. After being elected ..."

Sam leans forward. "A lawyer?"

His father says softly, "Yes. Listen."

"... he made an immediate impression in the House. Many people thought that his maiden speech was the best they had ever heard. He had a glittering career ahead of him. His local Association had no doubt that he would one day be a Cabinet Minister."

"Do you have any clue why he might have acted as he did? There's an obvious suspicion that it may have been suicide."

"None at all. I can't believe that Jonathan would kill himself. He loved being an MP. He was on tremendous form at his lunchtime meeting today and showed no signs of having any concerns or worries. He told me just a few days ago that this was the happiest time of his professional career. I can think of no reason why he would take his own life: no reason at all. I'm devastated. This news is just unbelievable. I'm so sorry for his wife Denise, and their two children."

The news report finishes: "In an additional development tonight, Police have issued an e-fit picture of a man they hope might be able to help with their enquiries. He may have been on the train or have been seen with Mr. Coombray. If anyone has seen this man or has any information, they are asked to phone the number on the screen but not under any circumstances to approach him. He is thought to be armed and dangerous …"

The picture shows an innocuous looking middle-aged man. White, in his forties, hair brushed back. It is an unremarkable face apart from - the eyes. The eyes are small, dark and deep and they do not smile.

Sam's heart pounds. The face from the poster!

The face he never wanted to see again!

Donovan Chatsworth!

He groans. He should have realised that the quiet summer had been too good to last. Chatsworth has claimed another victim.

Within minutes of the report ending there's knock on the door. It's Edward and Jan James. Maddy is with them. Helen Wright ushers them into the house.

"Did you see?" asks Edward James.

"We saw" says Sam's father.

"You know what this means?"

"Another one gone. Poor Frank".

"Donovan Chatsworth!" exclaims Maddy. "Again. But why?"

Her mother explains. "Jonathan Coombray was one of the prosecution team at Donovan Chatsworth's trial. Chatsworth would have targeted him, no question. That means the Judge has died, two members of the jury, one of the Police who caught him - and now the prosecutor. Then there was that horrible incident in Reading when one of the Police Officers was badly injured. The day you were there."

"But how could Chatsworth have been involved?" asks Maddy.

"No idea. I just know that he threatened revenge and this is the latest in a line of deaths. It can't be coincidence."

"And that was his picture they just showed. I saw a poster with his picture on it at the Guildhall" says Sam.

"Yes, it was. They probably have no idea whether Chatsworth was on the train or not – I reckon they're guessing that he was. But if you ask me, he was there. I'm sure this is another death connected with

Chatsworth and so are they. They're putting out his picture in the off-chance that someone saw him."

"Poor Frank" says Jan James again. "It looks like he's going to have to stay in hiding for a long time yet."

"But how could he make a man deliberately walk onto an electrified railway line?" asks Maddy. "It makes no sense".

"I've no idea" replies her father. "Blackmail, perhaps."

Silence.

But Sam knows. He can imagine all too vividly what happened on that train. Chatsworth follows Jonathan Coombray to Waterloo station. That's easy – the whereabouts of a Member of Parliament are hardly secret.

The train wouldn't have been crowded at that time of day. Sam imagines Coombray sitting by himself, perhaps reading.

The train is moving. The door to the carriage opens. A man walks up the central aisle to where his victim is sitting. Coombray recognises him immediately - Chatsworth! He starts and looks around.

Chatsworth smiles thinly. He sits next to his intended victim. "Good afternoon, Mr. Coombray. I am so pleased to meet you again." Or perhaps he doesn't say anything at all.

Coombray stands no chance. Chatsworth uses his mental powers to fill his victim's mind with despair. He destroys Coombray's will to live, just as he did with the guards in the prison van. He taunts the poor man. But he doesn't kill him, even though he could.

At the next stop, Jonathan Coombray staggers from the train and, with his mind no longer his own, finds the quickest and nearest way to end his life. He deliberately walks onto the lethal electrified third rail. As horrified passengers gather round to see what happened at the back of the train, Chatsworth walks to the front and, hat pulled down to shield his face, unrecognised by anyone, he steps onto the platform and slides quietly away.

From the moment Chatsworth joined him in the carriage, Jonathan Coombray's fate was sealed.

Sam shudders.

Chatsworth is evil! Sam will stay away from him. He has to.

And then Sam shivers again. Who is he kidding? The summer calm has been a lull and that's all it has been. Chatsworth hasn't given up. He'll never let go. He was simply pursuing other people on his list. Eventually he'll turn his attention back to Sam. Try as he might, Sam won't be able to avoid Chatsworth forever. He knows that Chatsworth will hunt him down.

Sam also knows that he can't let this killing continue. One day he will have to face his enemy. Sam is the only person in the world who might possibly be able to end this madman's mission of revenge.

And even though he knows he isn't ready, even though all his advice tells him no, tonight's news leaves him no choice. He must do something - anything - everything - he can.

Silently, Sam makes his decision. This is so personal that he won't even tell Ngozi. She would try to talk him out of it.

Despite M Cabrieres' instructions not to get involved, Sam now knows what he has to do. When the time comes, he will confront Chatsworth.

Even if it costs him his life.

As Sam reaches his unavoidable decision, fifty miles away a slightly built, innocuous looking, middle-aged man sits in an attic room lit by a single small lamp on a bare table. He has been watching the same news broadcast. But whereas Sam and his family are shocked to the core at what they have seen, this man smiles.

He is interrupted by his phone ringing. He checks the number of the caller and answers, affecting a calm and sincere voice. "Hello, my child. Yes, this is the Reverend."

He listens, making careful notes. "Thank you dear lady. That is most interesting. Yes, you were quite right to let me know. Yes: September 5th and 6th – I've made a note of that. You are right, of course. I will pray that he behaves properly in such a public place. You must pray for that too. Will you do that? Will you join me in praying for peace on those nights? You will? Bless you, my child."

He pauses, listening.

"Heavens no, my dear lady. Of course it wasn't a bad time for you to 'phone. There is never a wrong time for the Lord's work." He puts the phone down. "Oh how gullible some people are!"

"So, September 5th it is. A day that will be remembered for all time. I'll see you in London, Sam Wright."

CHAPTER 35 – DON'T GO TO SLEEP!

Something is wrong. It's four in the morning and whatever it is has woken Sam. He listens. Is someone moving in the house? Has someone broken in?

A burglar?

No, the house is silent other than his father snoring softly in bed.

A noise outside then? He slips out of bed and pads to the window. No, everything looks normal.

The street is deserted.

But something doesn't feel right. He can't put his finger on it. The house is looks normal. It wasn't a noise that disturbed him. If anything it is too quiet. There is something not there. Something that normally is there.

Ngozi!

He can't sense his friend.

"*Ngozi?*" Sam calls her.

No answer.

Asleep? She shouldn't be ... she's on night shift again this week. Normally she would reply even if it was to say 'call you back'.

"*Ngozi. I can't sense you ... are you alright?*"

Nothing.

Complete silence.

Sam tries the technique he used when he first spoke with his friend. Still he can't raise her.

He doesn't get back into bed. He can't lie there and relax ... not till he knows what is happening. This is important.

"Ngozi? Ngozi! Please answer me!"

Something is wrong. Something very serious. Sam feels panic rising in him.

Take a deep breath: stay calm.

For half an hour, pacing up and down his room, Sam calls Ngozi. Desperately he tries to think of alternative explanations to the one overpowering fear that is mounting in his head – what if the worst has happened and his telepathic friend is dead?

The thought terrifies him. It produces a sense of loss keener and deeper than anything he has felt before. It's his worst nightmare. Now he understands now how Donovan Chatsworth must have felt in prison when his partner refused to speak to him; when he was confronted with the dread realisation that he was finally, totally and irretrievably alone.

No wonder he went mad!

As Sam paces the room, worrying, the dawn sky is changing from black to red. But this morning he neither cares nor notices: he's thinking of the many conversations he and Ngozi have shared, how she advised him, how she'd been exasperated with him, how she helped him to rebuild his confidence and how she came to his rescue when he was in trouble. Ngozi is such an important part of his life now: how could he possibly cope without her? Will he be left alone in the world again, feeling lonely? But even lonelier than before because for a few months he had had a friend who was really close?

And, even more upsetting … if the worst has happened, Sam will have to bear the grief alone. He's never told anyone about his telepathic contact. How could he now explain that he's grieving for a woman in Nigeria that he's never met, and ask for understanding and sympathy?

"Ngozi?" he keeps calling his friend.

No answer. Still nothing but silence. What has happened?

He must be really tense - his chest hurts. He tries to breathe shallowly but it's becoming painful, as if a great weight is bearing down on him. Each time he takes a breath he feels a stabbing pain in his ribs. He breathes slowly to avoid the pain. "Relax" he tells himself. "You're working yourself into a state."

"Ngozi. Answer me. Please."

Nothing.

"Ngozi. It's Sam."

The pains in his chest are getting worse.

"Ngozi. Please answer."

The pains are almost unbearable. What is happening to him? A heart attack?

At fourteen?

It's not impossible - he's read about it. He's seen reports about footballers who suddenly collapse because of a heart disease they didn't know they had.

"Ngozi, where are you?"

"Sa-m?"

Sam feels like weeping with joy.

"Ngozi ... what's happening?"

"Don't know. Dark. Can't breathe properly. Dark. So dark. Oh!"

Ngozi is in pain and crying out. Sam realises now what is happening to him. The aches in his own chest – he's feeling what Ngozi is feeling. How can that be?

It doesn't matter. Understanding it will have to wait. This is no time to worry about himself. Ngozi was there for him when he needed her. Now their roles are reversed. This time he will help his friend.

If he can.

"Ngozi?"

No answer. She's gone again. But the throbbing pain in Sam's chest is still there. That has to be good, doesn't it? If it's an indication that his friend is still alive, Sam will tolerate the pain, and much more if he has to.

"Aarggh!" There she is again!

"Ngozi ... try to tell me what's happened."

"Not sure. At work ... hospital ... huge bang. Building shook. Middle of the night. Lights went out. Everything went dark. Feeling of falling. Something heavy on my chest. Can't move ... trapped."

It sounds as if the hospital where she works has collapsed and Ngozi is trapped in the debris. An accident? Terrorism? An earthquake? If it's a major incident it's likely to be on the television news.

Painfully Sam reaches for the remote and flicks on the television. The 24 hour news channels will be operating. Perhaps they will offer some information. He turns the sound down low so as not to wake the rest of his family.

"Ngozi. Hang in there. Obviously something bad has happened and you're trapped, but help will be on its way. Keep talking to me till it gets there."

Sam has no idea whether help is on its way or not. He has no knowledge of the emergency services in Nigeria and how quickly they might respond. But his friend is very weak. She needs encouragement. He'll try to keep her conscious.

From thousands of miles away, it is now his job to keep his friend alive.

Breaking news. The banner is running along the bottom of the screen … there are reports of a major explosion near Lagos, Nigeria. The cause is unknown.

There it is! The news …

First indications are that a number of buildings have been damaged including, it is feared, a hospital. There are no details yet about casualties.

"Ngozi. There's been an explosion. It's on the news."

"Need … to sleep."

"No!" Sam screams at his friend. *"Ngozi - do NOT sleep! You have to attract help. Stay awake: stay with me."* Sam instinctively fears that if Ngozi loses consciousness, she will slip away and then he will lose her forever. *"Ngozi … answer me!"*

"Sam … good friend … dark here. Can't see. Can't move. Cold. So tired."

"I understand. You're probably trapped in the rubble. But you're not alone. I'll stay with you for as long as it takes. Keep talking to me. Do NOT go to sleep!"

"Sleep."

"No, you can't sleep – not yet." Sam racks his brain for ideas – he has to keep Ngozi conscious and talking to him.

"Recite the three-times table with me."

"What?"

"Ngozi … do as I say. One three is three. Two threes are …"

"What?"

"Ngozi … what are two threes?"

There is a pause. Then: *"Six."*

"Good! Now … three threes are … Ngozi … what are three threes?"

"Three threes are … nine."

Relief! She is responding!

"OK … four threes are …"

"Twelve."

"That's better. Now keep doing this with me."

For an hour, Sam forces Ngozi to stay awake. Recite another table with me. What are the names of your husband and your children? How old are they? When are their birthdays? Where do you live? He knows all this, or course, but he needs subject matter to keep Ngozi concentrating on staying alive.

General knowledge questions. What is the capital of the United States … Australia … Egypt? Anything he can think of to keep his friend with him.

Six-o-clock. It's two hours now since he'd woken. Surely help will come soon?

Sam keeps watching the news. Information is slow. The bulletins go over and over the same material. But then come shaky pictures from a camera on a drone. It shows half a square mile of badly damaged buildings. And at the centre is the hospital.

The suspected cause is a gas explosion; the authorities had to delay any full-scale rescue attempt until the gas was switched off. But volunteers are now swarming over the rubble, lifting it away with their bare hands ... calling for help when it is too heavy. There are children trapped in there. Sick children.

"Ngozi ... it looks like there was a gas explosion. It's on the television. There are people all over the building, looking for you. You'll be out of there soon."

"Soon ... need to sleep."

Sam curses. He allowed himself to relax and Ngozi felt it. *"No sleep, Ngozi. Not yet. Let's do those tables again."* Again he bullies and cajoles his friend into staying awake and talking to him.

Seven-o-clock. Sam hears his parents moving about – his father going to the bathroom to shower and shave. He puts them out of his mind. *"Ngozi ... who is President of the United States?"*

"Don't know ... need to sleep."

"No. You can sleep later. It's President Monrow. Monrow – say his name back to me. Who is the President?"

"Monrow."

"Well done. Now tell me: what is the largest planet in the Solar System?"

"Oh Sam, I don't know. I'm tired. Why does it matter?"

"It matters because it keeps you conscious, Ngozi. Jupiter, Ngozi. The largest planet is Jupiter. Say it back to me."

There is a pause and then Ngozi slowly repeats the name.

"Well done! Now ... who was the first man on the moon?"

"Moon ... night time ... sleep..."

"Neil Armstrong, Ngozi, in 1969. Say it back to me."

Nothing.

"Ngozi ... say Neil Armstrong."

"Aargh." Ngozi moans in pain and Sam feels the stabbing pain in his chest grow worse.

"Sam ... I'm frightened. I don't want to die. My children ..."

"Of course you don't. Ngozi, you're not going to die. You're going to stay awake and that will keep you alive. Think of your family - you're going to fight

and stay alive for them. That pain in your chest ... I feel it too. Use the pain to keep yourself awake. Focus on it."

Ngozi doesn't answer but he feels an increased stabbing pain in his own chest. How can that be? No matter; if it helps his friend to stay alive, he'll take whatever pain is necessary.

The TV news shows people being carried from the rubble of the hospital.

"Ngozi ... which floor of the hospital were you on?"

"Six."

"How many floors are there?"

"What?

"How many floors are there in the hospital?"

"Six. Top floor."

Thank goodness! She's at the top! Otherwise she would most likely have been crushed to death straight away.

"OK. The TV pictures show people being carried away. Can you hear anyone?"

Silence. The pain in Sam's chest is subsiding. Does this mean she is losing consciousness?

"Ngozi! Answer me. Can you hear anyone?"

Sam doubles up – the pain in his chest is excruciating now.

"Voices."

"Can you call out?"

"No. Can't breathe properly."

"Can you make some other sort of noise? Can you get hold of something - anything?"

"Can't move ... wait ... something near my left hand. Bottle maybe. Can feel it. Can't move my arm though."

"OK. Can you get hold of the bottle?"

"Get hold ... I think so ... yes."

"Well done. That's really good. Now, I want you to tap with it. Make a rhythmical sound that the rescuers can hear."

"So tired."

"I know. But concentrate. Tap the bottle, Ngozi."

"Tap - I'll try."

"Good. Do it now, Ngozi. Think of your husband and children ... you're not going to leave them all alone. They need you. You are going to come through this and go home to be with them."

"Not ... leave ... them. Oh, chest hurts. Husband, children."

"Keep at it Ngozi! The rescuers have to hear you. Tap the bottle with me. Do it as I say – tap, tap tap. Pause. Tap tap tap. Pause. Tap tap tap. Are you doing that? Say it back to me as you do it."

Ngozi sounds exhausted: *"Tap tap tap. Pause. Tap tap tap."*

"And again."

Ngozi repeats the pattern.

"Good Ngozi ... keep at it. Make them hear you."

From downstairs comes a call. "Sam: do you want breakfast?"

Sam jumps. He has forgotten everything else to focus on Ngozi. He opens his door a crack "No thanks. I'll get myself something in a minute." Thank goodness it isn't a school day.

The pain is his chest is easing again. That's bad. It means that Ngozi is losing consciousness again. *"Ngozi. Hold on! Are you still tapping?"*

The pain comes back, but no reply.

"Ngozi?"

Then a searing, agonising stab in his ribs catches Sam unawares. At the same time his head feels like it is going to explode and he collapses backwards onto his bed.

CHAPTER 36 – THE BEST OF FRIENDS

Sam has to bury his head in his pillow to avoid crying out and bringing his parents rushing to his room to see what's wrong. It would be impossible to explain. He curls into a ball, holding his pillow close to him and tries as best he can to cope in silence. He hopes for Ngozi's and his sakes that it won't be for much longer.

"Ngozi?"

As he fears, there is no answer.

With some difficulty, and breathing shallowly, Sam lifts his head to see the television. Live pictures of the rescue are still coming in.

"Ngozi? Are you there?"

Sam can sense that his friend IS there, and if the pain he is feeling is an indication that she's still conscious, then that's good. But she isn't answering. Why?

"Ngozi – what's happening?"

Still no answer. It is totally frustrating to be unable to speak to her. But his ribs and head still hurt. He takes comfort from that.

"Sam. Someone … above me." Sam feels like weeping with relief.

"What happened?"

"Someone moved … rubble. Light came in. So bright. Lots of stones fell. Standing on top of me - ribs broken, I think."

That explains the pains in his head and chest.

"Have you called to them?"

"No. Can't … shout … chest … hurts."

"Tap the bottle again. Make them hear you."

"Yes … bottle. Tap tap tap. Pause. Tap tap tap."

"*Good. And again ... Ngozi ... again.*" Sam can only imagine the injuries and the terror that his friend is suffering. "*Not long now. Just a few minutes longer. Tap that bottle Ngozi. Tap tap tap, pause, tap tap tap.*"

"*Trying. Feel fresh air now ... helping. Sun is so bright - want to close eyes. Had been ... completely dark.*"

That explains why Sam thought his head was going to explode. He tries to imagine what it must be like to be in pitch blackness, trying to see, and then have bright sunshine flooding in. And the pain in his chest; Ngozi must have been in agony if someone was standing on the rubble on top of her ribs.

"*Concentrate on tapping. Make sure they know you're there.*"

It's down to the rescuers now. Will they hear?

Eight-o-clock. The TV news starts its hourly cycle. It's now four hours since Sam woke. Ngozi has been trapped all that time.

Sam picks up Ngozi's thoughts. She isn't talking to him though. "*Tap tap tap, pause, tap tap tap.*" She's concentrating her last energy on signalling with the bottle.

"*That's right, Ngozi. Make sure they hear you.*"

"*Tap tap tap, pause, tap tap tap.*"

"*Well done, Ngozi. You can do this. You'll be OK.*" Sam feels he can't do any more to encourage or cajole his friend – she's exhausted and she is giving it her all. He has to offer hope. That's all he can do now.

Another blinding pain in his head makes him groan. But the ache in his chest subsides. His breathing is easier now. Have the rescuers found her? Has someone lifted the rubble and let in more light?

"*Sam ... someone there. Must ... sleep.*"

Sam claps his hands with joy.

"*A few minutes more Ngozi. Keep tapping until they speak to you. Then tell the medics where it hurts. Thank goodness you're alright. Stay awake to tell them how to help you.*"

But he knows Ngozi hasn't heard him. He lies back on his bed and hopes she will recover. The pains in his head and chest are easing.

He will have to tell Emmanuel Cabrieres about this. Is this usual? Or is it another example of his mental powers developing in an unexpected way?

On second thoughts, perhaps he won't mention it.

A sense of relief washes over him. Ngozi is alive. Surely she will be alright now. Downstairs he hears his mother humming to herself. Is he transmitting his happiness and relief to her? Probably. He doesn't care. There must be some times when it's OK to relax.

As he lays back and closes his eyes, the silent TV news shows a survivor being lifted carefully from the wreckage of the hospital. A woman, the commentator thinks; it's difficult to make out from this distance. She must have been there over four hours.

A medic carefully wipes the white concrete dust from the woman's face and fits an oxygen mask. Another fits an intravenous drip. She is carried away.

"Was she speaking?" asks the first medic.

"Trying to. Couldn't make it out. Sounded like "Tap tap tap pause tap tap tap.""

"Must have been delirious. It's a miracle she managed to stay conscious at all with the weight of that beam across her."

"Good job she did. We wouldn't have found her in time if it hadn't been for that man over there" – he points to one of the rescuers – "hearing her tapping. She's almost gone as it is. Poor thing."

"Will she be alright now?"

"Depends whether there's any internal bleeding and if her lungs are badly damaged. If it's just broken ribs and bruising, she should be."

Sam moves gingerly as he showers and dresses. In the mirror, he sees an ugly red weal across his chest. It's the first sign of the extensive bruising he's suffered. How will he explain that if anyone sees it? Better make sure they don't.

But after this morning's experience he will certainly tell Emmanuel Cabrieres that the punishment he imposed on Donovan Chatsworth in prison had been wrong. Though he has no sympathy for the misery Chatsworth has caused and is causing, Sam knows now that to deprive a telepath of his partner and force him to lose contact completely with his closest confidant is an all-consuming loss. This morning he experienced a sense of loneliness more profound than anything he'd felt before. The only comparison he can make is bereavement – what it must be like for a widow to go to bed alone for the first time after a long marriage.

No wonder Chatsworth went mad! Today, Sam experienced the loss of Ngozi for only a short time, and it shook him to his core. Chatsworth received a life sentence of never-ending misery. It was a cruel punishment.

Too harsh.

Emmanuel Cabrieres was wrong to impose it.

For days Ngozi drifts in and out of consciousness. When she finally opens her eyes, she is lying in her bed at home, with her daughter sitting at her side.

"Welcome back, Mum."

"Hi." Ngozi tries to sit up.

"Don't move. You've got two broken ribs and internal bruising. You breathed in a load of dust, your lungs are damaged and you're very ill."

Ngozi puts her head back on the pillow. She's a nurse. She knows this is the truth and it's serious.

"We were so worried about you."

Ngozi smiles weakly and squeezes her daughter's hand.

"It must have been horrible, trapped there, in the dark. I can't bear to think about it. It must have been so frightening to be all alone like that."

Ngozi can only speak slowly and hoarsely. "I wasn't alone. I had a friend with me – the best of friends."

"Sam, thank you."

Her daughter looks puzzled. Her mother must have been dreaming.

A gentle smile plays round Ngozi's face and she allows herself to relax so that sleep overtakes her once again.

"Sam, thank you."

Sam is at the BMX track. He pauses in his riding. Ngozi's presence is growing stronger these days. But for now, she needs rest and most of the time she is asleep. That means that Sam is cut off from the network. He is isolated.

But Ngozi is going to be alright and that's what really matters. Sam smiles. They'll have plenty of time to talk again once she has recovered. He will wait for her to call him when she feels well enough.

Ashley looks at Sam with a puzzled look on his face. "Everything all right? You look like you're a thousand miles away."

Sam nods. "Yes, everything's fine. Let's ride."

CHAPTER 37 – AIDA, ACT ONE

"There – the last one!" For weeks Sam's sister has been marking off the dates on the kitchen calendar. "It's like an advent calendar – it's as exciting as Christmas."

September 5th; Rachel's big day. The Wright and James families have tickets to see her dance at the Royal Albert Hall.

Today, the girl who is rarely ready on time is dressed and waiting to leave a good half-hour early. Her rucksack is waiting by the front door, packed and ready to go. Sam smiles ruefully: see, she can do it if it matters enough to her. He'll remind her the next time she keeps the whole family waiting.

It's an early autumn morning; misty but with the prospect of a fine day once the early moisture has been burnt off. "You stay right by your Dad, OK? I'll see you this evening." Helen Wright hugs her daughter. "Have a wonderful time. Break a leg!"

"Thanks Mum."

"Keep in touch", Helen says to her husband as they set off, taking an early train to London Waterloo: Rachel needs to be at the Hall by 10-o-clock for rehearsals and costume fittings.

Sam and the rest of the party follow in the afternoon. Having left themselves plenty of time for the journey, in case the trains are late, everything runs to time and they arrive early.

"We've an hour to kill. It's a lovely day: we could take a walk in the park and look at the Albert Memorial. How does that sound?" Maddy's father points at the inviting open space.

It seems the perfect end to the summer holidays. The leaves on the trees have started to turn. Their autumn greens, yellows and reds match perfectly the golden glow of the Memorial as it reflects the rich yellow

September sun. Lately Sam has learnt to value the beauty around him and today is a day when nature is at its best.

For a few tranquil minutes, the peace of the setting drives completely out of Sam's mind the traumas of the previous weeks. He ambles slowly with Maddy, away from the rest of the party. "This is so lovely" she says. "In the middle of the City – it's beautiful."

Other people are milling round the park as well. Some, like them, are clearly passing the time, waiting to enter the Hall to take their seats. Others are members of the Hall staff, already in their uniforms, taking a break before the rush starts. Tourists are taking pictures of each other in front of the memorial.

Maddy nudges Sam: "Americans."

Sam looks at a woman who is photographing a man who is, presumably, her husband – he has his back to them.

"Looks like we're in the background of their photo. I usually try to get out of shot." They move away.

The American couple swap round. The man is now photographing his wife: he is tall, Sam notes idly, short cut fair hair, handsome craggy features and blue eyes. Smiling eyes. A big man but a gentle one. Military bearing.

Sam and Maddy walk past and sit for a few moments on a bench, relaxing. The adults smile at the obvious friendship that their children now share.

And then, to Sam's horror, on a sunny afternoon on a family day out and when he is least expecting it, he feels a brief snap of an artificial emotion - elation. A false emotion. Just for a moment. It's gone almost as soon as it comes. It's as if someone found the thing for which he was searching and then controlled himself.

There is only one person who could create such a sensation in Sam's head.

Chatsworth!

No! Surely not?

Not today – not here!

Please no – not on Rachel's big day!

There's no way he could know that Sam would be here!

But yes. Even though the sensation had lasted only for an instant Sam knows beyond doubt that his enemy is somewhere near. He looks at his friends: did they feel anything? No, of course not. They are totally unaware. It was over too quickly for them to notice.

"*Ngozi*", he calls. "*I'm in London.*"

As he expects, there is no answer. His friend is sleeping. It happens most of the time these days that she is out of contact as she recovers. Usually it doesn't matter. But right now it does. He cannot access the network. And that means he has no-one to turn to for advice, no-one to warn about what is happening.

Sam is isolated.

He needs to get a message to Emmanuel Cabrieres. That's impossible through Ngozi. He has the mobile number so he sends a text. For all the good it will do.

"Albert Hall, London. DC here."

Straight away his phone rings. It's the Frenchman.

"Sorry. Need to take this." Sam ducks away from Maddy.

"You say he's at the Albert Hall? How do you know?"

"I felt him."

"You are sure of this? Absolutely sure?"

"Of course I'm sure." Sam hisses, speaking quickly and quietly and turning his back to where Maddy is sitting. "I know a false emotion when I feel it. I've felt him before, remember? There's only one person who can generate the feeling I just felt. He's here and that means thousands of people are in danger. Remember what he did in Winchester, and that was out in the open."

"Are you his target?"

"I hope not. Shit, I pray I'm not. No. How could he possibly know I'd be here? He must be planning another spectacular. It has to be coincidence, doesn't it?" Sam is walking up and down, unaware of how animated he is getting.

"I wish I knew. It seems too much of a coincidence. There was no way he could know you would be at the cycle track, but he did. There was no way he could know you would be in Winchester City Centre, but he did. Perhaps somehow he is monitoring your movements. Look – I'm coming to join you."

"But you're in France!"

"No, no. I'm in England. I have been ever since you were kidnapped. A friend and I have been keeping track of you."

"What?" Sam feels annoyed. "Spying on me?"

"Not spying, Sam. I do not watch your every movement. But I stay nearby, in case you need assistance - if Chatsworth comes after you again. And it looks as if this may be that time. Do you not want my help?"

"Sorry. Yes, of course I do." Sam looks around, nervously, taking stock of the situation. He and his friends are out in the open. Wherever Chatsworth is, Sam and his party are visible to him - and therefore vulnerable. There are many people milling round that Chatsworth could inflame. But probably not enough to endanger their lives. Chatsworth will be biding his time.

Sam has a baseball cap in his back pocket. He puts it on, jamming it low over his eyes. From the bench, Maddy looks at him quizzically. He turns his back.

"Sam: do not go in. You and your family - you must leave, now."

"And how do I explain that?" Sam whispers intently into the phone. "My parents have been looking forward to this for weeks. My Dad and sister are already in there. I can't leave them. I'm sorry – believe me, I want to get away but I can't. I'm trapped."

"Then stay with your family. Do not attempt to face Chatsworth, if you find he is there. He will kill you. You know that."

"Believe me, he's the last person on Earth that I want to meet. Look: it's up to you now. Call the Police and warn them. They have to stop the show going ahead. Get them to empty the Hall. Tell them to get everyone out."

"You are right. I will do that. The thought of him loose inside a confined space - it's horrible."

"Right. I'll go, so you can do that. Let me know what they say." Sam hangs up. Whatever is to happen next, it's outside his control. Nervously he re-joins the others and they walk across the road to the Hall.

"Everything alright?" Maddy looks at him, curiously.

"I hope so."

"Sorry?"

"Oh. Yes: something just came up. It's under control."

Sam has seen the Royal Albert Hall on television, but only now does he realise how truly huge it is. He wonders how Rachel felt when she saw it for the first time that morning. She must have been nervous.

It is a spectacular setting. Sweeping galleries run round the auditorium in a giant oval that stretches from one side of the stage to the other, each level packed with steeply raked seats. Tonight the huge floor has chairs laid out on it as well. The impossibly high domed roof has 'magic mushrooms' hanging from it. The place drips with opulent reds and gold. This is a truly imposing building; architecture on a grand scale from an age when grandeur was a statement.

But the grand scale means ... thousands of people. "How many can this place hold?" he asks his mother.

"Not sure - about five thousand, I think."

So many? Sam groans in horror. Five thousand people in one building. Five thousand people at the mercy of a man who can manipulate them in ways they can't start to imagine.

Five thousand innocent people!

Can Chatsworth be so ruthless, so evil that he would risk the lives of so many? Surely not.

Surely ... yes. Sam tells himself not to be naïve. The man is mad. He'll find a way to justify to himself whatever he does. Chatsworth has already shown in Reading and Winchester that he has no compunction about causing chaos, misery and death. He is perfectly capable of doing it here, if it suits his purpose. He might be here to confront Sam, but his greater purpose could simply be to generate another disaster.

And that's the risk here – much worse than Reading and Winchester where the events were out in the open. This is a packed building. To get out, people will have to use the exits. Exits get blocked, especially when people panic. Donovan Chatsworth loose in this place ... it doesn't bear thinking about!

The two families take their seats in the first gallery. A few minutes later Sam's father joins them. "Rachel's OK. She's downstairs in a dressing room. There's a chaperone from the dance school with them. She's all kitted out in her slave-girl's costume. Rehearsals went OK" he breathes. "One of her friends said Rachel cried when she saw the size of this place, but she's OK now."

"Poor dear. I hope she'll be able to cope." Helen frowns with concern for her daughter. "The hall is filling up."

"Course she will – she'll love it once she gets going."

A cold shiver of fear runs through Sam at his mother's words: the hall is indeed filling up. He watches with mounting horror as more and more people walk in. in what looks like a never-ending stream. The hall is three quarters full and still they come.

Please - no more people – make it stop. Surely the announcement to empty the Hall will come soon? But relentlessly they keep coming, happy innocents looking forward to their evening out, unsuspecting music-lovers oblivious of the danger lurking somewhere in this famous place.

Sam's phone vibrates in his pocket. It's a text from Emmanuel Cabrieres. Thank goodness!

"Have warned police, but they won't clear hall. You must leave."

Sam has to leave his seat to have this conversation. He phones back: "Do you mean they're refusing to clear the Hall?"

"Yes. They say it would cause a panic in itself. But I think they want to capture Chatsworth."

"Then they're idiots!"

"They simply don't understand."

"There must be someone who does, surely?"

"Not that I know of, my friend."

"Try the Police in Winchester. They had a poster of him. Or Woking, where that MP died. Someone knows about him."

"I will. But get yourself out, Sam."

"How? Can you tell me what I could possibly say to persuade my family to leave? What reason could I give for them to walk out now, just when Rachel is about to go on stage? Tell them that I have a sixth sense that something bad is going to happen? Make them understand in two minutes flat what I haven't told them for months?"

"Could you say you're feeling ill?"

"I could. I expect one of them would come out with me and miss the show, that's all."

"Then we must pray that Chatsworth won't be so evil as to try something with thousands of people. He will cause pandemonium."

"If that's what he's planning to do, he'll do it. And he'll do it whether I'm in the Hall or not. My leaving won't make any difference. You told me yourself: he's obsessed, evil - completely mad."

"Then, if the Police won't empty the Hall, our only hope is that I find him first."

"Where are you?" asks Sam.

"I'm coming through the doors now."

"I'll come and help."

"No! If you confront him, all hell will let loose. The two of you fighting each other, using your powers, in a confined space? Both of you? It's impossible."

"Then get back onto the Police - if they won't listen, tell the Hall staff there's a bomb, or smash a fire alarm or something. Anything. Just get the people out of here."

"Then I will start a panic. Chatsworth will see what is happening and he will then add to it. People will still die, just as he intended, but I will then be blamed for it. No, I have no choice but to find him myself. I'm inside. I must go now."

Emmanuel ends the call.

Sam retakes his seat. Maddy leans over. "Secret girlfriend?" She looks concerned.

Sam blinks. "Sorry?"

"You're spending a long time on the phone. Problem?"

"Oh. Sorry. I hope not. No, not a secret girlfriend."

Why would she ask?

Sam misses the look of relief on Maddy's face.

"It's good to be out like this with our families. I wish Uncle Frank could be here though. One day you will have to tell me exactly how you worked everything out about him. It was uncanny."

"Keep telling you, I just put two and two together." says Sam. He forces a smile – the last thing he feels like at the moment – but he wants to rob the words of any offence.

The conversation, which could have been awkward had it continued, is stopped short. The audience is applauding for some reason. Oh hell, it's the conductor walking to his rostrum.

The lights dim.

Dammit, the performance is starting.

Sam has been looking forward to this moment for weeks. Now he dreads it. Will Emmanuel Cabrieres find a way to get the people out? Will he find Donovan Chatsworth?

Sam has never been to an opera before. He is surprised how much of the music is familiar to him. Twice in the first Act, Rachel and her friends have walk-on parts, slave-girls standing in attendance to the Royal family in Ancient Egypt. But Sam is too on-edge to enjoy the show. He is counting down the minutes, waiting for something awful to happen.

Thank God! The first Act has ended. As the audience applauds and Sam breathes a sigh of relief, his phone vibrates. It's a text message. "2nd tier bar. E"

Making his excuses, Sam finds his way as quickly as he can through the crowded corridors. A flight of stairs leads to the second tier and the balcony. Emmanuel Cabrieres is waiting for him. Beside him is the woman who was with him in Winchester.

The Frenchman makes no attempt to introduce them. He takes Sam's arm and drags him to a quiet corner. "Sam. There is little time. Have you sensed Chatsworth again since you came in?"

"No."

"Thank goodness. I have searched every row on the ground floor but have not seen him. I shall start on the galleries now."

"And what about getting the bloody place evacuated? There's five thousand people trapped in here with that madman. Why won't the Police do something?"

The Frenchman shakes his head. In the background Sam hears a siren wailing. "You hear that? They are doing something, but it is the wrong thing. They are surrounding the hall. They plan to capture him. He is public enemy number one, you understand and we have given them credible evidence on where he is. They are assembling hundreds of men to surround the place and ensure he cannot escape. Armed men. They will check everyone as they leave. But they refuse to stop the show. They say that would warn him that they are here."

"Idiots! They have to get everyone out right now. Don't they know what will happen?" Sam shouts the words in his frustration.

"No, the decision-makers here do not know what will happen. It is a well-kept secret. I spoke to the Winchester station but the senior people are off duty."

"Then smash one of the fire alarms."

"Then we will start the panic and Chatsworth will immediately add to it and we will be seen as the guilty parties. I cannot do that."

"What then?" Sam is agitated.

"I must find him ... I will continue to search."

"If you do, he'll kill you."

"That is a risk I must take."

"Are you armed?"

"No, of course not."

"Then what can you do against him? He'll kill you from across the room."

"I will try to talk to him, stop him from doing whatever he is planning. Or attack him by surprise. But you ... you must leave this building. If he is here because of you, he must not find you. You must leave now. Do not get involved, my friend. Leave this to me."

Sam nods but it is a lie. He will not do as he has been told. No more will he run away. He will not – he cannot - let Donovan Chatsworth create another disaster, unchallenged. That's the decision he made weeks ago.

Each of them has a sense of foreboding. Both are praying that nothing will happen.

Both feel it will.
The stage is set for disaster.

CHAPTER 38 – AIDA, ACT TWO

The bell rings to signal that Act Two is about to start.

"Where's Maddy?" whispers Sam as he retakes his seat.

"Ladies, I think."

"She'll miss the start."

"Must be a queue. Don't worry, she'll be back."

But she isn't. Act Two of the opera opens with the four slave-girls, of whom Rachel is one, sitting near the front of the stage, on the audience's right. Most people pay them barely a glance, assuming they are there merely to help set the scene. Sam recognises the music: Rachel has been playing it for weeks. Her dance is about to start. Maddy's going to miss it.

The conductor signals. Rachel and her three partners rise and start their ballet. For the next four minutes, five thousand pairs of eyes are on them and them alone.

Four thousand, nine hundred and ninety-nine.

No, four thousand, nine hundred and ninety-eight.

Two pairs are not watching the stage. Madeleine James' eyes are wide open, unblinking, unseeing, staring straight ahead. She is standing to attention, ramrod straight. Next to her, the other pair of eyes is concentrating as their owner taps a text message on her phone.

An audible "aaaah" ripples round the audience. Sam holds his breath, praying that the girls all remember their steps. They do. At the end of the dance, the crowd bursts into warm applause. The conductor pauses the orchestra until the noise dies away. The four little slave-girls have stopped the show and Rachel is one of them.

They bow and walk from the stage.

"Brilliant!" Sam beams at his parents. Both his mother and father are discretely wiping tears from their eyes, hoping no-one will see. They are bursting with pride, and rightly so.

But where is Maddy? She's missed it!

He has no time to think. His mobile phone vibrates. A text message.

Maddy's number.

Thank goodness!

"Top balcony. Come now or in five minutes she dies. DC." Attached is a photograph: it's Maddy. She doesn't look right.

No! Not Maddy!

Sam has no choice. Quietly he ducks out of his seat to walk up the aisle. Briefly he stops: "Dad, there's something wrong. Get everyone out. I'm going to find Maddy."

"What?"

"Dad, there's a fire or something. Get everyone out. I'll find Maddy."

"Sam?"

Sorry, he can't delay any longer. Sam runs up the aisle to the exit.

"Ngozi. Can you hear me?"

She's still asleep. Sam sprints into the corridor. Which way is the staircase to the gallery? Left? Right?

He turns left. He struggles to send a text to Emmanuel Cabrieres as he runs. "DC top balcony. Has Maddy."

There – stairs! Straight, half landing, double back, another half landing. They loop round taking Sam higher and higher. Sam leaps them three at a time as he dashes to find his friend. The steps are stone, worn smooth by hundreds of thousands of feet over a hundred years. Sam's foot slips on the shiny surface and he falls heavily, gasping for breath.

Ignoring the pain, he frantically resumes his flight. The steps echo his footsteps as he clatters loudly, up and up and up, round and round and round.

The stairs reach another landing.

This is it. The balcony.

One door. No choice.

"Stay calm!" Sam mutters to himself. He takes a series of deep breaths. "Move quietly – perhaps I can take him by surprise."

Sam eases open the door and slides smoothly through. He is in the topmost gallery of the hall. It curves round in a giant semicircle from one side of the stage to the other. There are no seats here tonight, just a few chairs set for no apparent reason against the back wall. Silently, he closes the door behind him. The music of the opera comes crystal clear from below – but that seems a world away now.

Looking down, Sam can see a sheer drop. The show is continuing, the rapt audience enjoying their evening out, unaware of what is happening far above them.

Maddy - where is Maddy?

But before Sam can find out, he hears a voice from the shadows. It is a calm, soft voice, silky and smooth and sinister.

"Good evening, Mr. Wright."

CHAPTER 39 – CONFRONTATION

O utside the Royal Albert Hall a tall man with olive-coloured skin and jet black hair, wearing a light coloured coat, is arguing with a senior uniformed police officer.

"Evacuate the Hall now. Stop the show before it's too late" he orders, waving a photograph at the officer.

"With respect Mr. – ah, Smith, you have no jurisdiction here. You cannot order me to do anything. I have an army of men assembling. We will catch him, have no worries about that."

"You will not catch him. You can't. If you don't stop the show and evacuate the Hall, hundreds of people will die. If you put them in his way, your own people will be among the casualties."

"That's melodramatic nonsense. I know you guys work in a rarefied atmosphere, but this isn't a James Bond movie. It's the real world and we are following correct practice. We have the situation under control. Now, you must excuse me, I have an important operation to direct and no more time to waste." The police officer stamps away.

The man in the light coloured coat swears and speaks urgently into a microphone under his collar.

Sam strains to see into the shadows, trying to make out the face that owns the voice. The speaker is hidden. But he knows who it is. Even though he's hot and breathing heavily from sprinting up the stairs, he shivers.

He knows what Ngozi would say if only he could contact her: you bloody fool! Get away from him. Run!

But he can't. Not till he knows what has happened to Maddy. Chatsworth has her here somewhere. Sam won't leave her to face this fiend alone. He looks round the gallery, trying to see if his friend is there.

Donovan Chatsworth continues to speak, his voice purring with satisfaction. "No response? I am disappointed in you. Sam Wright, I had the pleasure of not meeting you in Reading?"

Sam gives up looking for his friend and turns to face his enemy. "That's right, Chatsworth" he says, through gritted teeth.

"Ah! You speak at last. And you know who I am! I am honoured!"

"How did you know I would be here?"

"I make it my business to know."

"That's not an answer. How did you know I'd be here?"

"Hmm. An unexpected start to our conversation, when there's so much that is infinitely more interesting to discuss, but I suppose there is no harm in telling you. I knew in the same way that I knew you were going to be in Winchester City Centre and the same way I knew you would be at your cycle track. Your dear next door neighbour has been keeping me informed of your movements for some time."

The witch next door? Mrs. Jobson, the curtain-twitcher? So she's to blame?

"You look shocked. Don't be. Your neighbour is a very devout woman. A very caring person. But so easily led. She believes, with a little help from me, I must confess, that you are possessed of evil spirits, Sam. Yes, she really does! Evil spirits! She knows me as the Reverend Sherwood. She's had a troubled life, I'm afraid. Great wrongs have been done to her, just as they have to me. I understand her pain, you see. I have been counselling her by phone. Together we offer prayers for your salvation. I believe she may be even praying for you at this very moment. As well she might, incidentally."

The orchestra reaches a crescendo as the opera continues way below them.

Chatsworth walks slowly towards Sam. As he moves from the shadows, Sam looks into his face for the first time. Even though he has seen his picture, Sam is shocked that such an evil person can look so unremarkable. He feels a quiver of fear. This is death approaching.

Sam plays for time. "I know who you are, Mr. Chatsworth. And I know what you can do."

"Quite so. And that answers the first question that I intended to put to you when you were – staying – with my friends. But you left, so rudely, before I could get there."

"So you were responsible for my kidnap?"

"Oh yes. I assumed you knew? Surely the police told you?"

"No." Sam tries to hide the shock he is feeling. Did they really know? "My parents said it was a ransom attempt."

"Oh my dear, foolish boy – if we'd made some money from the exercise, it would have been a bonus but nothing more than that. Money was never my objective. No, my purpose was to meet you. The police have known this for some time. Are you seriously telling me that they didn't warn you?"

Sam's eyes widen.

"My, oh my! They didn't!" Chatsworth laughs. "How naïve you were to trust them. How utterly stupid of you." He pauses, a smirk playing round his lips. "I see it now. They've been using you as bait!"

Sam feels a sense of shock as the truth of Chatsworth's analysis rams home. The Police have known that Chatsworth intended to kill him, and they've said nothing. They've risked his life.

"Where's Maddy?"

"Ah yes, your lovely girlfriend. Over there. Let me show you. I'm afraid she is – how shall I put this - not well."

Chatsworth walks slowly round the balcony. There, in the dark and hidden by one of the large pillars is Maddy, standing stiffly to attention and with a glazed look in her eyes. Unseeing. Unknowing.

Sam runs to her. "Maddy!"

She doesn't answer.

Sam takes her hand and presses it. "Maddy. It's Sam. Speak to me."

There's no response. Not the slightest flicker.

Sam wheels round angrily to face Donovan Chatsworth. "What have you done to her?"

"The foolish girl defied me: I needed her to co-operate. It seems I overloaded her feeble little mind. It has, I would say, switched off. I've seen this before. Her body is alive, but her brain - it's out of reach now."

Maddy's greatest fear!

"Please, whatever you've done to her ... undo it."

"I can't do that, even assuming I cared enough. I'm telling you, dear boy, that there's nothing to be done." There is no compassion in Chatsworth's voice.

"You bastard. If you've hurt her …"

"You'll do what?" Chatsworth spits out the words. "Kill me? I don't think so."

"Why her? Why pick on Maddy?"

"I told you - she defied me."

"And that justifies - this?"

"She defied me!" shouts Chatsworth. It is clear that that is reason enough. "Her purpose was to bring you here. That was all. I needed her phone but the stupid girl tried to throw it over the balcony. I do believe she was trying to protect you. I think she has – well, had – a great affection for you. But she was very stupid to disobey me. Study her closely and learn: this is what happens to people who upset me."

"I begging you, please, undo whatever you've done to her."

"Begging now - I like that. I've already told you, that's not possible. She is shut off from me … from you … from everyone. She's gone. Her body lives, but her mind – it's no longer there."

Sam takes Maddy by the shoulders. "Maddy, it's Sam. Snap out of it. Speak to me." Frantically he shakes her. Below them the music swells to another crescendo.

Nothing.

He stands in front of his friend as if to protect her from Donovan Chatsworth.

"What do you want from me?"

"Your life, Sam. I want your life."

"But why?"

"Because you defied me too. In Reading. You stopped me from carrying out a plan that was important to me. I do not forgive people who do that. And, what's more, you are responsible for the arrest of my friends. You have angered me twice. And I want your life because I can take it and that is what I choose to do."

"But …"

Chatsworth raises his hand. "Let me explain. I warned Inspector Murphy that I had added you to my list of targets. I told him that if the police did not do as I said, I would kill you and stage another spectacular demonstration of my abilities.

"As it happens, you have given me the opportunity to deliver on both promises. You helped me select the scene for my greatest demonstration, simply by coming here."

Sam needs to buy some time. Where is Emmanuel Cabrieres? Surely he's received his text message by now?

"I reckon you killed that MP."

"Ah yes, the odious Coombray." Chatsworth's voice is calm and oily. "Such a tragedy! Only a few minutes earlier we were having a quiet conversation on the train, reminiscing on old times. I explained to him how – sad – I was at his role in sending me to prison. Finally he understood what a difficult time I had had there, all alone in such a horrible place. The poor man was overwhelmed with remorse and guilt and he killed himself." Chatsworth shrugs his shoulders nonchalantly.

"You killed him, you mean."

"Oh, no - I didn't lay a finger on him." Chatsworth is serious.

"You made him suicidal."

"Let us say that I helped him make an important decision."

"You murdered him."

"Not murder. It was just retribution. For what he did to me." There is an edge to Chatsworth's voice. He looks agitated. His actions are being challenged and he can't cope with that. Sam is worried that he will lose his temper.

This is no good. As Sam was told, Chatsworth can justify anything he does. He needs to try another approach. "There's no need for any more people to die. Surely you've done enough already to prove how powerful you are?"

Chatsworth smiles thinly. "You think so? People have short memories. They need constant reminding."

"What you did in Winchester – that was spectacular!"

"Yes, it was rather. But the City is recovering and people are forgetting."

Damn – that hadn't worked. Try another tack. "And I know what it must have been like for you in prison, not able to talk to your partner. I understand."

"You know about that?"

"Yes. My partner was injured recently and while she was unconscious I felt terrible. So lonely. That was an accident – but your loneliness was inflicted on you deliberately. The way you were treated was cruel." Sam means this. "It wasn't right."

Chatsworth looks surprised. "I confess that I'm gratified ..."
Chatsworth pauses for a moment, seemingly affected – impressed even.
"Those are kind words, Sam Wright. True words. It's a long time since I
received the understanding I deserve."

"Then ..."

"But kind words won't stop me. I now have the power to avenge
myself, and I choose to use it. Tonight."

"Please – not here. Not with all these people. You're a remarkable
man, but killing hundreds of people can't put right what you suffered.
They can't understand what it was like for you. But I can. I understand."

Chatsworth looks thoughtful. "To my surprise, Sam Wright, I find I
like you. In fact, you have astonished me. I believe you really do
understand how I suffered. You have a telepathic partner ..."

Sam nods.

"... so you appreciate my pain. No-one has ever understood me
before. Not my grandfather and his obsession with the mind, nor my
pathetic, hate-filled father nor my brilliant, holier-than-thou brother.

"Sam Wright, it occurs to me that you could be the caring relative I
never had. The first person ever to understand me. You could be my
friend." Chatsworth pauses, as if thinking. "Very well, I offer you your
life. Let us not fight. Instead, work with me. You and I are alike, you
know."

"Work with you? Killing people? I'd rather die!" The words are out
before Sam can think about them. Shit! Has he just signed his own death
warrant?

Chatsworth scowls. "Very well, Sam Wright, you have made your
choice. I was generous enough to offer you your life. As for me, my life
was ruined long ago. I won't stop until all those who turned against me
are brought to justice."

"Justice! You actually use the word 'justice'?" Sam gives up trying
to reason. His temper snaps and his voice rises as he speaks. Below
them the music grows louder again. "You don't know the meaning of
the word. You just want revenge."

"Justice – revenge – there's such a narrow line between the two."
Chatsworth too is also shouting above the noise of the music.
"Coombray received his just punishment and make no mistake, I'm
going to do the same to every one of them who conspired against me.
I'm going to destroy them all."

"Chatsworth. You're a raving loony."

Sam feels a stab of anger – Chatsworth's anger. But it passes – after years of practice this man is able to control his emotions well.

Chatsworth stands close to Sam. "And you are about to learn just how powerful a raving loony I really am." The music softens. Standing close to Sam and speaking slowly and softly, the madman continues: "In a few moments I shall kill you – rather slowly, I'm afraid. Soon, Sam Wright, you will be on your knees, begging me to stop, pleading with me to end your agony."

Chatsworth steps back again. "But first, let me ask you a question. Have you considered how irresponsible it would be if someone shouted 'Fire' in a crowded hall like this? Isn't that everyone's worst nightmare?"

Sam shrieks: "No! There are thousands of innocent people down there. You'll kill them! They won't stand ..."

But as he says the words, Chatsworth looks carelessly over the balcony edge towards the crowd below. Sam feels an irresistible sense of terror wash over him – an artificial fear created by the man in front of him.

"No! You can't!"

"But I can." Chatsworth smiles thinly. "And I do."

Way below them, the effect is like an explosion. From the previously silent audience, screams of fear interrupt the show. The orchestra and singers stop and run from their positions.

Chaos!

In blind panic people charge for the exits, frantic to escape, caring for no-one in their desperation to escape the unseen horrors that lurk in the shadows. Strong men throw women and children aside in their panic to get away. All reason is lost, all notion of human decency gone.

People fall in the doorways, blocking the exits, and are trampled underfoot by the terrified mob behind them. Piles of fallen opera-goers mount at every exit, blocking the way out. Shrieks of pain mix with the screams of terror.

As people panic in the hall below, Sam Wright faces Donovan Chatsworth. He understands what is happening. Knowing the emotion to be false, he is better able to cope with it, but he is too agitated to be able to stop it. In frustration he yells above the cacophony from below: "Stop! You must stop! You're killing innocent people."

Chatsworth is unmoved. He looks impassively at the pandemonium he is causing. "Yes. You're right, I am." He raises him arms to the heavens. "Look at them! They are sheep and I drive them where I choose. Let tonight be a lesson to any who defy me - a testimony to my power."

Sam rushes forward. He will kill Chatsworth with his bare hands if he has to. Chatsworth points and Sam stops in his tracks, falling to his knees, struggling now to control the even more powerful emotions that Chatsworth is projecting.

Chatsworth's face is a mixture of delight and expectation as he looks at Sam kneeling before him. "Even you, Sam Wright! Even you cannot resist me! You should have accepted my offer. You refused to join me and now I shall make sure you never defy me again."

"Please ..." Paralysed with fear, Sam is unable to move.

When Chatsworth speaks again it is quietly, malevolently. "Sam Wright, your future is hopeless – you must understand that by now." He walks slowly – menacingly – towards Sam.

Like a tap turned off, the feeling of terror is gone. In its place Sam feels a wave of despair wash over him. Despair - the most powerful emotion of all - the killer.

Life is futile. Why is he here? What could he hope to achieve by confronting this man? Sam sees it now: he can't live with this feeling. Best to end it now. Instinctively, he crawls backwards, trying to get away from the source of his pain.

In the hall below, people who had been frantic to push through the exits now stop struggling. Their terror is gone, replaced in an instant by the deepest, blackest sense of gloom. Many flop into the seats, sobbing. Others simply lie where they have fallen in the aisles, no longer caring what happens to them next, their fear replaced by morbid depression. Why were they wasting their energy trying to escape? It was futile; they'd never have been able to get away. It was ridiculous even to try. No, they'll submit to the inevitable and die where they are.

The sound of wailing replaces the screams of terror. And then ... what ... what is that? New noises. Over the cacophony of grief from below come screams and dull thuds. Men and women in the upper tiers are running to the safety rails and hurling themselves over, killing themselves as they crash onto the seats many metres below. Sam hears and feels the sickening, crunching impacts as their bodies break on the seat backs.

"Please - stop this!" Sam pleads.

Chatsworth smiles. "There goes one – oh, and another." He looks serious and pretends to care. "Ooh, crunch - that must have hurt!"

"I can't let you do this." Sam closes his eyes and forces himself to think positive, calming thoughts. Relax!

It's no good. At Reading he had been focussing on Maddy. Here, he has no-one.

He makes no impression at all.

Chatsworth places his hands on his hips, throws his head back and laughs out loud as Sam tries – and fails – to make any impression on the people below. He laughs the relaxed, maniacal cackle of a madman who is getting his own way – everything justified in his own twisted mind, his world in order, untroubled by remorse or conscience.

With a feeling of shock, Sam realises that his inevitable confrontation with Donovan Chatsworth has both started and ended in an instant. Emmanuel was right - he simply isn't strong enough. The showdown has come at a time and place he least expected. He wasn't prepared. His opponent is too powerful.

How long does he have to live?

"Oh my! Was that your best attempt? How pathetic!" gloats Chatsworth. "You dared challenge me? The most powerful man on Earth? You had the arrogance to try?"

A new wave of gloom washes through Sam's head. He cries out. It is taking all his willpower to fight the suicidal feelings that Chatsworth is forcing into his head. Round the hall the screams of despairing people jumping to their deaths continue.

"For pity's sake, stop!" sobs Sam, beating his fists on the floor in frustration. "Please. They're innocent!"

Chatsworth sneers at him. He is enjoying himself. He is killing people and he relishes the feeling of power that gives him. "You wish me to stop? Very well, I tire of this. I believe that you are considering whether to jump. If you do that, I need kill no more of those poor dupes down there. Once you are gone, then I may stop. Don't you think you should do the noble thing – for their sakes? Save their lives by sacrificing your own, Sam. Jump. Jump now."

Again, Sam feels an overwhelming sense of hopelessness wash through him. With the thought of jumping planted in his head, he crawls towards the edge of the balcony. It is so tempting - to end it, to end it all now. He never asked for this - he can stop feeling this misery.

Sam's senses are swimming; he can't hold out much longer. His mind ... his mind ... it's breaking. He's losing the ability to think for himself.

He struggles to control his own thoughts. I must do as Chatsworth tells me. No, no ... that's wrong. The edge ... walk to the edge. No ... stay down ... stay on the floor. It's safe down here. The floor is my friend. Don't stand up. If I get up, my death will be just a question of time ... a few minutes at most ... no more ... so sad to leave everything so soon ...

A door crashes open. Through his blurred vision, Sam can just make out the shapes of Emmanuel Cabrieres and the small dark lady who had been with him before. She is about 60 years old, her hair is grey and cut short. Her face is – sad. It is interesting that they should be here, but it's too late. Too late.

The woman is paying very close attention to Chatsworth and Sam. She has beads of perspiration on her forehead and is shaking under Chatsworth's mental onslaught. But she forces herself to speak.

"Donnie. You must stop this" she shouts above the noise.

Chatsworth blinks, his concentration broken. "Who's that?" And then, in wonderment: "You know me? You call me Donnie? Who are you?"

"Donnie, you know who I am" says the lady, speaking softly now. "You must stop doing this evil thing. You must stop now."

Another flood of misery washes over Sam. Emmanuel Cabrieres cries out and staggers against a pillar. The lady with him screams. Sam still on his knees, holds his head.

Then Chatsworth cries out. "That's right. I don't care!"

Where did that come from? Chatsworth is responding to something that no-one said. Sam senses that he is shocked.

"Donnie? Donnie? Only two people have ever called me that and my mother is dead. Now I recognise your voice." Chatsworth is talking aloud. "Alice? Is it you? MY Alice?" he asks in wonderment.

"Yes, Donnie. I am Alice."

"My dearest, sweetest Alice – you've come to me? Are you talking with me again?"

Briefly Sam feels a sense of ... happiness. The despair lifts.

"Yes, I'm talking to you – for one last time. I swore I would never do this again. But I am here now, and I am asking you – begging you - to STOP DOING THIS."

For a moment Chatsworth wavers.

But only a moment.

"No! There was a time when I would have done anything for you. You know that. I believed you cared for me. But you didn't. When I most needed you, you didn't answer. You left me all alone in that accursed place. You abandoned me. You are the cause of my misery! You made me like this! You!"

The brief moment of happiness is gone, replaced now by hate. "You were cruel and heartless, Alice. You, my closest friend, turned against me like the rest of them. My love for you is dead. It turned to hate, years ago."

As he speaks, for a few brief moments Chatsworth's attention is distracted. Emmanuel Cabrieres shouts. "Sam, get up! Fight! Stop kneeling there!"

Stiffly, Sam stands to face his enemy. Using Chatsworth's distraction he strikes: "You evil madman! The person you should hate is yourself." He concentrates on projecting a new emotion – self-loathing.

In the depths of the hall, the screams from the audience grow louder. Sam is affecting them, as well as Chatsworth. Now the crowd has conflicting emotions pounding into their heads.

"Hate myself." Chatsworth is looking at Alice. Has she just repeated Sam's words telepathically? He thinks she has.

As if to confirm what Sam is thinking, Alice shouts at him: "Don't stop, Sam. Finish this!"

"You can't live like this" shouts Sam, pointing at Donovan Chatsworth. "How you must despise what you have become."

"Despise myself. But Alice ..." Chatsworth is looking first at Sam, then Alice, then back again. It's true ... Alice is telepathically echoing Sam's words into Chatsworth's head.

Chatsworth takes an involuntary step back. Sam feels a strange wonder coupled with grim determination. Alice's arrival has given him a chance to fight back. But is he strong enough?

"You can't live like this." Sam continues to project his emotions at Chatsworth.

"Can't live ..." Chatsworth is looking pleadingly at Alice. He takes another involuntary step back. "Can't live ..." He is still resisting, but for the first time fear shows in his eyes.

Sam walks towards Chatsworth to emphasise his dominance, and Alice and Emmanuel match step with him. Now, with his own death the only other option, he resigns himself to what he must do. Tonight he will do what only he, Sam Wright, can - or he will die in the attempt. This is his one chance to rid the world of Donovan Chatsworth.

With icy coldness in his heart, Sam shouts "You don't want to live like this." He points as he projects his own deadly emotion. As he does, the noise of wailing rises again from the body of the hall. He steels himself, forcing himself to ignore it. He has to finish this. He has to finish it quickly or hundreds more people will die.

"Don't want to live like this" Chatsworth mutters. "No one cares for me."

Chatsworth looks pleadingly at Alice and staggers backwards, towards the stage end of the balcony, his mind weakening under the double onslaught.

Sam follows Chatsworth as he backs away. "Now we are doing to you what you did to the innocent people you killed." His mind is so icy cold he hardly knows himself. "Don't plead for our mercy; we despise you."

"Despise me." Alice's words have thumped into Chatsworth's head.

Chatsworth whimpers in fear. He is nearing the edge of the balcony. For the first time in his life, he knows what it is like to be the victim of an Emotist attack.

"Learn now how it feels. Feel despair, Chatsworth – we are stronger than you! You are a vile creature and don't deserve to live."

"Disgusting animal." Chatsworth looks forlornly at Alice. "Alice, please ... stop." He has clasped his hands together, pleading. He is teetering on the brink of defeat.

"There is no purpose left in your life. End it!" shouts Sam and projects despair at Chatsworth.

"Alice, no!" Chatsworth takes another involuntary step backwards. He is at the balcony's edge. He clutches the rail. With Sam's emotional attack and Alice's telepathic words, Chatsworth is fighting two people.

Sam dares not dwell on what they are doing to him. Instead he remembers that this evil man has attacked Maddy.

"You're not fit for this earth! Go! GO NOW!!" yells Sam, keeping up the emotional attack.

"Go now. No. Must not go now." Chatsworth screams. "I know what you're doing ... you want ME jump. I won't ... I won't ..." Abandoning his mental fight, he resorts to physical violence and makes a despairing lunge forward, his hands outstretched, aiming for Sam's throat.

He never makes it.

With tears streaming down his face, mixing with the sweat dripping from his forehead as he struggles against the emotions being forced into his head, Emmanuel Cabrieres staggers forward. He moves with robot-like precision.

With a supreme effort of will, the Frenchman pushes Chatsworth back to the edge and stoops. He grabs Chatsworth's ankles. With a single sharp motion, he silently, deliberately and ruthlessly lifts them. For a moment his victim lies across the balcony rail, balancing on the brink. Then Emmanuel jerks his hands upwards and with slow inevitability Chatsworth topples backwards and outwards over the edge and into the main body of the hall far below.

His enemy makes no sound as he falls, but nothing can block from Sam's mind Chatsworth's final, mind-numbing, blood-curdling telepathic scream of terror, nor stop Sam feeling the searing stab of agony as his enemy's back breaks on the seats below.

Sam screams in pain and falls to the floor.

The flows of terror and despair snap off.

The tunnel through which Sam is passing is long and spirals up and down. At breakneck speed he travels, sensing rather than seeing the cold, black walls rushing past him. He holds his hands to his side so as not to reach out and touch anything.

There is no sound to accompany his journey. Just the telepathic scream that Chatsworth made as he fell to his death. Eventually that becomes a distant echo and fades.

The walls rush past. This time Sam knows what is happening.

A new sound. He knows what it will be.

A dot of light appears at the end of the tunnel. It grows and grows, becoming larger, brighter. Abruptly the tunnel ends and Sam finds himself standing in the maternity ward of a well-equipped hospital. A young woman lies on a bed, her hand being held by a man. It is the moment of their baby's birth.

Sam has to act quickly. He knows what will happen if he doesn't intervene. The abilities of Donovan Chatsworth – the telepathic powers he had – will transfer to another person. The same had happened with Vincent Stewart.

The faint outline of Donovan Chatsworth stands in the room.

"You know I can't allow you to do this. I won't."

"You will. You're not a killer like me."

Sam stands between the outline of the man and the new born baby. "I won't let you steal this baby's body – its future, its life. You have to die now. It's your time, Chatsworth."

The baby takes its first breath. The moment has passed.

"You fool. Very well, not this child. But there are other options and I will find one." Chatsworth's image starts to fade, and his voice grows weaker as he speaks. "I promise you, Sam Wright, you will see me again and next time we meet I shall destroy you. I shall shred your mind into a thousand pieces." The voice reduces until it is barely a whisper: "The one you eventually face will wipe you out, and bring down pain and destruction on everything you hold dear."

The apparition disappears. Behind Sam, the baby is wrapped in a blanket and handed to her mother.

What did Chatsworth's words mean? Does he live on? Is that possible? Will they meet again? Sam chases for answers in his mind but these are questions he can't answer.

He turns his back on the scene.

Sam finds himself kneeling on the floor of the gallery where he fell. Alice is lying next to him, sobbing uncontrollably. "Donnie. Oh Donnie. We were so close. Now we've killed you. But I had to do this. Lord forgive me, I had to ..."

Carefully, gently, an ashen-faced Emmanuel Cabrieres brings chairs and helps the two of them to sit. "Young man. You have a frightening power. But you have defeated that evil man. You have won."

Sam doesn't react. Won? A victory? No. He feels numb, not victorious. He's just a fourteen-year-old boy from Winchester, and tonight he helped kill a man. No matter how evil Chatsworth had been, this is the opposite of everything he has been brought up to believe and value.

And how many innocent people died in the Hall tonight?

And how many were down to him and not Chatsworth?

His family - are they safe? Did they get out in time? What about his sister Rachel? Where had she been ... is she alright? What about ...?

"Maddy!" he croaks hoarsely. She must have been released now that Chatsworth is dead. Sam staggers across the balcony to her.

No! Oh God, no! His friend is still standing to attention, her blank eyes staring fixedly and unseeing into the distance. Chatsworth's death has made no difference to her.

Sam has lost her, forever.

CHAPTER 40 – THE NEVER-ENDING SCREAM

G ently, Sam takes his friend's hand. "Maddy! It's alright now. He's gone. It's over."

There's no reaction.

Taking Maddy's shoulders, Sam shakes her gently. "Maddy, he can't hurt you anymore. You're safe now. Let me help you."

Nothing. Maddy's eyes remain staring, unseeing.

"She's still the same! What did he do to her?" he asks Emmanuel.

"I do not know. If Donovan Chatsworth attacked her mind, he would have overwhelmed her."

"He did. He told me."

"Then I fear her mind is destroyed. Perhaps it will mend, in time."

"Is that theory or do you know that?"

"Neither. I am not expert in these things. If that wicked man destroyed her mind, I fear she will never recover. But people have – how do you say – mental breakdowns. They detach themselves from the world. They switch off. Sometimes they stay as Maddy is now ... it is like a self-made coma. I cannot know what is happening in her head. No-one can."

"A coma? Like Vincent Stewart?"

"No, that was different. He was the victim of an accident."

"But he was still alive! Underneath, his mind was still there! I heard him screaming for help as they switched off the machines. Perhaps I can make contact with Maddy too."

"But she's not one of us."

"I have to try. I owe that to her."

"No! It is too dangerous. You don't know what you will do to her – or yourself."

"I have to do something."

"Sam, my friend, I know how you feel about her. But there is nothing you can do. Her best hope is doctors and nursing care. Perhaps in time ..."

"No. They won't even know where to start. I must do it."

"Non!" Emmanuel Cabrieres lapses into French. He takes a deep breath. "Sam, listen. Who knows what you might do? Your powerful mind - you could kill her or damage her even more. Or yourself. I implore you ... what you are considering is not safe. It is too dangerous."

"She's already damaged, and it's because of me. She's only like this because of my involvement with Chatsworth. I can't leave her like this."

"I am sorry, I cannot allow this. You are dabbling in things you cannot understand."

Sam shakes his head. He is too tired to argue. "Look, I'm not asking your permission. This is my friend. I have to take the risk. I made her a promise."

Emmanuel Cabrieres raises his hands and shrugs his shoulders. This is way beyond anything he has previously experienced.

Sam faces Maddy again. "Maddy. Can you hear me?" He clicks his fingers in front of her face. He claps his hands.

There is no reaction.

Sam stands close. He puts his hands on either side of his friend's head and touches his forehead onto hers. Does he need to do this? He doesn't know – it just seems natural. He needs to reach out to her with his telepathy. He imagines himself back in the seaside hotel ... the room ... the dark wardrobe ... the blackness. He blanks everything from his mind except his search for Maddy.

"Maddy, are you there?"

He is standing in the blackness. He can see nothing. Slowly he inches forward ... into the dark ... seeking a way into Maddy's mind.

Another hesitant movement into the blackness.

And another.

And another.

In the distance ... through the darkness ... a sound! He turns and edges towards it. He focusses on it. Cautiously he moves deeper ... deeper ... deeper through the blackness, towards it.

Gradually the noise becomes louder, till it echoes through Sam's head.

It's a scream.

A never-ending scream.

A scream of terror, a scream of warning.

It's a wall of sound. Like a physical barrier, it is stopping him from going further. It is painful to hear. It is Maddy's voice. She is terrified, desperate. Is this how she defended herself when Chatsworth attacked her? If so she was strong. Determined not to be touched by him.

"Maddy. Is that you?"

The screaming intensifies. But that's good, surely? To react like that, she must have heard him. Sam pushes against the wall of sound. It feels as if he is breaking into private property. Invading someone's home. But this is his friend. He made her a promise.

He has to push through.

Sam focuses his attention on the wall. He pictures it as made from blocks – each brick individual. He selects one and pushes at it gently. *"Maddy: it's me, Sam."*

Nothing. He pushes harder. And again. As hard as he can now, he pushes with all his mental strength.

Abruptly the brick moves. He has punched a hole in the barrier. He looks through and realises he is seeing into Maddy's mind. Pictures flash past him; Maddy's memories. Images of her parents. Pictures of himself. The face of Donovan Chatsworth demanding that she give him her phone.

"No! Stay away from me. You can't have it. I won't let you hurt Sam. I won't let you control me."

That's what had happened between her and Chatsworth.

"Maddy. This is Sam. You're safe now. He's gone. You can relax – it's over." He tries to project positive thoughts to his friend.

Nothing.

"Maddy. Come back to us. Your family, your friends – we want you back. You're safe again now. He'll never hurt you again. Maddy – I promise you. The voice you're hearing now – it's Sam. I've come to bring you back."

The screaming inside Maddy's mind weakens. Is he getting through to her?

"Maddy. Please hear me. It's Sam, your friend. That man – he's gone. You're going to be alright. It's over. You can relax now. I promise you – you're safe now."

The screaming subsides. He sees a picture of himself smiling. He sees himself through Maddy's eyes scoring his first goal in the school football match. He senses a warm feeling. Affection ... love. For him! Had everyone been right about him and Maddy? It makes him all the more determined.

"That's right, Maddy, relax. It's Sam. I'm with you. You're going to be alright. We need you back. Your family ... they love you. I ... I love you too. I need you back. I couldn't bear it if I lost you."

The picture in Maddy's head changes again. He sees ... himself again, this time standing close to Maddy in the gallery of the Royal Albert Hall. He sees himself, as if through her eyes. He imagines her putting her arms round his waist.

No – that was real! She just moved! She's holding him.

"Sam?"

Maddy said that out loud!

"Sam? You came ... oh."

Sam catches his friend as she sighs and collapses. He lowers her gently to the floor. As carefully and as slowly as he can he severs his mental connection with her. She's unconscious now.

Has he saved his friend? Or has he finished the job that Donovan Chatsworth started?

Has his last action on this dreadful night been to kill his best friend?

Sam bows his head and wipes away the tears that are running down his cheeks. M Cabrieres puts his arm round him. "What happened? How is she?"

"I don't know. She said my name. I think she recognised me."

"I saw her move. What did you do?"

"I found a way through. I spoke to her."

"That is so wrong. To invade another person's mind. Her private space."

"What would you have had me do – leave her like that? For the rest of her life?"

Alice is kneeling beside Maddy, holding her wrist, feeling for a pulse. She nods at Emmanuel. Maddy is still alive.

"Very well. What is done is done. She is sleeping. I hope that is good. Let us pray you have not damaged her mind."

Sam nods. "God, I hope I've not hurt her. I tried to be gentle."

There is a moment's silence as they look at the unconscious girl. For the first time Sam realises not just how beautiful she is but also how frail she looks.

Emmanuel stretches out his hands: "But now, what about you, my friend? You have been so brave. No-one should have to experience what you have been through tonight." He turns. "And Alice. You did what you had to do. Your loss ... it is terrible, no?"

Alice nods. Her face is streaked with tears. She is still shaking. Sam understands. Evil or not, her one-time telepathic partner is finally gone.

Sam becomes aware of the cries of people in pain coming from the body of the hall below. They are now mixing with the frantic shouts of relatives and friends calling the names of their missing loved ones. He dares to peer over the barrier. The Hall staff and the first of the emergency services have arrived and are gently trying to usher out everyone fit enough to move.

Sam tries phoning his parents ... no signal. He will have to search for them. But not yet. He feels too ill.

Presently, the Frenchman says: "What has happened to my manners? Monsieur Sam Wright, I should introduce you. This is Alice Whatmore, from Los Angeles. She was ..."

"... Donovan Chatsworth's telepathic partner." Sam finishes the sentence. "I know."

"Quite so. When Chatsworth was convicted, I instructed Madame Whatmore to have no more contact with him."

Sam nods. "And that was wrong. It was a cruel punishment. Too cruel. It is a terrible thing to do to a telepath."

Emmanuel looks intensely sad. "Maybe so. I have agonised over that many times, my friend. But at the time ... I believed it was not our job to help a criminal avoid his punishment."

Sam shakes his head. "You were wrong. You actually punished him twice."

The Frenchman winces but continues "Be that as it may, I believed that Chatsworth would try to kill you. It was my judgement that you would ignore my advice to run from him but I did not know whether you could survive such an encounter. So I persuaded Alice to come from the United States and stay with me in the hope that she might assist when the two of you faced each other, as I knew eventually you must."

"You did help. Up to then – well, when you arrived, I was beaten. I couldn't have held out much longer" says Sam.

Alice nods.

"You were repeating what I was saying?"

"Yes. It must have been awful for him. You attacking him with the emotions and me screaming telepathically into his head."

"It worked."

"I know. I know. I helped to kill him."

Sam has been insensitive. She has lost her one-time best friend. He moves closer to her.

"You were very close?"

She nods, solemnly. "When he was sent to prison he kept trying to talk to me. All the time. All the time. All ... the time." Alice repeats the phrase over and over again with a faraway look in her eyes. Dark memories are plaguing her. She shakes her head, as if to clear it, and refocuses on Sam. "It was horrible. I had to listen to him ... his love, his hate, his thirst for revenge. Over and over and over again."

"That was terrible."

"You have no idea. I listened to a man going mad. I couldn't get away from it. I wanted to scream. Can you imagine what that was like?"

"No. How on earth did you manage?"

Alice sighs sadly. Sam has broken into private memories.

"There were times when I thought I would die. At first I couldn't get away from him. Then, when he stopped trying to talk to me, I was so lonely. I would go to public places – the cinema, a concert or the shops. Even among hundreds of people, I felt hopelessly alone. I cried every night. I thought of killing myself. But in the end, I managed. I had to. I adapted. I forced myself to change."

Emmanuel nods. "We understand."

Sam hauls himself unsteadily to his feet: "I need to find my family and Maddy's parents. They could be down there, dead." A desperate thought keeps churning through Sam's head. What if, in fighting Chatsworth, he helped to kill his own family? And Maddy's? How could he live with that?

Desperately beating down the urge to panic, Sam turns to pick up Maddy. He manages two steps, stumbles and topples forward. Just as at Reading, his legs are weak and his head is thumping like it will burst.

Emmanuel Cabrieres catches him. "You must take care. You are exhausted, my friend. I shall carry the young lady. The journey down – I am afraid it must be a slow one."

CHAPTER 41 – OUTSIDE THE HALL

Sam, Alice Whatmore and Emmanuel Cabrieres, carrying the unconscious Maddy, shuffle painfully slowly down the stairs.

"Merd! But I am a fool! How could I not think of this?" Emmanuel stops on one of the lower landings. "Please, remain here. Rest. I must leave you for a few moments. There is something I must do." He lowers Maddy slowly and sets her on the floor.

Grateful for the chance, Sam sits too. He is too tired to ask what is happening. He rests Maddy's head on his lap and gently, instinctively, strokes her hair. "Maddy - stay with us" he murmurs. "We're getting you out."

The Frenchman re-joins them a few minutes later. "Bien. All is well. Now we may continue."

Sam senses that M Cabrieres is puzzled, as if he has seen something that he did not expect. But he is too exhausted to care: he just wants to complete this interminable journey and get out.

Earlier in the evening, Sam had sprinted up the stairs in less than two minutes. It takes ten times that to get back down.

When the four of them emerge into the night, everything is illuminated in blue from the lights of the emergency vehicles. There are more police than he has ever seen before in one place. Everyone's identity is being checked as they emerge. It is an eerie sight; a famous landmark turned into an alien landscape.

"Urgh!" Sam gratefully sucks in the cool fresh night air and then wrinkles his nose in disgust. The smell of sick hangs everywhere, heavy and overpowering. People are throwing up on the pavement in shock after the terrors they experienced inside and, now, at the sights that greet them outside.

Police are crowding everywhere. What a mistake they made tonight - they should have cleared the place. This tragedy could have been prevented. Or at least reduced.

Paramedics are carrying injured people on stretchers to waiting ambulances. The victims' pale and bloodied faces are twisted, not only with physical pain but also from the mental stresses they have endured. But these are the lucky ones – they are still alive. Others are lying completely covered. A long row of bodies is being assembled carefully in the curved corridor inside the Hall.

Emmanuel shakes his head sadly. "This is bad. This is very bad. It is a disaster."

"And it's my fault."

The Frenchman grabs Sam's arms with an intensity that shocks him. "No" he hisses. "You must never say that again. Don't even think it. It is not your fault. You did not start this – you ended it. You know who did this. But say nothing more of it, not with so many police around."

Sam nods. He hopes no-one overheard.

Overhead, the throbbing of two helicopters adds further noise to the cries of the injured and the shouts of people searching for their loved ones. One is shining a searchlight down. Television, possibly.

Two paramedics approach them. Briskly, efficiently, they ask for their names, then take the unconscious Maddy and lie her on a wheeled stretcher. One sets about examining her. "No obvious injury. Do you know how she was hurt?"

"Caught in the crush." Emmanuel Cabrieres answers quickly.

"Another one. Never seen anything like it." The paramedic shakes his head. "What the hell happened in there?" It's a rhetorical question.

"Can you identify her, please?"

"Madeleine James."

"Age?"

"Fourteen."

"Address?"

Wearily, Sam supplies the information they need.

"Are any of you three hurt?" asks his colleague.

Emmanuel shakes his head. "Nothing serious. We will be alright, thank you."

"Then please walk across the road to the park. The emergency control centre is there."

"No." Sam speaks slowly, with difficulty. "I want to stay with Maddy. Till we find our families. How can we find out ... if they got out?" Even speaking is an effort. "I haven't been able to 'phone them. Does that mean ..?"

"No, Sir. The mobile networks were overloaded and they've been shut down. It's possible there was a bomb and we can't take the risk of another one being detonated using a phone. Please go to the memorial – we're asking all survivors who are separated from their friends and relatives to assemble over there. If your family got out alive, they'll have be told to go there as well."

Too busy to enter into a discussion, he turns away to tend to a new patient who has just been carried from the Hall, his face and clothes covered in blood.

The second paramedic has turned back to Maddy, having finished taking her pulse and blood pressure. "Is she going to be alright?" asks Sam, anxiously.

"Difficult to say. No obvious signs of a problem. Her vital signs are OK."

A tall man, wearing a light coloured coat, is walking slowly through the crowd. He has olive coloured skin and jet black hair and is showing people a picture. Idly, Sam notices that he is talking to the American couple who were taking photographs that afternoon at the Albert Memorial. That seems a lifetime ago. Many lifetimes ago. The man is staring at the photo fixedly, as if he's in a state of shock. The woman shakes her head when shown the photograph and shepherds her husband away. He looks completely disorientated.

The tall man reaches Sam and his companions.

"Have you seen this person, please?"

Sam freezes. It's Donovan Chatsworth. What can he say?

Again Emmanuel Cabrieres reacts quickly. "Let me see this. No, I have not seen this man." He shows it to Sam and Alice. "Have you?"

Following his lead they shake their heads.

"May I ask where you were seated?"

Sam fishes out his ticket and shows it to the man. "I need to find my parents."

The man shakes his head slowly. "I have to warn you – there was a big crush in the exit there."

"Is this the only way they could have come?"

"Yes, the only other option is for people who were taking part in the show. There's a tunnel that leads from the dressing rooms. Some people have come out there." He points to the other side of the hall.

"Rachel!" Sam shouts hoarsely. It's difficult – his head is thumping and he has to pause every few words: "My sister. My parents ... wouldn't have left without her. They would have gone ... to the dressing rooms. Please, stay here with Maddy."

He gives up trying to talk - it is too much of an effort. He starts a painful shuffle towards the tunnel. Someone behind him calls, but he ignores it.

Behind Sam the tall man steps away from Emmanuel Cabrieres and Alice Whatmore. He lifts the collar of his coat and mutters into it. "The Wright boy's here, no doubt about it. I've just spoken to him. He looks like death warmed up."

He pauses, listening to a voice at the other end.

"Yes, he recognised the picture. He froze when he saw it. But we knew that. He's seen it before.

"The Frenchman said they hadn't seen him. Don't know if that's true. Could be true - they wouldn't still be alive otherwise, I reckon ..."

He pauses again.

"The girl is unconscious. Just like hundreds of others. The boy's looking for his family now."

He listens for a moment more. "Yes, I've let him go. What? Because we've got nothing on him. It's Chatsworth we need to find.

"Yes, it could have been the Frenchman who phoned the warning. I hope it was. If so, he did the right thing. He tried to prevent this.

"I told them to empty the hall. They wouldn't listen. As a result hundreds of people are dead. Yes, you heard. No, I'm not exaggerating. This is a disaster zone."

It's like looking for a needle in a haystack. People are sitting and lying on the pavements, some injured, some resting, all ashen-faced and dazed. Sam searches for his family with mounting anxiety. It's a desperate feeling: hundreds of faces – but none are the ones Sam so desperately needs to see.

Hope fades the nearer he shuffles to the tunnel. This is just horrible!

"Sam? Sam!" He hears his name being screamed. "Over here!"

Sam turns, trying to find the person shouting his name. Who is it?

"Sam! Oh my God – look! It's Sam. He's over there! Sam! We're here!" To his right, he sees his mother running towards him. Behind her, on the steps to the Hall sits his father. He is holding Rachel, still dressed in her slave-girl costume. Maddy's mother is there too.

Helen throws her arms round Sam. "Are you alright?" She leads him back to where she was sitting.

"I'm OK."

"Have you seen Maddy?" Maddy's mother looks sick with anxiety. "Ted's gone to look for the two of you."

"Yes. She's over there with the paramedics." Sam points. "She's unconscious but she's alive."

Jan groans. "Unconscious? Oh my God! Show me, quick."

Feeling doubly weak with exhaustion and now relief, Sam shuffles slowly back to where he left Maddy. She is still lying on the stretcher. Emmanuel Cabrieres and Alice have kept watch nearby.

Jan breaks into a run when she sees her daughter and kneels beside her. "Maddy, it's Mum. Are you alright? Thank God you're out of there."

Jan cradles Maddy's unconscious head in her arms. "Maddy, you're safe. You're going to be alright." She looks up at Sam. "What happened to her? Why is she unconscious?" She turns to the medics. "What's the matter with her?"

"Don't know. There's nothing obviously wrong with her. Her vital signs are all normal. She should be awake. But a lot of people came out like this. You're her mother?"

"Yes. Can't you do something? I don't like seeing her like this."

"Not here. We need to get her to hospital." Gentle hands lift the stretcher.

"Can I ride with her?"

"Please do."

"Can I come too?" asks Sam.

"Are you direct family, Sir?"

"No. I'm her friend."

"Then sorry, that's not possible."

"But ..." She might need him when she recovers. He can't say that.

"Please understand - the hospitals will be full to overflowing tonight. They can't handle anyone other than the patients and their closest families." He pauses, seeing the concern on Sam's face. "I'm sorry, Sir, I really am – but it's impossible."

Jan turns to Sam: "Thank you, Sam. You should get back to your parents; they've been so worried about you. And when Ted gets back,

Could you tell him I've gone with Maddy, please? Tell him we've gone to ..." she looks at the medic.

"St. Thomas'" the man finishes the sentence for her.

"St. Thomas'."

Sam nods. "I'll tell him. I ... I hope she'll be alright. Will you let us know? Please?"

She squeezes his hands. "Of course. As soon as I know anything."

Sam watches sadly as the ambulance doors close and his friend is driven away. He should be with her. He should have insisted.

"Please be OK, Maddy. I couldn't bear it ..." he whispers softly.

He turns to Emmanuel Cabrieres and Alice. "Do you think she'll be alright?"

"I cannot say. I simply cannot tell." Emmanuel looks grim.

"But we hope so." Alice says, shaking her head at Emmanuel. There are times when the brutal truth is not called for. She takes Sam's hand for a moment. "At least she's still alive and, whatever you did, you brought her out of that trance-like state she was in."

"Yes, I did. I just hope..." Sam stops. There's nothing more he can say. "I have to get back to my family now."

"Of course."

"Thank you so much ... you saved my life."

"And you saved hundreds more." Emmanuel Cabrieres shakes Sam's hand. "I shall contact you when you are home."

Back at the steps, Maddy's father has returned. He looks exhausted but relieved to see Sam. "Sam, thank goodness ... your Dad said Maddy was unconscious. Do you know where she is?"

"In an ambulance on her way to hospital. St Thomas'. Mrs. James went with her."

Edward James reaches for his mobile phone and backs away, hoping to get a signal. It is futile.

For the first time Sam notices that his father is holding a once-white, but now red, handkerchief to his leg.

"What happened?"

"Caught in the crush downstairs. I was pushed onto a costume trolley on the way down to the dressing rooms to find Rachel. It was horrible down there ... the crowd ... nothing I could do. Cut it on a metal edge."

"Do you need stitches?"

"Possibly but it can wait till we're home. I'll live."

"And Rachel's OK?"

"Yes, she's fine. Down in the basement, she was shielded from what was happening upstairs. Thankfully she had the sense to stay where she was – otherwise we'd never have found her. We came out through the tunnel and missed the worst of it. What's it like back there?"

"Bad. Lots of bodies."

"Was there a fire?"

"Don't think so."

"Weird. People thought there was. Must've been something."

Now that he knows his family is safe, now that he can relax, Sam's exhaustion finally takes its full toll. The world spins and his mother reaches forward as he sits down heavily on the steps next to her. He feels like he's burning up. His body is bathed in sweat.

Emmanuel Cabrieres and Alice Whitmore wave goodbye. Sam wants to say something, but he can't form the words. M. Cabrieres shakes his head and puts his finger to his lips, indicating silence.

Sam watches them walk away. He watches as the woman he met for the first time that night, the woman who saved his life, merges into the crowd.

"Who were they?" asks Sam's mother.

Sam can't speak. He is barely conscious.

Gradually, Sam recovers. Had he passed out? Possibly.

As he sits on the steps of the Royal Albert Hall with his family, Sam thinks back with a sense of shock and wonder on how his life has changed in a few short months. From the day he was an innocent victim in a road accident, he discovered powers he never knew even existed. He now speaks regularly to a woman he has never met, in a country he has never visited.

He has solved the mystery of a dead man who is still alive, been kidnapped and rescued, attacked and survived. Now he has been party to confronting, defeating and killing an evil madman who had destroyed hundreds of lives.

Even so, Sam feels a chill of fear and guilt. He dreads to think how many others died here. How many of them were lost not because of what Chatsworth did to their minds, but because of what he did as they fought? How many people were caught in the crossfire?

Ngozi wasn't there to advise him tonight. He'd had to make all the decisions for himself. Had he made the right ones? Should he have done things differently?

What if he is destined to turn a monster like Chatsworth? Will he be able to handle his abilities without going mad as well?

Enough. This won't do. Too many questions: too much self-doubt. He must put such negative thoughts to the back of his mind. He did what he had to do to save Maddy. And he would have done the same even if Ngozi had advised him not to.

Reunited now with his family and friends, Sam wants nothing more than to sleep. And, with Donovan Chatsworth gone, at least he can look forward to living without constant fear of attack. Life can get back to normal - whatever that might mean for him now.

His head is throbbing and he knows it will continue until he's able to get some sleep. He lies back on the cold step and closes his eyes.

Sam's mother looks at him. Her relief at knowing her son is alive is immense. And yet, there is something strange about him now. A new inner confidence, yes. That's part of growing up. But there's something else and she can't put her finger on it. Something darker. Mysterious. Secretive.

Lying on the cold surface with his eyes closed, Sam knows there is now no turning back for him now. He'll no longer fight what he is. He'll learn to live with his abilities and control them. If he uses them, it will be to do good ... he'll try to make amends for the deaths he may have caused tonight.

For the first time in months, Sam Wright feels that he knows who he is, what he is and what he needs to do to order his life from now on.

His real self has emerged.

He has completed his journey.

Or so he thinks.

EPILOGUE

I f it is possible for a train to lean forward to shelter itself from the wind and rain, that's what it's doing. Its progress towards Winchester is painfully slow. Sam Wright and his family sit in silence in the open plan carriage, all lost in their own thoughts. Having waited for hours on the cold concourse at Waterloo station until the first train out, it now seems to be making no progress at all as it stops every few minutes, as often as not between stations.

The cause, though, is clear enough. Outside, the thunderstorm has broken and the rain is torrential. It beats against the windows and that, coupled with the condensation on the inside, makes it virtually impossible for the passengers to see where they are.

Sam gives up trying to monitor their progress. He rests his aching head as well as he can, trying to do nothing more than survive the journey without throwing up. He managed to get a drink at the station and his mother had some tablets with her, but they have only just started to cut in. It doesn't help that every few minutes a brilliant blue-white bolt of lightning generates another stab of pain and makes the pounding ache in his head re-intensify.

Sam has one constant thought. Maddy - how is she? Will she recover? What did he do to her? He curses himself for the hundredth time for letting the ambulance leave without him by her side. He gave in too easily. He should have gone with her.

A familiar noise. A phone ringing. His mother's.

"Jan! Thanks so much for calling. How is she?"

A pause.

"Ah."

"Oh my. Poor thing."

"Maddy?" Sam tries to interrupt, anxious for information. His mother nods and signals for him to be quiet.

"How strange."

She listens again.

"Sam? I wonder why." Instinctively Helen Wright looks at her son.

"Yes, of course. Get back to her. When she wakes up, please give her our love. I'll tell the others."

She hangs up. "The doctors think she's waking up. She's mumbling in her sleep. They say that's a good sign."

"You said something was strange?"

"What she's saying ... something about her phone. Telling someone to keep away. And she's talking about you ... not hurting you. She must be dreaming. The doctors say that's encouraging too."

Yes, it has to be a good sign. Dare he hope that she is going to recover? Did he really save her?

Pull out of it Maddy!

Sam watches the rain beating against the window. His body is demanding that he sleeps but he fights the urge. He mustn't give in to his tiredness: not until he knows what has happened to his friend.

But physical and mental exhaustion cannot be fought and slowly his eyes close. The noise of the carriage fades.

Sam dreams that he is lying on a strange bed. Someone is holding his hand.

Noises. Strange sounds. Machines beeping.

A voice. A woman's voice. "We're here, love. You're going to be alright. Open your eyes please, and say hello."

Who is it? It's a familiar voice, but distant.

"Come on love ... open your eyes for us."

Slowly, cautiously his eyes open. Bright lights in the ceiling. Everything's blurry. Can't focus. Shapes of people in white coats. Doctors? A familiar face. Maddy's mother. That's who's talking. Then a different voice ... weak, pained. "Hi, Mum."

Sam jolts himself awake. Despite his efforts to stay awake he must have been dreaming – a good dream, admittedly, in which Maddy regains consciousness. But a dream is not enough. He needs to stay awake ... stay awake ... wait for another phone call.

But he's too weary. Once again, believing that Maddy is alright, his body forces him to surrender to its exhaustion and he closes his eyes. Sleep overtakes him immediately.

In the darkness someone is calling Sam's name.

"*Sam? Sam? Are you here?*"

"*Hello?*" Sam realises he is still on the train ... he can feel its soporific movement. He keeps his eyes shut.

"*Hello?*"

He senses a moment of pure terror. Then calm.

"*Sam. Where are you? I can hear you, but I can't see you.*"

"*Who is this?*"

"*It's Maddy, Sam. What's happening to me? I heard you ... I felt you ... here ... inside my head. I can hear you now. Am I dreaming?*"

Sam gulps. Maddy's waking up – it had been for real! "*No, Maddy, you're not dreaming. This is really happening.*"

"*How are you doing this?*"

"*Stay calm, Maddy. I'll explain.*"

"*Sam, what's happened to me?*"

Sam remembers the terror he had felt when Ngozi spoke to him for the first time. That seems so long ago now.

He has to be careful. Take one step at a time ... use the words that Ngozi used when she first made contact ...

"*Maddy. Don't be afraid. Everything is alright ...*"

29642259R00200

Printed in Poland
by Amazon Fulfillment
Poland Sp. z o.o., Wrocław